Everyone LOVES

'Brooding and atmospheric – full ⟨...⟩
nothing is quite as ⟨...⟩
Catherine Cooper, *Sunday Times* ⟨...⟩
The Chalet

'Such a dark, atmospheric and comp⟨...⟩
Jackie Kabler, bestselling author of *The Pe⟨...⟩*

'Gripped me from the very first page!'
Louise Mumford, bestselling author of *Sleepless*

'Absolutely loved it!'
Laure Van Rensburg, author of *Nobody But Us*

'An immersive tale of past secrets and flawed family
relationships, all wrapped up with a … compelling narrative
that had me glued to my Kindle for most of the day'
Jenny O'Brien, bestselling author of *Silent Cry*

'Be ready to stay up at night until you're done!'
NetGalley reviewer, *****

'I LOVED THIS BOOK!'
NetGalley reviewer, *****

'Wow! This is a gripping debut novel about family, secrets and
lies … held me spellbound from beginning to end'
NetGalley reviewer, ****

'A real page turner. Kept me engrossed from start to finish.
Loved it'

KARIN NORDIN has been a compulsive reader of thrilling stories since childhood and discovered her love of Scandinavian crime fiction during summers spent visiting family in Norway and Sweden. She has worked in healthcare and education, including as a pharmacy technician, karate instructor, and an English language teacher for the Dutch military.

Karin completed the Creative Writing MSc from the University of Edinburgh with Distinction in 2019 and also holds an MA in Scandinavian Literary Studies from the University of Amsterdam. Born in 'The Biggest Little City in the World' and raised in America's Rust Belt, she now lives in the Netherlands.

Last One Alive is her second novel.

Also by Karin Nordin

Where Ravens Roost

Last One Alive

KARIN NORDIN

ONE PLACE. MANY STORIES

HQ
An imprint of HarperCollins*Publishers* Ltd
1 London Bridge Street
London SE1 9GF

www.harpercollins.co.uk

HarperCollins*Publishers*
1st Floor, Watermarque Building, Ringsend Road
Dublin 4, Ireland

This paperback edition 2021

1

First published in Great Britain by
HQ, an imprint of HarperCollins*Publishers* Ltd 2021

Copyright © Karin Nordin 2021

Karin Nordin asserts the moral right to be
identified as the author of this work.
A catalogue record for this book is
available from the British Library.

ISBN: 978-0-00-846205-5

MIX
Paper from
responsible sources
FSC™ C007454

This book is produced from independently certified FSC™ paper
to ensure responsible forest management.

For more information visit: www.harpercollins.co.uk/green

Printed and bound in Great Britain by
CPI Group (UK) Ltd, Croydon, CR0 4YY

For Feiko

Chapter 1

Lördag | Saturday

The wind swept the rain sideways. It was cold and each raindrop pricked the skin like tiny needles. Louisa turned her back to the spray and watched as her two colleagues hurried along the pavement under a shared umbrella towards the car park. They called out to her that they'd see her in the morning, but she could barely hear them over the hard splatter of water against the ground. She waved. Then she twisted the master key in the latch on the library door, checked to make sure it was firmly locked, and made her way to the back side of the building towards the shortcut for the bus stop.

The sky was dark, teeming with restless clouds, and a deafening clap of thunder quickened her pace. The path behind the library was muddy from the water rolling downhill. She should have walked the long way round through the car park. At least there it would be wet concrete instead of wet dirt.

Up ahead the headlights of the bus shone through the downpour. She would have to pick up the pace in order to catch it. If she missed the bus she'd have to wait thirty minutes for the next one. Or call her father to pick her up. But she didn't want to bother him. He already had enough going on without worrying about her every second of the day. And he did worry about her every second of the day, which was why she never called him unless it was absolutely necessary. At twenty-six years old she shouldn't have been treated like a child, but in her family's eyes she hadn't aged a day in eight years. To them she would forever be eighteen and missing.

Her shoe stuck in the mud. She stumbled, her foot sliding out of the discount faux-leather slip-on. Her tote bag fell off her shoulder and onto the wet ground. The bus pulled to a languid stop, the wheezing sound of the hydraulics buried beneath the rain. She tugged her shoe out of the mud and slipped it back onto her foot. She was soaked down to the skin. She picked up her bag and waved at the bus, hoping to catch the driver's attention.

'Wait!' she yelled. But her voice was drowned out by the clamour of rain. And by the time she made it up the hill the bus was already pulling out and continuing down the road.

She groaned and stood under the small overhang of the bus stop. Not that it would help. She was already drenched to the bone. Maybe she would call her father, after all.

'You just missed it. That's too bad.'

Louisa whipped her head around, surprised by the sound of another voice. A stranger stood beside her, too close for comfort. A sharp pinch pricked her neck and she tried to get away, but a hand gripped around her elbow. It was strong, the fingers bruising her through the thickness of her jacket. She tugged her arm, but it was held fast. She looked up at the figure, but couldn't get a clear glimpse of their face. They wore a mask. All she could see was their eyes. A cold icy stare that began to blur in front of her.

For a brief moment she thought she was dreaming that the stranger's face was melting. Then a wave of dizziness swept over her and she realised she'd been drugged. She wobbled on her feet until her knees gave out. Then she slipped down a tunnel of darkness.

Louisa awoke to her cheek pressed against cold damp concrete. She had no sense of time. No idea of how long she'd been out. Her head was spinning and a dull throb ached at her temple. The sharp scent of old petrol and oil stains filled her nose. It reminded her of her father's garage. She rubbed her eyes, hoping it would help her vision come back into focus. But the room was pitch-black. Her leg was asleep. She shook it and a heavy clanking rattled. She felt around in the dark. A metal clasp was fixed around her ankle. Her stomach dropped and her heart rate jolted. She reached around her, following the chain on her leg to an anchor bolted against the wall.

No, no, no.

An image of *him* flashed in her mind and she feverishly tugged on the chain. Her leg, still numb from whatever had been used to drug her, prickled at the sudden movement. She pulled harder, shoving her stronger foot against the wall for leverage and using the weight of her body to stretch the chain taut. It didn't budge. She crawled closer to the wall and felt around the bolt, nails digging at the cold wall in search of any weak points.

This couldn't be happening. Not again. It must be a nightmare. Because it couldn't be him. He was dead. They said he was dead.

She heaved on the chain. Tears streamed down her face. The muscles in her arms strained nearly to their breaking point, but she refused to stop pulling. She couldn't let it happen again. Not again. She'd never survive him a second time. Once had nearly killed her.

She wrenched her leg upward. The sharp edge of the clasp tore her skin. A white-hot pain shot up through her shin. She dropped her leg and the chain to the floor. She desperately tried to focus on escape, but her mind fought against her, surging forth with

3

the memories of eight years ago. Her breaths increased with the furious beating of her heart and her throat began to close up.

Don't you dare have a panic attack! Focus! Pull yourself together!

A door creaked open, letting in a thin sliver of yellow light. She winced and raised her hand to shield her eyes from the sudden brightness. She saw the legs first. Two thin shadows walking towards her. She couldn't make out any details. The figure was distorted by the jaundiced gleam from the light outside the room and her own panicked thoughts.

Dear God, please don't be him. Not him. Anyone but him.

The figure stopped just out of reach.

'You were out for a long time.'

The voice was jarring and she scrambled to place it, but it was unfamiliar. It wasn't him. She inhaled deeply at that realisation, holding her breath in her chest longer than necessary before breathing out a sigh. But there was no relief. The hairs stood rigid on the back of her neck. Because if it wasn't him then who was it?

'Please,' Louisa begged. 'What do you want? Money? I'll give you anything I can. Just please let me go.'

'I don't want money.'

A shiver crawled up Louisa's spine. Her eyes narrowed, trying to get a clearer look at the person standing before her. They were tall, lean-figured. But the voice was cold, just as those eyes had been. Mercilessly cold. And she almost wished it were him. He was at least familiar. He was a known entity. And everything aside, he had loved her in his own sick way. But Louisa had the impression that this person didn't love anyone. They didn't exude a single ounce of compassion. That was how she knew she would die.

'Then what do you want? Tell me, please. I'll do anything you want. Just tell me.'

The figure shifted their weight from one foot to the other before taking one step closer.

Louisa crawled back against the wall. The chain rattled along after her. She gripped her hands around the bolt on the wall. 'Please … What do you want from me?'

'I want you to give a message to Kjeld Nygaard.'

Louisa recoiled in shock. 'What?'

But before Louisa could process what had been said, her captor lit a match.

And Louisa screamed.

Chapter 2

Måndag | Monday

Kjeld swerved onto Föreningsgatan and parked his car along the kerb a block from Lilla Sam, the primary school building where his daughter, Tove, attended classes. He'd almost forgotten that she had a half-day scheduled because of a dentist appointment and had to race to the school to get there on time. In his haste he stepped out of the car and into a large puddle on the street, drenching his pant leg halfway up his calf.

'Goddammit,' he grumbled as he slammed the door shut and made his way down the pavement. It had finally stopped raining, but a damp chill lingered in the air and he turned up the collar of his coat against the wind. It was February and the weather couldn't seem to decide whether it wanted to wallow in the last remaining breaths of winter or fall face first into a wet spring.

Kjeld wished it would make up its damn mind.

From the outside, Lilla Sam looked more like a small mountain lodge than a school. The brown wood, ornately carved accoutrements along the windows, and stone foundation were reminiscent of a stave church. Compared to most other primary schools in Gothenburg, Lilla Sam was rather posh, a result of having once been a private academy. When the country removed tuition fees from its educational system, the private school became just another public one, but it still had a reputation for graduating the children of upper-class families.

In that respect, Tove was one of the exceptions. Kjeld had a particular disdain for institutions that were synonymous with wealth and societal standing, but Bengt had insisted that the school offered a system of learning that best suited Tove. It also had a very prestigious art curriculum and, being a fine art painter by trade, this was the ultimate tool in convincing Kjeld's ex-husband that no other school in the city would be good enough for their daughter.

Kjeld didn't begrudge Bengt's decision. When it came to Tove, Kjeld almost always gave Bengt the final say. Not just because he wanted to make Bengt happy, but because he knew that Bengt always put in the time and research when it came to their daughter. He always made the right choices as a father. Kjeld, on the other hand, was much less attuned to fatherhood. He loved his daughter, but he wasn't as attentive as he ought to have been. Kjeld didn't consider himself a complete failure as a parent. Nor did Bengt. At least, Kjeld didn't think he did. But Kjeld had a lot of making up to do for the last few years, both to Tove and his ex. And part of that compromise was admitting that Bengt was much more suited to the administrative aspects of Tove's life than Kjeld was.

Thunder rumbled in the distance and Kjeld hurried towards the school entrance. When he reached the gate, however, he paused, the corner of his eye catching a glimpse of another man helping Tove into a sharp black BMW SUV at the end of the street.

Kjeld immediately saw red. His body tensed as he watched the man and he had to clench his teeth to remind himself not to say something that would start a fight.

Liam Berg.

Bengt's live-in boyfriend and Kjeld's replacement.

Kjeld bit back his frustration and jogged over to the SUV. When Tove saw him her face brightened, smile stretching ear to ear. She was missing a front tooth, one of the many childhood milestones he lost out on by no longer being with Bengt, and when she spoke it was with a slight slur on her S's. 'Daddy! Look at me! I lost a tooth! And I got a pack of princess stickers from the tooth fairy!'

Kjeld smiled. A sense of unexpected pride warmed his face, but was hidden behind the scruff of his beard. 'That's lovely, sweetheart. You can tell me all about it when we get home. Come on. Grab your things.'

Tove was in the process of climbing out of the back seat when Liam stepped around the door.

Liam was a wall of a man. He was tall, at least two inches taller than Kjeld, with broad swimmer's shoulders and a physique that made it clear he prioritised the gym in his daily routine. His hair was styled in waves with a low fade and he had a full beard that was neatly maintained and natural. He hadn't had a beard the last time Kjeld saw him and that prickled Kjeld's already precarious temper. Kjeld saw that beard as an intentional act of revenge. Bengt had always insisted that he preferred a clean-shaven face when they were together, which was part of the reason why Kjeld had allowed his own ruddy-hued beard to grow out after they separated. But while facial hair made Kjeld look a bit like a scruffy lumberjack, Liam managed to exude the coolness of a men's style magazine.

At forty-seven years old Liam was showing some grey, particularly around the chin and mouth, but instead of making him look old, it gave him an air of timeless sophistication. And whether intentional or not, Kjeld saw that insufferable grin as an expression of smugness. The kind of smugness Kjeld couldn't help but associate with people like Liam. Doctors.

'What are you doing here?' Liam asked. He had a deep clear tone to his voice. The enunciation of the words was perfect, but inflected with a heavy English accent. *It's an East London dialect,* was how Bengt first explained it to Kjeld, but Kjeld wouldn't have been able to tell it apart from any other British accent. It did, however, make his Swedish sound a bit more serious and less sing-songy.

Kjeld hated that.

'Good to see you, too, Liam,' Kjeld said. He tried to offer a polite smile, but his teeth gritted too hard, making it more of a crooked scowl. Which better reflected his intentions because Kjeld didn't mean to be overwhelmingly civil. He glanced inside the SUV at the young girl with the curly red hair. 'Come on, Tove. Get your things. You're coming with me.'

'It's not your week, Kjeld. You've got your wires crossed.'

'No, I haven't. I had it written down on the calendar.'

'Then you wrote it down wrong.'

'And I'm supposed to take your word for that? As if I don't already know how much joy you took out of the last time I mixed up the dates.' Kjeld knew he sounded embittered and he was, but it was a struggle not to let Liam grate on him. Liam, whether consciously or otherwise, tested the limits of what little patience Kjeld had.

A light drizzle of rain began coating the ground as Kjeld helped tuck Tove's wild red curls back into the hood of her jacket. His phone rang in his pocket.

'Where's your backpack, Tove?'

'Here.' Liam reached into the front passenger seat for a bright blue and white-star decorated backpack. It was a new one that Kjeld hadn't seen before.

Kjeld snatched it out of his hands with a grumble.

His phone rang again.

'Do you need to answer that?'

'No.'

Tove jumped in a puddle, splashing water all over Kjeld's other leg. It soaked through to the skin. His phone continued ringing.

'Goddammit.' He took his phone out of his pocket and glanced at the caller ID. It was his partner at the Gothenburg City Police, Detective Sergeant Esme Jansson.

'Are you working this week?' Liam asked.

'What?'

'You heard me.'

'That's none of your business.'

'Actually, it is. Regardless of whether or not it's your week – it's not by the way – if you're too busy working then Tove shouldn't be going with you.'

Kjeld fixed Liam with a hard stare. 'I don't need you sticking your nose into me and my family's business.'

'They live with me, Kjeld. That makes it my business.'

The rain began to fall harder. Within seconds Kjeld's hair was matted down on top of his head. Liam, always prepared, took out an umbrella from inside the car and opened it up to keep himself and the half-open car door dry. Tove jumped in another puddle, laughing as she tried to increase the height of the splashes. Kjeld's phone continued ringing.

'Well, if you have a problem with it then you can take it up with Bengt.'

'Take what up with me?'

Kjeld turned on his heel. Heading towards them from the school's main entrance was his ex-husband and proof that Liam was probably right. Kjeld must have had the wrong week.

Bengt Olander walked briskly through the rain, a large umbrella protecting him from the sudden downpour. He wasn't normally the kind of man who commanded attention. At five foot seven inches he was a good deal shorter than Kjeld. He had dark brown hair with a streak of grey that started at his left temple near his parting and swept over to the right like a wave. His eyes were dark blue, not unlike a winter sky at twilight, which he hid behind a pair of black vintage-styled horn-rimmed glasses that made him look more unassuming than he actually was. As always, Bengt was clean-shaven and immaculately dressed. He had a penchant for form-fitting sweaters beneath fashionable blazers and occasional pin-striped vests, which he paired against jeans, somehow managing to be both unquestionably formal and respectfully casual.

Kjeld used to poke fun at Bengt's meticulousness when it came to his outward appearance. Now he just eyed him enviably, wishing he had the right to that kind of lover's banter. Bengt was a slim man, but he'd put on a healthy amount of weight since he'd been with Kjeld. Kjeld thought it suited him. Especially in the face, which is where he noticed it first. After the hair, that is. Kjeld always breathed a silent sigh of relief when he saw Bengt's hair. That meant he was still "in the clear".

'Tove left these in her classroom.' Bengt tossed a pair of pink mittens in the car before glancing at Kjeld. 'What are you doing here?'

'Kjeld's got his wires crossed again,' Liam interrupted. 'He says it's his week.'

'It is.' Kjeld looked to Bengt. 'You texted me yourself.'

Bengt raised a brow, confused. 'No, I texted to remind you that *next* week is yours. Starting on Friday. Besides, today is Monday.'

Kjeld swore under his breath.

'Daddy, can we go now? It's cold!'

'Hop back into the car, Tove,' Liam said. 'Your daddy is confused. We're going home now.'

Tove pouted and stomped back to the SUV. Kjeld felt like a heel. Worse, his mistake only made Liam appear more responsible. Which wasn't entirely untrue.

Kjeld lifted Tove back into the back seat, setting her backpack on the floor in front of her.

'But I want to go home with you and play with Oskar,' she said. The rain dripped down her face like tears.

'I know, sweetheart. But you can come over next weekend and we can do whatever you want. How does that sound?'

'Can we have a dance party and watch movies and order pizza?'

'Sure. Whatever you want.'

'No pizza,' Bengt said. 'And no ice cream either. It gives her an upset stomach. We're going to have her checked to see if she's lactose intolerant.'

Tove pouted.

'Maybe we can make pizza without cheese then,' Kjeld said, trying not to show his irritation. 'And sorbet doesn't have milk in it.'

Tove's face brightened.

Kjeld gave her a quick kiss on the forehead before closing the door.

'You know it's really difficult for her when you mess up like this,' Liam said, rigidly defensive. 'You need to get a better grip on your schedule.'

'Well, I wouldn't want to disappoint you now, would I?'

'I'm not the one you'll be disappointing.' Liam closed up the umbrella, shook it off, and made his way around to the driver's side of the vehicle.

Tove pressed her face against the tinted glass, smashing her nose until she looked like a pig. Then she started laughing. Kjeld cracked a small smile. When he turned his attention back to Bengt he was met with a disapproving sulk.

'I really wish you wouldn't rile Liam up like that. He's a good man, Kjeld. He just wants what's best for Tove.'

'So do I,' Kjeld said. 'I'm doing my best. I try not to let him get to me, but he's just so damn insufferable. I don't know what you see in him.'

Bengt frowned. 'I'm not having this conversation with you right now. You're drenched. Go home before you catch pneumonia or something. And don't forget about this weekend.'

Bengt pulled open the passenger side door of the SUV and climbed inside, slamming it shut behind him. Then he rolled down the window and peeked his head out. 'You know about Tove's dance recital, too, right?'

'Of course,' Kjeld hedged. 'It's on—'

'Thursday.'

'Right, Thursday.' Kjeld paused. 'Wait. *This* Thursday?'

Bengt withheld a sigh. 'It was rescheduled from last month after the instructor's grandmother passed away. Don't you remember?'

Kjeld didn't, but he nodded anyway.

'Anyway. Try to be there.'

'Wouldn't miss it for anything.'

But it was clear from Bengt's stony glare that he would believe it when he saw it.

'I'll be there,' Kjeld insisted. To this Bengt merely rolled up the window.

Kjeld stood in the rain, watching as Liam drove out of the parking space. Then he took a pen out of his pocket and quickly wrote a note on the side of his hand. *Thursday Dance Recital.* He wouldn't forget about it. Nor would he forget to pick up Tove from school next Friday. He couldn't. He wanted to be there for Tove. And to do that he had to prove he was capable of keeping his promises.

The SUV stopped at the next intersection, waiting for oncoming traffic to pass before turning. Kjeld watched as Tove craned her head backwards and waved at him.

His phone buzzed twice. Two text messages from Esme.

Potential homicide in Örgryte. On my way there.

Will send you the address.

A moment later she sent the address. He stared at it, wiping the rain off the screen to make sure he'd read it correctly. That couldn't be right. He recognised that address. He hurried back to his car and called her the moment he was inside.

The rain came down in buckets against his windscreen, nearly drowning out the sound of Esme's voice when she answered.

'I just got your messages,' Kjeld said. 'Are you *sure* that's the right address?'

Chapter 3

The address belonged to a small two-storey grey house at the end of Norströmsgatan in the Örgryte neighbourhood on the western side of Gothenburg. The house sat back from the road, which ended in a bicycle path that led to a children's playground in full view of the house's back garden. Örgryte was normally an upper middle class neighbourhood, but the lack of maintenance on the grey house defied the professional upkeep of its neighbours. The exterior paint was peeling and the hedges had grown wildly, concealing half of the house from view.

When Kjeld pulled his car up alongside the park he could see the boarded-up windows on the second floor and his heart began to race. A fire truck and two police patrol cars blocked neighbourhood traffic on the nearest side street, lights still flashing. Although it was difficult to see from his position, the back half of the house appeared blackened and burned out. An anxious dread crept through Kjeld's body as he watched the scene through the rain-blurred windscreen. He sat in the car with the engine running for a full two minutes, fingers clenched around the steering wheel until his knuckles turned white, before he turned off the car and climbed out.

Out of the corner of his eye he saw Esme's sporty green Volvo

66 DL parked on the side road, but she wasn't in it. The wind swooped the rain sideways, smacking him in the face and soaking his entire front before he made it to the police cordon and crossed the tape. The muggy odour of dampened smoke hovered in the air. Forensic specialists were already on the scene and had set up a tent on the bicycle path adjacent to the side yard. Kjeld followed their lead to the tent in order to suit up in protective gear before entering the house.

An oppressive sense of terror came over him as he stepped through the front door. The floor was wet from the firehose, but the scent of burning lingered. He turned to the side, allowing a crime-scene technician to pass, before making his way further into the house. There was no furniture and the walls were bare, streaked in scorch marks where the fire had torn through the rooms. The wallpaper, what was left of it, was ripped and curled near the ceiling. Someone had spray-painted profanities on the living room wall, but they were illegible from the damage caused by the flames.

The sounds around him faded into white noise as he passed through the corridor towards the kitchen. The fire damage was worse there. The walls were coated in a layer of crusty black that almost looked like tar dripping down to the wooden floor. The cabinets remained, but the once-white paint was marred black. Even through his mask he could taste the choking odour of smoke. Kjeld clenched his teeth and swallowed back a thick lump in his throat. Then he made his way to the door at the far end of the kitchen. No one told him where to go. He just knew. He'd been there before.

The cellar door was open and a surge of panic gripped him, his head pounding. Kjeld was halfway down the steps, remembering the last time he'd walked those creaking stairs, when Esme's voice cut through his thoughts, jolting him back to the present.

'That was fast,' she said, looking up at him from the bottom of the steps. Her small physique was framed in musty yellow light cast from a temporary lamp one of the technicians had fixed to the wall behind her. Her protective suit was at least a size too big for her. She'd rolled it up at the sleeves and the ankles, but she still looked like she was drowning in it.

'I was in the city centre,' he replied as he made his way down to the bottom of the steps. The fire damage on the walls became worse the further he went and he was surprised the stairs didn't collapse beneath his weight. 'Have we identified the body?'

'Not yet. Sixten was first on the scene. And we're still waiting for pathology, but …'

'But what?'

'It's a bad one.'

Kjeld steadied himself and followed Esme further into the cellar. At the bottom of the stairs was a large open space, but at the back of the far wall was another door leading to a smaller room. A room Kjeld remembered vividly.

'Kjeld!' an enthusiastic voice called out. 'Did the chief finally put you back in the field? I thought you were still on desk duty.'

Kjeld turned his head to see Sixten Andersson-Sund waving the two of them over from the doorway to the second room. Sixten was the newest member of their team in the Violent Crimes Division. Like Esme had been when she first arrived in Gothenburg, Sixten was fast-tracked to detective because of an exemplary service record working alongside members of the local drug enforcement team. He had one of those optimistic, go-getter personalities that always made Kjeld feel a little uncomfortable. He was the type of man to slap a colleague on the back for a job well done. But he was honest and he offered a pleasant contrast to Kjeld's sombre cynicism. He was also determined to prove himself to his new teammates, which meant he never shirked extra work. And in the last few months there'd been more than enough to go around.

'I've been cleared for a few weeks now,' Kjeld said, choosing not to elaborate. The Special Investigations Department hadn't been able to find any solid evidence connecting him to the Kattegat Killings. Nor could they prove that he'd had any foreknowledge of the crimes committed by his former police partner, Nils Hedin. As a result, the investigation into Kjeld's potential involvement had been dropped. But the stigma still stood.

Outside the wind battered the rain against the house. The howling echo resounded down the stairs from above.

'Where's the body?' Kjeld asked.

'Over here.' Sixten nodded towards the far corner of the room.

Kjeld ducked under the doorway, which was at least a foot lower than the cellar's ceiling, as he followed Sixten into the small room. A technician who had been setting up numbered placards along the wall left the room in order to make more space for the three detectives. From the scorch marks on the ceiling and the evenness of the burn residue on the walls, this room had been the obvious source of the fire.

Kjeld stepped around Sixten to get a better look at the scene. The body was curled up against the wall in a foetal position, face partially covered by a raised arm and pushed into a floor drain where the grate had been removed. The distinct discolouring on the limbs and torso were clearly the result of a fire. The body's flesh was charred black and crispy like a piece of meat forgotten on a grill; a charring that matched many of the scorch marks on the walls and floor.

Kjeld stepped closer and crouched down for a better look. A thick heavy chain had been clasped around the victim's ankle and bolted to the foundational portion of the cellar wall. Kjeld thought he saw remnants of nail marks in the concrete.

Christ. They'd tried to scratch the bolt free.

'Who found the body?' Esme asked.

'A neighbour saw smoke and called the fire department,' Sixten said. 'The fire department called us. I was in the neighbourhood when the call came in. I only live a few blocks away.'

'All of this water will have contaminated the scene.'

Sixten nodded. 'Once they realised what they had on their hands they tried to limit their focus to the fire. Sadly, this room was the source and as you can tell from the smell, there was definitely an accelerant used. Possibly some kind of oil. The fire chief said it's a miracle the house is still standing. Might not be if the neighbour hadn't called as quickly as they did. But whoever started it didn't do a great job of arson. When I spoke with the fire chief earlier his initial estimate was that it looks like they only covered the basement floor in accelerant. Otherwise you'd see more damage upstairs. Back of the house took a beating though. He said that was probably from the fire taking the path of least resistance through the house and maybe some accidental drip from the accelerant.'

'You don't think they intended to burn the house down with her in it?' Esme raised a brow.

Sixten shrugged. 'I think if someone wanted to go to the trouble of covering their tracks they could have done a much better job of burning down the house. This is an old wooden construction. It wouldn't have taken much effort.'

'Maybe the killer wanted her to be found.' Esme paused thoughtfully. 'Any identification on the victim?'

Sixten shook his head. 'Not yet. But we're still searching the house. We'll know more once Frisk gets here.'

Kjeld canted his head to the side, peering down at the victim's face between their raised forearms. Someone, possibly one of the firefighters, had turned the body enough to expose the part of the face that had been pushed into the drain. It was hard to look away from the contorted mass of burned flesh and muscle. The eyes were gone, melted in the heat. But even without them, Kjeld imagined the terror that must have been in their eyes. He thought of that fearful awareness they must have experienced in their last moments, knowing the end was near. And the sheer horror of realising their last thoughts would be of excruciating pain. God, he hoped they hadn't been alive when the fire was set. But the position of the body, curled up in self-protection told him otherwise.

It was a harsh reminder of how cruel and fleeting life could be. That was something Kjeld had been thinking about a lot, ever since he returned from Varsund. Ever since he'd learned the truth about his father. Facing his family's secrets and trying to navigate his relationship with those who were left had made him very conscious of the fact that life was short. And his father's dementia gave Kjeld a whole new meaning to the phrase "a fate worse than death". He'd never before considered the possibility of death being a reprieve, but now he wondered.

He shifted his weight to allow him a closer look at the victim's face. His thoughts turned to the last time he'd found someone in that cellar. A young woman on the brink of death. Emaciated and beaten, but alive.

Kjeld wasn't a religious man, but he silently prayed this wasn't what it looked like.

'This reminds me of Louisa Karlsson.'

'Who?' It was clear from her tone that Esme didn't recognise the name.

Sixten's attention perked up. 'What? You're kidding.'

A pit of dread tightened in Kjeld's stomach. 'Unfortunately not.'

Kjeld motioned to the technician waiting in the doorway to reposition the lamp that had been set up near the body. The technician hurried over and adjusted the light to shine more directly on the victim's face. Kjeld hoped it might reveal something that could identify the body. Some sign to confirm or deny his fears, but the body was too damaged. He couldn't even tell if it was a man or a woman, young or old.

'Who's Louisa Karlsson?' Esme asked.

Sixten frowned. 'She was from that case a few years back, wasn't she? The one with the serial murderer? I don't remember the details. Must have been – what? Five? Six years ago, now?'

'Eight.' Kjeld stood up, but kept his gaze on the body. The

19

corners of his eyes burned a little and he rubbed them against the inside of his shoulder.

'I didn't know you were on that case. Was that when you were partnered with—?'

'Yes,' Kjeld cut him off.

'Okay. Can somebody please catch me up to speed here?' There was an impatient edge to Esme's voice. The same tone she got when she felt like she was being ignored in a crowd of their male colleagues.

'Louisa Karlsson was the only surviving victim of Gjur Hägglund,' Kjeld said.

'Why does that name sound familiar?'

'I remember now!' Sixten said. 'The newspapers called him the Cellar Sadist. He'd pick up young women, usually first-year college students, and lock them in his cellar. Claimed he was searching for his soulmate. It was all over the news for months. I remember my cousin refusing to leave the house on her own for almost a year. The press had a field day with the whole thing when the bodies were found. How many were there?'

'Five that we uncovered in the backyard.' Kjeld pursed his lips. 'Two in a chest in the den.'

'They used to talk about that case at police college. Hägglund's house was basically a torture chamber. He starved a few of the women. Brutally beat the others. The media referred to them as his Basement Brides. It was disgusting. Louisa was the last one he took, wasn't she? It was lucky she was found.'

'There was no luck about it,' Kjeld said. 'He messed up. Made a mistake. And we caught it.'

Well, actually, Nils had been the one to catch it. But Kjeld was the one who followed through. He'd been the first one on the scene.

'And it wasn't just a house,' Kjeld said. 'It was *this* house. I knew the address was familiar when I saw it, but I wasn't certain. But this is definitely Gjur Hägglund's house.'

'Damn,' Sixten muttered. 'That's a creepy coincidence ...'

'I don't believe in coincidences.'

Esme turned her gaze towards Kjeld. 'You're the one who found her the first time around?'

Kjeld didn't look back at her. He could sense the concern on her face from where he stood and didn't want to let her see that it was warranted. He nodded. 'I wasn't the only one there, but I was the first to see her. And this was exactly how he'd planned to kill Louisa. He even said so in his statement to the police afterwards. Murder-suicide by fire. Purifying them both for the afterlife together or some such bullshit. Fortunately, he didn't get that far in his plans.'

Kjeld tried not to think about his old cases. Some of the images were too painful to recall. Too gruesome. Louisa was one of those images, burned into his memory. He'd never forget the way she looked at him when he entered that damp cubicle of space. He remembered the smell first. The rank odour of urine and faeces. The uncleanliness. The sharp stench of fear. Louisa had been so small then. Eighteen years old and half-starved. Eyes sunken, cheekbones jutting against thin sallow skin. She'd looked like a living skeleton. But it was that glimmer in her eyes that he remembered most. A poignant plea. *If you're not here to save me then kill me,* it seemed to say.

'Could Hägglund be behind this?'

Kjeld shook his head. 'No, he's been dead going on at least seven years now. He killed himself two weeks into his life sentence at Saltvik Prison.'

'And he didn't have any accomplices?'

'No, he was a loner.' Kjeld sighed. He turned his gaze back down to the body. A cold chill travelled down his spine.

He hoped like hell this wasn't Louisa. There weren't many moments in his career when Kjeld had been the bearer of good news for a family. Louisa had been one of them. But if this was her, he'd have to visit them again and deliver the news they'd expected to hear from him eight years ago. The thought of it made his stomach churn.

The sputtering sound of raindrops against the thin walls of the ground floor weakened. The storm was letting up, for now.

An awkward silence fell between them and while Kjeld still refused to look at Esme he knew she was watching him. She hadn't been there for Louisa's case, but she knew him well enough to worry. Despite his stubborn insistence that he always put his old cases behind him when they were over, he had the tendency to personalise some of them. Particularly the ones involving young women and children. Even before he was a father, those cases hit him hard.

'If it is her it's not fair,' Sixten said, breaking the breathless lull in the cellar. 'That's not how it's supposed to be. If you survive one horrific crime then you should be spared another. It's like getting struck by lightning twice.'

'Karma sometimes gets its fucking wires crossed,' Kjeld mumbled to himself.

'What?'

'Nothing.' Kjeld slipped off the gloves. 'Have the technicians send all the evidence down to the station. I'll call Axel and let him know to look out for it. Where's Frisk? He should be here by now.'

'He called just before you got here. Said he'd be on his way as soon as he finished up at an accident off the forty-five. Driver took an exit too fast and collided with a guardrail. You'd think with all this rain we've had that people would remember to brake.' Sixten rubbed the side of his mask to scratch his nose.

Kjeld cast one last glance down to the body. Louisa had fallen off his radar after Hägglund's trial. Part of that was Kjeld's own doing. He couldn't allow a case like that to ruminate in the back of his mind by keeping tabs on the people involved. If it was in his thoughts then he would obsess over it, tear it down bit by bit, second-guessing all of his actions and his decisions. If this was her it would bring all of that back. All of those internal questions. Could he have done more? Could he have done better?

Kjeld felt a twinge of guilt at not having kept in contact with her. Surely he could have spared a few minutes over the years to call on her and make certain she was doing well. He could have checked in on her. Asked her what she was doing with her life. And a dark voice at the back of his mind chastised him for his own selfishness. He'd saved her life, after all. Didn't that make him responsible for ensuring her continued safety?

Not for the first time a cold recognition gripped his conscience. The groundless thought that this person, whoever it was, might not have been there, dead in the same grungy cellar that had forever stained Louisa's life, if he'd picked up the phone and made a call.

Chapter 4

Kjeld couldn't get out of that house fast enough. The scene itself, while gruesome, wasn't what bothered him. It was the memory of his old case that made him ill at ease. And the fear that the victim might be someone he knew. Someone else who'd been there before. Standing in that confined space, seeing another body tortured and chained to that grimy slab, had been suffocating. It was as though the walls were closing in on him. He had to swallow back a gag reflex from the combination of it all – the choking odour of burnt flesh, the nail marks in the concrete, the memory of the day he carried Louisa out of the darkness and into the light. The second Kjeld stepped outside he tore off the protective forensics suit and gasped for fresh air.

He trudged through the wet grass on the overgrown lawn and ducked under the blue and white cordon tape, which had been pushed out further onto the small neighbourhood street to keep away onlookers. The rain had stopped, but there was still a misty wetness in the air and the dark clouds overhead warned of another impending shower. He pinched the bridge of his nose. A dull migraine was forming near his sinuses and he craved a cigarette. Just thinking about it left a tickle in the back of his throat. An itch he'd been trying to ignore since he'd decided to give up his nicotine addiction three months ago.

He searched his pockets for the pack of peppermint chewing gum he'd been using to help him overcome his need for a smoke. Empty. He must have left it in the car.

Kjeld was halfway to his vehicle when Henny Engström and her cameraman swooped in like buzzards. They seemed to come out of nowhere, rushing towards his blindside from the neighbourhood playground across the street. It gave Kjeld the impression Henny had materialised out of thin air or, knowing her, possibly the gloomy mist itself.

Henny was an amateur crime blogger with delusions of being an actual journalist. Her online blog, *The Chatterbox*, was started in protest after she survived a violent attack by a stalker that left most of her body scarred. After the incident she blamed the local police for not doing a better job of protecting her when she tried to file a restraining order against him before the attack. This brought her and her cause some attention, but it wasn't until she broke the news that Nils Hedin was the Kattegat Killer that she gained her true following.

But, in truth, her blog was little more than tabloid gossip. It was her YouTube channel, however, where she often reported live from active crime scenes, portraying the police as incompetent fools who preferred covering up the horrors of their colleagues to doing actual police work, which had earned her a popular following. And even though she was a nobody to the professional community, she made waves. Waves that had brought a fair amount of scrutiny on Gothenburg City Police and its administration.

And for reasons Kjeld still hadn't fully uncovered, she'd decided to take out a personal vendetta against him. Since Nils's arrest Henny had not only smeared Kjeld's name and reputation, but had begun posting about his family as well. And while being a police detective did make him a public figure, open to media criticism, it didn't give her the right to impose herself upon his crime scenes. Nor did it warrant the pervasive interference into his personal life. Kjeld could deal with people speaking badly about him, but her callous disregard for how her words affected Bengt and his daughter put her on his proverbial shit list.

'Kjeld Nygaard, is it true that you're off suspension and back to working cases in the field?' Henny shoved a microphone in his face.

'Turn the camera off, Henny.'

Karl the cameraman moved around so he could get both Kjeld and Henny in frame.

Kjeld turned to the side so as not to be looking directly down the lens.

'Nils Hedin's much anticipated trial is said to be starting in a few weeks. Do you have anything to say about that?'

'No comment.'

'But he *was* your best friend. Could you explain to our viewers how it's possible that you didn't realise your best friend was the Kattegat Killer?'

Kjeld turned his back on them and continued walking towards his car.

Henny followed along after him. 'Or is it possible that you *did* know and were protecting him instead?'

Kjeld stopped and pivoted on his heel to face her. Henny wasn't quite as tall as him, at least three inches shorter in fact, but she had a formidable presence about her. She was a confident woman who knew her own strengths. And she refused to back down.

'I'm not talking to you about Nils,' Kjeld said, biting back the urge to say more.

'What about Varsund?'

Kjeld flinched.

'Is it true that your sister was arrested on suspicion of murder?'

'No comment.'

'Was there a body in the house? Has the person been identified?'

Kjeld glared into the camera. 'Get that thing off me.'

'Freedom of the press,' Henny said.

'You're not the press,' Kjeld scoffed, returning his focus to Henny. 'You're a tabloid gossip columnist with a YouTube channel and your stories are nothing more than trash talk and hearsay.'

'Can I quote you on that?'

'I don't care what the fuck you say about me, but leave my family out of your garbage blog.'

'Vlog.'

'Whatever.'

'The people have a right to know about those who have sworn to protect them. They have a right to know if other members of the police are involved in the Kattegat murders.'

Kjeld refrained from flinching at mention of his previous case, but the tenseness in his posture was enough to show that Henny's insinuation hit hard. 'I know that you've been following my ex and my daughter. They have nothing to do with Nils or the police or anything.'

'I beg to differ,' Henny replied. She squared off her shoulders and stared at him directly in the eyes. 'They have to do with you and *you're* directly related to Nils.'

'I shot the son of a bitch. I didn't have anything else to do with him or what he did.'

'That remains to be seen.'

Karl moved in closer and the blinking red light on top of the mount flickered in the corner of Kjeld's eye.

Kjeld reached out and shoved the camera away. 'I told you to get that thing out of my face.'

'Hey!' Esme's voice called out.

Kjeld turned away from Henny in time to catch Esme storming past the cordon tape, heading directly for them. Just barely over five foot three Esme wasn't anywhere near as physically intimidating as Henny, but she had a seriousness in her tone that was unmatched by anyone else in the Violent Crimes Division. She also played by the book, which made her practically untouchable to reputation-destroying amateurs like Henny.

More importantly, Esme could always be counted on to save Kjeld's arse.

'You're not allowed to be here,' Esme said. 'This is an active crime scene.'

'Could you give us a comment on what happened here, Detective Jansson?' Henny's tone softened to a more polite and professional one than she'd used with Kjeld.

'Not at this time. Once we have more information I'm sure there will be a press conference. But until then you can't be here.'

'Isn't this the former residence of Gjur Hägglund, the Cellar Sadist?'

'No comment at this time.'

'Of course. My apologies. You know how it is. Always looking for that next big story. Gotta keep the people informed.' Henny cast Kjeld a sidelong glance and smirked. 'I'll be seeing you, Kjeld.'

'Not if I can help it,' he grumbled.

Henny nodded to Karl, who stepped off the road and back into the grass that lined the edge of the playground. He turned off the camera. Henny began making her way back across the park towards her car.

'Aren't you forgetting something?' Esme called out after her.

Henny turned, glancing back with a single raised brow.

'The camera footage,' Esme said, holding out her hand. 'You know how it is.'

Chapter 5

Once Henny and her cameraman were out of earshot, Kjeld gave an exasperated sigh. Then he tugged open the passenger-side door of his car and dug through his glove compartment for that packet of chewing gum. After he popped one of the pieces out of the packet and into his mouth, he slammed the door shut.

'You need to learn to control your temper,' Esme said. She wasn't being condescending. It was simply a reminder. Esme had learned a long time ago that demanding things of Kjeld only resulted in his stubborn refusal to listen.

'I know. But she really gets on my nerves.'

'Is the gum helping?'

'With Henny?' Kjeld scoffed. 'No.'

'With the smoking then?'

'Three months smoke-free but two kilos heavier. Win one battle, lose another.'

Esme gave him a quick once-over, her lips turning upward in a sarcastic smile. 'It's barely noticeable.'

Kjeld jokingly rolled his eyes. 'Thanks.'

'Frisk just called. Said he'd be here in about ten minutes. I was about to check in with the crime-scene manager and see what she's collected so far. I'm worried that we won't be able to get much from the body, but maybe we'll get lucky with trace and find something on the doorknobs.'

'Fingers crossed.' After a pause he continued, 'There's something unsettling about this murder, Esme. I'm worried about this one.'

'It's been a while since we've had a scene this violent.'

Esme didn't say which scene she was referring to, but Kjeld already knew. The Aubuchon case. The murders committed by his friend, Nils. The Kattegat Killer.

A high-pitched whistle cut through the air and they both turned back towards the house. Sixten waved at them from the side of the yard where the grass bumped up against the neighbour's driveway. In one hand he held up a tote bag, partly covered in mud.

'Found this in the neighbour's bin,' Sixten called out to them. 'It's got a wallet.'

Kjeld made his way back to the house, each step heavier than the last. Esme followed after him, double-stepping her pace to keep up. She handed Kjeld a pair of gloves from her pocket and he slipped them on just as Sixten removed a long magenta-coloured wallet from the bag. Kjeld took it tentatively, preparing himself for the name he might find.

He unsnapped the wallet. A vacant face on a driver's licence stared back at him through the clear plastic pocket. He read the name, just to be sure.

His heart sank.

Louisa.

Chapter 6

After finishing up at the crime scene and making arrangements with Frisk to meet up later for the results of the pathological examination, Kjeld and Esme drove to the police station while Sixten stayed behind to coordinate the evidence collection with the crime scene manager. While Esme was filling Axel, their data analyst, in on what to expect from the technicians, their chief, Johan Rhodin, caught Kjeld waiting in the corridor and called him in to his office.

Chief Johan Rhodin wasn't a large man, but he had a commanding presence. When he spoke, it was with the assurance of a man who'd spent most of his professional career telling other people what to do. Unlike some of the other police officials in the upper echelon of command, however, Rhodin wasn't a bully. And he had a soft spot for hard luck cases, which had been cultivated over the course of many years. And Kjeld was no exception.

'I heard you picked up a bad one today,' Rhodin said, perching himself on the edge of his desk with his arms crossed.

'We think it's Louisa Karlsson.'

'Shit.'

'My sentiments exactly.'

'Have you notified the family?'

31

'We've called them to identify some belongings we found at the house. They should be on their way here now,' Kjeld said.

Rhodin smoothed down his moustache with the palm of his hand. 'That's the last thing we need.'

'Sir?'

'I had a visit from Ardal over at Special Investigations this morning. He's been leading the inquiry into Nils's old cases.'

Kjeld nodded. He hadn't heard much about the investigation into Nils's history. They were keeping a tight lid on the flow of information. But everyone knew it was happening. The Special Investigations Department, or SU as they were commonly called, were in charge of investigating offences by police officials. They'd interviewed Kjeld on numerous occasions following Nils's arrest, scrutinising his every action to determine he hadn't been involved or had any foreknowledge of the killings linked to the Aubuchon case or the Kattegat Killer case as the media tokened it. Their investigation had been the basis of his suspension. Once they'd cleared him of any wrongdoing, however, he'd been able to return to work.

But with the trial approaching it was logical to assume they were searching through Nils's old case files for any sign of tampering. If they uncovered anything it could call into question hundreds of arrests. Anything linked to him had the potential of requiring re-examination. After all, how could they trust a serial murderer to follow appropriate protocol in the case of other killers?

Kjeld waited for Rhodin to continue, but he didn't. 'And?'

'And they've asked me about a particular case. A delicate one.'

Kjeld waited for Rhodin to continue, but he didn't. He merely stared at Kjeld as though looking for a sign of recognition before the fact.

'I hope you're not stalling for dramatic effect,' Kjeld said.

'Emma Hassan.'

Kjeld blinked. The memory of a teenage girl running out

into traffic flashed across his thoughts. His heart dropped into his stomach.

Rhodin must have noticed a change in Kjeld's demeanour because his face drew into one of grave concern. 'Is there something I need to know?'

Kjeld took a measured breath to compose his thoughts. 'Everything is in the case file.'

'Are you sure?' Rhodin reached behind his computer monitor and picked up an old file in a manila folder.

Kjeld's heart rate increased. It took him a moment to catch his breath and relax. Then he nodded, attempting to reassure himself as much as the chief. 'Yes. It was an accident. I don't know how it happened. It was thoroughly investigated and there wasn't any negligence found on our part.'

'On *your* part, Kjeld. That I believe. And even if you had left the door unlocked, I know it wouldn't have been intentional.' Rhodin smacked the file on his knee. 'But what about Nils? If SU has taken an interest in this case then they must have found something that we missed all those years ago. And if it wasn't you then that only leaves one other person.'

Kjeld furrowed his brows and racked his brain to remember the events of that day. It wasn't difficult to recall. It had been one of the great disasters of his early career. One that almost convinced him that he wasn't cut out to be a detective. Although he didn't think about it consciously anymore, it was a case that sometimes woke him up in the middle of the night. Because even though it had been proved an accident, something about it had always lingered. Something never did seem right.

He knew he'd locked the door. He just didn't know how she got out. And, at the time, Nils had seemed just as surprised as Kjeld when she threw open the back door of the police vehicle and leapt over the barrier to the oncoming leg of the highway.

'Kjeld? Is there something I need to know about the Emma Hassan case?'

'No, sir.'

'You're not covering for him, are you?'

The question took Kjeld off guard. It was a question he expected from one of his suspicious colleagues. Not from the chief who'd known him since his days as a rookie. 'No, sir.'

Rhodin sighed. 'You know I had to ask.'

'Was there anything else you wanted to ask?'

Rhodin eyed him with a hard stare that quickly wore off. 'No. Go on. Get out of here. And bring me the bastard who killed that poor girl.'

Rhodin shook his head. 'Louisa Karlsson, of all people. That's going to be a hell of a day when it hits the press.'

Chapter 7

'Take your time,' Kjeld said. Across the table were clear evidence bags filled with various items Sixten had uncovered in the bin of the house that bordered the property where the body was found. The body that they were reasonably certain had once been Louisa Karlsson. It was the wallet in the muddy tote bag that had practically sealed that belief in Kjeld's mind. Inside was a faded University of Gothenburg student card, a driver's permit, and a debit card, all of which had Louisa's name on them. There was also a mobile phone, a half-eaten bag of salted liquorice candies, a brush with blonde hairs caught between the bristles, and two library books.

Abel Karlsson took one look at the evidence bags containing his daughter's personal items and broke down. His sobs were uncontrollable, punctuated by deep panicked breaths and choking tears. The sound echoed throughout the small confines of the interview room. And it took almost twenty minutes before his eldest, now only, daughter, Danna, managed to soothe him down to a whimpering blubber.

Kjeld and Esme sat opposite Abel and Danna, waiting for the both of them to find the strength to continue. Esme had placed two cups of tea on the table in front of them, but they sat untouched, and had gone cold by the time either of them were prepared to speak.

'I'm so sorry for your loss,' Kjeld said. The words sounded flat, but he, too, could feel a thickness in his throat. This man had lost a daughter. A daughter he thought he'd never have to worry about again. Kjeld couldn't imagine how his own reaction would be if the situation had been reversed. 'And I know this is difficult, but I have to make an official confirmation before we can go further. To your knowledge, do these items belong to your daughter, Louisa Karlsson?'

Abel opened his mouth to respond, but only a raspy breath escaped. He dropped his head and gave a wordless nod.

Danna placed a hand on her father's back, then she looked to Kjeld. Her eyes were red, but she had yet to cry in front of them. Perhaps she'd already done so on the drive over. 'Yes. That's Louisa's tote bag. I recognise it. The hairbrush, too. I gave it to her for Christmas last year. It was in a gift set with—' She cut herself off realising it wasn't important. 'And that's definitely her phone. It used to be mine. I gave it to her when I bought a new one.'

Kjeld tried to offer a grateful smile, but it felt wanting. There was nothing he could say or do to relieve the unbearable agony they must have been going through in that moment. All he could give them was his attention, but even that was lacking. While he ought to have been focusing on Louisa, his thoughts drifted to the case Rhodin had mentioned to him as he left the station. Emma Hassan.

Kjeld had a very clear recollection of the day he'd informed her mother, Maja, that her daughter had passed. It was one of the first times in his career that he'd had to deliver the news himself. Nils had insisted. He remembered sitting on a sofa across from Maja. He couldn't recall what he said exactly, but he'd never forget the way she broke down in front of him, blubbering into the front of the plain formless dress meant to hide her large figure. Minutes later she'd pulled him into an awkward embrace, engulfing him with her sobs and weeping eyes smearing mascara on his button-up. A few days later she was threatening to sue the police department for neglect.

Esme pushed a box of tissues towards them.

Danna handed her father a tissue. 'What happened?'

Kjeld hesitated, his gaze averting to the bagged items on the table.

'We don't know yet and to be perfectly honest, we won't officially know it's her until the pathologist has a forensic odontologist compare the findings to Louisa's dental records. But from what we've seen and where the body was found, I think it's safe to say there's a high likelihood that it's her. And regrettably we are classifying it as a homicide,' Esme said. She had the perfect tone for these kinds of conversations. Calm, relaxed. Sympathetic but professional. Kjeld was always grateful when Esme took the lead on informing family members of the grievous circumstances surrounding the murder of their loved one. But in this case, he felt ashamed for not having the strength to speak up.

'She was found at his house?' Danna's face slackened.

'I'm afraid so,' Esme replied.

Abel's expression darkened, his eyes focused on Kjeld. 'Was it one of *them*?'

'Them?' Esme raised a brow.

'Gjur Hägglund had a small fan club for a while after his arrest,' Kjeld said, unable to hide his disgust. 'But it was mostly angry misogynists on the internet just looking to start arguments and rile people up. It died down after his death.'

'Dad got a few hate letters in the mail back then,' Danna said. 'But we haven't received one in years. Do you think it could be one of them?'

'It's too early to rule anything out, but so far there's no evidence to suggest that kind of involvement. It is, however, a lead we intend to follow up.'

'What about his family members? Someone who was angry

about his incarceration?' Abel stared at Kjeld, but Kjeld had the impression he wasn't really looking at him.

'What about the current owner of the house?' Danna said. 'Could they be responsible?'

Esme sent an uneasy peer in Kjeld's direction, searching his face for a clue into his thoughts.

Kjeld's expression remained firm. He was trying his hardest not to give in to his emotions. But in truth, with Gjur being dead, they were essentially starting this investigation with zero leads. Which was why this conversation with her family was so important. 'As soon as we have more information, you'll both be the first to know.'

An unwieldy silence filled the room. When it was finally broken it was by Abel trying to build up the courage through a raspy whisper. 'How?'

Esme fidgeted in the chair. 'We haven't received the results from the pathologist yet, but there was a fire.'

'Was she in pain?'

Esme bit her lower lip, struggling with how to answer.

'She's gone, Abel,' Kjeld interrupted. 'Whatever pain she might have experienced is over now.'

Abel groaned. He took another tissue from the box on the table and wiped his eyes. 'Thank God her mother isn't here for this.'

Kjeld turned to Danna. 'Where is Fru Karlsson?'

'Mum passed on last year,' Danna explained. 'Breast cancer.'

'I'm sorry to hear that.' And Kjeld was. Thankfully he didn't know what it was like to lose a child, but he did understand the pain of watching someone slowly wither away before him. Cancer had taken his mother. And it had almost taken Bengt.

Esme leaned forward. 'Was there anything different about Louisa recently? Any new people in her life? Conflicts at work? Anyone you can think of who may have wanted to harm her?'

Abel shook his head. 'She kept to herself. She didn't go out much.'

'She lived with Dad,' Danna said. 'Has ever since, well, you know. When she finished her studies, she got a job at the local library. Occasionally we'd go shopping together, but she bought most of her clothing online. Her routine was cautious and guarded. She went to work. She came home. That's it.'

'No significant others or close friends?' Esme asked.

Danna frowned. 'She tried to go out on a few dates early on while she was still studying, but they never worked out. She had a good friend her first year in college, but they fell out as well. She was too afraid to get close to anyone. Took her years to even open up to her therapist. She was getting better though. She ...'

The reality of what had happened seemed to hit Danna later than her father. She sank back into the stiff plastic chair as though hoping it would engulf her completely.

'She was working through her trauma,' Abel said. 'She'd even written a letter to that bastard during the trial, forgiving him of everything he'd done. Both to her and the other women. I hate to say it but I was furious when I found out. Why should she have to forgive him in order to move on with her life? And what good did it do her?'

Another lull fell between them and Kjeld found himself wondering why neither Abel nor his eldest daughter seemed to notice that Louisa hadn't been home for breakfast that morning.

'She hadn't been missing?' Esme asked, taking the words right out of Kjeld's head.

'She spent the weekend with Danna.'

Danna turned a confused glance on her father. 'No, she didn't.'

'Are you saying she lied to me?' Abel's face pinched in disbelief.

'No, I mean ...' Danna paused, trying to find her thoughts. 'She was supposed to stay with me. That was the plan. But when I last spoke to her she said she'd changed her mind. She didn't want to. Said she was too tired to deal with the kids.'

'When did she tell you this?'

'Saturday morning at the library. I took my kids there for a visit. We do that once a week. Not just to check on her, of course, but you know how it is when you worry. Anyway, the kids were really rambunctious and acting up. And Louisa was in one of her moods. You know, down. Depressed. Said she didn't think she could deal with a night of screaming kids and that she planned to go home after work.'

'And she didn't give you any indication that she might have something else planned? Or that she was going to make any stops on her way home?'

'She always took the bus home from work. The timetable doesn't leave much room for stops.' Danna shook her head. 'Oh, God, I should have asked her if everything was okay. I should have insisted that the kids would be settled down by the time she got off work. It's all my fault.'

'It's not your fault,' Esme said. 'You can't blame yourself for that.'

Abel clenched his fingers around the fabric of his shirt.

'We're going to have to come by and take a look at her room.' Kjeld didn't bother asking because he knew that this was something the family had already been through before. He also knew that Abel would do anything to find out what happened to his daughter.

Danna nodded, wiping the tears from her face.

'Inspector?'

Kjeld turned his attention to Abel. The look in his eyes, however, wasn't the tragic grief he'd expressed when he first saw Louisa's belongings spread out in evidence bags. And it wasn't sorrow, either. It was pure unadulterated rage.

'You find the son of a bitch who did this to my daughter.' Abel gritted his teeth hard. 'You find them and this time you don't make prison an option.'

Chapter 8

Breaking the news of Louisa's death to her family left a sour taste in Kjeld's mouth. Many detectives grew numb to the practice over time, but Kjeld became more sensitive to it. It rolled around in his empty stomach like a piece of undigested meat that secreted a foamy bile, threatening to squeeze upward and burn the back of his throat. Perhaps it was because he now had a child of his own that he'd become keenly aware of how fragile the thread of life was and how quickly it could be snatched away. He tried to maintain his stoic, standoffish disposition, but every time he had to look a parent in the eye and tell them their child was gone he felt a piece of himself crack off and crumble.

Fathers were the worst. Mothers leaned on their friends, their sisters, their therapists, other women who had lost children by birth or tragedy. They opened up and sought methods to help them grapple with their daily suffering. Fathers went into the garage and unloaded a round of buckshot into their heads. That's how they coped.

The floor of the Violent Crimes Division at Gothenburg City Police was bustling with officers, moving in and out. While they hadn't yet released Louisa's identity, news of another crime at the Cellar Sadist's house spread quickly. The persistent chatter of what had happened or who could have been responsible set Kjeld's limited patience to boil. And he'd already downed two paracetamol with a cup of rancid coffee in hopes of minimising his burgeoning headache.

Kjeld's phone buzzed on the desk, reminding him of an appointment with his therapist, Alice Pihl. The timing was almost too fortuitous.

'Can you believe Martin Stenmarck didn't qualify in the semi-final? Unbelievable!'

Kjeld glanced up to see Sixten following Esme from the department's kitchenette. He balanced three mugs of coffee in his hands and leaned in her direction when he spoke, giving him an awkward shoulder slump. Sixten was a tall, slim-figured man with a head of unruly blond curls that he tried unsuccessfully to slick down with gel that smelled like glue. He was the talk of the water cooler among many of the call operators and receptionists because of his charming smile and genuine politeness. He also had one of those faces that looked more suited for a lead singer in a boy band than a police detective, which no doubt endeared him to most of their younger colleagues.

Sixten set Kjeld's coffee mug down in front of him with a smile. 'What do you think, boss?'

Kjeld took a sip of the coffee and winced. Someone had put sugar in it. 'What do I think about what?'

'Mello.'

'What?'

'*Melodifestivalen*! The third semi-finals aired last night. I still can't believe Stenmarck was pushed to the second-chance round.'

'That's because he sang in Swedish.' Axel Lund, the forensic data analyst who often assisted their team, picked up his head from behind his extra wide computer screen. Axel had at least fifteen years on Kjeld and zero desire for professional advancement. He was distinctly unobtrusive, shorter in stature than most of the men in the department, and had a dry monotone voice.

He often treated his job like a chore, although he was one of the best forensic analysts in the department. Like Kjeld he usually found Sixten's youthful enthusiasm overbearing and trite, but their mismatched personalities often resulted in an amusing display of banter. One which had quickly earned them their office nicknames – Tweedle Lund and Tweedle Sund. 'You can't win *Melodifestivalen* unless you sing in English because that's the only way you have a chance of winning Eurovision.'

'I don't think that's true! Is it?' Sixten glanced to Kjeld.

'Don't look at me. I stopped watching Eurovision after the travesty of 2009.'

'But Norway's song was great that year,' Sixten said in disbelief.

'Let me guess.' Esme grinned. 'There weren't any metal bands in the grand finale.'

Kjeld shrugged. 'What can I say? I'm a sucker for a good rock ballad.'

'It's still a sham. How many non-English songs have won Eurovision in the last fifty years? Twenty?' Axel held up his phone. 'Forty-six per cent of winners since 1966 sang in English. Do you know what the percentage of Swedish language winners is?'

'No doubt you're going to tell me.' Sixten smirked.

'Two-point-nine per cent. Stenmarck didn't have a chance.'

'And, to be fair, there's no way the judges are going to send a song called "Let the Shit Burn" to the Eurovision contest,' Esme said, tucking a strand of unruly hair back behind her ear. 'I did like the song though.'

'If the people vote for it, they will,' Sixten insisted.

'No way. It's totally rigged,' Axel said before burying his face back into whatever he was working on.

Kjeld slouched in his chair and pinched the bridge of his nose. He was grateful for the temporary reprieve Sixten's conversation had given his thoughts, but the moment the conversation lulled he began mulling over the scene they'd witnessed that morning. It jarred him thinking about the state Louisa's body had been found in. That brutal image of her remains chilled him to the bone and left him with an aching sense of misplaced guilt that made it impossible for him to join in the office banter. He should have been there to protect her the way he had eight years ago.

He'd failed her. And it left him wondering who else he'd failed.

'Axel,' Kjeld said after gathering his thoughts. 'I need you to go through some CCTV footage around the Marksmyntgatan car park across from the Högsbo Library. We're fairly certain that's the last place Louisa Karlsson was seen. At least, that's the last location her family can place her at before she went missing. There's a pharmacy and a bank machine in that area which ought to have operating cameras so we should be able to determine what time she arrived and left work. If we're lucky we'll be able to get a glimpse of her.'

'We also need to interview her colleagues and find out if there'd been any changes in her behaviour at work,' Esme said. 'The Karlsson family seems to be very close, but it's possible Louisa told her co-workers things that she didn't share with her family. According to her family she didn't have a very diverse schedule so anything out of the ordinary is important. Particularly anything that could point us to a potential suspect.'

Axel nodded, immediately pulling up the area on his computer, including the contact information for the library. 'Has anyone considered the obvious?'

'The obvious?' Kjeld raised a brow.

'Someone related to the Cellar Sadist.'

Kjeld cringed at the name. He'd always hated the way the media painted killers in an extravagant light. Giving them colourful nicknames had always sat wrong with him. The focus should have been on the victims, not the psychopath. 'Esme made a call to the Land Registration Authority earlier. Apparently Hägglund didn't have any next of kin. The house was owned by a real estate company that was planning to remodel the home and put it on the market, but its reputation has kept it empty for years.'

'Did the family mention anyone with grievances against her?' Sixten asked.

Kjeld shook his head. 'Nothing. Which means we're starting from scratch just as we would any other homicide. Friends, family, close connections.'

'What about a copycat?' Axel rubbed his chin. 'You've got the same victim, the same setting, potentially the same method of killing—'

'Hägglund didn't have a single method of killing,' Kjeld interrupted. He thought back to when they found the other bodies on Hägglund's property. The ones who hadn't survived. Most of them he'd killed impulsively out of rage when they didn't appease his fantasy. Louisa had been smart. She'd indulged him just enough to stay alive. That was what kept her from being bludgeoned over the head with a saucepan or choked under the grip of Hägglund's meaty hands. 'And regardless of what he claimed he had planned for Louisa back then, he never got a chance to follow through with it.'

'And until we know the official cause of death, we shouldn't speculate on the idea of a copycat.' Esme turned a focused gaze on Axel. 'Most crimes are committed by someone close to the victim. Let's start there and fan outwards. Kjeld and I will be following up with Frisk at the pathologist's office and in the meantime we're going to need extra help manning the phones. The press is already onto the case and we need to make sure we stay on top of it.'

Sixten groaned. 'The phone lines are the worst. It's just a bunch of crazies looking for attention.'

Esme offered an encouraging smile. 'You'd be surprised how many cases get solved because one officer hears something on the tip line that everyone else ignored.'

Sixten's mouth upturned in that boyish smile. Kjeld thought he caught more than just a little admiration in the man's eyes as well, but Esme didn't seem to notice. Or, if she did, she pretended not to.

'The chief will probably be organising a press conference on this one before the end of the day so we need to collect as much information as we can before then. Crime scene technicians should already be on their way to the Karlsson residence to go through Louisa's belongings. I don't have high hopes that they'll find anything, but you never know.' Kjeld paused. 'And it goes without saying that Louisa's name doesn't leave this office. The last thing the family needs is the media tearing open old wounds before they've had time to grieve.'

Kjeld took another sip of his coffee having forgotten that someone, Sixten he assumed, added sugar to it, and spat it back into the mug.

A jolt to the back of his chair rocked Kjeld forward and he twisted to look up at the smug face of Kenneth Olsen, one of the mid-ranking detectives with whom Kjeld had never got along. Lately, however, Kenneth had been on loan to the organised crime department which meant he hadn't been around much to mock Kjeld with his snide barbs. Kjeld had enjoyed the reprieve while it lasted.

'Looks like your buddy is on the news again.' Kenneth sneered.

Esme shot Kenneth a hard glare, but Kenneth merely smirked and kept walking towards the group of detectives and officers congregated around the flat-screen television that was mounted to the wall near the kitchenette.

Kjeld focused his attention on the television, which showed a crowd of about twenty-five people outside the general court building, waving signs while court officials looked on baffled from the main entrance.

The camera swivelled back to an on-the-scene reporter from one of the major news networks. 'We're standing outside the Gothenburg general courthouse where these citizens have assembled to protest the incarceration of Nils Hedin. Deputy Commissioner Nils Hedin was arrested last October under suspicion of being the so-called Kattegat Killer, the serial murderer responsible for the deaths of at least four people including Roux Aubuchon, the French Ambassador to Sweden. The case had previously been postponed on account of medical reasons. Hedin sustained a gunshot wound during his capture. No reason as yet has been given as to why the courts have delayed the trial once again, but these protesters claim that Hedin was the fall guy for a larger conspiracy deep within the government. Regardless of what the general court decides to rule on the case, there's no doubt it will leave this city divided.'

A tense silence fell over the group that stood around the television as the reporter cut to the weather. A few peering glances were cast in Kjeld's direction, but he didn't give any of them the satisfaction of showing that he noticed. He kept a straight face, refusing to display any form of recognition that might allow them to presume he was bothered by their judgemental glares. He wasn't. Not really. He didn't need their reproachful sneers to make him feel guilty for what happened with Nils. He had enough guilt on his own.

The door to Chief Superintendent Rhodin's office swung open, slamming against the wall. The sound rattled through the room. Kjeld glanced up to see Rhodin's stocky figure in the doorway. 'Last time I checked gawking at the television never solved any crimes! Get back to work or all of you will be doing overtime on *Midsommar*!'

Chapter 9

Tisdag | Tuesday

Ove Frisk, chief medical examiner for Gothenburg's forensic department, dropped a toothed pair of forceps into a metal tray on the counter. Then he waddled back over to the body on the slab, stopping to hike his belt up over his round belly. One of the buttons on his dress shirt was missing, exposing his sweaty undershirt. 'The forensic odontologist sent his findings over this morning. The teeth have been sent to the lab for DNA confirmation, but from what he could see from the dental remains, this is indeed Louisa Karlsson.'

Kjeld's shoulders sagged, that tiny fragment of hope escaping in a sigh.

'The official cause of death is cardiac arrest, but as you can tell from the state of the body that was brought on by the severity of the burns.'

Kjeld huddled beside the slab. It was so cold in the morgue that he could see his own breath on the air. He tucked his hands into his pockets and pulled his arms in close to the sides of his torso to preserve his own body heat.

'Sorry if it's extra chilly in here today,' Ove said. 'The building supervisor accidentally turned off the heat yesterday. Not that we ever let it get too warm in here, but it is a bit more uncomfortable than usual.'

'I can't feel my fingers,' Sixten mumbled from the opposite side of the room.

Ove, not accustomed to a lot of humour from his visitors, nodded to the bench of dissection equipment. 'There are gloves on the counter.'

It hadn't been Kjeld's plan to bring Sixten along, but at the last minute the chief insisted that he and Esme take the younger detective with them. For the "experience", Rhodin had said, but Kjeld sensed it was because Sixten had been pestering him all morning and he just wanted the greenhorn out of his sight.

Kjeld took a step closer to Esme, who'd been quietly observing the cadaver with a quizzical gleam since they'd arrived.

In the centre of the frigid room, Louisa Karlsson's body, burned face unrecognisable in the bright fluorescent lighting, lay lifeless on the dissection table. Like her face, her torso was a brutally charred mass of flesh. What remained of muscle and tendons were red and raw. And her arms, already thin to begin with, were scorched down through multiple layers of tissue. The tips of her fingers and toes were burned nearly to the bone.

Kjeld tried not to imagine how long her body must have been engulfed in flames to elicit that result. Or how hot the fire had been.

'She was alive when this was done to her?' Esme's lips pulled taut in a grimace.

'Without a doubt. That was the first thing I looked at. Normally when someone dies from immolation, such as in a house fire, you find them in a pugilistic pose. They tuck their arms and knees together like a boxer. This is a result of the muscles contracting during the burning and the joints subsequently flexing.' Ove motioned to the length of the body. 'As you can see, Louisa's foetal

49

position is almost textbook in that regard. There's an extreme bend in the arms and legs, suggesting that she was on the ground when she succumbed to the fire. But there was also evidence in the skin, particularly on the back and shoulders, which indicates she was alive when she was burning. I've already sent some samples to the lab to test for trace elements of an accelerant and I'm waiting to hear back on the blood tests for confirmation of cardiac arrest. But at this point I think it's safe to say she was alive when she was burning and that the flames continued well after her death. Particularly where the lower limbs were concerned.'

From across the room, barely within view of the slab, Sixten gagged. Kjeld couldn't blame him. It was one thing to see the body in a dark basement, but under the bright examination lights the detail of her suffering was nauseatingly vivid.

'How could anyone do that to someone?' Sixten muttered.

Ove held up his hands and shrugged. With his round face, pink nose a tad too small for his face, cheeks rosy from years of late nights with a bottle of red wine, and bushy grey beard, he looked like a tired Santa Claus. 'That's an answer I can't give you.'

'My God,' Esme whispered.

Sixten scrunched his face into a squeamish grimace. Before they arrived at the morgue Sixten had been bright-eyed and eager. Now his face was a decided shade of green, not unlike Esme's car, which made Kjeld feel a little guilty about not welcoming Sixten more thoroughly into their team. He shouldn't have been so hard on the man simply because he was new, but Kjeld struggled with change. And he wasn't accustomed to having someone around who was full of pervasive enthusiasm. It made him wonder if there had ever been a time early on in his own career when his eagerness was so irritating. If so, Nils had never said anything. Then again, there had been a lot Nils didn't say.

'Can we cover her now?' Sixten asked, motioning to the cadaver's exposed lower half.

Ove rubbed his chin on his sleeve. 'This isn't a movie, kid. If you're going to stay in the murder business then you better get used to all sorts of parts dangling about.'

'I only meant out of respect ...' Sixten's voice trailed off, embarrassed.

'She's gone, son.' Ove's tone was brusque and a tad too pedantic. 'She doesn't care about respect anymore. If she could speak I'm certain the only thing she'd care about is you finding whoever did this to her.'

Kjeld almost felt sorry for Sixten. It wasn't easy dealing with Ove's overbearing gruffness. Then again, it could have been worse. Not that any murder was better. But it was always the ones where the faces had been mangled beyond recognition or bloated, full of insects eating away at the eye sockets, that made Kjeld's stomach churn. His own first homicide had him vomiting in the bin during the autopsy. In that respect, Sixten was doing fairly well keeping it together. But there was something about this murder that left him with a gut-wrenching nausea. It was gruesome because of her innocence. Because she'd already survived a circumstance worse than death once before. Because her murderer had treated her so cruelly. And because there was nothing about Louisa that warranted this level of torture.

'Fire is a horrible way to go,' Esme said. Her quiet tone suggested that she might have had some personal experience with that and, not for the first time, Kjeld wondered what else he didn't know about the woman he spent nearly every day with.

Kjeld straightened up and slipped his hands in his pockets. 'We need to make sure Axel prioritises the CCTV footage from the library where Louisa worked. If the killer found her there then hopefully we'll be able to see something of them on the footage. If not, then maybe we can at least get a timeline of her movements and find out where she went after work. We know she usually took the bus to and from work as well, so let's get in touch with whoever was driving that night. Maybe they saw something.'

Esme looked to Sixten and said exactly what was on Kjeld's mind. 'It'll probably be a full night of footage, if you're interested in the overtime. It's tedious work, but that's how most homicides are solved.'

'I'll get on it as soon as we get back.' Sixten smiled, grateful not to be ignored, but still holding back the urge to be sick.

Kjeld's phone buzzed in his pocket. He pulled it halfway out of his pocket to see the name of the caller. Bengt. He let it go to voicemail.

'Thanks, Ove. Let us know if you find anything else,' Kjeld said.

Ove placed his hands on his lower back and jutted his hips forward in a small stretch. 'I don't expect to find much more, but I'll give you a call when the bloodwork and toxicology get back to me. And I don't want to be *that guy*, but please don't forget to sign off on the examination documents in your inbox. The pencil-pushers in legal have been harassing me about your department forgetting to acknowledge receipt of evidence.'

'Don't worry, Ove. I'll make sure everything is filed properly.' Esme's mind was a steel trap when it came to organisation. Were it not for her Kjeld would have been buried beneath paperwork years ago.

Ove glanced back down at the body. That dry wit of his was replaced with abrupt solemnity. 'It really grates on me, you know. I remember those other women. The ones who didn't make it. Every time they brought another one in my heart just sank. We threw a party the day you caught that bastard.'

Kjeld frowned. His thoughts had drifted and he was only half paying attention. His phone buzzed again, the sound louder in that confined, windowless space. 'I know how it looks, but this doesn't feel like someone impersonating Hägglund to me. This is too planned. Too—'

'Practised?'

Kjeld shivered at the thought. 'Let's hope not.'

'Why's that?' Sixten asked.

'Because that would mean they've done this before,' Kjeld said, shrugging his shoulders against the cold in the room. 'And that they might do it again.'

Chapter 10

The bell above the door jingled.

Andrea didn't look up. Instead she tore open the plastic from the carton of filtered cigarettes the shit-for-brains supplier had wrongly sent to her. She'd ordered Marlboro Reds. They sent her Marlboro Golds. This was the third time this year that the supplier had misread her orders and it was only February. Andrea was beginning to wonder if the man was doing it on purpose because Andrea had refused to stock those cheap plastic earbuds that he offered her on discount before the holidays. Nobody bought earbuds from a convenience store. Not when there was a perfectly decent media store three blocks away and certainly not after eleven p.m. which was when she received most of her business. Cigarettes. Snacks. Low-alcohol cider. That's all anyone wanted after eleven. Everything else was just to make the shop look stocked.

No, he was probably jerking her around because she'd turned down his sleazy offer of a drink and a night out.

She should have opened a pub. That's where the real money was. Except Andrea had a record and there was no way she'd ever qualify for a liquor licence. Besides, her wife already complained that she wasn't home enough as it was.

She stuffed the packs of Golds into the slot on the shelf behind the counter until there wasn't any room left. Then she shoved the rest of the box underneath the register. She had enough Golds to last a full six months and almost no Reds. She was going to lose a profit there for sure. Maybe she could find another supplier. One with less of a misogynistic grudge. Or, at the very least, one who knew how to read an invoice.

Andrea ripped off the tape from the next box and gave a sigh of relief.

Thank God she'd had the foresight to order extra *snus*. Personally, the stuff disgusted her. She hated how it contorted people's faces like a cartoon rabbit when they stuffed it under their upper lip, protruding from their front teeth when they talked. And she hated how it left a gooey brown residue that sometimes dribbled out of the corner of their mouths when their lip loosened and lost its grip. Andrea had spent twenty-odd years in and out of the drug trade – pot, cocaine, heroin – and nothing grossed her out as much as cheap *snus* slobber.

She shoved the plastic snuff containers onto the empty slots on the shelf.

The doorbell jingled again. This time she looked up. No one there. She craned her head to peer out the window, but the rain streamed down the glass, distorting her view. Weird.

Two hours later Andrea's shift ended and she headed out into the still-dark morning. She'd lost her driver's licence a few years ago and never tried to replace it, but thankfully her shitty flat was only a twenty-minute walk from the store. Technically she could probably make it in ten, but Andrea was a dawdler. And she liked to smoke when she walked which, for one reason or another, always slowed her down.

Who was she kidding? She was just avoiding Ingrid. They hadn't been getting along recently and were bickering all the time. Hell, they were just looking for reasons to hurt each other. The last argument was about Andrea forgetting to bring home a new carton of milk after she'd accidentally bought one too close to the expiration date and it went bad before Ingrid could use it. Andrea didn't even drink milk. Why couldn't Ingrid buy her own damn milk?

If she followed the walking path she'd get to her place sooner, but Andrea liked cutting across the football field in Sunnerviksparken. There were two reasons for this. The first was that football fields always reminded her of the good memories of her childhood. Growing up in Strǎşeni had been a constant struggle for her family, especially when her father lost his job, but her brother always tried to improve her spirits by teaching her how to play football. Which worked until he died of an overdose at seventeen. The second reason was that it took longer to get home and gave her time to think. By "think" she meant stopping to get high. During the day, the park was full of children playing and local sports clubs practising. But once the sun went down it was a hub of degenerate activity. Andrea was simply one of many.

Except today. It was early and it was still raining, albeit less now than when she was stocking the store, and Andrea was alone.

Or, at least, she thought she was.

A figure approached her from across the field. At first she thought it was one of her junkie pals, hoping to bum a hit off her. But as the figure came closer she realised they were much taller than anyone she knew. Not freakishly tall, but leggy. And they didn't walk with that typical junkie hunch.

She slowed her pace and when the person was in closer view, she stopped.

'Andrea Nicolescu?'

The stranger was bundled up in a thick winter sweater and wore a balaclava over their face. For a split second, Andrea thought she recognised something about the voice, but she was distracted by the lack of emotion in the stranger's eyes. There was nothing. Not even a glimmer. Just an empty expression that caused the muscles in Andrea's stomach to clench involuntarily.

'Yeah?' Her hand trembled. She tried to hide her nerves by taking a drag on her cigarette. It didn't help.

The stranger didn't reply.

Andrea glared in annoyance. 'Who the fuck are you?'

The stranger raised their left hand quickly. Andrea flinched, her breath caught in her throat. Then she realised the hand was empty. An open palm. What the hell was this person playing at? But in her distraction she didn't see the other hand shoot out from the stranger's side.

Andrea's heart leapt into her throat. Her instinct was to run, but she was frozen in fear. The cigarette slipped from her fingers and landed in the wet grass. And her last thought as she stared down the barrel of the gun was that she should have just bought the damn milk for Ingrid.

Chapter 11

Alice Pihl's office was located at the end of a mostly forgotten corridor in the administrative wing of the Gothenburg City Police Department. While the police had always offered some form of counselling services to its officers and staff members, the decision to provide a full-time presence for them was relatively new. Alice was one of two part-time counsellors who took turns manning the oft-underused office. The first time Kjeld had met her was after his confrontation with Nils. All officers were required to attend a mandatory number of therapy sessions following the discharge of a weapon. And Kjeld had not only discharged his weapon, he'd shot a man. He'd shot a serial killer. He'd shot a friend.

When the investigation into Nils's involvement in the Aubuchon case intensified, Kjeld found himself on the opposite side of his colleagues – suspended while SU looked into the possibility that he was also involved in the brutal murders that had shaken the city to its core. And his time with Alice increased.

Kjeld took a sip of the chamomile tea Alice had steeped for him and glanced at the framed photo of a creamy white cabin in the woods, which sat on the shelf behind her desk. The room was sparsely decorated. There weren't many distractions aside from an oversized clock near the door. The style of the numbers, with its serif curvatures and pseudo antique colouring, was meant to look old-fashioned. Classic. But Kjeld would bet anything that it was plastic. There was probably an IKEA price sticker on the back. *Product of Sweden. Made in China.* Alice sat across from him in a single chair that matched the sofa in colour and design.

She said something, but he didn't hear it.

'What was that?'

'I asked if you felt guilty,' Alice repeated. She had long hair, ironed flat in that late 1960s style. Strawberry blonde was the phrase often used to describe the colour, although Kjeld never did quite understand that. Strawberries were red. Bright red. Like fire engines and sports cars. And blonde was blonde.

She caught him staring and turned her gaze down to her notepad where she scribbled something indecipherable from his position on the two-seater sofa across the room. When she was done she looked up at him from behind her glasses. Angular, thin-rimmed. Rose-coloured with a speckled pattern that brought out the pinprick polka dots on her blouse.

'Guilty about what?'

'You tell me.'

'Is this a guessing game? What are we talking about?'

'Let's start with Nils.'

Kjeld crossed his arms over his chest. 'I don't feel guilty about shooting Nils.'

'I didn't say shooting. I just said Nils in general.'

Kjeld pursed his lips and turned his attention to the window, collecting his thoughts. It was hard to say his ex-partner's name. He always unconsciously gritted his teeth afterwards. Sometimes hard enough to leave an ache in his jaw. 'I'm not responsible for what Nils did. Do I wish I'd seen it earlier? Yes, of course. But how can I feel guilty for something I knew nothing about?'

'You could feel ashamed for having been friends with the man.'

'It wasn't a real friendship. It was a façade.'

Alice tilted her head up from her notepad, expression blank. 'What makes you say that?'

'Because real friends don't kill people.'

Alice wrote something down, but Kjeld couldn't see what. 'What about your sister?'

Kjeld winced. 'I'm not responsible for the actions of others.'

Alice nodded. 'True, but that doesn't mean you might not feel responsible. The mind doesn't often work through trauma in a logical way. When a tragedy occurs, our emotions can cloud our ability to see our role in them clearly.'

'I can't change the past. Better to put it behind me and move on.'

'Assuming, of course, that you can move on.' And it was clear that Alice didn't believe he had. But before he could respond, she continued, 'How's your relationship with Bengt?'

'Better.'

Alice pushed her glasses up on the bridge of her nose in quiet disbelief.

'It's strained, but at least we're talking. Sort of. It's complicated.'

'Is it? Or are you just making it complicated?' Alice set her pen down and looked directly at him. 'You were in a relationship with someone. You were raising a child together. And then that person found someone else and moved on. There's nothing complicated about that. The only thing that's complicated are your feelings about it.'

Kjeld looked away from her and stared at the framed photograph of the cabin on her shelf. It made him think of his father's home in Varsund. A home that was empty ever since he'd moved his father to a care facility in Östersund. Eventually he'd have to go back to Jämtland and decide what to do with everything that was left behind. The house included. He'd also have to visit his father. He wasn't looking forward to that.

'Have you spoken to Bengt about how you feel?'

Kjeld laughed. 'What good would that do?'

'It might ease the tension between the both of you. It could also help him to understand why you've been having difficulty being a father to Tove. And it might give him the opportunity to see how much your relationship meant to you. Still means to you.'

Kjeld shifted uncomfortably on the sofa. 'Like you said, Bengt moved on.'

'Because he had to. You didn't give him any other choice. But you're making strides now. You're doing the right things. That might change his perception of the situation.'

Kjeld returned his focus to Alice. There was nothing but sincerity in her expression. No sympathy. No pity. Just simple honesty. Kjeld appreciated that. He knew he wasn't immune to emotions. He had his moments of fragility just like anyone else. But he struggled to let it be seen because he hated the response it elicited in people. It made him feel weak and incompetent. The same way he felt when he thought about all those years Nils had spent fooling him.

But Alice might be right. Perhaps it was time to finally open up to Bengt about everything.

'I'll think about it.'

The clock on the wall ticked into the new hour. Time was up. Kjeld pulled himself off the couch and grabbed his coat from the rack on the door. It was still wet and had dripped a damp puddle on the carpet.

'How's the case going, by the way?' Alice asked.

Kjeld slipped his arms into his coat. 'It's going to be a difficult one.'

'This is your first time back in the field after your suspension,' she said. It wasn't a question, but Kjeld felt like it ought to have been.

He nodded as he buttoned up the front of his coat, idly wondering why he hadn't listened to Esme about getting his zip-up winter coat from the back of his closet. He supposed he was just anxious for spring. 'It's fine. I'm ready to get back out there.'

'It's okay if you aren't, you know.'

'I am,' Kjeld said, his half-hearted attempt at a smile falling flat. It was the first thing he'd said to her during their session that didn't feel like the truth, but he needed to believe it.

Chapter 12

Esme rushed home after adding the pathology report that Ove provided them into the case file and typing up her notes on the events thus far. Normally she would delegate some of those tasks to the other team members, but she saw how shaken up Kjeld had been at the crime scene and wanted to make sure nothing slipped through the cracks. As a result, she ended up staying in the office longer than planned and didn't have time to do anything more than spray on a new layer of deodorant and change her shirt before she hurried out to meet her friends for dinner.

Esme was looking forward to seeing Tilde and Miriam, two friends she'd known since high school, as it had been months since they'd had the opportunity to get together and catch up on each other's lives. As it was, Esme had missed their last two planned outings because of work, which was always frustrating for Tilde who drove up from Malmö. But as she hurried to make it to the café on time, Esme caught herself thinking about the case they were working on and wondered if she shouldn't cancel again.

The lack of substantial evidence from Louisa's crime scene plagued her thoughts. It was still early days, but she was trying to reason what they might have missed in the initial examinations the entire way to the restaurant. Thirty minutes later as she sat at one of the tightly packed tables against the wall in Blackbird café, one of her favourite restaurants and her choice for their long-awaited girls' night out, she was still thinking about it.

Blackbird wasn't a traditional dining choice, but it was "very Esme" as her friends said. It was a vegan restaurant with a relaxed and welcoming energy. She'd thought it had been a good choice for their girls' night out. A comfortable location for a fun, casual dinner. But if she'd known Miriam was going to invite her friend, Britta, from her baby yoga class, she might have chosen differently.

'What is this exactly?' Britta poked at the meat substitute with her fork.

'They call it *lyckling*,' Esme said. 'It's one of their specialties. They make it from seitan, a wheat gluten. They marinate it in mango, ginger, lime, and coriander and then pan-fry it or heat it up in the oven. It's really good with the curry. Would you like to try some of mine? I ordered extra sauce.'

Britta turned up her nose. 'No, thank you. I'm on a strict paleo diet from my dietician. Mostly lean meats, fish, and nuts. It's supposed to help me get my pre-pregnancy figure back.'

Miriam laughed. 'My youngest is already sixteen months and I still haven't lost a single pound of my baby weight!'

'Tell me about it,' Tilde said. 'I swear I could be on a diet of water and rice cakes for an entire month and I'd still have this belly. But it's worth it, isn't t?'

Miriam and Britta nodded in agreement. Esme spread another layer of green curry mix on her ciabatta and took another bite. She didn't really know what to say.

'But it is nice to get an evening to ourselves for once.' Miriam smiled.

Esme noticed then that Miriam looked a little older around the eyes than the last time she'd seen her, but she still exuded that vibrant energy she'd had when they were growing up. She wasn't jealous, but she did feel a sense of misplaced yearning.

Like she was missing out on something that she'd been actively trying to avoid.

'It's so difficult to schedule things when you have children. I practically had to beg my husband to give me an evening off.' Britta waved over the waitress and ordered a glass of wine.

'Is merlot on the paleo diet?' Miriam grinned.

Britta shrugged. 'It's made from grapes.'

Esme had to force herself to laugh with the others in response.

'I'm just glad we were finally able to find a day that we all had free,' Esme replied. She felt a little left out of the conversation, but tried not to let it show. All of this talk about children made her think of the anguish in Abel Karlsson's eyes when he realised his daughter was dead and Esme found herself staring aimlessly into the ceramic ramekin that held her extra curry dressing. Like Kjeld, she'd hoped for the Karlssons' sake that the body wasn't Louisa's, but even if that had been the case it wouldn't have changed things. If it hadn't been Louisa it would have been someone else's loved one who was murdered. Either way someone would be hurt. And either way Esme would still have to find the killer.

'Oh God, yes! It's about time we got together again,' Tilde said between bites. 'Not that I don't love being a mum, but I sometimes feel like I'm going to rip my hair out. All those late hours waking up in the middle of the night. I'm so glad that Marit was able to take off a week to watch Violet so I could come up and visit you guys. I still miss her though. Let me show you this video Marit sent me the other day!'

Tilde took out her phone and played a thirty-second film clip of a tiny infant squeezing her index finger. Both Miriam and Britta made exaggerated expressions of admiration followed by the proverbial "awws" and "how adorables". Esme gave a small smile. Violet truly was a picture-perfect baby but seeing how Miriam and Britta reacted to the image left Esme with an odd sense of estrangement. It wasn't unlike holidays with her family. She spent nearly every family gathering shrugging off her aunt's questions of when she planned to settle down and have children. In the beginning, when her cousin started having children, Esme would laugh off her aunt's insistence. Later it made her angry. Nowadays she tried to work the holidays to avoid the conversations altogether.

It wasn't that Esme didn't like children or want them. She just didn't know if being a mother was in the cards for her. There were other things she wanted to do first. And she knew that was nothing to be ashamed of. Yet still these kinds of conversations made her feel like a disappointment.

'What about you, Esme? Any chance that you'll be joining us at baby yoga soon?' Britta asked, completely ignorant of the insensitivity of her question. She pushed aside the *lyckling* on her plate to stab at her salad instead.

'What?' Esme had been lost in her thoughts and missed the question.

'Will we be seeing you at baby yoga soon?' Britta repeated.

Esme didn't know what bothered her more, Britta's rude question or the fact that she wouldn't even try the food. But it was clear from Britta's expression that she had no idea how hurtful her question could be.

'I don't think so,' Esme mumbled in between bites.

'Don't you want children?' Britta looked at her like she was from outer space.

Esme's face burned with embarrassment.

'Esme is great with kids,' Miriam interrupted. 'She watched my eldest two a few times when they were younger. They loved her.'

'Esme's just more practical than us. She wants to make sure she's found the right partner and is properly settled before she dives into family life. I know I would have had it easier if I'd saved up some money beforehand.' Tilde smiled.

Esme knew it was meant to be a compliment, but she couldn't help but feel like there was an unintentional barb to Tilde's words. Of course, Tilde would have been devastated if she'd known she'd hit a painful chord with Esme. Which was why Esme just replied with a half-hearted chuckle.

'I don't really work the greatest hours at the moment,' Esme said, suddenly even less interested in her meal than Britta was. But all of this talk of babies and families made her chest tighten. She suddenly felt like the walls were closing in on her. She sipped her mineral water to distract herself, hoping that the cool wet taste would ease some of her nerves.

Miriam leaned across the table. 'But surely there must be someone at your work who's interesting.'

Esme took another bite to avoid having to respond.

'Police officers are really fit.' Britta grinned. 'There's one who goes to my gym. I swear if I weren't already married ...'

'You would not!' Tilde laughed.

'I absolutely would. That man looks like he was cut from marble.' Britta paused. 'From what I can tell anyway. Sometimes he lifts up his shirt to wipe the sweat off his brow. Half the gym has a membership just to see it. I swear.'

Tilde snorted. 'You're unbelievable! But seriously, Esme, there must be some hot guy or girl at the station. I think I watched every single crime drama on Netflix in the last two months of my pregnancy. And everyone on those shows was gorgeous. That's gotta be based on truth, right? Tell me it is. Are all your colleagues so good-looking that it's impossible to choose between them?'

Esme shook her head. 'Not really.'

'Tilde! You make it sound like she works on the set of a soap opera!' Miriam waved over a waitress and ordered another Ramlösa citrus water. 'But now I'm curious. There's *no one* at work you're even slightly interested in? Not even for a one-night stand?'

'I don't think it's really a good idea to get involved with someone I work with.'

'What about your detective partner? What was his name?'

'Kjeld?'

'Sounds sexy already.' Britta winked.

'Why is that name so familiar?' Tilde asked. 'Have you talked about him before?'

'You probably saw him in the papers.' Miriam took out her phone and pulled up an article on *The Chatterbox*, holding it up for everyone at the table to see. A photo of Kjeld standing in the rain in front of Gjur Hägglund's house stared back at them.

'Girl! He is hot! Let me see that!' Britta took the phone from Miriam. 'I would jump that in a second. Wouldn't you?'

'Hell no, I'm way too gay for that.' Tilde grinned.

'He's married. Is that it?' Miriam teased.

'No.' Esme pursed his lips. 'He's just complicated.'

'But you do agree that he's smoking, right?' Tilde passed the phone across the table to Miriam.

Esme combed her fingers through her fringe, pressing it down to cover as much of her forehead as possible. 'No. I mean, yes, he's good-looking, but it wouldn't work. And I'm not interested in him like that. We're just friends. And I like it that way.'

Miriam looked as though she might press the issue further, but the waitress returned to ask if anyone was interested in dessert. Miriam and Tilde both ordered the chocolate brownie with milk-free whipped cream. Britta ordered a lemon *dammsugare* and a cappuccino. Esme had been thinking about the infamous chocolate and coconut pastry that she often ordered to go on the weekends. One of the few sweet indulgences that she'd been looking forward to. But she didn't feel very hungry anymore. In fact, she felt a little sick. She ordered a peppermint tea hoping it might settle her stomach.

The conversation quickly returned to talk of the other ladies' families and children. Esme sat there quietly and listened, her thoughts distracted. After a few minutes she found herself peeking at her phone under the table, hoping for a message from work that would give her an excuse to leave early. But all she'd received in the last two hours was an apologetic text from her aunt asking her to call when she got a chance and an email from her mobile phone provider reminding her that she only had five days left to upgrade to a new plan before the monthly deal was over.

She sighed and slipped her phone back into her pocket. Then she turned her attention back to her friends and tried to enjoy the stories she couldn't relate to. She even smiled once or twice, but she wasn't listening properly. She was thinking about how much anger a person would have to feel in order to burn someone alive.

Chapter 13

Onsdag | Wednesday

By the time Kjeld arrived in the incident room the next morning, Esme had already set up a whiteboard with the evidence they'd collected thus far. It was depressingly sparse. She'd posted a map of the city, pinning the location of the library where Louisa worked, as well as the location of Gjur Hägglund's house. Axel had also printed off a snapshot of Louisa from the CCTV footage, depicting her leaving the library at closing time. But there was nothing else. No suspects. No leads. Nothing but a dead girl and a grieving family who was waiting for answers that Kjeld didn't have.

'Where are we on the evidence collected from Louisa's room?'

Axel lifted up his head from behind his computer screen, twirling a pen between his fingers. 'Zilch.'

'Nothing?'

'No social media, no personal emails, the most minimal of texts. The only people she's really been in contact with for the last few years are her father, sister, colleagues – but she only messages them about work – and her therapist. The girl was a shut-in.'

'Got you a coffee, boss.' Sixten held out Kjeld's personal office mug, the one he kept in his drawer and often forgot to wash more than once a week. The aroma of a dark roast brew filled his senses. Not the normal cheap brand that was stocked in the station kitchenette.

Kjeld accepted it with a grateful nod. He used a tissue to remove the piece of chewing gum he'd hoped would stave off his cigarette craving and tossed it in the bin beneath his desk. Then he took a sip. No sugar this time. 'What about CCTV?'

'Security cameras from the pharmacy across the street show her arriving for her shift a little after nine in the morning.' Axel pulled up another clip of video footage on his computer screen, depicting the main entrance of the library. 'Here you can see her coming around the corner of the building from the back.'

'Not from the direction of the car park?' Kjeld asked.

Axel shook his head. 'The nearest bus stop is on the street behind the library. She shortcuts through the grass instead of walking around via the car park.'

'I called the library and the head librarian said Louisa worked the entire day. According to her, she didn't seem upset or distracted. In fact, she said Louisa was in uncommonly good spirits,' Sixten said. 'But she did confirm that Louisa's sister had been in that morning with her children and that Louisa was a little distracted afterwards.'

Axel fast-forwarded the surveillance footage. 'As you can see, Louisa leaves the library thirty minutes after her shift along with two of her colleagues. The two head for their cars in the car park. We have footage of them driving off separately. Louisa waves them off, locks up, and then heads back around the building to the shortcut.'

Kjeld leaned forward to get a better view of the image on the screen. 'What about the bus stop? Any cameras there?'

'Nothing. There aren't any businesses up there. And it's a small neighbourhood bus stop.'

'So, something happened between the library entrance and the bus stop.' Esme chewed on her lower lip in thought. 'She doesn't double back to the library?'

'I watched it ahead five hours on both cameras. There's nothing.'

Kjeld glanced at Sixten. 'Have we contacted the bus service? Do we know if the driver picked anyone up from that stop?'

Sixten took out a small notepad from his pocket. 'I called the transportation services in charge of that line and they didn't have any verified check-ins from that bus stop between three o'clock that afternoon and seven the next morning. I spoke to the driver that evening and he said he didn't take on any passengers on that stretch during the time we think Louisa went missing. He also claimed not to have seen anyone, but it was raining pretty hard.'

'Dammit.' Kjeld pinched the bridge of his nose. 'What about the toxicology report?'

'Frisk just sent that over a few minutes ago,' Esme said, searching through a stack of papers on the desk. 'Traces of ketamine in her system. He said the state of the body made it impossible to determine the route of administration. He was unable to find an entrance point for a potential intravenous injection, but he wouldn't rule it out at this point.'

Kjeld sighed. 'Do I even want to know what forensics recovered from the scene?'

The rest of the team went quiet, which told him everything he needed to know.

They'd found nothing. It was back to square one.

'They're still collecting evidence,' Esme offered. 'But the fire destroyed a lot. And the presence of the firefighters didn't help any.'

Kjeld stared at the near-empty board, gaze darting back and forth between the map and the photo of Louisa leaving the library. 'Then we do it the old-fashioned way. We talk to everyone. Neighbours, family, colleagues.'

'We've already talked to the family.' Sixten frowned.

'Then we do it again. We've missed something. Louisa was

a known victim of a heinous crime. This is not some random killing. Someone planned this carefully. The execution of it is too clean. But no one commits a perfect murder. Whether they're aware of it or not, someone knows more than they're letting on.'

The door to the incident room opened and a young intern hurried in, breathless. She inhaled deeply, face red and frazzled as she gasped for her words. 'Sorry to interrupt, but you need to see this.'

The intern held up a tablet displaying a rainy scene of what appeared to be an empty football field. It was livestreaming on YouTube. The number of viewers and likes were increasing by the second. When the camera turned away from the field, it centred on a woman. Henny Engström's face filled the screen. She was speaking straight into the camera and even though he knew it wasn't the case, Kjeld felt like her words and that simpering smirk, were directed at him.

'This is Henny Engström reporting to you live from Biskopsgården where it appears yet another body has been found and the police are nowhere to be seen.'

Chapter 14

The crime scene was located in Sunnerviksparken, a small grassy area crammed in between a section of lower rent apartment housing on the eastern side of Biskopsgården not far from the Lundby neighbourhood line that mostly consisted of a children's sized football field and a rusting swing set. By the time Kjeld and Esme arrived on the scene, three major media vans and two local press vehicles were already blocking traffic in both directions on the main road. A pair of uniformed officers were arguing with reporters to move their vehicles to one of the side streets in order to allow general traffic to pass safely while another officer pushed back the steadily growing crowd of photographers trying to snap pictures of the body before the crime scene technicians put up a tent.

It was a disaster.

The torrential downpour of that morning had lightened up to a drizzle, but the wind pummelled it horizontally against Esme's face as she pushed through the crowd, yelling at everyone to move back. Most of the journalists took a respectful step backwards, hoping it might endear them to her or Kjeld in exchange for a statement. It didn't, but Esme appreciated the gesture. Unsurprisingly, the lone individual who refused to follow the will of the group was Henny. While the others stepped back, she stepped forward, shoving a handheld camera in Kjeld's face.

'Inspector Nygaard! Can you tell us if this murder is related to the body found the other day?'

'We won't know anything until you let us pass.'

'Can you tell us why it took so long for law enforcement to arrive on the scene?'

Kjeld shot her an accusatory stare. 'Can you tell me how you were the one to find it?'

Henny brashly stared him out before continuing with another series of rapid-fire questions. 'Is it true that the crime committed at the Cellar Sadist's house might be the work of a copycat killer? Was someone close to Gjur Hägglund involved in the murder of the person discovered a few days ago? When will the police be releasing the identity of the body?'

The uniformed officers were using the media's distraction to put up a line of cordon tape stretching between their two vehicles. Kjeld held up the tape for Esme. She ducked under it, quickly followed by her partner who allowed the tape to snap down as a barrier between them and Henny.

Henny leaned over the tape. She was so close to Kjeld's face that if Esme hadn't known better she would have inferred that there was more to their history than Kjeld let on. But Esme knew that wasn't the case. And Henny's hissing threat only cemented that fact. She was just out for a story and would get it any way she could. 'If you don't tell me what I want to know I will find out another way. This is your chance to improve your standing with the media.'

Before Kjeld could make a scene with his response, Esme brought her fingers to her lips and let out a high-pitched whistle. An officer trying to hold back the wall of journalists glanced in her direction before jogging over.

'Kindly escort Fru Engström down to the station. We're going to have a few questions for her when we finish up here.'

The officer nodded and made his way to the other side of the police line to lead Henny towards a patrol car.

'How dare you! You bitch! You don't have any right to detain me!'

'I'm not detaining you, Henny. I'm giving you the opportunity to talk to us voluntarily before someone starts to get suspicious about how you keep ending up at the wrong place at the right time.' She paused. 'Or would you rather I read you your rights?'

Henny fumed.

'Doesn't always pay to be the first at a scene. Looking forward to having a chat about that.' Esme fixed her with a hard stare before waving off the officer and following Kjeld to the tent that the crime scene technicians finally managed to erect. Behind her she heard the clicking clamour of cameras flashing at her back.

Esme was the first in the tent after gowning up in protective gear, but from the state of the scene it didn't look like it would do much good. The weather had already had its way with the scene. Even worse was the erratic mess of footprints, in various sizes and shapes, that were scattered around the area. Half the reporters in the city had probably already snapped close-up photographs of their victim. She sighed when she realised her caution on approach to the scene was unwarranted. Another pair of muddy prints wasn't going to make much of a difference.

Esme exhaled a tired breath, disappointed and annoyed. Unlike Kjeld who was a downtrodden realist, she'd always tried to err on the side of optimism in most situations. Kjeld never expected the best of people. But she wanted to believe that, given the opportunity, people would do the right thing. Like not trample over a crime scene in order to get their picture on the front page.

In the middle of the football field, sprawled almost bullseye of the field's centre circle, was the body of a woman. Her skin was a deathly shade of purple that was enhanced by the gloom of the low-hanging clouds. She lay on her back, arms and legs naturally limp and bent as though she'd merely fallen backwards and never gotten back up. Her wavy black hair was matted along the sides of her face and in the muddy grass. And dead centre of her forehead was the explanation for the shock on her face.

A bullet hole the size of a small coin.

'We're going to have to get shoe and fingerprints from everyone on the road. There's no telling which of them ran out here for the money shot. And who knows if they touched the body or not.'

Kjeld shoved his hands into the pockets of his coat. Esme heard his phone vibrate, but he didn't answer it. He didn't even look to see who it might be. He merely stepped around Esme to the side of the body.

'Another woman,' Esme said, more out of sadness than observation. She felt an odd sense of defeat at that realisation.

Esme drew her brows together. The dead woman's eyes were open and cloudy. She was fully clothed and didn't appear to have been in a struggle. It reminded her of a few comments an old colleague of hers back in Malmö used to make. The kind of comments that began with 'Well at least she didn't suffer.' As if murder wasn't bad enough.

'This looks like a gang killing. We used to get a lot of those down in Malmö.' She felt a tiny caffeine headache begin to pinch at the front of her head. 'On the way over here I was really worried that this was going to be another Louisa, but this MO is completely different. This doesn't look like the same killer.'

'You're right, it doesn't.' Kjeld crouched down and angled forward on his haunches. There was what appeared to be a frothy foam at the corner of the cadaver's lips, but it was too minute to determine whether it had come from within the body or was a result of exposure to the elements.

'The location is weird, too. It's so open. Anyone could have witnessed the murder.' Esme took a careful step forward. 'Hopefully Frisk will be able to give us an accurate time of death.'

Kjeld stood up and glanced around the scene. He had a look on his face that Esme had grown all too accustomed to seeing.

That vague sense of recognition where he tried to puzzle out a question he wasn't ready to ask.

'What is it?'

'Who walks through a football field in the middle of the night?'

Esme shrugged. 'Maybe she was a night owl or had trouble sleeping.'

'It was raining pretty hard last night.'

'Maybe she works late. She could have been heading home.'

Esme glanced down at the ground. Heavy foot traffic in combination with the rain had made the grassy area around the body muddy and soft. Softer than might have been expected. But that aside she couldn't see anything out of the ordinary. Deep in the mud was the remains of a half-smoked cigarette. She waved the crime scene photographer over to take a picture before getting a technician to bag it up.

Kjeld stepped outside the tent and she followed. He walked a short distance away from the crime scene and stared off at a row of old flats that bordered the edge of the field. Esme narrowed her eyes, trying to see whatever it was Kjeld saw, but she drew a blank.

'If she was heading home then she probably lives in one of those buildings over there. Seems counterintuitive to walk through the grass though.'

'Maybe she was shortcutting to somewhere else.'

'Maybe.' Kjeld shoved his hands in his pockets. 'I used to work this area a lot when I first started out. It was almost nonstop domestic calls.'

Esme frowned. 'What kind of calls?'

'Domestic abuse, gang violence, drugs. I'm certain there were more than a few murders as well,' Kjeld said. 'I think there even used to be another row of flats where this park is. The city probably thought that by tearing them down they'd reduce the amount of crime in the area.'

'It probably just pushed the crime to another neighbourhood.'

Esme thought back to the woman's face, blue lips open, eyes frozen in fear.

'We need to find out who this woman is.'

'I'll make sure Frisk rushes the fingerprints, but first we need to talk to Henny Engström. I don't believe for a second that it was a coincidence she was the first on the scene. She knows something.'

A chill swept through Esme's body. The murders didn't appear to be related, but she still felt wary. Two murders in the span of a week would draw a lot of attention to their department and after the debacle with Nils that was the last thing they needed. The public would be watching their every move. They'd have to be extra careful and thorough. And stave off any baseless rumours that this could be a serial murderer.

But most importantly, they couldn't afford to make any mistakes. Certainly not in view of the press.

Chapter 15

Kjeld hated the press.

When they entered the room, Henny was leaning back in the hard-plastic chair, arms crossed impatiently. She all but ignored Esme, who sat down and immediately began arranging a file and notepad on the table in front of her. But her eyes were glued on Kjeld in a firm glare.

Kjeld took a seat beside Esme before acknowledging Henny with a glance.

'Would you like anything to drink?' Esme asked.

'No, thank you.' Henny's lips pursed in a thin line.

Kjeld watched her carefully, but Henny either hadn't yet realised how serious this conversation was or didn't care. She was in defiant mode and probably hoped that by crossing her arms and sneering her disdain she might distract them from their questions.

Esme opened up the notepad to a blank page and unclipped a pen from her shirt pocket.

'Am I under arrest?' Henny asked.

'No,' Esme replied.

'So, I don't have to answer your questions if I don't want to?' Henny shook her hair back over her shoulders.

'You don't have to, but if you don't it will be noted. And if we discover later that your failure to cooperate in any way impeded our investigation then that'll be a different matter.'

'Do I need a lawyer?'

Esme raised a brow. 'Have you done something illegal?'

Henny hesitated. 'No.'

'Then you don't need a lawyer.' Esme pressed the record button on the table. The camera in the corner of the room flashed green. 'This is Detective Sergeant Esme Jansson interviewing Henny Engström. Also present is Detective Inspector Kjeld Nygaard. The time is 6.32 p.m.'

Henny tapped her fingernails along the side of her upper arm. 'I suppose you'd like to know how I found the body.'

'That would be an excellent place to start.'

Henny fidgeted in her chair. She crossed her legs in the opposite direction and clicked the nails on her thumb and middle finger together. She was nervous. She suddenly refused to make eye contact with Kjeld and he tilted his head to the side, watching to see if she offered any signs that she wasn't going to tell the truth.

Esme watched her as well, but with a more formal expression. She held her pen above the empty notepad as though she planned to write, but Kjeld didn't think she would. Esme didn't need to take notes while the recorder was on. She was doing that on purpose to ease Henny's nerves. To make her forget that this interview was being taped.

Henny sighed before finally giving up an answer. 'I got a tip that someone had dumped a body in the football field.'

'What kind of tip?' Esme asked.

'Someone called me. I didn't recognise the voice and the number came up unknown.'

'What did they say exactly?'

'I can't remember exactly, but it was short. Something like: "There's a body in Sunnerviksparken. It's the same person who murdered Louisa Karlsson."'

81

Her answer jolted Kjeld out of his thoughts. He shared an uncertain glance with Esme who showed signs of surprise, but also disbelief. Was it possible there was a link between these two cases? Kjeld didn't think so, but he immediately began running through the crime scenes in his head, trying to find any mental clues that might connect them.

Henny uncrossed her legs and scooted the chair closer to the table. 'Is that true? Was the other body Louisa Karlsson?'

'The caller mentioned Louisa Karlsson by name?'

'Yes.' Henny focused an urgent look on Esme. 'It's true then?'

'I can't verify that at the moment.' Esme scribbled something on the pad of paper. 'Was the voice male or female?'

Henny looked down in thought. 'Male.'

'You're certain?'

'I had the impression he might have been trying to disguise his voice, but it was definitely a man. But like I said, it was a short message. There wasn't much to listen to. Once he gave me the information he hung up.'

'And you didn't try redialling?'

'The number came up unknown. I couldn't redial.'

'Can you show me?'

Henny took out her phone and pulled up the call log, holding it up for Esme to see.

Esme reached out and took Henny's phone, scrolling through it.

An uncomfortable silence filled the room and Henny shot a glare at Kjeld. 'Are you going to say something or are you just going to sit there like a creep?'

'Calm down, Henny,' Kjeld said.

'Fuck you. Don't you tell me to calm down. I have a civic duty to inform the public of your incompetence. That's why I do what I do. Because the people of this city have the right to know that the police don't give a shit about them.'

'All right. So, a strange man calls you, a man you claim you don't know, and tells you that the killer has murdered someone and you just trust him?'

'I had no reason not to trust him.'

'If you thought he was telling the truth why didn't you call the police?'

Kjeld didn't need her to answer that question. He knew the reason. It was because she wanted the headline. She wanted the story. She wanted to be a real journalist instead of a two-bit crime blogger. Or worse, she wanted to find the person responsible for the murders before the police, proving that they were incapable of properly doing their jobs. Which would, naturally, get her even more exposure. More headlines. More attention. But Kjeld also knew she would never admit that. She couldn't because then they could charge her with obstruction.

'I thought it best to verify the credibility of the information before involving the police. Wouldn't want to send you lot on a wild goose chase over nothing. Not that it would matter. Seeing as you're so busy doing shit-all to protect the people of this city.'

'You were livestreaming to thousands of viewers before informing us.'

'Yes, well, that wasn't intentional. Shortly after I arrived at the scene other journalists from established stations began swarming the area, snapping photographs and setting up links to their networks. I assume they received messages similar to the one I did. And you know how cut-throat this industry is. Especially for someone working from the ground up.'

Bullshit, Kjeld thought.

Esme placed Henny's phone on the table and Henny snatched it up, shoving it back in the pocket of her coat. She looked over at the two-way mirror. Kjeld thought he saw an anxious glimmer in her eyes. Then she returned her focus to the table, twirling a long strand of hair between her fingers.

She looked rattled.

Good.

'You got to the other crime scene pretty quickly, too. How did you find out about that?' Esme asked.

'My cameraman, Karl, heard about it from a friend of his who works for SVT Väst,' she said. She didn't look at either of them when she spoke and Kjeld sensed she was lying. 'I took a chance that he wasn't giving us the run-around and drove out there. Turns out it was a good lead.'

Henny turned to Kjeld and the corners of her lips curled in a pointed smirk. 'You have a very obvious tell. Do you know that? You tug at your ear. The one with the scar. I bet you're a shit poker player.'

Kjeld clenched his fist beneath the table. He could feel Esme's eyes on him and knew that he had to keep his calm. If not for his own sake then for the sake of the investigation. One day he'd have the opportunity to tell Henny what he really thought of her. But now was not the time.

'Do you think you would recognise the voice if you heard it again?' Esme asked.

Henny shrugged. 'Maybe.'

Esme slipped a card across the table. 'If you hear from him again, call us first.'

There was a pleading tone to Esme's voice that surprised Kjeld and he wondered how much of it was pretence.

Henny reached for the card, but Esme held on to it, forcing Henny to pay attention to her next words.

'I'm serious, Henny. This isn't a game. If you want to help protect people then make the right decision next time.' Esme let go.

Henny shoved the card into the same pocket as her phone. 'Is that it? Can I go now?'

'Interview terminated at 6.57 p.m.' Esme pressed the stop button on the recorder. 'You can go.'

Henny snatched up her purse from the floor and crossed the length of the interview room in two long strides. She stopped at the doorway as though she might say something else, but didn't. She left without looking back at them, the door slamming behind her.

Esme slouched back in her chair with a sigh.

Kjeld leaned forward on the table, casting a sidelong glance in her direction. 'Well?'

'I don't disbelieve her,' she said.

'But you don't believe her either?'

'She's holding back.'

Kjeld tugged absently at his earlobe. Then he was reminded of Henny's jibe and stopped. 'Is it possible that these two murders could be connected?'

'It doesn't seem likely, does it? Louisa's murder was so gruesome and personal. This other one was the complete opposite. Not to mention the murder weapons were different, as well as the scenes.'

'But we can't discount that there could be something to what she's saying. We need to figure out who the woman in the field is and see if there's something that connects her to Louisa.'

Esme clipped her pen in the spiral of the notepad. 'We can't rule out that Henny's informant is just trying to give us the runaround either. Or that Henny isn't telling us the whole truth.'

'She might know more than she's letting on.'

'That could be it.' Esme furrowed her brow. 'Or it could be that she's just not comfortable talking in front of you.'

'Me? I didn't do anything.'

'That's your problem, Kjeld. Sometimes you don't have to.'

Chapter 16

Jonny rolled over in bed and slipped his mobile phone out of his pillowcase. Technically he wasn't supposed to have the phone. It was a fragment of his old life, a memory of the existence that almost killed him. There weren't really any hard-and-fast rules about possessions at the commune, but every resident was expected to do their best to purge themselves of the person they'd been before. And Jonny was completely on board with that. But every time he tried to throw out his phone he felt a twinge of uncertainty twist in his gut. What if he changed his mind? What if he decided he did want to return to his old life? His family? His friends?

He was being overly dramatic, of course. There was nothing forcing him to stay at the commune. There weren't any armed guards at the gates or vicious dogs let loose from their leashes at night to scout the perimeter. It wasn't a cult, after all. It was a respite. A place that offered people like Jonny the opportunity to rediscover themselves again. And then, if they chose to, the opportunity to start anew.

And Jonny desperately wanted to start anew. To have a second chance at the life he was given. He'd already made great strides in doing so. He'd been clean and sober for almost six months.

No drugs. No alcohol. He hadn't even smoked a cigarette. But he still had his mobile phone. Because that's where he had his mother's number, videos of himself with his girlfriend who was dead going on four years now, and photos of his dog. He felt bad about leaving his dog. But the dog had been a gift from his mother after the incident. The *event* as many people referred to it. And as such the dog was a constant reminder of his life before. The life he didn't want anymore. The life that he'd barely survived.

Malte, the twenty-seven-year-old former car thief he shared a room with, rolled over in bed, turning his back to Jonny. Malte knew Jonny had a mobile phone with internet access, but he didn't tell anyone. He hadn't made it past the third step yet either, the one about material possessions, and so he knew it wasn't his place to judge. He had his own shit going on – although Jonny had never asked him to his face what had brought him there. He simply assumed they'd all fucked up somewhere in their before-lives and Malte was probably no exception. Malte also mostly kept to himself. Jonny appreciated that.

One of his first concerns about joining the commune was the fear that it would be like any other rehabilitation centre. That everyone would be trying to tell him what to do and how to live. But that wasn't the case. The commune let you follow your own path. For some people that path led to a chance at a new identity. For others it led them back to the person they'd always been.

But Jonny knew he couldn't go back. There was nothing but nightmares and pain in his past. He wanted something different for his future.

He tugged the duvet up over his head to block the dim light of the phone's screen from disturbing Malte's mumbling sleep. He scrolled through his messages, most of which were from his mother begging him to come home. He swiped the messages away without answering and pulled up the local news page. That had become one of his more compulsive tendencies since the incident. An unabating obsession to know what was going on. To make certain *it* hadn't happened again. Not that it could. They were all dead, after all. He was the only one left. But he checked just the same.

The breaking news alert at the top of the page jolted him. His fingers stiffened on the phone, clenching it like a knife. The headline was bold and black against the white background: CELLAR SADIST'S FINAL VICTIM MEETS TRAGIC END IN POTENTIAL COPYCAT KILLING. Beneath the headline a photograph of Louisa stared back at him with sad blue eyes and Jonny's heart skipped a beat.

No, no, no, no, no. She couldn't be dead. She couldn't be. Not after everything she'd been through. Not after the promise they'd made to each other.

Jonny scrolled through the article, his heart racing in his chest when he realised it was true. And worse, the police had no leads and no suspects in custody. A horrifying panic gripped him, flooding memories of the incident to the forefront of his mind.

Because if Louisa wasn't safe then none of them were.

Chapter 17

'One shot. Point-blank. Bullet was still in the skull.' Ove shook a small dish that held the blood-stained bullet before setting it down on the counter. The bullet rattled against the metal edges for a few seconds before finding a resting spot against the side of the tray. 'Sorry it's still cold as a boar in here. The thermostat says it's two degrees warmer than yesterday, but I think it's broken.'

'That suggests she saw her killer.' Kjeld crossed his arms over his chest, tucking his hands up into his arm pits for warmth. Despite Ove's assurance that it was a few degrees warmer, the temperature in the morgue seemed colder than it had been the other day and it assaulted his gloveless fingers with a bitter chill.

'It's a good shot, even at close range,' Esme said. She leaned over the head of the body to get a better look at the entrance wound. 'I'd say she definitely got a good look at the person.'

'But it was early morning. Still dark. Who allows someone to walk up to them so closely like that?'

'She could have known them,' Esme said. 'Or they could have surprised her.'

'She was found in the middle of a field. Hard to surprise someone when you're at the centre circle.'

'Maybe she was meeting them there? Something happened. Things went wrong.'

Kjeld glanced over at Ove. 'Anything to suggest that there was a physical altercation before her death?'

Ove shook his head. 'No offensive or defensive wounds. And no bruising. Nothing recently anyway. She has a few track marks on her left arm though and some old scarring. But there's nothing to indicate she got into a physical fight. In fact, in all my years working forensics, this is the closest I've come to seeing what looks to be an honest execution.'

'It's not a professional hit though,' Kjeld said.

'What makes you say that?'

'A professional wouldn't risk a single shot to the head. They could miss and lose their opportunity. Or the victim could survive.'

Esme canted her weight to the opposite leg. 'You said track marks on her arms. What about a drug deal gone awry?'

'That would be the most likely explanation. What about her identity? Have we gotten a name for her?'

'Ah, yes! I almost forgot.' Ove hiked up his belt and waddled over to the side table where he kept an antiquated laptop that looked like it weighed more than a brick. The keyboard was covered in a layer of plastic. Without taking off his gloves he pulled up a screen with an arrest photo of the woman on the slab followed by a list of aggravations. 'I had forensics do a rush on the fingerprints. Took them less than a minute to come up with a match. Lady and gentleman, I present to you … Andrea Nicolescu. Convicted of armed robbery, drug dealing, resisting arrest, and former resident of Högsbo Institution, prison for inmates of drug and substance abuse.'

'Which increases the possibility that this is drug-related.' Esme tucked her hair back behind her ear. 'This has to be unrelated to Louisa's murder.'

'But what about the tip Henny received? The one who said

this was the same killer.' Kjeld didn't know if or how this murder was linked to that of Louisa Karlsson, but he felt in his gut that there was something about this homicide that wasn't as easy as it seemed. It was too cut and dried. And even though there was no evidence at the moment to suggest a connection, his instinct told him it wasn't a coincidence that someone had tipped Henny off to the crime.

'Maybe it was simply someone who wanted to yank our chain? You know how people get when a high-profile crime is committed. Everyone wants their fifteen minutes of fame. Or maybe it's someone who wants to send Henny on a wild goose chase. You can't be the only person she's burned in the last few years.'

'I don't know. Anything is possible, but the timing doesn't feel right. So close to the other murder? I agree that it's unlikely to be the same killer. But even though the method isn't the same there are similarities. Both are women, both were discovered with little evidence as to who else might have been involved. And we have to consider the possibility that Henny is telling the truth and someone, the killer perhaps, told her about the link between the two crimes.' Kjeld stared down at Andrea's face. She was older than Louisa, but couldn't have been much older than himself, if that. It was difficult to tell because of the lines around her eyes and lips. She looked as though she'd lived a hard life. But Esme was probably right. This crime could have been a coincidence of timing. Just what they needed. Two difficult and unrelated murders.

'Tox screen?' Esme asked. 'Just to rule out any possible connections?'

'I've pushed it ahead to the front of the line, but it's still going to take some time. My good looks only get me so far.'

Esme glanced up at Kjeld. 'We should look into her drug arrests, see if she had any enemies or connections that might also link back to Louisa.'

Kjeld nodded in agreement, but he didn't think they would

find anything. Louisa didn't strike him as someone who would get into drugs. And even if she had, she wouldn't have been able to hide it from her family. They had been obsessively protective of her. They practically had her under a microscope.

'What happened to her hand?' Kjeld asked. 'Is she missing a finger?'

'Ah, yes. That's an older injury. Fairly clean cut. Looks like whoever stitched it up did a decent job. There's a scar, but it's mostly faded. Hard to tell how it happened, but definitely not related to the shooting.'

Something about the missing finger felt familiar to Kjeld. He was almost certain he'd seen that before. 'Hm.'

'What are you thinking?' Esme asked.

'I'm not sure,' Kjeld said after a pause. 'But we need to find out where Andrea was before she ended up in that field.'

'There weren't any cameras in that neighbourhood. She could have come from anywhere.'

'Then I guess anywhere is where we start.'

'Sure, let me just type "anywhere" into Google Maps and see what pops up.' Esme's heavy-handed sarcasm was a gentle reminder to Kjeld that he needed to lighten up a bit. And it wasn't undeserved. He'd been a bit of a grump since, well, since he shot a colleague.

'You know what I mean,' he said, failing to hide the small quirk of a smile. 'Let's find out if Andrea had any living relatives who might be able to give us an idea of her movements over the last few days before her picture ends up on Henny's gossip rag. Then we'll work on finding a connection between her and Louisa, if there is one. I feel like we're missing something here, but maybe that's just wishful thinking.'

'Sounds to me like you could use a holiday.' Ove sniffled against the cold of the room and tugged on the waistband of his slacks, which had slipped below his belly again. 'You wind yourself up any tighter and you're liable to snap.

'Kjeld just got back from holiday,' Esme said.

'Oh yeah? Go anyplace nice?'

'Jämtland,' Kjeld said flatly.

'Jämtland?' Ove shook his head. 'Who the hell goes to Jämtland on holiday?'

Chapter 18

A few hours after Kjeld and Esme had shared the pathological findings with Axel and Sixten, Kjeld finished typing up his part of the initial report on the Nicolescu case and headed home. The microwave pinged and he took out the ready-made meal with his bare hands. He'd left it in for a minute longer than the suggested directions on the packaging and the plastic tray nearly burned the tips of his fingers. He tossed it on the counter before ripping off the plastic sheath. The steam that exhaled from the package carried with it the scent of overcooked lasagne and burnt cellophane.

Oskar, Kjeld's overweight ginger cat, waddled up to his legs and brushed against his calf. He let out a pathetic mewl as though he hadn't eaten in days despite the fact that Kjeld had fed him less than ten minutes ago.

'I'm not falling for that trick, Oskar. The vet says you need to lose weight. No more between-meal snacks.'

Oskar slumped onto his side, blocking Kjeld's path to the silverware drawer.

'Don't be so dramatic.'

Kjeld stepped over Oskar and snatched a fork from the drawer. Then he used a paper towel to pick up the microwave dinner by the edges and made his way to the living room to sit on the couch. He had a kitchen table, but it was covered in paperwork and boxes that he'd brought back from his father's house in Varsund. Boxes he'd meant to go through months ago, but still hadn't touched. They reminded him of the guilt he felt for not having gone back to visit his father for the holidays. He'd tried to call at Christmas, but the nurse on duty said his dad was extra confused that day. He missed his house and his routine.

Putting him in a care facility had been the right decision, but Kjeld regretted not doing more. And just when he'd forget about the shame he felt for the unresolved tension with his father, he'd see those boxes and old wounds would tear open again. For all his attempts at moving forward, there were some things he simply wasn't prepared to put behind him.

Kjeld's apartment was unremarkable. It was a two-bedroom flat in the Majorna district that he'd moved into after he and Bengt separated. Normally it would have been out of his price range, as it was completely remodelled on the inside, but the previous owner had died under uncomfortable circumstances and gossip frightened away most of the prospective buyers. He'd always intended for it to be a temporary living situation, until he found something with a more appropriate outdoor space for Tove. Three years later it still looked like he'd only recently moved in.

The living room, which was open plan to the kitchen, was the only space that looked remotely lived-in. And that was a term he used lightly. He had a stack of IKEA Billy bookshelves on one wall, filled to the brim with books. On the floor he had a row of vinyl records and the record player itself sat on a low side table beside the television. In the corner of the room stood a fake Christmas tree, brightly illuminated with multicoloured lights that twinkled to a tune that didn't play anymore. The string of paper Swedish flags that wrapped around the plastic branches had been tugged off by Oskar and dangled to the floor, half eaten.

Kjeld meant to take the tree down after the holidays but left it up because Tove liked it. This led to a new tradition they'd created over the last few weeks where Kjeld sometimes hid a present beneath the tree on her weekends with him. He wasn't sure if that was a sign of better parenting on his part or bribery, but Tove enjoyed the surprise. And he enjoyed seeing her happy.

He stabbed his fork into the lasagne and used the edge like a knife to cut through it. The top layer of pasta was hard and crispy and he had to leverage the plastic tray against the coffee table to push the fork through. He took a sip of beer while he waited for the lasagne to cool. Spread out across the coffee table were the documents he'd asked Axel to compile: Louisa's phone records, recent emails, work schedule, as well as the transcripts of statements from the family and the neighbours who'd discovered the fire.

There must have been something in all of this that could give them a clue as to who was responsible for Louisa's death. Or, at the very least, why someone would want to kill her. He refused to believe what the media were speculating – that she was a target simply because of her "fame" of having been the final and only surviving victim of the Cellar Sadist. That insinuated a killer who had no reasoning behind the crime other than notoriety. But Louisa's death felt more personal than that. She hadn't just been killed, she'd been tortured. And while Kjeld couldn't ignore the possibility that this was simply a copycat looking for recognition, he felt that there was more to it.

He took a bite of lasagne. The inside was still scalding and it burned the roof of his mouth, but he chewed through it anyway and swallowed it down with another sip of beer. The rain pattered against the metal overhang on his outdoor patio. Oskar meowed in the kitchen, tapping his paw on the lip of his empty food dish so it clinked against the floor.

Kjeld scanned through the printout of Louisa's work schedule. Her entire life was so organised. So monotonous. On paper it looked as though she did the same thing every day. She worked the same shift Monday through Thursday and rode the same bus line to and from the library. On Friday mornings she had group therapy. And, if her family was to be believed, and Kjeld had no reason to suspect otherwise, she spent most Saturdays and Sundays at home reading. She didn't go out with friends. Correction, she didn't *have* friends. She didn't join her colleagues for a drink at the pub after her shifts. She rarely went out to public places and when she did she was almost always accompanied by her father and sister. And her online presence was less than minimal. It was almost non-existent.

Axel was right. She was a shut-in. He could have probably set his watch to her schedule. And it wouldn't have taken much for someone else to figure that out.

But as Kjeld read more carefully through Louisa's recent work shifts he noticed some irregularities he hadn't seen earlier. On at least four separate occasions over the last month her shift was filled by another one of her co-workers, Linnea Thorsen. The first had been on a Thursday and the other three had been on subsequent Tuesdays.

Kjeld flipped through the documents, but couldn't find anything to account for Louisa not attending her shifts. No dentist appointments. No therapy sessions. And while Sixten had spoken to Louisa's manager, the head librarian, and the two female colleagues who'd last seen her the night of the murder, none of them had the name Linnea. Which begged the question, who was she? Why was she covering Louisa's shifts? And, more importantly, where had Louisa been on those days if she wasn't at work?

Chapter 19

Torsdag | Thursday

The next morning Kjeld called Högsbo Library and learned that Linnea Thorsen was working the early shift. When he caught up with Esme at the coffee machine, he found out she'd spent her evening tracking down Andrea Nicolescu's next of kin. It hadn't been as easy as she'd expected. Together they agreed it would be best to cover more ground. While Kjeld drove to the library on his own, Esme and Sixten set off to deliver the bad news to Andrea's family.

When Kjeld arrived at the library, Linnea was waiting for him. It was early and there weren't any patrons as of yet. The library was usually quiet until after lunch, Linnea explained, so they sat down at a study table near the children's book section. Normally Kjeld preferred to talk to witnesses and suspects without warning. It gave them less of an opportunity to plan their answers. But it was impossible to hide the investigation into Louisa's death. Even if Linnea hadn't known that all of her colleagues had already been questioned, she would have been able to guess from the media's persistent chatter and speculation about the case.

'This was Louisa's favourite part of the library. She loved helping children find new books to read.' Linnea's words were solemn and sympathetic, but her expression was difficult to read due to her serious face and the thick-lensed glasses that unnaturally magnified her eyes. 'She ran the Monday morning reading hour for pre-schoolers. She was quite popular with the parents.'

'What about with her colleagues? Did Louisa get along with them?' Kjeld asked.

'Sure. Everyone liked Louisa. She was polite and she always cleaned up at the end of her shifts. She didn't gossip like some of the other ladies who work here. That's what you get sometimes when you work with all women. I know. I used to work in a crafts store and it was the same thing.'

'What kind of gossip?'

'The usual thing. Family, boyfriends, annoying customers.'

'Did Louisa have any peculiar customers? Anyone suspicious or someone who might have been bothering her?'

Linnea shook her head. 'I don't think so. She didn't talk to people much. Except the kids. She was good with kids. I'm not. I prefer working in the adult science fiction and fantasy section. Most people who read those genres leave you alone.'

It didn't surprise Kjeld that people might avoid trying to talk to Linnea.

He took out the piece of paper that showed the shifts Linnea had covered for Louisa. He'd circled all four of them with red pen. 'You covered four shifts for Louisa over the last month.'

'That's right.'

'Why?'

'Because she asked me to.' Linnea's gaze slipped to the side and Kjeld got the impression she wasn't telling him the entire story.

'Wasn't it odd for her to take a day off? Let alone four days off in a single month? According to the head librarian she almost never missed a shift.'

Linnea snorted a laugh. It was high-pitched and echoed

loudly in the quiet space. Then she shrunk back into her chair, embarrassed.

'Is something funny?' Kjeld asked.

'Just this idea that everyone thinks Louisa was so perfect and innocent.'

'Wasn't she?'

Linnea chewed on her lower lip. 'I shouldn't speak ill of the dead.'

Kjeld leaned forward, resting his arms on the table. 'No one's going to judge you, Linnea. Whatever you have to say could be helpful in finding Louisa's killer.'

Linnea ran her fingers over the back of her neck where her hair was buzzed short. Kjeld noticed the skin was raw and wondered if this was a nervous tic of hers.

'The first day I covered for her wasn't planned. She didn't show up for work at all. She called me and asked if I could work her shift for her. I asked her why and she said she wasn't feeling well, but she sounded fine on the phone. I was annoyed because I had plans to play D&D with some friends. We're running a big campaign right now and—' She cut herself off and gave Kjeld a critical look. 'You know, the game, Dungeons & Dragons.'

'I know what D&D is.'

'Anyway, I felt bad. Because it's Louisa. No one ever talked about what happened to her, but we all knew. I didn't want to seem callous so I said I'd go in for her.' Linnea looked down and fiddled with the sleeve of her shirt around her wrist. 'When she called me the second time the next week, I was mad. I thought she was taking advantage of me for being so easy-going the last time. I told her I didn't believe she was sick. Especially since I knew she'd worked the day before. I said she had to give me a better excuse if she wanted me to cover for her again.'

'What did she say?'

'She said she'd made some friends. People who were helping her work through some trauma. She said her therapy sessions weren't working anymore and she felt like her family was suffocating her. This was the only chance she had to feel like her own person.'

'Did she tell you who these friends were?'

Linnea shook her head. 'No. But I think one of them came into the library a week later.'

'Why do you think that?'

'Because he didn't look like the kind of person who goes to a library.' Linnea paused. 'That sounds bitchy, doesn't it? What I mean to say is that he came in, asked if Louisa was working, and left without checking out any books.'

'You said he didn't look like someone who goes to a library. What does that mean?'

'He was really – what's the word for it? Alternative? No, that's not the right word. He looked like Eminem back in his early days. His hair was bleached blond and shaved close to his head. He had a runic tattoo on his neck like something you'd see in that *Vikings* television show. And he wore a hooded sweatshirt. No coat. In *January.*'

'Did you hear anything he and Louisa talked about? Any names? Any places they were planning to go to?'

'No. Like I said, I mind my own business. Gossip isn't my thing.' Linnea hesitated. 'But I did see him tape a flyer to one of the lamp-posts in the car park when I was taking out the rubbish.'

'Which one?'

'Right outside the entrance. People do that all the time, but they're not supposed to. The city usually takes them down when they see them. But they do it anyway.'

Kjeld walked out the front entrance of the library towards the car park. A frigid mist coated his face. The air smelled like there might be frost in the forecast. Kjeld shrugged his shoulders against the chill and tucked his hands in his pockets as he made his way to the first of two lamp-posts positioned over the southern side of the car park.

Posted to the pole were a handful of flyers, most of which had either been torn in half or were washed out from the recent rain. The only two flyers that were even remotely legible were one for a missing dog, a Pekingese, and another for what appeared to be some kind of local worship group, but half of the flyer's information had been smeared by the rain. Kjeld took out his phone and snapped photos of both the flyers. Then he made his way around the back of the library to the grassy shortcut leading up to the bus stop. He scoured the ground for anything that might have been missed by the crime scene technicians who'd been sent to the scene, but he came up empty-handed.

Kjeld walked up the muddy slope of the small hill to the bus stop. A teenage girl sat on the bench beside the timetables, her focus buried so deep in her mobile phone that she didn't notice him. Down the road he caught a glimpse of the bus slowing into the right lane. Kjeld tried to imagine the scene in the evening, the sky dark, the rain coming down hard. If Louisa had been late getting to the bus stop – if she'd slipped or slowed down – she wouldn't have had a chance of being seen.

The bus rolled to a stop and the girl climbed aboard without giving Kjeld a glance. The driver shot him an impatient look, but Kjeld waved him off. Then the driver closed the doors and continued down the road.

What had happened to Louisa in those moments between locking up the library and coming into contact with her killer? Could it have been this mysterious friend Linnea mentioned? Or had she been so inattentive of her surroundings that she didn't notice a stranger sneaking up on her?

Kjeld turned his gaze back down the shortcut. It couldn't have shaved off more than a minute or two from the normal walking path. And that's all it took for a young woman's life to change. Two minutes for a predator to catch their prey.

Chapter 20

'What's up, Jonny! I thought you'd quit?' The bartender stretched over the edge of the counter and held out his fist.

Jonny bumped knuckles with him, eyes darting from side to side to make sure no one was listening in. It was a ridiculous concern. DJ Trix was on the playlist and the club was a pulsing drone of bass. Jonny could barely hear himself think.

'Yeah, well, maybe I had a change of heart,' Jonny said, loud enough for the bartender to hear. Then he leaned in closer. 'You seen Rask around?'

The bartender snatched two empty beer glasses from the counter and dunked them into the soapy sink. 'He was making the rounds here earlier. Had a new girl with him. Damn, she was hot. Weird, but hot.'

'When did you last see him?'

The bartender wiped off the counter with a wet rag. 'About thirty minutes ago. Try the car park out back.'

'Thanks, man.'

'No problem. Oh, and don't buy that glowstick shit off him. That stuff's lethal. Especially if you've been on the wagon.'

Jonny nodded, bumped the bartender's fist again, and made his way through the employee corridor of the club to the back entrance. True to his word, Rask was outside, leaning up against the exterior wall of the building in front of a small group of clubgoers. It wasn't raining anymore, but the air was damp and Jonny wished he'd dressed more appropriately for the weather. But there'd only been one thing on his mind when he left the commune.

Relief.

Vidar Rask was a gangly man with a bald head and scraggly brown beard. His eyebrows were wild and took up most of his forehead, doubly accented by the charcoal-coloured eyeshadow that circled both above and below his buggy eyes. He dressed in an oversized tracksuit and seemed to have no shame that he looked one part white trash hustler and two parts hobgoblin. But that didn't bother Jonny. He wasn't interested in what Vidar looked like, only what he had.

'Jonny, my boy!' Vidar called out, shoving a pair of scantily clad clubgoers to the side so he could make his way to Jonny. He slapped him on the shoulder a little too hard and Jonny winced. 'Oh, man, I'm sorry. You still got that bum arm? I keep telling people. Cage dancing ain't for the faint-hearted.'

'My arm is fine,' Jonny muttered.

In the background Vidar's girlfriend, a much younger woman with her head half shaved revealing a brightly coloured Japanese koi fish tattoo on her scalp, her face covered in more piercings than Jonny could count, chewed on a piece of gum with her mouth open. She shot Jonny a bland but slightly suspicious stare that looked cloudy in the yellow light above the back entrance.

'So, what can I do for you, Jonny boy? I gotta say I'm a little surprised to see you. I thought you'd gotten clean and shacked yourself up with that second coming sect.' Vidar squeezed Jonny's shoulder, fingers digging into the meaty spot near his neck.

'They're not a religious cult,' Jonny said, surprisingly defensive of the commune. Partially because it was true. They were neither a religious group nor a cult. That was just trash that the media spouted about them in order to fill their quota of bullshit stories. But Jonny thought he might have also been uncharacteristically protective of them because up until he saw Louisa's photo online they'd really helped him. They'd shown him that it was possible to start anew. And they'd taught him how to get clean.

Now he was standing inches away from his old dealer about to make a really bad decision.

And Vidar knew it.

'Okay, okay. Don't get your acolyte robes in a bunch.' Vidar released Jonny's shoulder and a sharp-eyed smirk crept over his lips. 'Tell me then. What is it Uncle Vidar can do for you? You've been out of the game for a while so maybe you want to start off with something easy. You want a few joints? I'll give you one on the house just because you're an old friend. Or how about some pills to help you sleep at night?'

'I want something stronger.'

The girl with the koi tattoo glanced up inquisitively, a single brow raised unnaturally high on her forehead.

Vidar stared Jonny directly in the eyes. There was a flash of hesitation in his look, but Jonny couldn't tell if it was from honest concern for his well-being or if Vidar was simply searching for a sign that he might be setting him up. But Vidar's pause was fleeting, quickly replaced by a more intense stare. 'How strong are we talking?'

'Strong enough to make me forget.'

Chapter 21

Ingrid Nicolescu sucked on her cigarette like a swimmer coming up for air after holding their breath under water for two laps. She didn't have a naturally stern face, but there were dark circles under her eyes and her jaw was set tight like a vice, which pulled the skin around her lips into a permanent scowl. When she exhaled the smoke filled the small living room of her cheap third-floor apartment in the centre of Biskopsgården, a short drive away from where Andrea's body had been found. The building was one of many early Eighties prefab constructions, built quickly and affordably to accommodate the growing population of Gothenburg that was pushing the city out into the suburbs. The walls were paper-thin and Esme could hear the upstairs neighbours' argument as clearly as if she were in the room with them.

Ingrid took another sharp drag and exhaled in Esme's direction. Esme turned her nose away from the smoke. There were times when her keen sense of smell was more disadvantageous than it was worth.

'I'm sorry for your loss,' Esme said. She sat beside Sixten on the small flower-print sofa, her hands placed politely in her lap. The sofa was actually too small for two adult people and Sixten's thigh kept inadvertently bumping her leg as he tried to find a comfortable position in the lumpy cushions. Esme sat closer to the edge so she could keep her feet firmly planted on the shag carpet. It forced her posture to be unnaturally rigid, but at least it prevented her from sliding towards the centre of the sofa and into Sixten's lap. Sixten, for his part, didn't seem to notice the awkwardness of their positions. His gaze was fixed on Ingrid, the not-so-grieving widow.

Ingrid leaned forward from her tattered armchair and flicked the ash from her cigarette into an antique carnival glass bowl. The original colour was pink, but the centre of the dish was stained a rusty orange.

'I always knew Andrea would get herself killed eventually. Granted, it was supposed to be drugs not—' Ingrid cut herself off with a deep sigh. Esme saw a glossy shine to her eyes and realised she might have been premature in judging Ingrid. She was holding her grief in, steeling herself in front of strangers. Ingrid coughed, loosening a thick wad of phlegm in her throat that she swallowed back down.

'Do you have any idea who may have wanted to harm your wife?' Esme asked.

Ingrid scoffed. 'Besides me?' She flicked the ash from her cigarette into the carnival glass. 'Sorry, that's not what I meant. It's just … She couldn't even put the fucking dishes in the dishwasher, you know? The sink is still full of her mess.'

'Andrea wasn't acting oddly or out of the ordinary? Any arguments with colleagues or friends?' Esme took out her pocket-sized notepad and jotted down a few things in her illegible scrawl.

Ingrid shook her head. 'Andrea wasn't exactly the brightest bulb in the box, if you get my meaning. She was barely keeping that job at the petrol station as it was. The only reason the owner kept her on was because she was willing to work the night shifts. They called it a management position on paper, but all she did was sell cigarettes and clean up the toilets. But it was better than letting her work days. She had a short fuse. Everything pissed her off. And she pissed off everyone else in return.'

Esme paused her note-taking to look directly at Ingrid. 'What about her drug involvement? Was she still in that?'

'Dealing, you mean?' Ingrid shrugged. 'I don't think so. Wish she had been. Then maybe I wouldn't have had to live in this dump.'

'Did she ever have any dealings near Sunnerviksparken?'

'I don't know. Maybe? If there was good business then she might. Andrea would sling just about anything if it meant she could get high herself. She used to do some really stupid shit for a kick. That was a while ago though. Back when things were really bad. When she was on the junk. But she stopped with the hard stuff more than a year ago. Tried to get clean, for what good it did her. What is it they say? Once a junkie, always a junkie.' Ingrid wiped the back of her hand over her eye, smearing thick clumps of mascara over her cheek.

A sudden pounding of heavy footsteps trampled overhead. Ingrid grabbed the handle of a broom that rested against the nearby wall and stabbed it into the ceiling above her. 'Shut the fuck up!'

A high-pitched shriek yelled back at her through the ceiling. Sixten flinched. Esme couldn't understand the erratic exchange of screams from the neighbours above, but it didn't take much to guess that this was a normal occurrence.

Esme scribbled in her notepad. 'What about the last few days? Did Andrea go anywhere without telling you?'

Ingrid snorted a laugh. 'Andrea was always staying out, coming home late. The only time I'd notice is if she'd forget to leave money on the table for the rent. Just because we were married don't mean we had each other on a short leash. I didn't care what she got up to as long as she didn't bring it home with her.'

Esme raised a brow. 'You think she was seeing someone?'

'I don't think it much matters.' Ingrid paused. 'But no. She wouldn't do that. Not after the last time. We'd been arguing, sure, but not over that. She knows I … She *knew* I would have left her if I caught her messing around with someone else again.'

'When was the last time you saw her?'

Ingrid coughed out another puff of smoke, gaze wandering across the room before she answered. 'Tuesday morning before I went to work. She was supposed to go to a group meeting with her therapist that afternoon. That's a condition of her parole. I assume she went or I would have gotten a call. And then she worked last night. I know she worked because she called me from the petrol station phone to ask me to save my dinner leftovers for her. She'd eat them when she got home around breakfast time before passing out on the sofa for the rest of the day.'

'And did she?' Sixten asked.

'Did she what?'

'Eat the leftovers.'

Ingrid stared at him as though he'd just insulted her. Then she flicked another clump of ash in the bowl. 'No, as a matter of fact she didn't. I had them for lunch today.'

'So, as far as you're aware Andrea didn't come home after her shift, which started on Tuesday and ended early Wednesday morning,' Esme said.

'If she did I didn't see her.'

'What about Andrea's old contacts? Any reason to believe that they might have a grudge against her?'

A brief flash of fear crossed Ingrid's face. She tried to hide it by drawing another long drag on her cigarette, but her eyes deceived her, quickly breaking contact with both Esme and Sixten to look at the ground. It was always difficult to judge a person's reaction after receiving tragic news, but despite Ingrid's almost cruel amount of apathy towards her murdered spouse, Esme sensed that she was more broken up than she let on. And she wondered if Ingrid's sudden aversion to look them in the eyes was more than just a desire not to show weakness in front of the police.

'I don't know,' Ingrid said. 'That was all so long ago. And who can say how long someone might hold a grudge? Andrea didn't get along with a lot of people. And, yeah, she was involved in a pretty rough crowd when we first met. But she wasn't one of the big fish, you know? She wasn't worth anything to anyone dead. We argued about stupid shit all the time, but she would have told me if she had dirt on anyone. And if she thought her life was in danger she would have said something. If she wasn't too high to forget …'

Ingrid's brows pinched toward the centre of her forehead in the first show of real emotion since Esme and Sixten had walked through the door. She sucked on her cigarette hard, fingers trembling. And when she exhaled it was with an exasperated wheeze.

Esme relaxed her shoulders. She'd been hoping for more. For some clue as to who might have executed Andrea on her way home with seemingly no real motive.

Sixten leaned forward, resting his elbows on his knees. 'What do you remember about this rough crowd she was in?'

Ingrid smudged her cigarette into the makeshift ashtray and took another out of the pack on the side table. 'Not much. It was a long time ago and I was high most of the time back then, too. I'm pretty sure it had something to do with bringing in merchandise from other countries. Romania, probably. Maybe that's how she got involved? There was a guy back then she dealt with who sometimes stayed over. Couldn't speak a word of Swedish. But I got the impression he was just a runner. Whatever they were doing, he and Andrea made good money. Enough to buy a high-end TV and computer. She even bought me some new clothes. Anyway, one day it just stopped and Andrea went back to the small-time shit. Then she got caught by an undercover narc and had to do a stint in Högsbo. That's when she got clean. Well, mostly.'

Esme looked up from her notes. 'How long ago was it that she stopped running with that crowd?'

'Ah, hell, I don't know. More than ten years ago, I reckon. Maybe fifteen.' Ingrid struggled with her lighter. When she couldn't get more than a spark she tossed it on the coffee table and took out another from the end table drawer.

'What happened to her finger?' Sixten asked.

'That was a weird story, actually. It wasn't long after we met. Andrea was running drugs back and forth for this big boss back in Romania. One of the deals went bad and he sent two of his guys out here to make an example of her. That was their thing. Cut off a finger as a reminder that they wouldn't accept any more mistakes. Well, Andrea didn't let them take her finger easily. And one of the guys pulled a gun on her. But there was this young cop in the area ticketing cars that were parked in a towaway zone. He heard the commotion, barrelled into the building, and by some stroke of luck she managed to escape.' Ingrid gave an awkward laugh, but there were tears in her eyes. 'She still lost the finger, but Andrea always said she owed her life to that cop.'

'Do you remember who the officer was?'

'I wasn't there and Andrea never told me. I don't think she knew either.'

'One last thing,' Esme said, removing her phone to show a photo of Louisa Karlsson. 'Have you ever seen this woman around Andrea?'

'Isn't she the one from the news? That girl the serial killer had locked up?'

Esme nodded.

Ingrid shook her head. 'No. She's not really the type to be found around the likes of us though, is she?'

Esme closed up her notebook and placed one of her police cards on the coffee table. 'We might get in touch later this week. If you think of anything that—'

'Was it quick?' Ingrid asked.

Esme hesitated for a moment before answering. 'The patholo-gist said it was probably instantaneous.'

Ingrid brought the cigarette to her lips, lighting it with an unsteady hand. 'It's just fucking typical.'

'Typical?'

'Of life,' Ingrid said, exhaling a queasy cloud of smoke. 'No matter how much you survive, you never make it out alive.'

Chapter 22

Bengt craned his neck, peering over the rows of seats towards the doors at the back of the auditorium. The performance would begin in less than five minutes and the chair to his left, the one he'd saved for Kjeld, sat empty.

Liam took his hand, entwining their fingers together. Then he leaned in closer and placed a kiss on Bengt's cheek.

Bengt tried not to shy away from the affection, but he could feel his muscles tense. Public displays of intimacy, even those as simple as handholding or an almost platonic peck on the cheek, made him uncomfortable. Liam knew that, but he still persisted in trying to bring Bengt out of his shell. It wasn't that Bengt didn't want to flaunt his affections or share his feelings, but it had never felt natural for him to do so within view of others. Strangers in particular.

Liam was the exact opposite of him in that respect. Liam was open and warm with everyone. He wanted his love for Bengt to be on display for all the world to see. That was his way of showing his commitment to their relationship, by making it clear to everyone how he felt. Liam was an extrovert in all the ways that Bengt wasn't and it was one of the reasons why he'd been attracted to him in the first place. But he still couldn't get used to sharing his emotions publicly. Not because he feared being judged or harassed by those who might not approve, but because his private life was no one else's concern.

That had been the one easy thing about being with Kjeld. Kjeld, too, had a cold exterior when it came to public affection. Although, in Kjeld's case, Bengt suspected that the reasons for his standoffishness stemmed from something much deeper than simple apprehension about revealing too much of himself in the eyes of other people. Kjeld never would have kissed him in public. Not simply out of respect for Bengt's unease about such exposed tenderness, but for his own unspoken anxiety when it came to showing his feelings. In fact, the only time Bengt could clearly remember Kjeld ever kissing him in public was when they signed their marriage licence at city hall. And even that was only in front of two witnesses and a local civil servant.

Of all his past relationships, Kjeld had been both the easiest and the most difficult. Love didn't come easy for Kjeld, but he made his passion for the people who were important to him clear in subtle ways. Ways that took Bengt too long to understand. In the end, however, it wasn't enough. For as closed off as Bengt was he needed something more than what Kjeld had been willing to give him. Something that he thought he could get from Liam.

'Forget about him, *älskling*,' Liam said. His British accent seeped through the way he pronounced that term of endearment. *Darling. Sweetheart. Lover.* It warmed Bengt's cheeks to hear someone speak to him that way and mean it. Which was not to say that no one had ever meant it before, but Liam had a way of making it sound so normal. So true.

But also so underwhelming.

'He promised he'd be here.' If it had been for himself, Bengt wouldn't have thought twice about it. But it was a promise Kjeld had made to their daughter. She would be expecting him. And if he didn't show then Bengt would have to deal with the disappointment and the heartbreak Kjeld left in his wake.

Liam scoffed, the sound of which was halfway between a laugh and a disbelieving sigh. 'Kjeld is always making promises.'

Liam wasn't wrong. Kjeld was a master of saying he'd do something and then failing to follow through. Not with everything, of course. If that had been the case then he and Bengt would never have lasted as long as they had. When it came down to the wire's edge, Kjeld was perfectly capable of making good on his commitments. But Kjeld had an infuriating habit of confusing his priorities. Truth of the matter was Bengt didn't appreciate being second place to Kjeld's work. But it was seeing Tove play second fiddle as well that had pushed him over the edge. And until Kjeld could learn to put his family first then they would never be able to have the relationship that Bengt had always hoped for. That he sometimes – guiltily – still hoped for.

'I know, but this time will be different,' Bengt insisted.

Kjeld hadn't told Bengt everything about what had happened in Varsund, but Bengt had put together enough of the pieces through hearsay to have a good idea. He'd actually thought about calling Kjeld up and asking if he wanted to talk about the situation with his father, but then thought better of it. Taking care of Kjeld wasn't Bengt's job anymore. Nor was it a job he really wanted to take back. But for all of the hurt and resentment between them, Bengt did worry about Kjeld. He was Tove's father, after all. Whether they liked it or not they would always be a part of each other's lives. And if Bengt's cancer were to come back with a greater vengeance then Kjeld would be all Tove had. That in and of itself was reason enough for Bengt to be concerned.

But it was also the reason why Bengt hoped Kjeld would be there tonight for Tove's recital.

The lights dimmed on the audience and a yellow lamp cast a bright spotlight on the centre stage. Bengt turned in his seat again, looking back over the shadowy heads of other parents for any sign that Kjeld was there. Perhaps he was standing in the back, too late to make his way up to one of the front rows. But

Bengt didn't hold his breath as he scanned the room for a lone figure in the dark.

The music began to play and the curtains opened. Liam squeezed his hand and Bengt turned forward in his seat. The beginners ballet group from Stella's School of Dance stood posed for their debut performance. Tove was poised at centre stage, proud in her pink leotard, tights, and tutu, wild curls done up in a matching bow. She had the biggest smile of the group.

Bengt frowned, craning his neck one last time to the back row, hoping he might catch a glimpse of that familiar head of reddish-blond hair. But he wasn't there. He sighed.

A murmur to his left drew his attention from the stage. One by one the shadows in the row stood up for a figure, trying to squeeze his way through the seats to the empty chair beside him. Bengt recognised that familiar scent of cologne in the darkness.

'Did I miss anything?' Kjeld whispered, turning his focus to the stage.

Bengt's heart skipped a beat. 'No, you're right on time.'

Chapter 23

Kjeld returned from Tove's dance recital in uncommonly good spirits. Not only had he enjoyed the performance, despite the fact that one of Tove's fellow dancers stood on the side of the stage weeping through most of the numbers, he even refrained from getting into an argument with Liam afterwards. Most rewarding, however, was the look on Tove's face when she saw him in the audience applauding her solo. It was more than happiness in her expression, it was pure love. She hadn't looked at him like that in more than a year. And neither had Bengt. Although Kjeld suspected he wasn't supposed to notice that glimmer of affection in his ex's eyes.

He knew it was conceited to be proud of himself for doing something that was basically the bare minimum where most parents were concerned, but it was another step towards fulfilling the promise he'd made to himself when he returned home from Varsund. That he would do better as Tove's father. And he would show Bengt that family and fatherhood were important to him. Just as important as his career. No, more so.

It felt good to feel good. Even his microwaveable lasagne, still overcooked and burnt on the edges, tasted better than it had the day before. Maybe those therapy sessions with Alice were finally paying off. Because for the first time in a long time he felt like he was doing something right.

The frantic knocking on the front door broke his thoughts. Kjeld walked barefoot across the cool laminate floor to the foyer. When he opened the door he was surprised to see Esme, drenched and shivering from the cold rain. She shoved past him and into the welcoming warmth of the flat.

'What's wrong with your intercom? Is it broken? I was standing outside for at least ten minutes before your neighbour let me into the building.'

Kjeld glanced at the intercom, tapping the speaker button. It didn't light up. 'Maybe it needs new batteries.'

'I was calling you, too.'

'Ah, shit. I turned my phone off during Tove's recital.' Kjeld reached into the pocket of his coat and removed his phone, setting it to vibrate.

Esme huffed and shook the rain out of her hair. Her fringe was wet, swooped sideways to reveal a rare glimpse of her forehead. It always surprised Kjeld how much older she looked without that thick mop of hair covering her eyebrows. He might have suggested she grow it out, but he knew Esme was particular about not drawing too much attention to herself.

'What's going on?' he asked. 'You want something to drink?'

'I can't. I have a—' Esme cut herself off. 'I'm meeting someone.'

'A date? In this neighbourhood?' Kjeld raised a brow. 'Do I know them?'

Esme snorted. 'Do you know *anyone* in this neighbourhood?'

'Fair point.' Despite living in his flat for going on three years now he'd never introduced himself to his neighbours. And any interactions he'd had with them had been limited to in-passing pleasantries at the ground-level postboxes. 'So, what's up?'

'Ballistics came back on the bullet.'

'And?'

'Perfect match to a previous case.'

118

'Which one?'

Esme reached inside her coat and removed a manila folder. She flipped it open and brought forth a printout from a case dating back sixteen years. 'Tobias Hedebrant.'

'Why does that name sound familiar?' Kjeld took the printout and skimmed through it.

'Because it was a case you worked. Tobias was involved in a very profitable trafficking outfit, transporting drugs into Sweden from Eastern Europe, until his business partner, Emil Hermansson, shot him dead in one of their warehouses for attempting to push him out of their most recent deal. Emil served five years before he was killed by another prisoner in the lunch line. Apparently he made one too many ethnic slurs to his cellmate.'

Kjeld raised a brow. 'Let me guess. The bullet that was used to kill Tobias—'

'Has an identical striation pattern to the one used to murder Andrea Nicolescu. Which increases the likelihood that it came from the same gun.'

'Which means the possibility that Andrea's death was drug or gang-related just became our primary focus.'

'And it also increases the probability that Henny's supposed tipster is a crank. Like we said earlier, it could simply be someone who's trying to give her or us a hard time. Someone who gets a kick out of the police or the media spinning their wheels over nothing.'

Kjeld ran his hand over his chin as he mentally added this new piece of information to the puzzle. There was a flaw in Esme's theory. He remembered the Hedebrant case, but not because of the men involved or the conviction. He remembered it because of how he'd found the gun. Emma Hassan, the girl who mysteriously managed to unlock the back door of his police car, had it in her possession when he picked her up. 'But it can't be the same gun because that gun is in evidence.'

Esme double-blinked in surprise. Then she leaned over to look at the file again. 'What? Are you certain?'

Kjeld didn't have to reach back into his memory to remember. The event was clear in his mind. They'd received a call from an administrative worker at Emma's school that one of the other students saw a gun in her backpack. That was why they picked her up in the first place. And that was how they linked the gun back to Emil Hermansson. 'I'm positive. I put that gun in evidence myself. It should still be there. And if it's not …'

'… Then someone with police access removed it.'

'You might want to reschedule that date, Esme.' Kjeld grabbed his coat off the wall. 'It's going to be a long night at the office.'

Chapter 24

Fredag | Friday

Therese Grahn, senior officer in charge of evidence, used a specialised key card to open the door to the property room while Kjeld and Esme waited on the opposite side of the counter. She returned a few minutes later with the box from the Tobias Hedebrant case, but before she turned it over she requested both of their signatures on two different forms. Then she placed an itemised list of the box's inventory in front of them.

'Which item are you interested in?' she asked.

Kjeld glanced at the list. 'Item B-3. The pistol.'

Therese opened the box.

Kjeld watched in anxious anticipation, fully expecting the gun to be missing. But before he could express his prediction to Esme, who was also waiting eagerly, Therese took out a bag and placed it on the table.

'SIG Sauer P226 service-model pistol with a single 9x19 millimetre Parabellum cartridge. One bullet missing. But the bullet is labelled as item number C-2.' Therese searched through the box

121

again and retrieved a tagged plastic bag containing the bullet uncovered from Tobias Hedebrant's skull.

'The gun is here,' Kjeld said, surprised. He realised he was stating the obvious, but his thoughts hadn't quite caught up to his words.

'Has anyone checked on this file recently?' Esme asked.

Therese glanced at the requisition forms. 'Not since 2003.'

'That would have been about the time of Emil Hermansson's trial.'

Therese nodded. 'And you were the last officer to sign off on both pieces of evidence.'

Kjeld leaned closer to get a better look at the forms. 'Can I see that?'

Therese showed him the chain of custody document along with all of the transfers. True enough, Kjeld's signature was the last one on the list before it was turned in to the evidence manager.

'Is it possible that someone could have removed it and replicated your signature on the original documentation?' Esme asked.

'Impossible,' Therese interrupted. 'The property room is under twenty-four-hour surveillance on minimally rotating shifts. And the key card system ensures we know exactly who and when is accessing the room at all times. Everything is recorded digitally. This box is from before the new system was in place, but the paperwork is clean. And as you can see from the bag, it still has the original seal. No one could have been in this box without my knowing it.'

'Maybe it's the wrong gun. Maybe this gun wasn't used to murder Andrea Nicolescu.' But even as he said it, Kjeld didn't feel right about it.

'But according to the initial ballistics report the striation patterns matched this case identically. Do you know what the odds are of it being a different gun?' Esme was frustrated.

'I know, but how do we account for this one still being in evidence?'

Esme scrunched her nose up in thought.

'I don't know what they've told you down in ballistics,' Therese said. 'But *this* pistol hasn't left the property room in sixteen years.'

'Microscopic striations change over time,' Axel said after Kjeld and Esme had caught up the rest of the team on their findings. 'I know it's unlikely, but if the make and model of gun is the same and they came from the same production line it's possible that with time and use the striations between two firearms could be similar.'

'You're correct,' Esme said. 'I asked the ballistics specialist about that and he said that would normally be true. But he pointed out a distinctive groove on the edge of both bullets. He believes this is the result of an aberration in the barrel. Possibly something missed in quality control before it reached the market.'

'Which means the likelihood that the bullets were fired from two different guns would be astronomical,' Sixten said, his mouth half full of the cinnamon roll he was eating.

Esme nodded. 'Assuming no other weapons came out of the manufacturer from the same time with the same defect then it would be anomalous to that gun only.'

Axel reached over for the file, flipping it open to the last page. He removed a full-colour photograph of two bullets, side by side, displaying their various striations. 'Maybe ballistics made a mistake?'

'We'll have to have the bullets re-examined.' Esme huffed.

'We should have the gun from the Hedebrant case tested as well,' Kjeld said. 'If it was used recently there should be residue. And we can fingerprint the evidence bag to check for tampering.'

'Who was the last person to log into evidence for that file?' Sixten asked.

'The on-duty evidence clerk was the last signature on the documentation. Before that the forensics analyst and then myself. We checked the chain of custody. It doesn't look like it's been touched in years.' Kjeld leaned back in his chair, steepling his fingers beneath his chin in thought.

There was a collective pause among the team as though they were all holding their breath. And Kjeld knew why. They were expecting him to say someone else's name. Someone they knew could be blamed for obstructing the course of justice. Nils. Which made Kjeld wonder if SU hadn't been right. Was it possible that someone else in the department could have been working with Nils during the Aubuchon case? If another officer had been involved in the murders then that would explain why it had taken so long for the evidence to lead back to Nils. Could something similar have happened here?

'But we have to consider the possibility that it was. If someone was smart enough to remove the gun and return it without anyone noticing, then they'd be smart enough to cover their tracks.'

'Does it bother anybody else that this is the same kind of weapon many of us were issued?' Sixteen asked.

'It's not the only service pistol the police use. I have a P229,' Esme said. She glanced at Kjeld.

'Same, but my first model was a 226.'

'It could just be a coincidence,' Axel offered. 'It's a common firearm for duty use and concealed carry in multiple countries.'

Kjeld ran his fingers back through his hair. He didn't believe in coincidences. Nor did he think the investigators at SU believed in them. And the moment anything even tangentially related to the Emma Hassan case came under suspicion, they could lose the entire investigation to SU.

'What about Louisa? Any chance that she could be connected to Andrea?' Axel asked.

Esme leaned against the side of Kjeld's desk. Her eyes were tired and bloodshot from too much caffeine. 'Doesn't appear to be. They couldn't have been more different from each other and there's no suggestion that their circles crossed. They're from different areas of the city, different social standing, different careers. Not to mention the fact that Louisa practically never left her house except to go to the library. She had no history of drug abuse or any known connections to people in the drug trade. And Andrea's wife didn't recognise her.'

'But we still haven't accounted for Louisa's whereabouts on those four days she didn't go to work.'

Esme crossed her arms over her chest and pinched the bridge of her nose. 'I know we all want these two cases to be linked, but I think they're unrelated. And I think we need to treat them as such. There's nothing to suggest this is the same killer. Hell, for all we know Ingrid killed Andrea.'

'She didn't seem that broken up about it,' Sixten added.

'Okay, let's go through it again from the beginning,' Kjeld said. 'Starting with Louisa.'

Esme ran down the list of evidence – or the lack thereof – starting with Gjur Hägglund's house and leading up to the pathological findings. While she spoke, Kjeld's thoughts drifted back to Emma. They'd picked her up at school. The gun was still in her backpack. They put her in the back seat. Kjeld had the backpack in the front, on the floor between his feet. They drove onto the highway. The traffic was bumper-to-bumper. The door opened. Was there an unlocking click? Fuck, he didn't know anymore.

Axel began walking them through the CCTV findings for the umpteenth time.

Kjeld sighed. His eyes were beginning to cross from going over the same ideas over and over. As much as he agreed that Esme was right, that these cases weren't linked, he couldn't help but feel like there was something they were missing. Something *he* was missing.

He took out his phone and pulled up the photo of the flyers he'd taken outside Högsbo Library. He zoomed in on the number for the missing Pekingese and dialled it on his desk phone. Esme shot him a look as though to question why he wasn't paying attention, but didn't say anything. A few seconds later an older-sounding woman answered the phone. Kjeld spoke with her for a few minutes only to discover that the woman had indeed found her missing dog and forgotten to take down the neighbourhood flyers.

He rang off and then zoomed in on the other flyer. There was no phone number or address. At the top of the flyer was a drawing of a pair of opening palms, which met at the wrists in a V-formation. In between the hands was what appeared to be a sun, its rays stretching upwards. Underneath was a single question without an answer: *Are you ready for your second chance?*

Kjeld frowned. What was that supposed to mean?

Axel groaned. 'This is impossible. We need more evidence. I hate to say it but I think we need to lean in on the tip line. Maybe we'll get lucky.'

Sixten rolled his chair up beside Kjeld. 'Thinking about joining the collective, boss?'

'Hm?'

Sixten nodded to the image on Kjeld's phone. 'Second Life Wellness Respite. To be honest you really don't strike me as the type, but to each their own.'

'Wait – you know what this is?'

Sixten tossed a gummy Bilar candy into his mouth, which he'd taken from the jar on Axel's desk. 'Sure. I saw a documentary on them a few years ago. They claimed to be a kind of commune for people who'd gone through traumatic experiences or were trying to kick drug habits. Like an alternative form of a rehabilitation clinic. Residents lived on their campus until they were healed from whatever ailed them. But some of them stayed on, which started these rumours about the place being a cult.'

'A cult?'

Sixten chewed the gummy candy in between talking. 'I don't think it's a *real* cult. That's just something people started saying because some of the former residents admitted to going by different names, refusing to use modern technology, and practising meditation. You know, hippy stuff. But after the bad press you stopped hearing about them in the news.'

'And this is one of their flyers?'

Sixten nodded. 'Yeah, looks like it. That was part of the reasoning behind them being a cult. Because their flyers were so vague and always consisted of a single question. I think the idea behind it had something to do with need and determination. If you really *were* ready for a second chance, for example, then you would find a way to get in touch.'

'So, it's a religious group?'

'Holistic, I'd say.' Sixten held up a handful of candies. 'Bilar?'

'No thanks.' Kjeld pulled thoughtfully at the beard hair on his chin. He needed a trim. 'How would someone go about finding this commune?'

'I'd start with Google.'

'I thought they didn't use technology.'

'Have you ever known a cult not to be hypocritical?'

Chapter 25

Sixten was right. While Second Life Wellness Respite, or Second Life as it was more commonly called on the internet, didn't have a phone number or an email address, they did have a website. And that website did very little to hide their location. There wasn't a physical address for the commune, but they did have driving directions listed at the bottom of the page with a statement that claimed, 'Due to the delicate nature of the healing and self-discovery process, the administrators and residents of Second Life are not available for public interviews with media or television personalities.' There was, however, contact information for their private attorney. A fact Kjeld found suspiciously unsettling but it didn't stop him and Esme from driving out to the commune on their lunch break.

Second Life's compound was located off route 190 near the southwestern edge of the Änggårdsbergen Nature Reserve about twenty minutes from Gothenburg city centre. The area was sparsely populated and dotted with small hard-to-find houses on dirt or gravel roads that weren't indicated on any map or GPS. Even the driving directions Kjeld had copied from the website were hard to decipher once he reached the area. In fact, were it not for a small hand-painted sign Esme saw on the side of a road near the town of Gunnilse, depicting the same open hand and sun gesture that was on the flyer outside the library, they may not have found the commune at all.

Although "found" was a relative term.

The final road that Kjeld thought would take him up to the gate stopped at the edge of a densely wooded area. Outside the air was frosty, the sky bleak with low-hanging snow clouds. He grabbed a pair of gloves from the centre console and climbed out.

There wasn't a distinct path to the commune, but the direction they needed to follow through the dense woodland was easy enough to find. Someone had marked a series of low-hanging tree branches with red ribbons that fluttered in the wind. The terrain wasn't difficult to traverse, but large protruding roots and thick brambles that stuck to their clothing if they got too close slowed their pace. In the end it was at least a fifteen-minute hike through the woods before they came upon the entrance.

From the outside there wasn't much to see. A wooden fence, about eight feet high, surrounded the entire commune. And a single door, stark white in colour, offered the only passage in and out. It wasn't locked, but when they stepped inside they were immediately met by a woman who appeared to be in her mid to late forties and was wearing a beige-coloured tunic and green linen slacks. Her auburn hair, which was pulled back in a loose bun, was gently matted down by the rain.

'Welcome to Second Life Wellness Respite,' she said. 'I'm Sister Löv.'

Esme introduced them both, showing the woman their police identifications. Sister Löv didn't display any surprise. If anything, she acted as though they were expected and with little more than a 'follow me' she led them across a large open field to a row of buildings.

Inside the commune walls it was eerily quiet. No voices. No doors slamming shut. Only the occasional whistling chirp of a blackbird, perched hidden in the trees. The layout reminded Kjeld a bit of Skansen park in Stockholm, the small houses made to look like older farm dwellings. They were all painted in traditional Falun red and a few of the houses had grass roofs, although Kjeld suspected they still had modern plumbing and electricity. Most of the buildings were close together, like one might expect in a suburban neighbourhood. There was, however, a central gazebo with rows of outdoor amphitheatre-styled seating built into the ground and a large vegetable garden, which had been wilted by the excess rain.

Sister Löv escorted them into what appeared to be an indoor communal area. The room was open and spacious with amber-coloured walls that were interrupted every few feet by long pieces of tie-dyed cloth that dangled from the ceiling like wispy tapestries. There weren't any tables or chairs in the space. Only a circular spiral-designed carpet and a smattering of beanbags. It reminded Kjeld of the photos from a yoga retreat pamphlet that Bengt had tried to con him into years ago.

A few young people, both men and women, passed them by in similar loose-fitting robe-like garments, politely nodding their heads in acknowledgement. Kjeld did his best not to show how ridiculous he thought all of this was and pursed his lips to prevent himself from making any sarcastic comments. Esme, for her part, didn't seemed fazed by the utter absurdity of what appeared to be a commune of hippies in the middle of the woods outside Gothenburg proper. Then again, she was a little more accepting than he was. Or perhaps she was simply better at hiding her opinions. Probably both.

Sister Löv led them towards the beanbag area of the room. 'Brother Björk will be with you shortly. Would you like any water or herbal tea in the meantime?'

'Do you have any coffee?'

'We refrain from stimulants here.'

Kjeld made a face.

'No, thank you. We'll be fine,' Esme said.

Sister Löv nodded. 'You're welcome to make yourself at home while you wait,' she said, motioning to the beanbags. Then she wandered off, leaving them alone.

Kjeld nudged one of the beanbags with the toe of his boot. 'Are these people for real?'

Esme shot him a warning stare. 'Play nice, Kjeld.'

'I am playing nice, but come on. If this isn't a cult then I don't know what is. No one else would wear that much linen.'

'You're just jealous you wouldn't be able to pull off that beige tunic with mint-green slacks.'

'They'd have to pry my blue jeans from my cold dead hands.'

'Someone really ought to.' Esme smirked. 'You've been wearing the same pair since we met.'

'When it comes to a good pair of denim I'm fucking loyal.'

'I think the word you meant to use is "stubborn".'

'Well, we can't all look like we rolled out of bed and into a Vero Moda catalogue.'

Esme rolled her eyes. 'Says someone who's clearly never stepped into a Vero Moda in their life.'

Esme walked over to a far wall where a framed photograph hung between two swaths of sheer fabric. It was a small group of people, all dressed in commune garb. At the centre stood a tall man with a soft face and thin blond hair. Above the photo someone had printed a quote and taped it to the wall: "Every second chance begins with a first one."

Kjeld stepped up behind her and eyed both the photograph and the quote dismissively. 'Sounds like a load of bullshit to me.'

'That's what most of the people in that photo said at first,' a voice said from behind them.

Kjeld and Esme turned around to see a man approach them – the same man from the centre of the image, only quite a bit older. Brother Björk appeared to be in his early to mid-sixties. He had an oval-shaped face, marked by loose jowls along the sides of his jaw. His eyes were small and his nose long. He had blond hair that was thinning and combed backwards, revealing a broad forehead dotted with sun spots. Although he didn't wear any earrings, Kjeld could see that his left ear was pierced. And there were faded remnants of an old tattoo on the side of his neck that disappeared under the Nehru collar of his tunic.

Björk offered his hand to Esme first. 'I'm Brother Björk.'

'Esme Jansson. And this is my partner, Kjeld Nygaard.'

Kjeld shook Björk's hand as well and was surprised by how firm it was. The grip was stronger than he'd anticipated and he could see the tendons in Björk's wrist tense just before he dropped the handshake.

Björk nodded to the photograph. 'Our first cohort. That must be about ten years ago now. Most have moved on, but some are still here.'

Esme pointed to a young woman in the front row. 'Is that Sister Löv?'

'She's been with us from the start.'

'Why stay?' Kjeld asked. 'I thought this was a wellness centre. Isn't she well?'

Björk smiled, but Kjeld sensed a taut impatience at the corner of the man's lips. 'For some people, the act of helping others helps them. Sister Löv was in a dark place when she joined us. A place that was heightened by her connections in the outside world. By remaining here she ensures that she won't fall back on bad habits. And instead of taking that risk, she's devoted herself to helping others find their way to a new life.'

'What's with the names? Löv? Björk? Are you sure you aren't a tree-hugging society?'

'We're all family here. And we're all equal. Hence the brothers and sisters. As family we accept each other's difficulties and burdens without judgement. As for the plant references, well, nature is an instinctive source of rebirth and renewal. By giving each other new names we offer our residents the opportunity to be the person they were always meant to be. It's not required, but it is encouraged. You'd be surprised how much of a person's identity and trauma is wrapped up in a name. A name given to us by someone else at the moment of our birth. A name that might not even truly reflect the people that we are. From the moment we're born we're trapped into someone else's idea of us. And that can make it challenging for people to move forward. That's what we try to do here, help others rediscover their true selves. Their better selves. The past is not important to us here. Only the present.'

'And the future?'

Björk looked Kjeld directly in the eyes. 'That's up to them.'

Esme took out her phone and held up the image of the flyer Kjeld had snapped outside the library. 'Is this one of your recruitment flyers?'

'Recruitment? You make it sound like we're an agency or a cult. I assure you, we're neither.'

'My apologies,' Esme said. 'But is it one of your flyers?'

Björk leaned in closer, narrowing his eyes. 'Yes, it does appear to be one of ours.'

'It seems a bit counterproductive to post a flyer offering to help people but not providing any contact information,' Kjeld said.

Björk peered at Kjeld. The corner of his eye twitched and there was a familiar intensity to his gaze that made Kjeld wonder if they hadn't met somewhere else before. After an uncomfortable pause Björk answered, 'As I'm sure you're both aware, we've had some difficulty with the press recently. And we're only here for the truly devoted. For the people who are ready to put their old lives behind them. Completely behind them. And people who are that desperate for a new start have no trouble finding out how to contact us.'

Esme removed a photo of Louisa Karlsson from her pocket and held it up for Björk to see. It was one of the photos Louisa's father had provided them for the press conference. 'Have you ever seen this woman before?'

Björk held Kjeld's gaze for a split second longer than necessary and then averted his attention to the photograph. 'That's the poor girl from the news, isn't it?'

'Louisa Karlsson,' Esme said. 'We have reason to believe that one of your residents may have been in contact with her.'

Björk shook his head. 'I'm sorry. I haven't seen her.'

'Are you certain?' Kjeld took the photo out of Esme's hand and held it closer to Björk's face. 'Look again.'

The muscles around Björk's jaw tensed, but he looked at the photo again. Longer this time. Afterwards he shot Kjeld an unwavering stare. 'I haven't seen her.'

Esme cleared her throat with a cough and Kjeld took a step back from Björk, passing the photo to Esme as he made his way over to a window. There was a light rain outside, but that didn't seem to stop two women from working in the garden.

'Would it be possible to talk to your residents and see if any of them have seen Louisa?' Esme asked. Kjeld could hear in her tone that she was purposefully being extra polite, perhaps to ease any tension Kjeld might have created.

'Naturally if anyone wants to speak with you, that's their business. This isn't a prison. Everyone here is free to speak to whomever they want. But I don't think you'll get much out of them. Even if they had seen that poor girl, they wouldn't have any information about her murder.'

'What makes you so certain?'

'Because that's exactly the kind of thing people here are trying to get away from.'

Kjeld perked his attention back up and glanced at Björk. 'Are you saying that you're hiding murderers here?'

'No,' Björk said. 'I'm saying that people who come here are escaping personal traumas and tragedies. Many of them have been abused or in violent relationships. Some have even been victims of unimaginable crimes. They wouldn't put themselves in the position of getting hurt again. And if they had seen something, they would have already called the police.'

'Is that one of the tenets you practise? Call the police when you witness something criminal? Because that doesn't quite jive with what the news has to say about Second Life.'

'Kind of like what the news has to say about you, Detective?'

A heavy silence fell between them and Kjeld felt his face burn with anger.

'Thank you for your time, Brother Björk. I'm sorry if we interrupted your day.' Esme shot Kjeld a look, but he didn't see it. Then she turned an apologetic expression to Björk. 'I hope you don't take my partner's gruffness personally. We're anxious to bring some peace to Louisa's family.'

'Of course.' Björk offered a sympathetic smile. 'There's nothing more tragic than the loss of a child.'

Chapter 26

When they returned to the station, Esme immediately set about looking into the commune's history in order to verify the information they'd received from Brother Björk while Kjeld put on a new pot of coffee. He watched the coffee machine absent-mindedly as he rewound the conversation with Björk in his mind. Kjeld couldn't pinpoint exactly what it was about the man that seemed off, but his gut told him Björk had been lying. Whether he'd been lying about the commune or about seeing Louisa, Kjeld couldn't say. But something about the man felt untrustworthy. And Kjeld was certain he was withholding something.

The coffee maker shuddered and started to fill the carafe when a harsh shove to Kjeld's arm drove him out of his thoughts.

'What the hell were you doing at Second Life?' Kenneth Olsen glared, the tips of his ears red with anger.

A flash of annoyance crossed Kjeld's expression. 'I have a better question. Why do you care?'

'Don't fuck around with me, Kjeld. You do not want to go head-to-head with me.'

'Don't I?' Kjeld opened the cupboard to remove a clean cup for Esme. Then he rinsed out his own mug, still stained from last night's multiple-cup marathon, in the sink.

136

'You wouldn't stand a chance. Unlike you I actually have friends in the department.'

'Friends or cronies?'

'Just answer the question.'

Kjeld lifted his shoulders in a nonchalant shrug. 'Maybe I was having a crisis of faith.'

'Cut the crap, Kjeld. What's your interest in Second Life?'

'Sounds to me like the answer is in the name. Maybe I'm looking to heal from my past trauma and start anew.' Kjeld eyed Kenneth closely. 'What's your interest in them?'

'They've been under investigation for the last five years on suspicion of drug trafficking with a cartel out of Eastern Europe. We've been trying to build a case against them, but every time we get close to proving their involvement we get waylaid.'

'Yeah, well, I'm investigating a potential double homicide. One of my victims might have been a convert. And the last time I checked murder trumps drugs.'

'Not when Interpol is involved.' Kenneth smirked.

'You've got to be fucking kidding me.'

'We're working with Romanian police to bring down the Sandu cartel. We know they've been edging into Sweden through the ports for the last couple of years, but we haven't had the evidence to prove it. Now that we're close we're sure as hell not going to lose our edge because you *think* there might be a connection to your homicide.' Kenneth paused.

'Did you say the Romanian police?'

'Maybe you didn't hear me. I said stay off my turf, Nygaard.'

'How did you even know I was there? Are you monitoring my social media check-ins again?'

'Very funny,' Kenneth scoffed. 'The organised crime team has had the commune under surveillance for months. No one gets in or out without our knowing about it. My guys called me as soon as you pulled up on the commune's borders.'

The coffee maker beeped that it was finished. Kjeld pursed his lips in a disgruntled sneer before removing the carafe and filling up the two mugs, his to the brim and Esme's enough to still add creamer. 'Look, I'm not interested in getting between you and your investigation. I just want to find my victims' killer.'

'I don't care what you want. Second Life is off limits. You got a problem with it, you take it up with someone higher up the food chain.'

Kjeld opened his mouth to protest when Esme hurried into the kitchenette. She was slightly out of breath as though she'd just sprinted across the room. And the look on her face told him whatever she was about to say wasn't good.

'Your phone is off again. Bengt just called,' Esme said. 'Tove's in hospital.'

Chapter 27

Kjeld rushed into Sahlgrenska Hospital, his hair damp from running through the rain from the car park. After checking in with the receptionist, he jogged down the corridor and made his way to the children's surgical ward where Tove was registered. His heart beat wildly in his chest, the internal pounding so loud it drowned out his thoughts.

When he stepped into the room he didn't know what to expect. He'd dialled Bengt multiple times on the drive from the station to the hospital, but it kept going to voicemail. Bengt was always very compulsive about answering his phone. When he didn't, Kjeld's nerves responded by twisting into a tangled ball of terror that sat heavy in his gut. And when he saw Tove sitting up on the bed, her face flushed but smiling, he almost threw up from the sheer anxious panic that had tormented him on the drive over.

'Look, Daddy! It's pink!' Tove held up her arm, which was encased in a cast that started at the centre of her palm and stretched halfway up her forearm.

Kjeld's mind was a buzz of questions, the least of which was the fact that Tove was in this room alone, but before he could ask any of them, Bengt walked in from the hallway. Kjeld whipped his head around and stared at his ex-husband, who appeared inexplicably calm with a cup of hospital coffee in hand. On closer inspection, however, Kjeld noticed that his shirt was untucked, his hair dishevelled, and his eyes puffy. Composed, but not calm.

'What happened?' Kjeld asked. 'I must have called you a dozen times since Esme gave me your message.'

Bengt stepped up beside him, taking a sip of the coffee before setting the paper cup on the bedside table. 'I was talking with the doctor and couldn't answer my phone.'

Kjeld sat down on the edge of the bed and tried to catch his breath.

Tove raised her cast-covered arm close to his face. 'It's really heavy! The doctor said I can have the kids in my class write their names on it. Look! Papa already wrote his name on it.'

Kjeld gently held her arm in his hand and glanced down at the pink cast where Bengt had drawn a heart and signed "Papa" beside it with black marker. Then he carefully – as though it were made of glass – placed Tove's arm back in her lap. He turned his attention back towards Bengt who watched them both with what looked to Kjeld like a kind of desperate longing. He must have been mistaken though. It was probably just sympathy.

'What happened?'

'She fell in the school playground and fractured her wrist.'

'She *fell*?'

Tove answered before Bengt could continue. 'Hugo Blum said that girls can't climb as high as boys can and I said that was stupid. Then he said, "If I'm so stupid why don't you prove me wrong?" So, I climbed up the big tree behind the school. But one of the branches broke.'

Bengt sighed. 'The teacher's aide said she was only out of her sight for a few minutes.'

'I climbed higher than Hugo. He even said so himself!'

Kjeld tried not to look upset, especially when Tove was so proud of herself. But he still felt like his heart was beating a million miles a minute. 'You have to be careful, Tove. That was really dangerous. You could have really hurt yourself.'

'I did hurt myself!' She knocked her knuckles on the cast. 'I don't feel it anymore though.'

'I told her she's not allowed to climb trees without telling an adult first,' Bengt said, pulling up a chair and sitting down across from Kjeld.

'What did the doctor say?'

'The cast will probably have to stay on for five to six weeks.' Bengt reached into his pocket and removed an instructional pamphlet on how to care for the cast and what types of activities to avoid while wearing one. 'So you know what to do this weekend.'

Kjeld took the pamphlet and frowned. 'This weekend?'

'When Tove comes to stay with you. 'I know you were supposed to pick her up this afternoon, but tomorrow morning might be better. I want her to stay home tonight so Liam and I can keep an eye on her. Just to be safe. Bengt paused. 'You didn't forget, did you?'

'No, of course not. I'm just a little rattled.'

'You're not working this weekend, right?'

Kjeld could feel Bengt's peering eyes upon him. 'Not if it's my weekend with Tove.'

Bengt nodded, but didn't say anything. He took a sip of his coffee. When the silence between them became too uncomfortable he cleared his throat with a cough. 'I'm glad you came. She was crying for you when I got to the school.'

Kjeld looked up at Bengt, trying to decipher his expression. At first, he couldn't tell if that was a quiet jab at his lack of presence in Tove's life or an honest expression of gratitude. But when Bengt failed to meet his gaze he decided it was the latter.

A flutter of anticipation caught in his throat. 'Bengt, I've been meaning to tell you—'

But Kjeld's comment was cut off by the sound of the door opening. He turned to see Liam stepping through the door, tall and respectably handsome in his white physician's coat. Kjeld's heart sank.

'I just spoke with the surgeon. Everything looks good. Tove is cleared to go home. I've asked for the rest of the afternoon off as well.' His eyes narrowed just a fraction when he glanced at Kjeld. Then he gave him a curt but acknowledging nod. 'Should I get the car?'

Bengt pursed his lips. There was a distant sadness in his face that Kjeld couldn't quite place. It tugged at the corners of his mouth. But when he looked up it had been replaced with a forced smile that was almost – but not entirely – convincing. 'Thanks, Liam. We'll meet you downstairs.'

Liam left and Kjeld wanted to ask Bengt if everything was all right, but it didn't feel like his place to intrude. And before he could work out how best to phrase his question, Bengt was getting up and collecting Tove's shoes and coat.

Tove waved a marker in front of Kjeld's face. 'Will you sign my arm, Daddy?'

Kjeld smiled. 'Of course, sweetheart.'

Chapter 28

Esme stood in front of the vending machine that had recently been installed in the newly renovated corridor that led to the Violent Crimes Division. She'd been on the phone with forensic technicians ever since Kjeld rushed off to the hospital. She hoped the frequent calls might hurry along their processing, but they had nothing new to report. Even ballistics said it would probably be at least another day, maybe even longer, before they could get back to her on the weapon from the Hedebrant case. She didn't want to think that someone in the department could be responsible for these crimes, but she knew that until they found out if that was truly the gun used to kill Andrea she would be cautious of everyone.

That impatience and suspicion, compounded by concern for Kjeld's daughter, had her craving something fattening. After a few minutes, she was still debating how much she really wanted to cave in to her sweet tooth when she caught a glimpse of Kjeld heading towards the administrative wing.

'Kjeld!'

He stopped in his tracks and blinked, as though caught in mid-thought. Then he stepped around two colleagues who were exchanging paperwork in the middle of the corridor before making his way towards her. He glanced at the vending machine contents.

'Doesn't look like your usual breed of snack,' he said.

Esme surveyed the selection of potato crisps, salt liquorice candies and chocolate with inherent boredom. Kjeld was right. Nothing in the machine was tempting her. In fact, most of it didn't even satisfy her – admittedly halfhearted – attempts at being vegan. She still snuck a bit of creamer into her coffee now and again, after all. But something about these two cases was giving her unhealthy cravings throughout the day. If she wasn't careful she'd put on five kilos before they caught this damn killer.

'You're right, but someone in the office ate my carrots and hummus dip.'

'My money is on Sixten. That man is always snacking on something.'

'And not gaining a single pound, by the looks of it.' Esme shoved her loose change back into her pocket.

Kjeld turned to leave.

'How's Tove doing?' Esme asked before Kjeld could get too far. 'I didn't expect you to come back to work afterwards.'

He turned around, holding back the exasperation she knew he felt. 'She's okay. Broke her arm falling out of a tree trying to show the class bully that girls can climb better than boys.'

'Well, at least her intentions were noble.'

Kjeld gave a small chuckle. 'If this is how she is at six I don't know if I'll survive sixteen.'

'Can't help you there. I was a teenage terror.' Esme smiled. 'Where are you going?'

'I was going to ask Alice if she might have any insight into the case.'

'Insight?'

'Maybe help come up with a profile of Louisa's killer.' Kjeld paused. 'Want to join me?'

Esme's lips pursed into a thin line. She'd been thinking about introducing herself to the station counsellor for a few weeks now, but every time she had the urge something stopped her. It wasn't difficult for her to pinpoint that insecurity, however. She'd seen so many counsellors and therapists as a child that they left a dark memory on her past. And she secretly worried that talking to one now might allow her past to come flooding forward from the deep pit of her mind where she buried the truths she wasn't willing to confront.

She shook her head. 'No, thanks. But before you go I wanted to ask you something.'

Kjeld quirked a brow. 'What's that?'

'Who's Emma Hassan?'

Kjeld flinched. Esme was surprised by his reaction. She stepped closer.

'Where did you hear that name?' Kjeld asked.

'Rhodin called me into his office yesterday. Someone from SU wanted to ask me some questions about you. They wanted to know if you'd ever brought up Emma Hassan in conversation.'

'And what did you say?'

'The truth. I'd never heard her name before.' Esme gave Kjeld a moment to respond, but when he didn't immediately, she continued. 'Then I was going through the Hedebrant case again trying to figure out if we'd missed something about the weapon and discovered the gun wasn't found at the crime scene. It was uncovered later after you and Nils were called to a school where one of the students potentially brought a firearm to class. That student is named in the case file as Emma Hassan.'

Kjeld looked down at his feet and ran his fingers back through his hair.

'What's going on?' Esme asked. 'Who is she and why haven't you brought her up before?'

Kjeld checked to see if the couple in the corridor were within listening distance, but they'd already split up and gone their separate ways, leaving him alone with Esme.

'She was part of an investigation that Nils and I worked on. It was years ago. Early in my career. I'd just been promoted to detective. It was one of our first cases together.'

'What happened?

Kjeld crossed his arms over his chest. 'You already know about the murder committed by a man named Emil Hermansson. Emma was on our list as a potential witness or unwitting accomplice. She was a teenager, only sixteen at the time. We suspected she might have been tangentially involved because her father, Jan-Erik Hassan, also had some dealings with Hermansson. They were both into drug trafficking. We picked Emma up after someone at her school called the police claiming they saw a gun in her possession. We thought it might be the same gun used in the murder. Turns out our hunch was correct.'

Esme listened carefully as Kjeld told the story. She could see that there was something about the case that bothered him. His eyes refused to focus on her when he spoke, gaze continually falling to the floor. What was that expression in his face? Shame? Regret?

'We were driving back to the station when we got stuck in traffic on the exchange above the E45.'

Esme nodded. 'I know where you mean.'

'Well, Emma jumped out of the patrol car and made a dash across the highway into oncoming traffic. I chased after her, but I wasn't quick enough. She was hit.'

'Oh my God,' Esme muttered under her breath. 'Right in front of you?'

Kjeld's mouth twisted into an uncomfortable frown, but he didn't reply. Esme recognised that look now. Remorse. And uncertainty.

'But how did she get out of the vehicle? It should have been locked.'

'It *was* locked. I don't know how she got out.'

Esme ran her fingers over the coins in her pocket. The sensation of cold metal against her fingertips focused her thoughts.

She tried to put herself in Kjeld's position. A suspect escaping from the back seat of a patrol car only offered a few explanations. Only three which she could reason: mechanical failure, human error, or malicious intent. The door was broken. Someone forgot to lock it. Or someone purposely made sure it was unlocked.

Two of those possibilities were unfortunate, but not criminal. The other ...

'What happened afterwards?'

'It was investigated and determined to be an accident. We did manage to put Hermansson away for murder as you saw in the case file, but we couldn't connect anything to Emma's father. He fell off the radar not long afterwards. We suspected he might have left the country. Sadly, her mother committed suicide shortly after.'

'Because of her daughter's death?'

Kjeld nodded. 'She drove her car off the Lemmingsgatan bridge and into the river.'

'Have they reopened the investigation? Is that why SU is asking around about it? Do they suspect foul play in Emma's death?'

Kjeld shrugged. 'All I know is that they're looking into it.'

'I wouldn't worry about it.'

'Easy for you to say.'

'It is. Because I know you, Kjeld. You wouldn't make a mistake like that. You're too careful.'

Chapter 29

Kjeld paced back and forth in front of Alice's desk, shoes threatening to burn a path in the thin carpet. He stopped at the window and peered out into the street. The rain had stopped and a foggy chill began to ice the corners of the glass where there was a draught. Outside a pedestrian slipped on the pavement, but quickly got up and continued on their way undeterred. Alice had a small space heater beneath her desk that whirred as it rotated, jetting out a small whoosh of heat. It often took the radiators in the older section of the building time to warm up. The electric kettle jiggled on its stand, wheezing when it finally came to a boil, and she poured them both a cup of chamomile tea. Kjeld was embarrassed that he was growing accustomed to the scent and he instantly felt more relaxed.

He stepped away from the window and slumped down on the sofa. Alice placed a mug in front of him, the steam wafting up from the liquid, tea still steeping.

'I'm stuck. These cases are eluding me. They've out-thought me at every turn.'

Alice sat down in her chair and took a small sip of her tea before setting the mug down on the low table in front of her.

'Have you considered the possibility that they haven't out-thought you but are simply ahead of you?'

'Isn't that the same thing?'

'Not necessarily. Say, for instance, that you and your friend decide to go on a road trip in separate automobiles, but your friend gets half a day's head start. It's not that your friend knows the way any better than you do. It's just that they're ahead of you on the journey. And there's always the possibility that your friend will make a wrong turn or stop to fill up the tank and give you the opportunity to catch up.'

'If they were really my friend then we would have travelled together,' Kjeld said blandly.

'It's a metaphor.'

'I know, but I don't need metaphors. What I need is a profile of the type of person who would re-enact a crime that a gruesome serial killer had planned for their last victim. I need to get in their head so I can figure out what's motivating them. I need to know *why* they're doing this. Then I can stop them from killing anyone else. Because they will do it again. I can feel it.' Kjeld picked up his mug and took a sip. He'd let the teabag steep too long and it gave the chamomile an almost chalky taste. He took out the bag and set it in the small dish at the centre of the table. 'Who do you think could be behind this?'

'I'm not a forensic profiler.'

'Humour me. If you had to guess based on the events so far. What kind of person would you be looking for?'

Alice crossed her legs. 'Well, and this is purely speculative, mind you. And you only have one victim, thus far, correct?'

Kjeld nodded. 'The other case is another problem, but at the moment it's being deemed unrelated.'

'In that case, your victim is a woman. That usually indicates a male killer. Her death was incredibly violent which would also play in favour of a man. But if we're considering the possibility of a serial killer then for men there's usually a sexual component.

149

Female serial killers are more pragmatic in their motivations.'

'There's nothing to indicate a sexual motivation. None that we've found so far.'

'It could be a delayed gratification on the killer's part. Maybe he waits until after the killing to indulge his sexual cravings.'

Kjeld leaned forward, resting his elbows on his knees. He hadn't considered the possibility of there being a sexual connection to Louisa's murder, but that might have been because he hadn't wanted to see it. Alice had a point, however. There had been a lustful component for Gjur Hägglund when he chose his victims. If this new killer saw Hägglund as a kind of inspiration then he might have a similar design on his victims. And there was a torture aspect to the crimes that couldn't be ignored. It wasn't a stretch to consider that the motive could have a sexual factor to it.

'It's also someone who is familiar with Louisa's history. They've replicated the original crime almost exactly,' Kjeld said.

'But the original crime didn't end with Louisa's death. Which means the killer believes it should have. Like he's finishing what someone else started or setting right what went wrong in the past.'

Kjeld's forehead furrowed in thought. Was it possible that's what the murderer was doing? Editing a past crime and giving it a new ending? Revising it to match what the original killer had intended?

'But why Louisa? And why now?'

Alice shrugged. 'I'm afraid that goes beyond my ability to speculate.'

Kjeld could still speculate, but beyond what Alice had already hypothesised ran into the realm of thinking too far. And, unfortunately, one death wasn't enough to form a basis for any reliable conclusion. They would need another murder to compare it to. And potential ballistics error aside, Andrea's case didn't have the same level of execution and planning to it. Which meant that the only thing connecting the victims was Henny's mysterious tipster. But that was a flimsy connection at best.

'I heard SU is looking into your old cases,' Alice said, cutting through Kjeld's thoughts.

'They are.'

'Is that something you want to talk about?'

Kjeld sat back and ran his fingers through his hair. 'It wasn't about me. Not really. They're going through all of Nils's old cases to make sure he didn't tamper with evidence. If he's convicted then every investigation he was involved in will be called into question. They're trying to get a head start before the trial.'

'That must be difficult for you. Because they weren't just his cases. They were yours as well. If they discover that he falsified evidence or lied on his reports then people might question how you didn't notice it.'

'People can think whatever they want. I know I didn't do anything wrong.' As much as Kjeld hated to admit it, if Nils had done something illegal in their past cases together then Kjeld simply didn't catch it. Not because he wasn't a good detective. Not because he wasn't smart. But because Nils was better. And Nils was smarter. And because Kjeld had trusted him.

'Still, it can be difficult going through your old cases and wondering if there was something you missed or something you got wrong. Even if it was accidental.'

Kjeld thought back to the Emma Hassan case. For years he'd racked his mind over that. Had he made a mistake? Had he gotten it wrong? He'd been replaying the event over and over in his thoughts every day since the chief asked him about it. The more he thought about it, the more uncertain he became. But he remembered clearly how he'd felt after it happened. He'd been adamant that he hadn't made a mistake.

I locked that door. I know I did.

He shook the thought away.

'I didn't get anything wrong,' he said. But in truth he didn't know if he could trust his memories.

Chapter 30

Lördag | Saturday

Esme stood in front of the whiteboard in the incident room with her arms crossed. She'd been staring at their depressingly sparse collection of evidence for the last hour, trying to find a clue to jump-start their search in either case, but she kept coming up empty. It frustrated her not to be able to see the way the pieces fit together. She had a knack for visualising information in her mind. It wasn't quite a photographic memory, but it was close. She referred to it as puzzling because it was a lot like spreading out the pieces of a jigsaw puzzle, picture side up, and looking for patterns before attempting to fit the pieces together. She was actually quite good at jigsaw puzzles for that exact reason. If she stared at the pieces long enough she could find their proper places with very little effort.

But these cases were confounding her. She'd drawn a line down the centre of the whiteboard. On the left she'd scribbled the information from Louisa's case in blue dry-erase ink. Close to her family. Last seen by her colleagues at the library. Didn't make it to the bus. Unaccounted for on at least four work days.

Potential relationship with someone from Second Life Wellness Respite. Extreme fire damage to her body. Toxicology had indicated ketamine in her system, but pathology added a caveat that the damage to the tissues from the fire could have masked or distorted the results and therefore the presence of unknown substances couldn't be ruled out entirely.

On the right side of the board she'd written down the information from Andrea's case with a green pen. Drug connections. Tense relationship with her wife. Gunshot wound to the head. Last seen on CCTV at the convenience store petrol station where she worked. Possibly still involved in the drug trade. Bullet matched to the gun in the Hedebrant case, but gun was found in evidence room in original bagging. She made a side note on this final point that the firearm was being retested and added three question marks for extra emphasis.

Then she stepped back and looked at all of it from a distance. From the outset they looked like two completely different cases. The only apparent connection between them was the note Esme had written in red at the top of the board: Henny's Tipster.

Esme picked up the red pen and circled those two words. Then she stepped back again. She twirled the dry-erase marker between her fingers. She ran down the basics in her mind again. Louisa survived a serial killer and was murdered in the exact same manner the original killer had planned for her. She was close to her family, but didn't tell them about her whereabouts on the four days she skipped work. She may have known someone at the commune, but Brother Björk claimed she'd never been to the commune. Andrea, a former drug dealer, was executed point-blank on a football field. The bullet striations were identical to the bullet that killed another man sixteen years ago, who was also involved in drug trafficking. What was she missing? What didn't she see?

'You're still here?'

Esme glanced over her shoulder to see Sixten in the doorway.

153

He slipped his arms through the sleeves of his jacket as he made his way to the whiteboard. Once he was beside her he stopped and observed the list she'd made.

'That's not a lot of information,' he said.

'I know.' Esme returned her gaze to the list, hoping it would suddenly reveal the thread she was looking for.

'I worked this case once when I was a beat officer. The till at this lingerie store kept getting robbed to the tune of almost twenty thousand kronor in a single week. For a month I kept getting called there because they were certain it was a particular customer who came in regularly because the money always seemed to go missing on days when this woman would come into the shop. I talked to her and she seemed genuinely surprised that anyone thought she would steal from them. But there weren't any cameras inside the shop and so there was nothing to suggest she'd done anything wrong. Then one day we get a call to this pub that was across the street from the lingerie store saying that one of their regulars had smashed up the place. It was the same woman I'd interviewed at the shop. She'd had one too many drinks and gotten into a brawl with another woman for insulting her. When her purse was knocked over a stack of wrapped five-hundred kronor notes fell out along with three pairs of lace panties. Later we looked at the CCTV footage from the pub and discovered she would always leave the lingerie shop and head directly over to the pub. She was spending all the money on drinks and appetisers.'

Esme furrowed her brow. 'Is this a morality tale about the danger of spending your stolen fortune in the same place?'

Sixten chuckled. 'No, it's a lesson about looking in the right direction. I was so focused on the lingerie shop that I didn't think about the other places in the area. And if I'd looked across the street I might have realised that the pub had security cameras, which clearly depicted the woman leaving the shop and going directly to the pub.'

'I don't think anyone can fault you for being focused on the lingerie.'

Sixten blushed. 'I'm just saying that sometimes we have tunnel vision and don't even realise it. Sometimes we get so focused on the who that we forget about the how and the why. And if we start with the how and the why, often times the who is obvious.'

Esme glanced up at Sixten, surprised by the solemn composure on his face. She was so accustomed to him cracking jokes and playing the part of the idolising newbie that she often forgot he'd had a successful career in another department before transferring to their division. With his jaw set and mouth drawn in a neutral state of contemplation, he lost that boyish quality and seemed to age ten years. Serious looked good on Sixten and Esme was embarrassed to catch herself paying such close attention to how handsome his face looked. And how good he smelled.

She looked away quickly, her cheeks warm with chagrin.

Sixten didn't notice or, if he did, had the good grace not to react. Esme appreciated that.

'So, how do we know that Louisa might be connected to the commune?' he asked.

'Because her colleague told Kjeld she saw her talking to a young man who posted a flyer for the commune outside the library.'

'And why don't we know who he is?'

'Because the library doesn't have CCTV.'

Sixten crossed his arms over his chest. 'But the library isn't the only thing in the area, is it?'

'Dammit,' Esme cursed beneath her breath. She turned around and sat down at Axel's computer, quickly pulling up the surveillance footage from the ATM that sat diagonal to the library. She searched through the files until she found the date that Louisa's colleague claimed she'd been visited by a young man. The man who posted the flyers on the lamp pole in the car park.

Sixten watched her curiously, but didn't say anything. Everyone on the team knew never to interrupt Esme when she was thinking.

It took her a few minutes to locate the file with the correct date and time, but when she fast-forwarded through the footage she felt a heavy weight fall from her shoulders. A weight that was replaced by an anxious flutter in her belly. A young man matching the description Linnea Thorsen gave Kjeld flashed on the screen. And not only that, it was a face Esme recognised. Not from either of the cases they were investigating, but from one she and Kjeld had four years ago.

Jonny Lindh. The sole accidental survivor of a tragic murder-suicide that had rocked the city as much as the Cellar Sadist case.

It wasn't a stretch of the imagination for Esme to believe Jonny Lindh might seek out Second Life to help him recover from the gruesome scene they'd found him at. He must have been the man posting the flyers. The one who'd visited Louisa. And, in Esme's mind, that meant one of two things.

He was connected to the killer.

Or he was next on the list.

Chapter 31

Jonny's head was pounding as though it had been pressed against a bass speaker for the duration of a rock concert. A wave of nausea surged up from his stomach and he rolled over onto his side to vomit, but nothing came out. Just a gagging heave. There was a sour taste in his mouth, but his lips were dry, dehydrated. He'd never been so thirsty in his life. Fuck whatever it was Vidar had given him. He'd never touch that shit again. Hell, he'd never touch another drug for as long as he lived.

You've said that before, the condescending voice of his subconscious reminded him. And he was right. He had said that before. And then he got himself clean and sober for six months. Six months that he pissed away because he saw a picture of a girl in a news article. A girl he barely knew. But an article that scared the shit out of him.

The ground was damp and cold. Wooden planks ran horizontal to his face. It was dark in the room, but a thin glimmer of daybreak shone through the partly drawn curtains. A few feet away from him were the remains of yesterday's dinner, which he must have heaved in the middle of the night. He couldn't remember that.

But the putrefying pile of vomit explained the rotten taste in his mouth and the woozy sensation in his head.

You wanted to forget.

And he did. He forgot the hours from when he shot himself up with whatever poisonous concoction Vidar had sold to him when he woke up on that cold unfamiliar floor. But he didn't forget what had happened to him. That he still remembered. That would never go away no matter how many joints he smoked, veins he collapsed, or detergents he sniffed. He would always wake up and his first thought would be the same.

Bodies. Bodies everywhere.

He pressed his palm against the floor and pushed himself up. His finger slipped and a tiny piece of wood from the planks jabbed into his skin.

'Dammit,' he cursed under his breath as he sat up. He narrowed his eyes to see the splinter, but it was too dark. His legs were tired, half asleep. He crawled closer to that thin stream of light from the window and raised his hand. Then he squeezed at the pad of his finger to try to squeeze the splinter out. No such luck.

He slumped. It was then that he realised he wasn't at the commune. A slow creeping terror that began at his lower back idled up his spine until it pinched the nerves in the nape of his neck. It was the same walls from his memory. The same musty odour of wet wood and rainy pine nettles. The same dingy curtains. The same floor, now empty, where his friends had puked up their guts just before spasming to their deaths. He remembered their eyes, glossed over, protruding in horror as their mouths foamed, pink with blood.

He was overcome by another dry heave, his throat clenching up and cutting off his air supply until he inhaled a deep breath through his nostrils.

Along the wall was a pop-up camping table and at the centre was a punch bowl. *The* punch bowl. Filled to the brim with a sweet-smelling reddish liquid.

He crawled to his feet and made his way over to the table. A single cup sat beside the bowl.

Oh, God. Please be dreaming. Please don't let this be real.

'It's the only way out.'

Jonny's head snapped to the side. There was a figure in the corner, shrouded in the shadows. He hadn't noticed them before. They were so still. Could they be real? Or was this just another hallucination?

'I can't,' he whimpered. 'I don't want to die.'

'But you don't want to remember either,' the voice said.

That was true. He wanted to forget. But nothing helped him forget.

'You were supposed to join them. You were never supposed to be here.'

Jonny's heart sank because he knew that was also true. He could still remember his girlfriend convulsing on the floor. He'd watched the light go out of her eyes. He'd watched as she went from laughing to choking to dead in a matter of minutes. The fact that she was dying hadn't even processed in his mind. It was all too fast. Too sudden. She was laughing, celebrating. And then she was dead. Then they were all dead.

'It's not a shame to wish you'd been with them,' the voice said. There was a lilting quality to the tone, convincing.

'I can't die.'

'You can't live either. You've tried that. How successful has that been?'

More truths. This must have been a dream. His subconscious was reaching out to him with the answer to the question he'd been struggling with for the last four years. How did he move on? How did he live when his every thought circled the concept of death? A death he'd avoided by pure happenstance.

'Will it hurt?' he asked.

'No more than life,' the voice replied.

And wasn't that the hardest truth of all?

He picked up the cup and held it above the bowl. His fingers trembled. Then he steeled himself, tensed the muscles in his arm, and dunked the cup in the punch. One sip and the nightmare would be over.

Bottoms up.

Chapter 32

To say the downpour that morning had been torrential was an understatement. The rain flooded over the flimsy awning above his back patio like a raging waterfall. The small playground at the bottom of the hill was completely underwater. Even the swings skirted the top of a free-formed stream that surged through the lots. Kjeld had no desire to go outside, but after being stuck indoors for two days in a row watching animated princess films, he was willing to endure any weather conditions just to get out of the house.

Luckily for him, Gothenburg was home to Universeum. Complete with a replica rainforest, space experience, chemistry laboratory, and one of the biggest aquariums in the world, it was certain to provide a full day of entertainment for Tove. And with Tove's newfound interest in sea creatures, something Kjeld had only learned that weekend, he was guaranteed to win a few fatherly bonus points.

Much to his dismay, however, half the parents in Gothenburg had the exact same idea as him. The narrow corridors were packed with screaming children and frantic parents, accidentally pushing prams into the backs of his calves whenever he stopped in the middle of the walkway because some random child decided to have a tearful fit in front of him. Or bumping against his shoulder when he slowed his pace to catch sight of Tove when she darted off to another exhibit. The dark corners, illuminated only by the hazy blue lighting from the glass of the aquariums and the phosphorescent gleam of certain species, darting about in the deep water, made it difficult to keep track of her.

Kjeld wasn't the biggest fan of open water. It wasn't a phobia, but more of an unsettling apprehension of things he couldn't see. He'd never been comfortable on boats or in the ocean. There were too many unknowns. Too many opportunities for things to go wrong. And while he was certain there was nothing to fear from the thick glass that separated him from those aquatic creatures, the combination of children screeching in enthusiasm and people crowding the dimly lit pathways caused his heart to race from nervous claustrophobia.

He almost didn't notice when his phone rang. Fortunately, he caught it on the third ring, just before it went to voicemail. It was Esme. He chalked up the sudden silence on her end to her shock that he'd actually picked up.

'Give me a minute,' Kjeld said, switching his phone from his left hand to his right to avoid inadvertently whacking a young mother with his elbow. 'I need to get some place where I can hear you.'

Kjeld skirted around small groups of families and children who ran up and down the corridor, yelling at their parents, 'Mama, see this! Papa, look at that!' The room was dark aside from the blue glow of the tanks and the vibrant colours of exotic fish. In contrast, the people were all black shadows, unrecognisable until they pressed their faces close to the glass and caught a reflection of the lights that shone down from above the water.

Tove skipped up ahead with another young girl she'd made friends with, pointing at all of the brightly coloured fish and giggling. Her wild head of curls, which Kjeld hadn't had time to put up in a ponytail that morning, bobbed with each step, helping him keep her in sight.

162

Kjeld followed them around a corner towards the aptly named Shark Tunnel, a curved tank that surrounded the corridor like a dome, allowing viewers to feel like they were in the tank itself. It reminded him of a trip he and Bengt had taken to Aruba early in their relationship. It was supposed to be romantic with its sandy beaches, crystal-clear water, and all-you-can-drink cocktails. But Kjeld had read too many statistics on unexplained ocean deaths, and after an uncomfortable scuba diving incident on the first day he kept himself firmly planted in the hotel room for the rest of the trip.

Needless to say, he had misgivings when it came to the ocean. And being beneath 1.4 million litres of water and carnivorous fish didn't endear him to it any more than that ill-fated trip had. His abdominal muscles tightened as he walked through the tunnel, avoiding the sideways stares of a shark that followed along to his right before disappearing into the darkness of the tank. He kept his focus aimed towards the ground and the groups of clamouring children, periodically catching sight of Tove as she jumped up and down in the crowd to get a better look at the sharks.

'Can you hear me better now?' Kjeld asked, but Esme's voice was garbled in response. 'Shit.'

A young boy bumped into his leg just as Kjeld caught a glimpse of a sting ray crossing overhead. The illusion of being underwater set him off balance and he cursed again under his breath. Maybe he should have tried to have this conversation outside the exhibit. Not that it would be any less noisy in the café.

'Don't go too far, Tove!'

Tove beamed at him with the biggest smile he'd seen in years and were it not for Esme continually calling his name from his phone, he might have forgotten she'd called at all.

He pushed himself up near the glass of the corridor and brought the phone to his ear. 'Sorry about that.'

'Where are you?' Esme asked. 'You sound like you're in a tunnel.'

'Technically I'm underwater,' he said, watching as a school of blue and yellow fish swam overhead.

'We've found another body.'

'What? Where?'

'The Estuary. Ove's on the scene and gave us a quick time-of-death estimate. According to him the murder could have taken place as early as this morning. Sixten and I are on site now.' Esme paused. 'We just missed him, Kjeld. We were so close.'

'Who called it in?'

There was a moment's hesitation on Esme's part before she answered and Kjeld caught his shoulders tensing in preparation for her response. 'I did.'

'What?'

'I was going through the CCTV footage again and I came across an image of a young man who matched Linnea's description of the person Louisa had been speaking to at the library. I recognised him. It was Jonny Lindh.'

It took Kjeld a moment to make the connection between the name and Louisa. Two survivors of violent serial murderers. 'Jonny Lindh from the graduation massacre? And you didn't call me?'

'It was your day off. And with the scare you and Bengt had with Tove I thought it was best to let you be until we had real results to share. It all happened so fast.' Another pause. This one felt more apologetic than the last. 'But you need to be here for this one.'

Tove turned a corner, chasing a blacktip reef shark that was skirting along the inner edge of the tank. Kjeld followed after her, trying to keep his focus on her instead of the millions of pounds of pressure pushing against the glass all around him.

'I've got Tove with me for the rest of the day. Bengt is out of town until tomorrow evening. I don't have anyone who can watch her.' But he was already mentally running down the list of people he knew who might be able to keep an eye on her for a few hours.

There was a pause on the other end of the line. When Esme finally spoke there was a fearfulness in her tone that shook Kjeld from his thoughts. 'It's the same MO, Kjeld.'

'Fire?'

'No.' Esme sighed. 'It matches the graduation massacre. It's the same method of death Jonny's classmate intended for him four years ago.'

Chapter 33

The Nordre älv estuary was a 7000-hectare nature reserve that sat at the mouth of the Kattegat and Göta rivers, twenty-six kilometres from the centre of Gothenburg. In the summertime it was a popular destination for hikers, birdwatchers, and sport-fishing enthusiasts. But in the wet rainy months of winter, the reserve was almost entirely abandoned. Many of the hiking paths that skirted the water's edge were blocked off from overflooding and the favourite picnic spots for families became boggy pits of mud and grass.

Normally, Kjeld would have been able to drive the distance in less than thirty minutes. But the heavy barrage of sleet against his windscreen forced him to drive more slowly on the back roads, increasing the time to a nerve-racking hour. At one point his visibility had been so low that he nearly drove the vehicle off the road when he hit a slick patch where the rain coated a layer of black ice. Tove let out a laughing scream like a kid on a roller coaster. Kjeld, on the other hand, drove the rest of the way white-knuckled, shoulders hunched over the wheel as though leaning forward might help propel his car forward and protect them from the elements.

When he reached the nature reserve entrance nearest the

popular bathing locations, he pulled his car off to the side of the road and parked. Up ahead he could see officers taping off a section of the trail, which Kjeld knew led to one of the park's abandoned utility cabins. The one that had hidden one of the city's most devastating discoveries four years ago.

Kjeld took a deep breath, held it in to a count of six, and exhaled. It was a trick Esme taught him. It was supposed to calm the nerves. It worked, although he'd never admit it. He glanced down at his phone. He'd already called Bengt three times since leaving the museum. Each time it had gone directly to voicemail. He even tried getting hold of Liam, albeit he only called him once, also to no avail. It was then that Kjeld realised he didn't have the numbers to any of Tove's friends' parents, teachers, or dance instructors. He didn't even know the name of her regular babysitter and when he asked her she could only tell him that she called her Ducky on account of some cartoon they watched together.

As a result, he had no other choice but to bring her with him. A tiny voice inside of him warned that it was a bad idea, but short of leaving her with his next-door neighbour, who was basically a stranger to him even after sharing a wall for nearly three years, there was nothing else he could do.

Tove sat in the back seat, clutching a stuffed hammerhead shark puppet that Kjeld had bought for her as a bribe for having to leave the science centre early. She kicked the back of his seat.

'Can I come with you?' Tove asked.

'No, sweetheart. You have to stay in the car.'

'But Papa always says I'm not allowed to be by myself in the car. Not even when we go to the supermarket.'

'You're not going to be sitting by yourself. One of my colleagues will be here to sit with you.' Kjeld peered through the blurry windscreen towards the row of police and emergency vehicles up ahead that were blocking the lane to the car park. The rain hit the windscreen sideways and he turned on the wipers to get a better view. Esme had texted him that Sixten would wait in the car with Tove until Kjeld got back, but so far there was no sign of him.

'But I want to go with you! I never get to go with you. Emelie Gunnarsson got to go with her mum to work one day. She told the entire class about it!'

'What does Emelie Gunnarsson's mum do?'

'She's a dog walker.'

Kjeld blinked. 'A what?'

'She walks dogs for people.'

'Well, that's completely different than my job. It's a lot less dangerous.'

'She told us that one time she got bit by a dachshund and had to get six stitches,' Tove said, matter-of-factly.

Kjeld checked his phone for any missed messages. Nothing. Where the hell was Sixten? 'I'll be really quick, I promise. I just have to go check on something and then I'll be right back.'

'Was it a car accident?' Tove traced her finger over the heart Bengt had drawn on her cast.

'I don't think so. But that's what I have to go find out.'

'Is it safe? Is there a bad guy out there?'

'There's no bad guy. Esme is already there. It's perfectly safe.'

'I want to see Esme!' Tove smiled, her red ringlet curls falling in her face.

'Maybe she can come see you afterwards.'

'Daddy?'

'Yes, Tove?'

'Did somebody die?'

Kjeld was taken aback by that comment. Although he and Bengt had explained death to her when she was younger, when Bengt was very ill and things looked as though they wouldn't improve, he hadn't expected Tove to remember it. Let alone make the connection between his work and death. It seemed like such a grown-up question. One he wasn't prepared to answer.

Fortunately, a familiar figure jogging towards the car saved him from having to come up with something on the spot.

'Don't think about that right now. Just sit here with your shark. Sixteen is going to watch you for a bit and I'll be back in a few minutes.'

Sixten tugged open the passenger side of the car and climbed in, pushing back the hood of his parka to reveal his wild blond curls, half matted with rain.

'Sorry about that. The press are starting to crowd the edges of the cordon tape. Some of them even walked the edge of the beach to get closer.' He turned and glanced back at Tove with a toothy grin. 'You must be Tove.'

Tove moved the mouth on her shark puppet. 'Obviously.'

'Just keep an eye on her until I get back.'

'Sure thing, boss.'

Chapter 34

Kjeld stared down at the body of the young man that lay askew on the cabin floor. His skin was pale, almost transparent, and his lips were a deep shade of purple. The rest of his body appeared untouched. It was as though he'd simply fallen over and died. But even if Kjeld had come across this scene unexpectedly, he would have known that wasn't the truth. Anywhere else in the park and it might have been an accident. But not here. And not now.

Esme had caught him up on the events he'd missed during his weekend off while he'd suited up. After Esme recognised Jonny on the CCTV footage outside the library, she and Sixten immediately put out an attempt-to-locate on Jonny. They'd driven to Jonny's mother's house first, hoping to find him there. When his mother confirmed that Jonny had been living at the commune, they checked there as well. But Sister Löv said he hadn't been there in a few days. After that there was only one place Esme thought to go, and fearing the worst she drove directly to the scene of the crime from four years ago. But they'd been too late.

Inside the cabin there was an eerie silence, but outside was the muffled sound of officers holding back a small crowd of journalists that had somehow made their way past the cordon tape. The clicking of cameras sent a chill down Kjeld's spine. After a moment their voices melded with the clamour of rain, filling the background with a monotonous din that allowed Kjeld's thoughts to retreat into a memory. A memory of standing in the middle of that cabin once before. The ground littered with the bodies of dead teenagers.

'I never thought I'd be here again.'

Esme nodded. 'I know.'

Kjeld's shoulders sagged. Four years ago, Jonny Lindh had been the sole survivor of a mass murder-suicide. It had been early in Kjeld's partnership with Esme. One of the first and most gruesome crimes they'd investigated together. A group of high school students decided to celebrate an end-of-term party out on the nature reserve, using the abandoned cabin as a base for their party. One of the party-goers was a quiet student, the kind who never spoke up in class, received adequate grades, and was brutally bullied throughout his entire childhood. In revenge against the classmates who had tormented him, he'd laced the alcohol with antifreeze. Kjeld still remembered the look on Jonny's face when he told his story. The sheer terror he experienced as he watched each of his friends double over in pain just before coating the cabin in vomit and convulsing on the floor. It had been a particularly gory scene. One of the worst in Kjeld's recent memory. The bullied teenager ended the night by shooting himself in the head. Jonny only survived because he'd stuck to drinking soda the entire night, unbeknownst to the student who'd dosed the cider.

Kjeld clenched his eyes shut to shake away the image of the dozen other bodies that had once covered the floor. When he reopened them only Jonny was left. He glanced over at the table with the punch bowl. It was still half full and Kjeld could smell the sickly-sweet contents. On the ground lay an empty cup a few feet from Jonny's fingers. Used, by the looks of it.

Esme watched him with an intense look of concern.

'Christ,' Kjeld grumbled. A thickness caught in his throat as he surveyed the scene. He didn't know what was worse, finding another one of the survivors from his old cases dead in the manner originally intended to kill him or the fact that Jonny's expression looked almost relieved. 'Have you notified his family yet?'

Esme shook her head. 'Sixten and I were going to head over there after we finished here.'

Kjeld nodded. 'This is going to break his mother. Maybe I should go, too. I was there before, after all. It only seems right.'

'That's actually something I want to talk to you about.'

'What's that?'

'A theory I've been thinking about all morning.' Esme canted her head. 'I'm concerned about a potential pattern I'm seeing here.'

'What pattern is that?'

'Louisa was one of your cases. Andrea was potentially murdered by a firearm used in another of your previous cases. And Jonny's crime was also one that you investigated.'

'What are you trying to say?'

'I'm saying it feels like a pattern.'

'But Andrea was never a victim in a case I investigated. I agree, it's peculiar that the bullet that killed her matches one from the Hedebrant case, but we still haven't heard back from ballistics on the gun. It could have been an error. And I've worked so many cases over the years, you could probably throw a stone and hit someone who was related to one of them.'

'I know. I just have a feeling. And it worries me.' Esme turned to face Kjeld. 'If there's a link between you and these murders, even if it's just two of them, then we have to consider the possibility that you're at risk.'

'If the killer wanted to get to me they could have. They didn't have to kill two other people to do so. Besides, I thought we agreed Andrea's case was unrelated.'

'I'm still not certain about Andrea. It could be a coincidence. But maybe Louisa and Jonny were just meant to get your attention. Maybe that's what the killer is building up to. And I know

172

you don't want to think about yourself as a possible target, but I'm serious. This changes everything. Whether we like it or not, there is a potential connection now. And you know what the chief is going to say—'

'I am not walking away from this case simply because it looks like the killer is going after people from my old cases. For all we know it's an attempt to misdirect us. Maybe it's a sign that we're getting close to catching this person.'

Esme didn't respond directly. She gave Kjeld a reflective look, as though thinking about bringing up something, then looked away. 'Jonny changes the pattern. We're not just looking for someone who's targeting women. We're looking for someone who's targeting survivors of high-profile cases. We're going to have to go back to the drawing board and refocus. Maybe we can find another similarity between them.'

'If that's the case, this killer is trying to make a statement about these survivors. They're not just restoring the old crime scenes, they're finishing them. Giving the old crimes new endings, if you will. That's where we're going to find the answer.' Kjeld turned his attention back down to the body, forehead wrinkling in thought. 'Is it possible that we could be looking for a survivor as well?'

'What do you mean?'

'The killer. If you're correct and this person is seeking out survivors, is it possible that they also survived something? Something that maybe they didn't want to survive? Or someone whose life became worse afterwards?'

Kjeld thought of Louisa and the course of her life after being rescued from Gjur Hägglund's cellar. He'd saved her life, but had she been better off? Was a life spent hiding from the world and fearing the worst in everyone around you a life at all?

Esme wrinkled her brow. 'Like an angel of death? Someone who thinks they're doing these people a favour?'

'I don't know, but this doesn't feel like someone who's killing

173

for the sake of killing. This person wants attention for something else. Something we're not seeing.'

But what kind of message could the killer be sending about these victims? That they weren't safe? That no one was? Kjeld caught himself thinking of the day he'd found Louisa eight years ago. There'd been a defining look in her eyes back then, but it wasn't a look he ever would have associated with a survivor. It was the look of someone who'd given up.

Jonny had that same look in his eyes now.

'Daddy?'

At first Kjeld thought he heard his daughter's voice in his mind. Then she said his name again and he turned sharply on his heel to see Tove standing just inside the doorway of the cabin. She was staring at the lifeless form of Jonny Lindh, her eyes wide in fear and confusion. A second later Sixten scrambled into the cabin, panic-stricken.

'Oh my God,' Esme gasped.

'I'm sorry, Kjeld!' Sixten panted between gasps of breath. 'She just jumped out of the car and made a run for it.'

Kjeld rushed over to Tove, blocking her view of the scene.

'What's wrong with that man, Daddy?' Tears welled up in her eyes.

'Nothing, sweetheart. Come here.' Kjeld picked her up, turning her away from the scene and carrying her out of the cabin.

Tove buried her face into his shoulder. 'I'm sorry, Daddy. You were taking so long and I didn't want to sit in the car anymore!'

Sixten and Esme followed after them.

'I'm really sorry, boss. Honest. I didn't see her get out until it was too late. And she was just so damn fast.'

Kjeld shot Sixten a glare as he stormed past him, ducking under the cordon tape. 'Don't talk to me, Sund.'

A camera flash nearly blinded him on the other side of the tape and Kjeld caught himself in a dead stare with Henny Engström, the gleam on her face pleased and predatory.

Chapter 35

Söndag | Sunday

'What happened?'

Kjeld stood in the narrow entranceway of the upscale flat Bengt shared with Liam. His face was cold and numb. The rain that had been soaking the city for weeks had let up again, but the temperatures had decided to drop to frigid levels. Now the mist that coated the air was like little pieces of ice. And suddenly stepping into a warmer space left him flushed.

'Kjeld, what happened?' Bengt adjusted his glasses that were always falling forward on his face. He was dressed more casually in a sweater and jeans, a pair of boiled wool house slippers on his feet. Kjeld thought he saw dark circles under his eyes, but that might have been from the dim lighting in the hall. 'Tell me.'

Kjeld hung his head in shame, stuffing his hands in his pockets as he tried to find the words to explain what had happened without looking more irresponsible than he already was. Tove had run off to her room the moment they arrived, slamming the door shut behind her. She wasn't angry with him. She was just confused and upset because Kjeld was upset. And because she didn't fully understand what she'd seen.

'There was an incident today.'

'An incident?' Bengt raised a suspicious brow.

Kjeld lifted his head and glanced past Bengt. Through the doorway in the corridor, he could see that the entire living room and kitchen space had been remodelled to an open floor plan. The furnishings and décor were modern and streamlined, styled in the way Bengt had always talked about. It barely even resembled the home it had been when Kjeld lived there. And in the centre of it all was Liam cutting up vegetables for dinner. The sight of him filled Kjeld with a regrettable longing. And he turned to the side so as not to be facing that direction. He didn't need any more distractions that could potentially set him off.

'Tove came upon a crime scene,' he said in a hushed whisper.

'Tove came upon a – what?'

'She was in the car. I asked a colleague of mine to watch her for a few minutes while I was on the scene and she snuck out of the car when he wasn't looking to come and find me.' Now that he said it aloud it sounded even worse.

'What are you saying, Kjeld? What did she see?'

Kjeld wiped his hands over his face, fingers jabbing deep into the sinus points along the sides of his nose until a dull pain spread through the ridge of his brows. 'I'm not certain.'

'You're not *certain* what she saw?' Bengt's expression was fraught with horror. 'What kind of crime scene was it?'

Kjeld knitted his brows together. Neither apology nor explanation would be enough to make up for this blunder. The words to express how he felt simply didn't come to him. He'd never felt more ashamed in his life.

But Bengt had always been able to read him well. And Kjeld's silence said enough.

Bengt shook his head. 'I don't believe it. You allowed our daughter to see – to see what? A murder victim? A body? What

176

the hell, Kjeld? She's a child. Do you know what that could do to her?'

'I know and I didn't allow it! It was an accident. Honestly. I told her to wait for me in the car. I left someone with her—'

'Who?' Bengt interrupted. 'What kind of idiot did you leave in charge of our daughter while you went gallivanting around a murder scene?'

'Gallivanting? Oh, come on, Bengt. You make it sound like I was at a fucking strip club.'

'*That* I would be able to explain to her. Strippers I couldn't give a shit about. But a dead body? She could be traumatised for life!'

'It's possible she didn't see as much as I think she did. And there wasn't any blood or anything.'

'You've got to be fucking kidding me. Kjeld, this is serious.'

'I know it's serious.'

Bengt scratched his fingers through his hair, digging at his scalp. 'I'm going to have to find a therapist for her. We have to get on this right away. We can't wait. And *you* have to explain this to her.'

'What?' Kjeld wasn't prepared for that. He could barely explain it to Bengt. How was he supposed to explain it to Tove? Bengt had always been so much better at these things than he was. Bengt had a natural way with Tove. He understood her needs so much better than Kjeld ever did. Or ever would. 'I can't.'

'You have to.'

'I don't know how.'

'Figure it out. And do it now before it's too late.' Bengt took a deep breath and glanced back towards the kitchen, a glimmer of panic on his face. 'I'm not going to tell Liam. This would enrage him beyond belief.'

'Thank you,' Kjeld said.

'I'm not doing it for you. I'm doing it for Tove. I told you I want her to have you in her life. Regardless of how reckless and foolish you can be, that's important to me. I know you're

… trying. But if Liam finds out about this he will be livid. He cares a lot about her.'

'I care about her too.'

'Which is why you need to be the one to talk to her.'

'Dinner will be ready soon!' Liam called out from the kitchen. 'If Kjeld's staying tell him to take his shoes off before he comes in!'

Kjeld flinched at the sound of his name. Even more so at the politeness that he knew probably infuriated Liam as much as it did himself.

Kjeld slipped off his shoes and started down the corridor towards Tove's room. 'I'll do my best.'

Bengt nodded. 'You better.'

Chapter 36

Kjeld sat on the edge of Tove's bed, but Tove remained hidden beneath her pink polka-dotted duvet, a curled-up lump beneath the blanket and a soft whimpering sound the only signs that she was in the room.

The bedroom was picture-perfect for a little girl. Bengt – and Liam, much as Kjeld didn't like to admit it – spared no expense to make her room every girl's dream. Between the flowered curtains, the unicorn collection, and the heart-shaped picture frames boasting photographs of Tove with her friends at school and her dance lessons, it was a tad too girly for Kjeld's tastes. But it was artfully done and it was a considerable step up from the spare bedroom at his place, with its second-hand IKEA furniture and bare walls.

He was working on finding a new place for them though. Somewhere Tove could have a proper room like the one she had with Bengt. He'd seen a house for sale on Järntorgsgatan that would be perfect. It was in a much nicer neighbourhood, closer to Bengt and her school. It was a bit out of his price range even with his recent inheritance. Well, out of the range he wanted to pay. But its location would allow him to better support Tove during her weekends with him. And that would be worth the price.

'Tove, could you come out for a minute? I want to talk to you.'

Tove squirmed underneath the duvet, her voice muffled in the bedding. 'I don't want to.'

'Not even for a quick second before I have to leave?'

Tove peeked her head out from beneath the blanket, concealing everything save for her eyes. 'Are you leaving?'

Kjeld brought the duvet down beneath her chin. Then he swept her wild head of red curls from her face. 'I have to go home soon. You have to eat dinner and I have to feed Oskar.'

'I forgot to give Oskar a treat yesterday.'

'Should I give him one for you?'

Tove nodded. 'And tell him it's from me.'

'I will.' Kjeld smiled. How was it that children could appear so resilient? He felt like he was falling apart on the inside and Tove seemed, all things considered, the picture of composure. 'I wanted to talk to you about what you saw today.'

'About the man in the cabin?'

'Yes. About the man in the cabin.' Kjeld took a deep breath. 'You know what Daddy does for a living, right?'

'You catch bad guys.'

'That's right. But sometimes the bad guys get away or they're too fast for me.'

Tove pursed her lips. 'And they hurt people.'

Kjeld's stomach clenched with nerves. He wished Bengt were there beside him to reassure him that he was doing this properly. That he was saying the right things. 'Yes.'

Tove looked down at her duvet, fidgeting with the button on the end of the cover. 'Did a bad guy hurt the man in the cabin?'

'Yes. And I wasn't there to help him. But that's why I had to be there. So I could find some clues to help me catch the bad guy before anyone else gets hurt.' Kjeld placed a hand over his daughter's, gently squeezing her fingers. 'I'm sorry you saw that. It must have been really scary.'

'It was a little.'

180

Kjeld took a deep breath. He wasn't prepared to explain murder to a six-year-old.

'Will the bad guy hurt us?'

'No, sweetheart. Absolutely not. I would never let anything happen to us. You know I'll always protect you.'

'And Papa and Liam?'

'Them, too.'

'And Oskar?'

Kjeld let out a small laugh. 'Oskar especially.'

Tove crawled out from beneath the covers and sat up. Kjeld hadn't noticed it earlier, but her hair was getting so long. It was well below her shoulders now. It reminded him of how quickly she was growing up.

'Papa might take you to someone to talk about what you saw. Would that be okay?'

Tove looked away. 'Are you angry with me?'

'Of course not. Nobody is angry. It wasn't your fault, Tove. I shouldn't have taken you there.'

'I'm sorry I got out of the car.'

'It's all right. There's nothing for you to be sorry about.'

Tove nodded, but Kjeld could see in her expression that she didn't quite believe him.

Kjeld glanced over to her nightstand where a snowglobe with a unicorn inside sat perched in a place of honour beside a lamp. He picked it up and shook it, watching as the sparkles spiralled around the inside of the globe. 'I didn't know you still liked unicorns.'

'I don't,' Tove said in that pragmatic tone only children were capable of. 'But Papa likes to buy them for me.'

Kjeld smiled, setting the snowglobe back down. 'It's a very nice gift.'

Tove pulled her stuffed hammerhead shark puppet out from beneath her pillow. 'I like my shark better.'

'Well, if I see a shark snowglobe I'll be sure to get it for your birthday.'

Tove leaned forward and wrapped both her arms around him as best she could with the cast. Kjeld held on to the hug for as long as possible, wishing he could have spent the rest of the night with her instead of going back home to his bleak apartment and his guilt-ridden conscience.

'I love you, Daddy.'

'I love you too.' He placed a kiss on the top of her head. 'And I always will.'

Chapter 37

Esme opened the front door of her apartment and was immediately embraced in a semi-wet hug by Miriam.

'Miriam, what are you—' But Esme cut herself off. She'd forgotten that she'd invited Miriam over at the end of their girls' night out, which sadly hadn't been much of a night out. In fact, they'd all made excuses to go home early after dinner, leaving Esme with another evening alone on her couch in front of the television to binge-watch another mindless show on one of her five different streaming services. 'Can I take your coat?'

But Miriam was already hanging the dripping coat on the rack by the door. 'You completely forgot that I was coming over, didn't you?'

It was then that Esme realised her entire kitchen table was a spread of files and images from the recent crimes she and Kjeld were investigating. She rushed over to organise them.

Miriam turned and watched sympathetically as Esme quickly tried to cover up the mess of crime-scene photographs and paperwork that had taken over her kitchen table. Esme knew Miriam wasn't judging her forgetfulness, but she was still embarrassed for not having written it down in her agenda.

'I'm so sorry, Miri. I'm a little scatter-brained lately. This case has really been getting to me.' Esme scurried over to the kitchen which, unlike the table, was immaculately clean. Most of her apartment was organised to the nth degree. Every piece of furniture in its proper place. Every surface spotless. Even the air in the flat was refreshing, a peaceful scent of citrus pumped out by an electric air freshener in the corner of the living room. Esme had always believed that keeping an obsessively clean and almost systematically arranged environment helped give the mind structure and order. But in actuality it had become a crutch to hide the fact that she felt like a total mess on the inside. 'Would you like a drink? Wine? Juice? I might have a beer leftover if you'd prefer that.'

'I'll just have a glass of water.' Miriam caught a glimpse of one of the photographs on the table and cringed. 'Holy shit, Esme. Is this how you spend your evenings?'

Esme ran a glass under the tap and brought it over to the table. When she saw the images of Louisa Karlsson's crime scene she quickly turned them upside down. Then she grabbed a tablecloth from a drawer and covered the table and the files. 'I'm so sorry. I didn't mean for you to see that.'

Miriam gave her a look of concern that reminded Esme of her cousin. The kind of look that suggested she thought something was terribly wrong, but didn't know how to bring it up.

'Was that the girl from the serial killer case years back? I saw something about it on the news. They were asking for anyone with information to call the police line.'

Esme nodded. 'Yeah, she's one of the cases the chief has my team working on. It's been a bit of a shit show to tell you the truth.'

'I don't know how you do it. Surround yourself with all of this death and violence.'

'It's my job.'

'Sure, but this is your home. Aren't you afraid that you're – I don't know – inviting bad karma or something?'

'Someone is killing innocent people. And it's not like I have

184

kids at home to take care of or anything. So, no. I'm not worried about bad karma. I'm only worried about not catching the person responsible for all of this before they strike again.' Esme hadn't intended to sound short-tempered, but her words came out more harshly than she'd expected. 'I'm sorry, Miri. I'm just really over-whelmed. It was a rough day. We found another victim and there was a thing with my partner's daughter and …'

Miriam sat down at the table and sipped at her water. 'I heard about that. Britta sent me a link to a YouTube video. That poor child.'

'It's not what you think. It was an accident. This stupid jour-nalist keeps twisting everything around and making our jobs even more difficult than they already are.'

Esme sighed and slumped down in one of the kitchen chairs. She could still see the outline of the files underneath the table-cloth and she smoothed over the edges in a feeble attempt to make it less noticeable.

'Is this really what you want to be doing?' Miriam asked.

'What do you mean?'

'You're witty, smart, attractive. But when you're not at work you hide yourself away in your apartment obsessing over these horrifying cases. Tilde and I hardly ever hear from you anymore. You haven't even been to my new house yet. How long are you going to keep going like this?'

Esme frowned. 'This is my career, Miri. This is what I do.'

'I know, I know. And I get it. I guess. Well, kind of. But what about *you*? What about your life outside of your career? Don't you want to date someone? Settle down? Have kids?'

Esme shifted uncomfortably in her seat. 'I date.'

'Late-night hook-ups on Tinder is not dating.'

'Well, maybe I'm not interested in anything more than that.'

'Bullshit.'

'It's not bullshit.' Esme chewed on her lower lip. 'I don't know that I want those things. Sometimes I think I do and sometimes

I think I'm too selfish for a relationship or for kids. It's not like getting a bad haircut and saying, "Don't worry it'll grow out." My career is important to me. And I enjoy the freedoms I have right now.'

Miriam laughed. 'Are you saying that being a parent means you're not free?'

'I'm saying that relationships change a person. Parenthood changes a person. You're never the same again. And what if I don't like the person that makes me? What if it doesn't fulfil me? What if it bores me or makes me boring?'

It had already taken Esme a long time to learn who she was as a person and accept that she didn't fit into the traditional moulds that society crafted for people. Women, in particular. If she welcomed new challenges in her life – a relationship, children, change in career – then she'd have to rediscover who she was in those new roles. And she didn't know if that was something she was willing to explore. Even if she did sometimes feel like an anomaly among her friends and colleagues.

When Esme looked up at Miriam she was surprised to find herself met with a hard stare.

'The change is worth it. I wouldn't be anything without my family. They make life worth living. I wouldn't change that for the world.'

'I'm not saying it isn't worth it for some people,' Esme said, struggling to find the words that both explained her own confusion about parenthood and relationships without minimalising the joy it gave Miriam. But she sensed anything she said would only make it worse. 'I'm just saying I don't know if it's for me. I don't know that I can identify with that. Being biologically bonded to another person for the rest of my life. Being responsible for them. Sometimes I try to imagine myself as a mother and I wonder how it can be worth it.'

'Wow, Esme. Way to make me feel like crap.'

Esme blinked. 'What? No, you don't understand. I'm not

186

speaking for all women. Just myself. I just don't know that I'm meant for that.'

Miriam pushed out her chair and stood up. 'Well, you should probably figure that out. It's not like you're getting any younger, after all.'

Esme frowned. 'Why are you so upset?'

'Because you make it sound like being a parent means you have to give up your entire life and identity. That it makes you boring and dissatisfied and ugly. And that's not true. Being a mother gave me meaning. Is it a struggle sometimes? Yeah, Esme. It can be fucking hard. Harder than sitting around looking at nasty photographs of dead people. But at least I'm not coming home to an empty house. At least I don't have to pick up a stranger to give me an hour's worth of pleasure.'

'Don't be a bitch, Miriam. That's not what I meant.'

'Well, that's what it sounds like. And you know what? Some change would probably do you good. You're not a teenager anymore. Do you want to be that same moody goth girl with the black lipstick and the fuck-the-world attitude for the rest of your life?' Miriam grabbed her coat from the rack on the wall and headed for the door. 'It's like I don't even know you. And, honestly, a real friend wouldn't have forgotten the plans we made together.'

Esme stood up and followed her to the door. 'I told you it's been a rough week.'

'With you it's been a rough decade. Do you know how many times you've cancelled on me in the last year?'

'I told you—'

'I know. Work is crazy. Well, that's the trade-off, Esme. If you give all of yourself to your job then there's nothing left over for anyone else. And as much as I enjoyed our friendship when we were younger I think we're just not on the same page anymore. I want friends who make time for me.'

'Like Britta, I suppose.' Esme fought against the urge to roll her eyes.

'Yes, like Britta.'

'She's not even that nice.'

'But we have a lot in common. She doesn't forget about me when we make plans. And she doesn't make me feel like shit for … how did you word it? Giving in to society's pressures on women? Give me a break.'

Esme's cheeks flushed with anger, but she didn't say anything. Instead her face and neck grew warm despite the cold that rushed in from outside when Miriam opened the door. There were a lot of things she wanted to say – maybe even yell – but the words never made it to her lips. She was too afraid of making things worse. And when she did finally find something to say, she was embarrassed by how pathetic her voice sounded.

'I'm sorry, Miri. Really. Please. Can we talk about it?'

'Maybe some other time, Esme. But right now I'd rather spend time with my family.' Miriam turned up the hood on her coat and continued to her car.

Esme watched her drive away, her hands shaking. Then she closed the door and made her way back to the table. The anxious sensation of misplaced guilt caught in her throat as she removed the tablecloth, folding it up neatly and setting it back in the drawer. But she quickly realised it wasn't guilt so much as anger that she felt. It was bad enough that Miriam didn't understand her, but to attack her in her own home for her way of life? Esme was seething. She had the sudden impulse to do something with her hands. Something to keep her busy. She considered vacuuming, but she'd just cleaned her apartment the other day. Instead she flipped over the photographs, one by one. Louisa. Andrea. Jonny.

She'd call Miriam tomorrow and properly apologise. Perhaps with a clear head she could explain her feelings better. But for now she had to focus. That would soothe her nerves. Find the killer. Solve the case. Then she could give herself time to breathe and to figure out how she could fix the friendships that kept falling apart around her.

Chapter 38

Måndag | Monday

'I'm taking you off the Karlsson case.'

'What?' Kjeld stared at Rhodin in disbelief, certain he'd misheard him. But Rhodin looked back at him with a weary exasperation that told him otherwise. 'Why?'

'You know why, Kjeld.'

'I want to hear you say it.'

Rhodin sighed. 'Well, Henny Engström for starters.'

'What did she do this time?'

'Her job.' Rhodin turned his computer monitor around. Zoomed in at full screen was Henny's newest piece of gossip trash presented as truth. A photograph of Kjeld holding his crying daughter on the opposite side of the blue and white cordon tape, a blurry image of the crime-scene tent in the background. But as devastating as the picture was, the headline was even worse. "Top Cop Takes Baby to a Bloodbath" was printed above the photo in bold black lettering. What followed was a half-arsed article based on hearsay and half-truths. As always, Henny used dramatic imagery and slanderous buzz words to get readers onto her website. Not that Kjeld imagined many people actually read her articles. It didn't take half a brain to realise there was nothing in her writing that was either factual or based on concrete evidence. She was just in it for the publicity. Other people's lives and reputations be damned.

'It's not true,' Kjeld insisted.

'It doesn't *matter* if it's true. The picture itself is damning. Not to mention all of the other nonsense she's managed to string together. Some of which isn't exactly *untrue*, by the way.' Rhodin shook his head, defeated. 'The truth doesn't make a difference at this point. Nobody does their due diligence when it comes to things they read online. And this is just the article! You should see the video she posted to go along with it. People will see it and they'll believe it. And regardless of the facts it makes us look like chumps.'

'I didn't take my daughter to a crime scene. She was being watched by another officer and—'

Rhodin held up his arms. His eyes were practically begging Kjeld, but Kjeld couldn't help but feel personally attacked. And not just by the media and Henny's inflated articles, but also by his own colleagues.

'I know, Kjeld. I *know*. But I've got the bureaucrats breathing down my neck. You know how tense things have been since the situation with Nils. And with the proceedings on his trial delayed it's only putting more stress on the police administration. The longer that arsehole sits in prison without being convicted, the more we look like incompetent fools. And the press, as infuriating as they can be, aren't wrong.' Rhodin dropped a pen into a cup on his desk. 'We fucked up. We missed a serial killer in our ranks. And I'm not saying that's just on you. That's on all of us. We deserve to be nit-picked by the media. They should go through us with a fine-toothed comb. And everything we do is under their scrutiny. Everything. So, I know how angry you are. I'm fucking livid myself. But we can't afford headlines like these. Not now.'

190

Kjeld took a deep breath and resisted the urge to raise his voice. He knew it wasn't the chief's fault. He knew how the system worked. But there were circumstances, such as Henny's blatant slandering of his name, where he thought the system was also an impediment to his ability to do his job. 'Henny Engström is a liar. She's a half-rate gossipmonger who gets away with libel on a daily basis. But I get it. For better or for worse, we have freedom of speech in this country. How am I supposed to stop her from publishing a shitty article that has no shred of truth in it whatsoever?'

'By not doing anything that she can use against you and, in turn, against this department. We can't handle any more bad press. And you know that.'

Kjeld pursed his lips in frustration. 'This is completely insane. What about how this affects my life? What about my privacy? What about my family? Do you think I want to see my daughter's face plastered all over the internet? Where's the protection for her? You should be berating these journalists instead of reprimanding me. I was just doing my job. It was an *accident* that she saw the crime scene.'

But Kjeld knew the argument was futile. He knew Rhodin only had so much sway with the people above him. This was coming from higher up the chain. It was a matter of protecting one detective over the rest of the department, and Kjeld knew that no amount of friendship or trust between them would be enough for Rhodin to sacrifice his own career. Let alone the careers of everyone else in the department.

'I just need you to stay out of the limelight for a while,' Rhodin said. 'And I'm not taking you off the Nicolescu case.'

'I owe it to Louisa's family to find her killer.'

'And if it were just Louisa then I would agree with that. But the death of Jonny Lindh changes things.'

'Changes things how?'

'Both Louisa and Jonny have direct connections to you. Is it a thin thread? Yes. But I can't take the risk of keeping you on a case where the killer might be purposefully seeking out your old cases as starting points for their murders.' Rhodin smoothed down his bristly moustache. 'Besides, if there's any chance that the life of one of my officers could be in danger …'

Kjeld snorted. 'Danger? Oh, come on. This is Esme talking, isn't it?'

'She has a right to be concerned, Kjeld.'

'My life is not in danger. If the killer wanted to come after me then why would they be wasting their time going after anyone else?'

Rhodin pursed his lips and Kjeld could see he was trying to restrain his temper. 'Like I said, it's a risk I'm not willing to take.'

'You know that's a bad choice.'

'But it's my only choice. The only choice you or Engström or anyone has given me.'

'There are no solid leads on the Nicolescu case,' Kjeld insisted. 'What do you expect me to do?'

'Your *job*. I expect you to put in the work like you used to. Like you did before you let Nils get to your head. Axel has hundreds of hours of video footage yet to go through and we've received almost a thousand calls from the public claiming to have information on all three of these murders. I don't have the manpower to go through all of them as it is. And you know that at least eighty per cent of cases are solved behind a desk. So that's where I need you. Doing your best work behind a computer screen.'

'Screening crank calls?'

'Investigating. Going through the evidence. Catching the bad guys. You know, being a fucking detective.'

Kjeld placed his hands on his hips and turned sideways to the chief's desk, staring out the window into the main work space of the department. He had an intense desire to hit something. Not because Rhodin was wrong about anything he'd said. He was absolutely right. Whether deservedly or not, Kjeld was a liability to the department right now. No, he wanted to lash out because Kjeld felt like he was being purposefully backed into a corner. Like with Bengt or Liam or his father, he felt as though someone was threatening to take away the few things that made him whole. But it could have been worse. Rhodin could have put him on a full suspension again. And his career, tenuous as it was, would have struggled to survive two of those in less than a year.

He simply had to remind himself that being remanded to a desk didn't mean he was being punished. It was for his protection.

'Are you changing the SIO for Louisa's case?'

Rhodin's lips stretched into an uncomfortably thin line. 'For the time being I'm going to put Esme in control of the day-to-day operations of the investigation. She's always been better at answering questions from the press anyway.'

Kjeld nodded. He couldn't argue with that. He hated holding press conferences. They only agitated his temper. 'Who's going to assist her in the field?'

'Sixten is the obvious choice.'

Kjeld withheld a groan but it was clear from the way his stance loosened that he disagreed. 'He's so green.'

'Everybody's got to start somewhere.' Rhodin paused. 'I could probably get Lindén to assist.'

Through the window Kjeld caught a glimpse of Esme on her phone. She looked tired and exasperated, but determined. She rang off with the caller and shoved her phone in her pocket. Then she fiddled with her fringe, making sure it covered her forehead. They were all on edge.

He glanced back over at Rhodin. 'Is that it?'

Rhodin nodded. 'Yes.'

Kjeld made for the door.

'One more thing!'

Kjeld stopped. When he craned his head over his shoulder he saw an affectionate concern in the chief's bristly face. It was the same look he'd given him when the forensic results came back on the Aubuchon case, proving that Nils was the killer they'd been looking for. The kind of fearful look that said he was worried about what Kjeld would do.

'How's your daughter?'

'She's fine. Kids are incredibly resilient, you know.'

'And you?'

The corner of Kjeld's lip turned upward in a half-smile. 'I'm fine, too.'

'Really?'

'Really.'

Kjeld left the office, tugging the door shut so it wouldn't roll open on its crooked hinges. Was he fine? No. Nor was it the first time he'd lied to the chief about how he was feeling. It was, however, the first time he felt guilty about it.

Chapter 39

'Nothing changes,' Esme said, a tad louder than planned. She was reassuring herself as much as she was the rest of the team. It was the first time she'd been put in charge of an investigation and even though they all knew each other well and she undoubtedly had the team's support, she felt like she needed to appear more confident. More firm in her ability to handle this responsibility. She cast a sidelong glance to Kjeld who sat slumped in his chair, his focus intent on the contents of his coffee mug. Esme cleared her throat. 'We continue as we have been. We now have two murders that have a high likelihood of being committed by the same killer. Our priority is to go through everything we know about Louisa and Jonny. Try to find a connection between them. We've already established that they were both involved in previous high-profile murder cases. What else do we know?'

'They were both Kjeld's cases,' Sixten said.

Kjeld shot Sixten a discerning look, but Sixten's focus was solely on Esme and the whiteboard.

'That's true. He was the secondary investigator on the Cellar Sadist case and he was lead on the Graduation Massacre.' Esme wrote Kjeld's name at the centre of the whiteboard between the columns she'd already made for Louisa and Jonny. Andrea's column had been erased and moved to the corner of the board. 'What else?'

Axel stretched backwards in his chair. 'They were both survivors.'

Esme quirked a brow. 'What do you mean?'

'Louisa was the only surviving victim of Gjur Hägglund and Jonny was the only student who didn't drink the poisoned cider. They weren't just victims of old cases. They were survivors of old cases.'

'And not just survivors,' Sixten added. 'They were literally the last ones alive when they were found.'

'That's interesting.' Esme tapped a finger against her lips. She turned back to the board and wrote "last one alive" beneath Kjeld's name. She stared at the phrase thoughtfully. There was something about it that left her with a cold chill at the back of her neck. 'What else do we know?'

'They both appear to have struggled with getting over what happened to them,' Sixten said, less confident about this theory than his earlier statement. 'We know Louisa basically became a recluse and according to Jonny's mother he was a completely different person afterwards.'

Axel popped his chair forward and leaned his arms on his desk. 'How else would they be? They were traumatised.'

'I'm just saying that could be a connection. They both had trouble getting over their tragedies.'

'The commune,' Kjeld said.

They all glanced over at him, anticipating more to his thought, but he didn't continue. Instead he turned his focus onto his computer screen. Axel and Sixten both looked to her expectantly.

Esme could feel her confidence wavering. She kept pushing back an anxious worry that she wasn't capable of handling the lead on an investigation. Kjeld always made it look so easy. So natural. He was always relaxed, almost nonchalant, when he was telling other people what to do. Meanwhile that quiet insecure part of herself she perpetually fought to keep hidden from her colleagues made her feel like she needed to ask permission to be direct and authoritative.

'Right. They both potentially have Second Life in common.' Esme added that to the list. 'That could also go hand-in-hand with them struggling to recover from their traumas. Maybe they both saw it as a last chance to help them move forward with their lives.'

Sixten scratched the back of his head. 'But you said Brother Björk denied ever seeing Louisa at the commune.'

'He's a cult leader,' Axel mocked. 'He was probably lying.'

Sixten nodded. 'We should talk to him again.'

'We'll need more than just an assumption that he's lying before we talk to him again. We'll need some actual proof that Second Life is a viable connection to both of them. Hearsay isn't going to get us through the door a second time.' Esme dropped the pen on the whiteboard tray. 'I know this might sound like a long shot, but I think we should look into Kjeld's old cases.'

Esme looked at Kjeld, but his focus remained glued to his computer. It bothered her that he was so quiet. Granted, he wasn't technically on the case anymore, but that didn't mean he couldn't lend her some support. And yet again she found herself mentally comparing the two of them and wondering why she doubted her ability to take command.

'And look for what exactly?' Axel didn't sound convinced.

'A profile that matches our other two victims. Someone who either survived being the victim of a serial murder or a group killing.'

'With Second Life as a connection, too?' Sixten took out a pad of paper and began jotting down notes.

'Not necessarily. But if we find a connection to Second Life let's make sure we put that file at the top of the line.'

Axel scoffed. 'You do realise that if we find anything we might end up stepping on SU's toes. Half of Kjeld's old cases are under investigation. No offence, Kjeld.'

Kjeld responded with an indecipherable grumble.

'SU isn't going to impede a murder investigation. We're all on the same side here. We all want these cases solved and the killers brought to justice. It's good for the department, but more importantly it's good for the community and the people of this city.'

'Survivors of multiple murders by a single killer?' Axel shook his head. 'Well, at least it can't be a very long list.'

'What about one of Nils's victims?'

The room went deathly quiet and Esme felt the air between them tense. Sixten's face flushed, no doubt instantly regretting his question. Axel purposefully looked down at the desk to avoid catching Kjeld's gaze. But Kjeld didn't flinch. If anything, he acted as though he hadn't heard anything. That bothered Esme more than anything. Kjeld didn't usually have the patience to curb his temper when Nils came into the conversation.

'Nils didn't have any surviving victims,' Esme said, interrupting the silence. 'Not that we're aware of. And besides, he's not in a position to be committing these murders.'

'I'll start compiling a list of potential targets from the old case files. And maybe the crime scenes themselves could be a link to the killer? I can get us a map.' Sixten added this to his notes.

'That reminds me,' Esme said. 'Where are we on fingerprints from the cabin?'

Axel sighed. 'Nothing. Technicians combed the entire area and the only prints they recovered were Jonny's.'

'What about on the punch bowl and cup?'

'Also Jonny's.'

'Toxicology?'

Sixten shuffled through a few sheets of paper in search of the document Ove had sent over. 'No traces of ketamine or any other incapacitating drugs normally used in kidnappings. He was chock full of recreational drugs, however. Uppers and downers. And, of course, antifreeze.'

Esme narrowed her eyes. 'What are you saying?'

The door to the incident room flung open and Rhodin stepped in. His face was haggard and his skin sallow. Esme noticed that he was wearing the same shirt and tie from Friday and it looked as though they hadn't been washed since.

'Suicide,' Rhodin said, dropping a file on the desk in front of Esme. 'Frisk just sent over his findings and there wasn't anything to indicate that someone else was involved in his death. The medical results read like a suicide. Poor boy took his own life.'

'But—'

Rhodin cut Esme off by raising a hand. 'I know. The original crime was made to look like a mass suicide as well. I get it. But unless you lot can prove someone else was in that cabin holding a gun to Jonny's head, forcing him to drink poison, then this case is closed.'

Rhodin turned to leave, but stopped beside Kjeld's desk to exchange a glance with him. Then he shook his head and left.

Esme frowned. This turn of events potentially threw a spanner into their theory. 'I still say we move forward with the idea that the killer is choosing their victims from similar cases. The person responsible for Louisa's death is smart. They know how to cover their tracks.'

'But the chief just said—'

'I know what the chief just said,' Esme interrupted.

Sixten looked down, embarrassed. Esme felt a twinge of guilt for snapping at him.

'He said we have to prove someone else was in that cabin forcing Jonny to drink that poison. To do that we need to know more about where he's been and who he's been around. Someone knows something. No killer is this careful. There's always a witness. We just have to find that person before the murderer goes after their next victim.'

'This could be our excuse for talking to the commune again,' Sixten said. 'We know Jonny was posting flyers for them. And his mother was under the impression he was living there.'

'That's a consideration, but I feel like we need to know more if we're going to confront Björk again.'

'What about someone else from the commune?'

'I don't know who else we could get to talk. If Björk is telling the truth then one of their principles is to not get involved in these kinds of things. But it's something to look into. Axel, maybe you can find someone who was recently involved in the commune?'

Axel shrugged. 'I can try.'

Esme turned her attention to Kjeld, hoping for some backup, but again he said nothing. 'I know it feels like we're at a dead end, but we're not. We have a more substantial theory of the type of victim the killer is targeting. And we have more evidence now than we did a few days ago. There's something in all of this that'll bring the pieces together. We just have to find it.'

Axel and Sixten nodded, quickly picking up the phones and getting started.

Kjeld took a large gulp from his mug and stood up. Then he left without saying a single word, leaving Esme fuming.

Chapter 40

Kjeld refilled the coffee machine and set the pot under the drip, waiting for it to brew. He had a dull throb at the back of his head, no doubt spurred on by the stress of the case, the situation with Tove, fear that he'd already screwed things up with Bengt again, and his intense craving for a cigarette. Chewing gum wasn't cutting it. He tossed two paracetamol in his mouth and swallowed them dry. Then he rinsed his mug out in the sink.

Esme jabbed her bony fist into the fleshy part of his upper arm and Kjeld whirled around, spilling some of the water from his mug onto his shirt. 'For fuck's sake, Esme. What's that about?'

'Why didn't you back me up in there?' She placed her hands on her hips and blocked his path to the coffee machine.

'What do you mean? I didn't disagree with anything you said.'

'But you didn't agree with me either. You just sat there staring off into space. You could have at least given me some support in front of the other guys.'

The red light on the coffee machine blinked that it was ready and Kjeld manoeuvred around her to fill one of the cannisters. 'I didn't think you needed me to do that. You had it all under control. You know you did.'

'It would have been nice to have some encouragement.'

'Since when have you needed my approval or my encouragement? You know you have my every confidence. And the others know that, too. You're going to be a great SIO.'

'Really?' Esme frowned.

'I wouldn't have told Rhodin so if I thought otherwise.' Kjeld screwed on the lid to the coffee cannister and filled his mug. Then he set it back on the warmer.

Esme's shoulders relaxed. 'I'm sorry. I'm just nervous. It hasn't been the best week. And this case is really getting to me.'

'I know how you feel.' Kjeld would struggle to admit it, but he hadn't been sleeping or eating well since the start of this case. He seemed to be functioning solely on coffee and brash obstinance.

'How's Tove doing?'

'As well as can be expected, I suppose. It's difficult to tell if she's already forgotten about it or if she's just pretending because she knows how much it upsets us.'

'And Bengt?'

'He's upset, but not as much as I anticipated.'

'I'm sure he knows it's not your fault.'

'Maybe.' Kjeld took a sip from his mug.

Esme leaned up against the side of the counter. 'Tell me your thoughts.'

Kjeld made a face. 'On Bengt?'

'On the case.'

'I think you're right. I think someone knows something and they either don't know it or they aren't saying it.'

Esme chewed on her lower lip. 'I've been thinking about that call that Henny Engström received. The one that allowed her to find the second crime scene. What if it wasn't a tip?'

'What are you saying?'

'I asked around with some of the other journalists who were on the scene of Andrea's murder and none of them received a mysterious phone call. They were all prompted to the location because of Henny's broadcast. I also talked to a couple of the reporters who were on site at Jonny's crime scene and they all agreed that Henny was one of the first ones there after the police. Perhaps even *the* first one.'

Kjeld tried not to roll his eyes out of disgust. 'That could just mean she has a source inside the department somewhere. A receptionist. An intern. That doesn't mean she's getting phone calls from the killer.'

'But have you seen her recent blog articles? Or her YouTube videos?'

Kjeld shook his head. 'I've been told to stay as far away from that woman as possible and I intend to. She doesn't know news from a hole in the ground. She's nothing but a bloodsucking slanderer.'

'Some of the things she writes suggests she knows more than she's saying.' Esme paused. 'And she was also the survivor of a heinous crime. Not unlike the other victims.'

'But she wasn't one of my cases.' Kjeld paused, his expression drawn into a serious sulk. 'You're not suggesting that Henny could be the killer, are you?'

'She does have a grudge against the police. And she's had a personal vendetta against you for the last year.'

Kjeld considered the possibility. Henny did have a grievance against him that he didn't entirely understand. And it wouldn't take much to go from grievance to vengeance. But he couldn't rationalise the idea of Henny killing other people to get back at him. Particularly people who'd suffered crimes as well. Why would she willingly murder other survivors when she was one herself? That seemed to go against everything he knew about her personal story. It was the crime committed against her, her survival, and her belief in the police's incompetence that inspired her foray into amateur crime reporting. Murdering others who'd had similar experiences seemed contradictory to her message.

'I don't think Henny is involved in these deaths. Not directly. But do I think it's possible that the killer has contacted her?'

Kjeld canted his head from one side to the other in thought. 'That sounds more plausible. It makes sense that a killer who has gone to such extremes would want some kind of media attention. We've seen that before. And if there is a component of hatred towards me involved then Henny would be the perfect person to get under my skin.'

'If only we could find out who's been calling her,' Esme said. 'But unless we can uncover proof that the person she's speaking to is connected to these crimes or find substantial evidence that she's actively impeding the investigation, there's nothing we can do.'

'We know she believed the voice belonged to a man. And we know it's someone who's familiar with her vlog. We could have Axel do a search of her social media accounts and go through her followers. Check the comments on her videos for anything suspicious. Maybe we'd get lucky and find some similarities to the information we already have.'

'That's not a bad idea. Why didn't I think of that?' Esme took out her phone and quickly sent a message to Axel. 'What are you going to do with the Nicolescu case?'

'I'm going to dig deeper into Andrea's history. She was involved in the drug trade for a long time before she supposedly stopped. If this is drug or gang-related then maybe she has a contact who has information. Or at least someone who knows whether she was back in the business or under threat.'

'Keep me posted,' Esme said. 'Hopefully the ballistics results will be back soon and we'll have more to go on.'

Esme reached around him, removed a clean mug from one of the upper cabinets, and filled it halfway. She took a sip and winced at the taste.

'No milk?'

'It's going to be a long night,' she said. 'I'm going to need all the caffeine I can get.'

Chapter 41

A few hours later, after most of the team had gone home for the evening, Kjeld went to the Espresso House on Linnégatan, hoping that a change of scenery might help inspire some new ideas about the case. He sat at a corner table near the window, his back to the wall. The stream of traffic outside was muffled by the smooth jazz music playing over the loudspeakers. Kjeld turned his gaze to the window. Over the course of the last hour the rain had turned to sleet and the ground was covered in a thin layer of ice. He checked his phone but he didn't have any new messages from Esme about the investigation. And nothing from ballistics on the firearm examination either. He had, however, missed another call from an unknown number. Damn those telemarketers. They were relentless. He reached into his rarely used satchel bag and removed his work laptop.

He quickly connected to the internet through his phone and pulled up Andrea Nicolescu's arrest record. The general consensus at the station, both among his teammates and others in the department, was that Andrea had been murdered in a drug deal gone wrong. Kjeld had to admit that did feel like the most likely possibility. But the peculiar connection to the Hedebrant case, albeit unconfirmed, coupled with Henny's mysterious tipster gave him the impression that there was more to the story. Could Andrea have been involved with Emil Hermansson and his drug trade all of those years ago? What about Olsen's comment about Second Life potentially being involved in a trafficking case out of Romania? And what about the drugs in Jonny's system and his connection to Second Life? It felt like too much of a coincidence for Kjeld to ignore. But whatever the missing piece of the puzzle was, he was blind to it.

Kjeld scanned through Andrea's file. She'd had a history of drug abuse and trafficking almost from the moment she arrived in Sweden. She'd served a short stint in a women's prison for dealing, but there was an indication that she'd gotten clean or, at the very least, stopped selling after she got out. There wasn't so much as a parking ticket on her record in the last five years.

Kjeld scrolled down to the information on known associates and saw a lot of familiar faces, many of whom were either serving time or dead. One, however, gave him pause.

Vidar Rask.

Kjeld scratched the side of his neck as he stared at the photo of the man with the bald head, close-set eyes, and scraggly beard. He'd had a few run-ins with Vidar in the past. The man was more a nuisance than an actual criminal, although he'd had brushes with the law going back to childhood. He'd come across Kjeld's path when he was still a beat cop. Vidar wasn't a good man, but he wasn't one of the really bad ones. He was the kind of person who did what he had to in order to survive. And if helping the police served his own agenda then he did so. That was how Kjeld had come to know him. Vidar wasn't technically an informant, but he'd occasionally provided Kjeld with the odd tip over the years. Most of which had been helpful.

The last Kjeld knew, Vidar was working at a sleazy tattoo parlour in Strömmensburg. He glanced at the time on his phone. It was too late to go tonight. The shop would be closed. He made a mental note to pay Vidar a visit tomorrow. Perhaps he'd heard something about Andrea that could shed some light on her death.

'I'll have a large salted caramel latte without whipped cream,' a familiar voice ordered.

Kjeld glanced up to see Henny paying in cash before stepping off to the side near the waiting end of the counter. Then he shifted position in his chair so his back was turned to the counter. The last thing he needed was another confrontation with her in a public space. He kept his head down as though focused on his work and hoped she wouldn't see him.

Then her phone jingled and Kjeld caught himself listening in on her conversation.

'When?' Henny asked. She reached into her purse to remove a pen and paper. 'Are you certain?' She wrote something down. 'How did you get this number anyway?' A pause. 'No, I'm not going to call the police.' Another pause. 'It's none of their business. And it's none of *his* business either.'

Kjeld strained to hear better, but between the background music, the coffee machine steaming the milk for her latte, and the couple chatting at the table in front of him it was impossible to make out everything she was saying, let alone hear the voice on the other end.

'I don't know if I can do that,' Henny said to the caller. 'I've already got too many eyes on me. If I do that then people will know I was involved.' She hesitated. 'Do you promise you can arrange it for me?'

Kjeld frowned. He wondered what she was referring to. It sounded like she was being purposefully vague, as though fearful, and rightfully so, that someone might be listening in on her conversation. He didn't want to jump to conclusions, but it quickly crossed his mind that she could be talking to her tipster. Or worse, the killer.

'I'll see what I can do,' Henny said. 'Don't tell anyone else.'

'Large salted caramel latte to go!' the barista called out.

Henny rang off and reached across the counter for her beverage.

When she turned to leave, however, she caught a glimpse of Kjeld. Their eyes met and her face flushed a panicked shade of white. 'Are you following me?'

Henny tried to get a look at his laptop, but Kjeld quickly reached over to close it before she could see any of the information on the screen.

'Is there a reason why I should be following you?'

Henny narrowed her eyes. 'This is an invasion of my privacy. I could file a harassment complaint against you.'

'This is a public coffee shop.'

'There are a dozen other coffee shops in this neighbourhood.'

'I like this one.'

Henny's lips curled into a jeering smirk. 'I heard a rumour that someone lost his spot on the Karlsson case.'

Kjeld narrowed his eyes at her. He knew she was baiting him. He knew he shouldn't fall for it. But her mockeries riled him more than they should have. And he wondered how she could have learned that so quickly. 'Where'd you hear that?'

'A little bird told me.'

'Is this bird an actual person or have you resorted to planting voice recorders on pigeons?' Kjeld said, his tone heavy with sarcasm. 'Because I wouldn't put it past you. A bit of advice, if your informant spends most of its days pecking trash off the street and shitting on lamp poles, no one is going to take you seriously. Definitely not going to get you into the journalistic big leagues either.'

Henny's face turned a heated shade of red. 'Don't disregard me, Kjeld. My last article had over ten thousand clicks in less than an hour. You're more photogenic than I gave you credit for. Or maybe it was just the image of you putting a poor child in danger that inspired so much public interest.'

'If you post one more thing about my family I'll—'

'You'll what? You're a public servant. The people deserve to know what kind of person the city has hired to look out for their welfare. I wonder how long it'll take before someone from child services sees that photograph.'

Kjeld shook his head and looked away from her. He'd already let this conversation go too far.

Henny smirked. 'You'll get what's coming to you eventually. And I can't wait to be there when you do.'

'You have anything else to say, Henny? Your latte is getting cold.'

'Yeah, I do. If I catch you following me again, I'll make sure the entire city knows about it.'

'I wasn't following you. I was here first.'

'That's the great thing about the media, Kjeld. You can always spin a story two ways.'

Chapter 42

Tisdag | Tuesday

A temporary reprieve from the rain fell over the city just as Kjeld pulled his car up front of Skin Deep, a walk-in tattoo parlour nestled between a second-hand clothing store and a sushi takeaway in the south-eastern corner of Strömmensburg just north of Härlanda Park. Kjeld slammed the car door shut and made his way to the entrance. A little bell jingled above his head, announcing a potential customer with apathetic fanfare.

From the outside Skin Deep wasn't much to look at. Bars on the windows provided the first clue as to the kind of trouble they'd had in the past. The hand-painted logo on the door was mediocre at best in its design, which didn't bode well for the talent of its artists and was chipped from weathering. And with the backdrop of dully coloured block apartments, the entire image screamed two-star Yelp review.

Likewise, the inside reflected a lacklustre ambience. There was no welcome desk in the foyer. Simply a poster on the wall with a list of prices that someone had routinely crossed out in marker over the years and adjusted in incremental increases instead of reprinting a new sign. A coat rack stood in the corner, the mish-mash of jackets and scarves collecting dust on the hooks giving off a distinctly used odour. From the musty scent Kjeld assumed the items had been purchased at the shop next door and were never washed. The floor was cheap linoleum in a black-and-white chessboard pattern, although many of the white squares had a distinctly ashen hue from not being properly mopped in years.

Further into the shop were four parlour chairs, each surrounded by its own set-up of ink and tools, the range of disarray distin-guishing the various artists. On a Saturday night it could have been a hopping place, but at ten a.m. on a Tuesday morning it was practically abandoned. Kjeld wiped his boots off on the ratty floor mat, which smelled like wet dog shit, and stepped deeper into the parlour.

A younger woman with her head half shaved revealing a brightly coloured Japanese koi fish tattoo and her face covered in more piercings than Kjeld could count lumbered out of the back room. She wore a tight pair of black vinyl pants, platform boots, and a purple bra covered in a fishnet crop top. She chewed on a piece of gum with her mouth open and stared at Kjeld with a bland, hazy glare that could have either been from intense boredom or coming off a weak high. Kjeld's guess was both.

'What do you want?' she asked. Her tongue was split down the middle like a snake's causing her to lisp some of her consonants.

Kjeld kept his focus on her eyes, glossy and smeared with an overuse of eyeliner, so as not to cringe at the way her tongue went in two different directions as she spoke. 'I'm here to see Vidar.'

The woman rolled her eyes as though she'd expected this and yelled towards the back room. 'Vidar! Fucking swine is here to see you!'

Then without so much as another glance she crossed the room and slumped down into one of the studio chairs.

A minute later a gangly man stumbled into the main area of the parlour. He had a bald head and scraggly brown beard. His

211

eyebrows were wild and took up most of his forehead, doubly accented by the charcoal-coloured eyeshadow that circled both above and below his buggy eyes. He tripped over his own feet as he zipped up his loose-fitting jeans, freezing when he glanced up and met Kjeld eye to eye.

'Ah, you've got to be fucking kidding me,' Vidar groaned. 'Whatever it is, I didn't fucking do it. Go ahead and put that in your little report and—' Vidar paused. 'Where's your little firecracker friend with the funny fringe? Couldn't she deal with your bullshit anymore?'

'She just didn't want to deal with your smell.'

'It's a medical condition.'

'Is that what they call it these days?'

Vidar's mouth spread into a sarcastic grin, teeth crooked and yellow. 'Oh, you are a funny one today, Nygaard. I'll give you that. Now seriously, what the fuck do you want? You know it's bad for my reputation to have a cop in my place. Not that we're doing anything we shouldn't be, mind you! I've been out of the racket for a good six months. Swear to God. Even Siri will vouch for that. Won't you, sweetheart?'

Siri raised her middle finger from across the room.

Vidar beamed. 'True love, man. It's a beautiful thing.'

Kjeld held back his urge to say something cruel. Vidar Rask had been a pain in his side for years. The man was notorious among the police for getting himself involved in low-level street crimes, half-arsed racketeering schemes, and general malfeasance. Kjeld had crossed paths with him early on in his career and, like the cockroach he was, Vidar kept coming back. He was like a bad apple that somehow kept finding its way into the fresh produce, infecting everything it touched. Not that Vidar was evil or really all that bad. He put on a good show and made a considerable effort to be more bark than bite. That being said he was still in and out of the system. He couldn't stay clean to save his life. But he had connections and, for the right price, he could be a very useful informant. Or at least he had been in the past.

Which was the only reason Kjeld put up with him and his notably pungent body odour.

'I'm not here about any of that,' Kjeld said. He took out his cell phone and opened it up to a photograph of Andrea. 'I just want to know about this woman.'

Vidar's lips turned downward in a fake pout. 'Are you always this demanding or am I just special?'

'Just look at the photo, Vidar. I don't have all day.'

Vidar snatched the phone out of Kjeld's hand and held it up to his face, close enough for his eyes to cross. Then he handed the phone back to Kjeld. 'That's Andrea Nicolescu. Andy Nic is what most people call her. What do you wanna know about her?'

'Let's start with how you know her.'

Vidar rolled his eyes. 'You wouldn't be here if you didn't already know that.'

'Humour me.'

'She's a dealer sometimes. And an addict. Which makes her a pretty shitty dealer because on any given day she's more apt to use up all her own stock than sell it.'

'Did you ever work with her?'

'Why? Is this a set-up? You trying to pin something on me?'

'She's dead, Vidar. I'm trying to find out who killed her.'

Vidar's gaze wandered away from Kjeld. He scratched the side of his neck, inadvertently leaving deep red marks along his tattoo. 'Are you sure she didn't just OD?'

'I'm certain.'

'I don't know. I really don't want to get involved.'

'There must be something you can tell me,' Kjeld said, his patience wearing thin. 'Have you seen her lately? Did she make any new enemies? Was she trafficking again?'

'I think I saw her a few weeks ago. Maybe less. Was she trafficking drugs? I don't know. But she was selling a bit of weed here and there. Nothing big. Probably from a personal stash.' Vidar chewed off the chipped black polish from his thumbnail. 'You know she used to be involved with that cartel out of Romania, right?'

'Sandu?'

'Yeah. That was the name.'

'How do you know that?'

'Missing finger. That's kind of their thing. Someone fucks up, they chop off a finger. Someone fucks up again and they chop off the finger of someone they care about.'

'Is Sandu still operating with someone here in Gothenburg?'

Vidar shrugged. 'I don't know anything for certain, but there's been some new product moving around lately.'

'I thought you weren't in the business anymore.'

'I'm not in *that* business. I don't get into it with foreigners, man. You know that. That's heavy-level consequences if you fuck up. And I'd like to keep all of my body parts attached, thank you very much.' Vidar rolled his head from one side to the other. 'But there's definitely another player in the game. And Andy, well, like I said. She's an addict. Was an addict. And she never learned. She always fell back into her routine. She liked familiar. And she liked her own people.'

'You mean Romanians or drug dealers?'

'Is there a difference?'

'Hey! My grandmother's half Romanian!' Siri yelled from across the room.

'I was just joking, babe!' Vidar called back.

Kjeld ran his finger over his ear, running over the divot of scarred missing cartilage. 'What about the Second Life Wellness Respite? You know anything about that?'

'What, the hippy commune?'

'I heard they're under investigation for international drug trafficking. Could that be with the Sandu cartel?'

'Hell, man. I don't know. I don't get on with any of that

weird-ass guru shit. The only thing worse than dealing drugs for foreigners? Getting involved with anyone into peace, love, and brainwashing. I saw that fucking Jonestown documentary. I ain't getting anywhere near that place or those people.'

'What about Andrea? Would she?'

Vidar pinched his face in thought. 'Nah, man. I don't think she'd buy into that either. She was trash and she was mean. But she wasn't crazy. Only crazy people get involved in that nonsense.'

Kjeld nodded. Then he made his way back to the parlour door.

'Hey!' Vidar called after him. 'What about me? What do I get for giving you all these answers?'

Kjeld glanced back over his shoulder. 'How about a bit of free advice? Get yourself to a dentist, Rask, before all of your teeth fall out. And take a bath.'

'Yeah, yeah.' Vidar waved a dismissive hand at Kjeld. 'Always the wise guy. Next time you come in I hope it's for a tattoo! There's nothing I'd like more than to stick a fucking needle in that pale arse ginger skin of yours and watch you bleed.'

'Keep dreaming.'

'You better watch yourself, Nygaard. One day someone is going to get the fucking better of you and I sure as hell hope I'm there to see it.'

'You're going to have to get in line.'

'You can bet your arse I'll be the first one to buy a ticket when they go on sale.'

Kjeld shoved open the door but stopped in the entrance to send Vidar an obnoxious smirk.

'To quote someone much wiser than you …' Kjeld raised a middle finger to Vidar.

Chapter 43

Kjeld returned to the station after speaking to Vidar and spent the rest of the day going through the tip line, searching for anything that might be even remotely related to either of the cases they were working on. Unfortunately, it had been another dead end. Nothing but crazies, crank calls, and people just looking for attention. When dinnertime rolled around, he ate one of Sixten's sandwiches from the communal fridge, leaving a handwritten IOU on his desk, and spent another hour going through the evidence from Andrea's murder again from the beginning. When that resulted in nothing more than a headache, he drove home. Fifteen minutes later he was fitting the key into the lock of his apartment complex's entrée when he heard a car door slam shut behind him. He didn't pay it any attention until he heard a harsh voice calling out his name.

'Kjeld! You son of a bitch!'

He didn't need to look to know who it was. The use of an English expletive, accompanied by that heavy accent, told him it was Liam. And he was furious.

Kjeld hurried inside the building foyer where the postboxes were housed. He attempted to shove the door closed behind him, but it was on a slow-moving lever and Liam jabbed the toe of his shoe in between before it could shut. Then he pushed the door open further to let himself in.

'This is a little far out of the way from your place in Lindholmen, isn't it? Or are you here providing house calls for another one of your better-looking patients?' Kjeld couldn't help the spite in his tone as he shoved his key in the postbox for his flat. He took out a few envelopes, refusing to meet Liam's eyes. He shoved the utility bills in his pocket and dropped the junk mail in the bin beside the stairwell.

'You're a real piece of work, you know that?'

'I've been called worse.' Kjeld turned his back on Liam and made his way to the stairs.

Liam caught him by the elbow, spinning him around.

Kjeld had a short temper and his first instinct was always to lash out. Physically, verbally. Any way he could. But recent events had taught him that he needed to learn to tone down that bad habit. As such he'd been trying to restrain that initial compulsion with people. His success had been mixed. Suffice it to say, when Liam grabbed him it took nearly every ounce of self-control he had not to land his fist square on the good doctor's face.

The anger, however, which shot up from his gut and spread a heated glare across his face was not held back.

'Let go of me, Liam.'

'Not until we've had a little chat.'

'You wanna chat? Call my office. Make an appointment. Or better yet, write me a letter so I can have something of yours I can put through the shredder.'

Kjeld tugged his arm out of Liam's grip. The man's fingers around his elbow had been firm and Kjeld thought he might have a small bruise in the morning.

'I'm sick and tired of you interrupting our lives with your shit problems. I don't know if it's out of need for attention, a cry for help, or if you're just incapable of recognising that Bengt has moved on without you. But it has to stop. I've done my best to stick to the side-lines and not get involved. For Bengt's sake and for Tove's. But you've gone too far.'

Kjeld gave a curt laugh. 'My relationship with Bengt and my daughter is none of your business.'

'It's every bit my business. I care about them both. I care about Tove as if she were my own daughter.'

'She's not your daughter.'

'And I can't stand by anymore watching you inflict this kind of damaging trauma on her.'

'Trauma?'

'I saw the photograph in *The Chatterbox*.'

Kjeld gritted his teeth together so hard that the rigidity in his jaw travelled upwards, forming an early tension headache in his temples. 'I would have thought a professional, such as yourself, would know to do a little fact-checking before believing what he reads on the internet.'

'There was a picture of her at the crime scene. That tells me all I need to know.'

'It's being dealt with.'

'Dealt with?'

'Bengt and I have discussed it and talked about it with Tove. It's under control. It has nothing to do with you.'

Confusion flashed across Liam's face. And Kjeld knew that Bengt had kept his word about not telling Liam his plans to have Tove meet with a therapist. Liam, however, recovered quickly, hiding his surprise behind a cruel, mocking laugh that echoed in the small space of the entranceway. The sound grated on Kjeld's ears. And it really pushed his temper to the furthest edges of its patience.

'Under control? That's a laugh. Nothing is under control with you. You're a parasite. You latch on to other people, *good* people, and suck them dry of everything they're willing to give you. Then when you've taken everything from them, you guilt them into feeling bad for you.' Liam stepped in closer, blocking the way to the door.

Kjeld backed into the wall between the postboxes and the stairwell. He didn't like being cornered. Liam was close enough for Kjeld to smell his aftershave. It was one of those musky devil-may-care scents. Handsomely expensive, no doubt. But worse than the uncomfortable closeness of being pushed between a cold brick wall and his ex's insufferable paramour was being forced to listen to Liam's well-practised speech. Not simply because the words were razor-sharp, designed to cut with every syllable. But because no one had spoken to Kjeld that way before. No one had ever said those things to his face.

And he had to stop and wonder if there was any truth to Liam's words. Had he been guilting Bengt over the years? He'd been angry, yes. And Bengt had been the one to break the vows they'd made to each other. But Kjeld had always recognised his own fault in their short-lived marriage. Kjeld put his work before his family. And as upset as he'd been with Bengt for stepping out on him, he was more upset with himself. If he'd been more cognisant of Bengt's needs, Liam might never have entered the picture.

Parasitic, however, seemed a bit harsh.

Liam's dark eyes bored into Kjeld. 'I'm not falling for your woe-is-me routine. I've seen you for what you are from the beginning. A user. Always taking. Never giving. And I won't have it anymore. I'm done dealing with Bengt's misplaced shame and Tove's tears. I want to take the next step with them and for that I need you out of the picture.'

Kjeld blinked, struck by the turn in Liam's words. 'What?'

'You heard me.'

Kjeld tried to sidestep around Liam, but the other man extended his arm in a motion that would have clotheslined Kjeld if he'd been moving more quickly. As it was, Kjeld just bumped into Liam's forearm, shadowed in the dim yellow lighting of the ingress.

'I swear to God, Liam, if you touch me one more time …'

'I'm going to ask Bengt to make it official.'

The words sounded weird to Kjeld. Almost foreign. Maybe it was Liam's stuffy accent. Or maybe it was just the way he said *official*, as though whatever he currently had with Bengt wasn't real. As though it were a game. Then again, it might have just been the look on Liam's face, a bizarre combination of arrogance and formality that in no way signalled affection for the person he spoke about, which Kjeld found uncomfortable.

Or he could have been honest with himself and admitted the truth.

He was jealous. And he was angry.

'Why the hell should I care what you and Bengt decide to do in your free time? You two want to go ahead and play house? Fine. Whatever. But that doesn't change anything with Tove.'

'Actually, it does. The difference between you and me is that I want a family, Kjeld. And if Bengt agrees to it then I want to be more than just his partner. I want to be the second father that Tove needs. The one she deserves.'

Kjeld shook his head. He wished he couldn't hear what Liam was saying. The thought that Liam would try to take Tove away from him caused his blood to boil. 'Tove isn't your daughter. She's mine and Bengt's. He and I will decide everything when it comes to her. Not you. Just because you're fucking my ex does not mean you have any say in situations that concern our child. And I would never fucking agree to that. Never.'

'Well, that might not be your choice to make. I'm quite certain a judge will only have to take one look at that photograph and article to realise you are wholly incapable of raising a child. In fact, I'd go so far as to say that the courts might even consider you a liability to her physical and emotional health.'

Kjeld's fist collided with Liam's face before he knew what he was doing.

Kjeld hadn't intended to get into a fight with Liam. All he'd wanted was to go upstairs to his apartment, have a drink to stave off his nicotine cravings, watch the recording of the women's league football match between Sweden and South Africa he'd missed a few weeks ago, and maybe – if he was lucky – have a few hours of sleep before he headed back to the station.

But his short fuse and oppressive envy got the better of him.

What Kjeld wasn't prepared for, however, was Liam's equally obstinate loathing for him.

Which was why Liam's punch took him by surprise.

The fist landed on his cheek and slid up into his left eye, knocking him with a dizzying sting. Kjeld was in reasonably good shape. He was strong and athletic. But Liam was bigger. Stronger. Fitter. He had the upper hand. He also had the benefit of being more cool-headed and collected, despite the fact that Kjeld had pushed him over the edge as well. And the fight might have ended there, with that swimming rattle of his brain inside his head, if Kjeld could have latched on to some of that collectedness himself. Instead he responded to Liam's punch by ramming his entire body into the man, an act that sent them both off balance and crashing to the wet tiled floor.

But for all of Kjeld's scrappiness, it was Liam's weight that won out. Liam quickly rolled Kjeld onto his stomach like a judo grappler, pinning him down to the floor, his sore eye pushing into the slick immobile tile. A dull pain shot up through his head and he groaned.

'You're going to stay away from Bengt,' Liam hissed in Kjeld's ear. 'No more coming around uninvited when I'm not there. And if I find out that you've put Tove in danger again, I'll make sure you lose more than just your weekend privileges.'

'I could have you locked up for assault on a police officer,' Kjeld grumbled against the floor.

Liam pressed his forearm hard against the back of Kjeld's neck, pushing into a soft pressure point in the hook where his neck met his shoulder. 'But you won't. Because you're not an upstanding member of the police force. You're the arsehole who's made a name for himself by getting on the bad side of the media. And you're the inspector who covered for a serial killer.'

'I didn't—'

Liam jabbed his elbow into that soft spot in Kjeld's neck. A sharp pain shot through Kjeld's shoulder, nearly numbing his arm.

'No one in family court would give a shit about anything other than what they can see. An unreliable man who consistently prioritises work over the well-being of his daughter.'

Liam climbed off him and Kjeld continued to lie there, using the clammy chill of the floor against his face and the gritty indentations between the tiles where his fingers scratched to distract him from his urge to go after Liam. When what little was left of his good sense returned to him he slowly pushed himself up off the ground.

Liam stared down at him with a mixture of satisfaction and disapproval. For all of Kjeld's hatred of Liam, he'd never honestly considered the doctor to be a bad man. But that look sent an uneasy chill down the back of Kjeld's neck.

'Are we in agreement?' Liam asked.

Kjeld's face throbbed, but the sight of blood at the corner of Liam's lip was worth the pain. He felt a sweet moment of vindication. Later, when he was pressing a bag of frozen vegetables against his face, he would regret it all. He would curse his stupidity and his short fuse and wish he'd had the self-control to not allow Liam to get to him. But it was easier to be angry at Liam than at himself. Or at Bengt, for that matter. Easier to hate the man who came between him and the only real relationship Kjeld had ever wanted to work out than to recognise his own complicity in pushing Bengt away.

Easier to pick a fight than to have a difficult conversation with someone he loved. Or to admit that Liam might have been right. He might not have been the person his daughter needed in her life.

'Fine,' Kjeld said under his breath.

'What was that?'

'I won't stop by unannounced,' Kjeld spat, sounding more sarcastic that he'd intended.

'Good. I'm glad we could settle this.' Liam made for the door. When he opened it a rush of cold damp air filled the corridor. 'And don't forget what I said about Tove. You pull a stunt like that with her again and I'll make sure you won't be allowed to see her until she's eighteen.'

The thumping of Kjeld's heart, quickened by rage, pulsed in his head. He could barely hear the sound of Liam's voice over his own ragged breathing. Even when the man left, Kjeld found himself seething, both in anger and fatigue. Liam may not have been right about everything he'd said, but he was correct about one thing. Something had to change.

Chapter 44

Onsdag | Wednesday

Kjeld woke up the next morning with a splitting headache that felt like a hangover. His eye throbbed and a dark purple bruise had begun to form a crescent moon shape that curved along his orbital ridge to his cheekbone. It was sensitive to the touch, but not nearly as swollen as it could have been and he immediately regretted not leaving ice on it longer the night before. He could only imagine the look Esme was going to give him at the station. Axel and Sixten would believe the good old *I walked into a door* excuse without question, but not Esme. Nothing got past her.

He swallowed two paracetamol with his first gulp of coffee. The dark, long-roasted liquid nearly burned the roof of his mouth because he didn't wait for it to cool. He chased it with half a slice of buttered toast and cheese while Oskar mewled at his feet for breakfast.

'One of these days we're going to have to talk about this whining behaviour of yours, Oskar. Better enjoy this kibble while you can, too. The vet's probably gonna put you on a gross diet brand after your next appointment.' Kjeld bent down to the lower cupboard and scooped out the kibble. Oskar was already sniffing and licking at his wrist before he poured it in the bowl. Then he refilled Oskar's water dish.

He took another swig of coffee and glanced over at the clock. Shit, he was running late.

Without finishing his breakfast, he grabbed his coat by the door and picked up his car keys from the credenza in the foyer. Then he headed out of the apartment.

He thought about his conversation with Vidar as he jogged down the stairs. The more it rolled around in his mind the more he began to wonder if they weren't wrong about Andrea's murder. Was she connected to Olsen's drug trafficking case at the Second Life commune? And, if so, did that mean they were wrong about Louisa's murder? Could she have been involved in drugs as well? Was that the murderer's motive? Something about it didn't sit right with Kjeld, but he couldn't help but wonder if he hadn't been too quick to ignore the possibility that Louisa could have turned to drugs in order to help her cope with her trauma. She was an intelligent young woman. If she'd wanted to hide it from her family, she could have. And Kjeld, of all people, should have been more open to the possibility that her family members might not have seen what was directly under their noses. Kjeld hadn't recognised the deceptions in his own family, after all. Not until it was too late.

Once outside his phone rang in his pocket. Kjeld took it out and looked at the caller ID. It was that unknown number again. He grumbled. He was sick and tired of these telemarketers. Didn't they have anything better to do than hound him until he picked up? Maybe if he finally answered and gave them a piece of his mind they'd leave him alone.

He stood on the pavement in front of his building and pressed the answer button.

He brought the phone to his ear just as he removed his keys

from his pocket. 'Who the hell is this? And why do you keep calling this number?'

There wasn't an immediate answer, but Kjeld could hear breathing on the other end of the line. He waited for a car to pass before stepping out into the street.

'Hello? Are you going to answer me?'

A voice began to speak as Kjeld pressed the unlock button on his key fob. But he didn't hear a word they said. They were drowned out by the deafening boom of his car exploding.

Chapter 45

The thick forking vein on the side of Rhodin's temple pulsed hard enough for Kjeld to see it from across the room. Rhodin paced behind his desk, sweat dripping from his brow despite the fact that the room was cool. He wiped it off with his sleeve. 'I don't even know where to begin.'

Kjeld and Esme stood side by side in the centre of his office. Kjeld felt like he was back in school, waiting to be reprimanded for skipping class or getting into arguments in the playground. Esme was quiet but concerned. Kjeld knew she was purposefully avoiding looking at him. Not because he'd done anything wrong, but because she knew what the chief was going to say.

'It's fine,' Kjeld said.

Esme cast an incredulous glance his way.

'Really, it is. It doesn't have to change anything. And my insurance is covering for a temporary rental car.' Kjeld glanced at the clock on the wall. 'It should be ready to pick up in an hour.'

'Are you fucking insane?' Rhodin placed his palms on his desk, leaning towards them. 'Someone placed a bomb under your car, Kjeld. You're lucky we're not scraping pieces of you off your neighbours' windows right now.'

'I'm not hurt. Barely even a scratch.'

'Your eye says otherwise.'

'That was—' Kjeld shook off the rest of that comment. The last thing he needed was to tell his boss he'd just gotten into a brawl with one of the city's most well-respected oncologists. That wouldn't exactly stand in his favour. 'I'm good to continue working the case.'

Rhodin snorted in disbelief. 'The fuck you are. First of all, we don't even know who put that bomb on your car. It might not even be related to either of these cases. Secondly, you being at risk puts the entire team at risk.'

'You can't suspend me again.' Kjeld turned to Esme. 'Tell him I'm fine.'

Esme's brows knitted at the centre of her forehead. 'You could have died, Kjeld.'

'But I didn't!' Kjeld understood that there was protocol to follow, but he couldn't help but feel personally attacked. At the very least he'd expected Esme to take his side.

'Esme, talk some sense into your partner.'

'I think you might be in shock,' Esme said.

'I was checked out by paramedics on the scene. They said there was nothing wrong with me. No concussion. No signs of external or internal injury. I was far enough away from the blast. Can't say the same for my neighbour's Peugeot, but it needed a new paint job anyway.'

Rhodin hung his head over his desk. When he looked up again his skin appeared sallow, almost jaundiced in tint. The dark bags under his eyes were more prominent than they'd been over the last few days. 'I'm not going to suspend you because I know your record can't handle that. I am, however, going to put in a request for leave.'

'I don't need a holiday, chief. I need to solve this case. A case. Any case. Don't send me home.'

'You have plenty of days leave left to spare. If anyone asks I'm going to say that in light of your daughter's recent injury you've decided to take some time off to spend with your family. Which, all things considered, is something you probably should have done on your own.'

'This is absurd.'

'No. Someone blowing up your car outside your apartment is absurd. A serial murderer going after victims from your old cases is absurd. Taking time off to rest, recuperate from everything that happened last year, and get your shit together is not absurd.'

'Chief—'

'No. I'm done. This is final.' Rhodin turned a weary gaze to Esme. 'The Nicolescu case is yours if you can handle it. If you can't, I'm passing it off to Olsen. He's already asked for it.'

Esme bit her lip. She knew that if she allowed Olsen to take on the case, Kjeld would never forgive her. 'We can handle it.'

Kjeld shot her a disappointed stare.

'I'm sorry, Kjeld,' she said, her shoulders drooping. 'I agree with the chief. You need to step away from the job until we figure this out.'

Chapter 46

Kjeld stormed out of Rhodin's office and made straight for his desk. He could feel his temper flaring, burying beneath it the delayed shock of what had happened. Esme was right, he could have died. But that's not what angered him. Nor was he angry at the chief. He knew Rhodin's hands were tied. And he wasn't angry with Esme, either, although he was a little annoyed. But he recognised the hypocrisy of being irritated with Esme for not supporting him when he'd been less than helpful to her when she'd been placed in charge of the Karlsson case.

In truth he was just angry and he had been for months. Up until recently, however, he had a focus for his anger. Nils, his father, his sister, Bengt. There was always someone he could pinpoint as the reason why his life was going off the rails. But there wasn't anyone left to blame but himself. Alice was right. If he wanted things to improve in his life then he needed to be the one to initiate changes. He couldn't expect the universe to wave a wand and magically put everything in his favour. People who found happiness in their lives worked hard for it. Kjeld clearly hadn't worked hard enough.

He was cleaning out some of the personal items from his desk when he caught a glimpse of one of the station's front desk liaisons standing beside a woman near the doorway; straw-thin blonde hair, anxious complexion, and a visitor's badge on her sweater. She glanced tentatively from side to side. When her gaze met Kjeld's, she frowned as though guilty of not knowing where to go.

Danna Karlsson.

Kjeld looked back to Rhodin's office, but Esme was still inside speaking with him. He might have been off the case, but he was still on duty until he left the building. So he quickly crossed the room to meet Danna at the entrance. He nodded to the liaison, who returned to her duties. 'Danna, what are you doing here? I told your father that if I had any new information I would deliver it in person.'

Danna sniffed, her nose red from coming inside from the cold. 'I know, but there's something I wanted to talk to you about.'

She hesitated before staring at the dark bruise that had begun to form around his eye. 'Are you all right?'

'I'm fine. Would you like a tea or coffee?'

She shook her head.

Kjeld led her to an empty office at the far side of the room, away from the commotion of officers and detectives going about their daily routines. Once she was inside he closed the door to give them privacy.

Danna sat down in one of the chairs in front of the desk. Kjeld sat in the other beside her.

'Is everything all right?' Kjeld asked. 'How's your dad holding up?'

'He's struggling, but I think he's going to be okay. It's difficult. I know my parents never had favourites, but Louisa always got so much attention because of what happened to her. I don't mean to speak ill of her or anyone. That's not how I feel. But sometimes I don't know how to speak to my father. It's like he saved all of his love for Louisa. It makes me feel a little estranged.'

'It's not easy being the one left behind. I know a bit about

231

being estranged from my father as well,' Kjeld offered. 'Give him some time.'

She nodded and took a centred breath, but when she exhaled it sounded heavy and exhausted. She fiddled with a loose thread on the thumb of her glove.

'You wanted to talk to me about something?'

'About Louisa. I remembered something that I should have mentioned earlier. But when I thought of it I just shrugged it off as nothing.'

'Before we go any further I need to be honest with you. I've been taken off your sister's case.'

Danna's expression turned grief-stricken. 'What? Why? That's … no. We want you to be on the case. Dad says you're the only one he trusts to find the person who did this.'

'I know. I'm sorry. And I haven't given up on catching the person. But there's some behind-the-scenes bureaucratic nonsense and, well, the department doesn't want me in the limelight on this one.'

'Because of the Kattegat Killer?'

This time it was Kjeld's turn to look surprised.

'Dad has kept up on your career. He's a little … Obsessed isn't the right word. But after everything I think he sees you as one of the family.'

Kjeld looked away. That made him feel worse about not keeping in touch.

'Do you trust the person they've put in charge of Louisa's case?' Danna asked hesitantly.

'Absolutely. She's the best I know. Better than me in fact.'

Danna nodded. 'If it's all right with you I'd still like to tell you personally.'

'Of course,' Kjeld said. 'What do you remember?'

'A few weeks before Louisa's death I took the kids to the library. Louisa was in a really good mood. Too good. I hadn't seen her so excited in years. I almost didn't believe it.' Danna smoothed out the thread on her glove, pushing it back into the fabric so as not to distract her. 'At first I thought she must have met somebody because she had a glow about her. The kind you get when you're interested in someone. You know what I mean?'

'Yes, I know. Go on.'

'So, I asked her what she was so happy about and she told me that she'd found a group of people who might be able to help her. I didn't know what that meant at first. I thought maybe she'd found a new therapy group or something. I admit I was a little distracted because I had the kids with me and they were a little crazy.'

'Did Louisa say anything about this group?'

'No, not really. She said that they had weekly meetings and she'd been to one of them. She said it was people just like her. People who'd experienced trauma and tragedy. She said that for the first time since her kidnapping she'd finally found people who understood her. Who knew what it felt like to be the only one.' Danna tucked a strand of hair behind her ear. 'I should have questioned it more. I should have pushed her to tell me, but the kids were screaming and she just seemed so happy. I didn't want to turn it into a downer. That happened sometimes. Whenever we questioned her about her moods, she'd think we were judging her. I always tried to be careful with the things I said when she was around.'

There was a pause and Danna leaned forward in the chair. 'I don't know. Maybe it's nothing. Maybe I'm just looking for something to help since I feel so helpless.'

Kjeld thought about her words for a moment before snatching a piece of blank paper from the desk and drawing the rising sun between two open palms symbol that he'd found on the flyer posted outside the library. 'Have you ever seen this symbol?'

Danna frowned. 'Yes, actually. Louisa would doodle that some-times when she came over. She would babysit for me and she and the kids would draw pictures. I saw her draw that a few times. What does it mean?'

'Have you ever heard of Second Life Wellness Respite?'

'I don't think so.'

'It's a kind of rehabilitation commune for people trying to move on from tragedy or trauma. This is their symbol.'

'What are you saying? That Louisa might have been involved with them?' She paused. 'Could they be behind her death?'

'I don't know, but I promise you I'll do my best to find out.'

'Detective?'

'Hm?'

'Does it make me a bad person if I feel like Louisa is in a better place?'

Kjeld gave her a pointed stare that slowly relaxed into one of sombre acceptance. 'No, Danna. That doesn't make you a bad person. That just makes you an honest one.'

Chapter 47

Esme twirled the dry-erase pen between her fingers while she listened to Kjeld reveal the information he'd learned during his conversation with Danna Karlsson. Esme was frustrated and the explosion of Kjeld's car had her rethinking the potential motives behind these murders. Was Louisa's killer targeting him? Was it unrelated? Normally an attack like that would come with a clear message, but not even Kjeld was certain who was behind it. And that worried her. There could have been any number of reasons why someone might want to hurt Kjeld or send him a warning. The least of which was persistently on the news awaiting trial.

She pushed aside her thoughts on the threat to Kjeld's life and tried to focus on this new thread Danna had provided them. If she was correct, then they might finally have a direct link between both Louisa and Second Life and Louisa and Jonny. But with Second Life under investigation for international drug trafficking crimes, it would be a precarious line to investigate. Especially if they were wrong. Then not only would they be wasting time on their own case, but they might also impede the work of the officers in the organised crime department. And while she agreed that Björk didn't seem trustworthy, they'd need more if they wanted to push him to reveal something new.

'I just don't think it's enough to go on, Kjeld.'

'What do you mean it's not enough to go on?' Kjeld held out his hand and began counting on his fingers the points in favour of his lead. 'First, we can place Jonny in the area of the library on surveillance camera. Second, Linnea Thorsen admits to seeing Louisa speaking with a young man matching Jonny's description. Third, Jonny was posting flyers for Second Life—'

'*Allegedly* posting flyers for Second Life,' Esme interrupted. 'Forensic analysis wasn't able to retrieve fingerprints from the paper. It had been too weathered by the rain.'

'Didn't you receive confirmation from his mother that he was living at the commune?'

Esme sighed. 'Yes and no. His mother was vague on the details. Apparently, he had a lot of difficulties this past year. He was in and out of a lot of rehabilitation facilities. Nothing seemed to stick. Eventually he stopped coming home. She thought he was purposefully trying to be difficult to reach. But she blamed that on herself for not trying to get him help sooner.'

And what good would returning to the commune do without more substantial evidence? Björk could easily lie to them about Jonny.

Kjeld gave a thoughtful look. 'That sounds a little similar to something Danna said. According to her, Louisa told her she'd found a new group that was going to be more successful in helping her overcome the trauma of her experience with Gjur Hägglund. Second Life is known for appealing to people who have lived through difficult tragedies. It's right there on their website for anyone to see. Also, Danna claims Louisa was doodling the Second Life symbol around their house. What more do we need?'

Esme set the pen down in the whiteboard tray. 'I'm not arguing with you that the evidence suggesting that Louisa might have attended one of the Second Life meetings is strong. It is. But even if that's true, we have no evidence suggesting that Second Life was involved in the murders. It could simply be a coincidence.

And if we go barging into Second Life asking questions about a second homicide and we're wrong then we've just messed up two investigations instead of one.'

Kjeld huffed and placed his hands on his hips, turning his attention to the whiteboard and the list of potential victims the team had collected from old case files. There weren't many, but there were more than Esme had anticipated. It would take time to go through each of them individually. And if the killer continued at the rate they were going, time was something they didn't have enough of. They'd have to pick the most likely targets. Then cross their fingers and hope intuition and sheer luck were on their side.

'And not that I want to split hairs,' Esme continued, 'but you're not on Louisa and Jonny's case. Hell, you're not on any of the cases. So, unless you have a connection between Second Life and Andrea Nicolescu there's no way the chief is going to approve any of us going there again.'

'I talked to a guy who says that Andrea used to be involved in the Sandu cartel. That's the same group organised crime thinks Second Life is involved with. If Andrea was still working for Sandu, then there could be some evidence at Second Life that she'd been there. Someone may have seen her.'

'Who's this guy you talked to?'

'Vidar Rask.'

'Rask?' Esme almost laughed in disbelief. 'You know that guy isn't trustworthy. He'll say whatever he thinks you want to hear just to get you off his back.'

'He's been helpful in the past.'

'But not without consequences. And anyway, just saying Andrea might have been involved with a cartel that might be working with Second Life isn't enough. The chief would never go for it.'

'You could convince him.'

Esme found herself in a difficult position. Normally she trusted Kjeld's hunches, but this was her first time in charge of an investigation and she didn't want to disappoint. 'I don't know, Kjeld.'

Kjeld propped himself on the edge of Sixten's desk. 'Our investigation should take priority over whatever nonsense Kenneth Olsen suspects is going on with Second Life. Drugs? I mean, come on. We've had three homicides in a matter of weeks.'

'I know, but you heard the chief. Without more direct evidence, we don't have purview there. And as much as we're all sick of hearing it—'

'—we still haven't gained the city's trust after the Aubuchon case.' Kjeld heaved a frustrated sigh.

Esme watched him carefully. There were dark circles under his eyes from lack of sleep and it looked as though he hadn't shaved his neck in almost a week. She knew the team was tired – hell, they'd all been working extra hours – but Kjeld looked more than tired. He looked haggard. And it was clear that more was weighing on him than just the case. And she suspected the bruise that had formed over his left eye had something to do with it.

'I'll see what I can do,' she said. 'Just promise me you won't go to Second Life on your own making accusations.'

'Not unless I have a good reason.'

'I mean it, Kjeld.'

'I know.'

She sat beside him on the edge of the desk. Her feet didn't reach the floor, but it brought their shoulders closer together and made Esme feel a bit taller. A bit more on his level. She thought again about how she shouldn't be comparing herself to Kjeld. She was just as competent an investigator as he was. She was more than capable of handling both cases. And it wasn't as though she was working alone. She still had the team backing her up. Maybe she was being too hard on herself.

'If there's anything you ever want to talk about. Anything outside of work. You can talk to me about it. You know I won't judge you.'

Kjeld canted a sidelong glance at her. Was that suspicion in his eyes?

'And if there's anything I can do to help I—'.

'I'm fine, Esme. You don't have to worry about me.'

Esme grew quiet, drawing into herself as though she'd just been scolded for saying something wrong. She knew that was an overly dramatic way of thinking about it, but she couldn't help but feel hurt by Kjeld's refusal to talk to her about his private life. It was as though he was drawing a line in their relationship. And while that had never bothered her in the past, it bothered her now.

She changed the subject.

'What about Henny? Has she done anything peculiar lately?'

'I ran into her at the coffee shop the other day and overheard her talking to someone. She was agitated. It sounded like whoever was on the other end of the line wanted her to do something she wasn't comfortable with. It felt suspicious because she was very particular not to mention any names. Maybe it was nothing. I don't know. If she's involved then she's being careful.'

Kjeld nodded to the whiteboard. Esme had created a list of potential victims from his old cases. 'Who did you come up with?'

'There weren't many that fit the requirements. Assuming of course that our theory is correct. We narrowed it down to five but one no longer lives in the country. None of them appear to have any connection to Second Life and only one could be considered a true survivor of a mass killing.' Esme stood up and circled a single name on the board.

Daniel Santelmann.

'He was the one from that financial conglomerate, wasn't he?'

Esme nodded. 'He was helping a firm launder money from their clients. It was a type of pyramid scheme. They were taking off small increments at first, but over time the money added up. Lots of people went bankrupt because of the fake investments. One of the investors burst into the boardroom and shot everyone before shooting himself. Daniel survived by hiding under the body of the company's CEO and pretending to be dead.'

'I remember he was still there when we were called to the scene.

Scared the shit out of me when we saw him move. I thought he was dead.'

'Sixten and I are going to drive over to his house and speak with him. Ask if he's seen anyone unfamiliar in his neighbourhood. He works from home so if he is on the killer's list that's where he'll be most vulnerable.'

Kjeld nodded but didn't say anything. Esme took that as quiet approval.

An awkward silence fell between them. Almost a minute passed before Kjeld spoke up.

'When are you speaking with him?'

'Tomorrow, I hope. We've been trying to get a hold of him, but no luck. We sent a patrol car over to his house this morning but the officer said it looked like he wasn't home. No signs of any foul play and the neighbour confirmed he travelled a lot. I just hope we're not too late on this one.'

'Let me know if I can help.'

Esme quirked a small smile. 'And have the chief take me off the case and put me on the phone lines? I don't think so.'

Kjeld leaned into her, playfully bumping their shoulders against each other before standing up. 'You'll be fine, Esme. It's the right choice. It's the same thing I would do.'

'I know you would. Because I'd be the one telling you to do it.'

Kjeld grinned. 'You always were the smarter of the two of us.'

An unexpected warmth glossed her cheeks and she untucked her hair from behind her ear to hide it. 'Obviously.'

Chapter 48

Torsdag | Thursday

Less than three hours into his so-called holiday, Kjeld realised he couldn't let the case go.

After he left the office, he walked to the Sixt car rental services at the central station and picked up the mid-size sedan his insurance was covering until he found a replacement. Then he returned home and tried to fill his time with everyday chores that were never finished because he was always working. He tossed out all of the past-date food in his fridge, threw in a load of laundry, and made an appointment with his barber for a trim next week. Still he couldn't switch off his thoughts.

He was halfway through writing up a grocery list when his mind started running through the evidence. Ever since Kjeld had spoken to Vidar he'd been thinking about the information he gave him. Andrea, Olsen's investigation into Second Life, and Jonny's death all had a drug connection to them. There were simply too many coincidences to ignore. And even though Esme and Sixten had already spoken to Jonny's mother when they notified her of his death, and Kjeld had gone over their notes before he was officially removed from the case, it wasn't enough. There had to be more to the story. And he was determined to find out what that was.

He was driving back from the supermarket when he decided to call Jonny's mother, Monika Lindh. She remembered him immediately, which made talking to her easier. He didn't lie to her. The chief had technically closed the case because of lack of evidence. All indications pointed to a suicide, even if nobody believed that. Kjeld admitted that he wasn't technically on her son's case, but because of his history working the previous investigation Jonny was involved in he wanted to reach out to her and make sure there wasn't anything his colleagues had missed. Monika admitted that she would be home for the rest of the day, but the tone of her voice indicated she didn't have high hopes that it would improve her spirits. Kjeld drove directly to her house anyway, forgetting about the perishables in the back seat.

The last time Kjeld had seen Monika Lindh, she'd been a vibrant woman with a full head of thick blonde hair and a fresh modern style. She was the kind of mother that teenage boys used to tease their friends about. The kind of woman pubescent boys considered too attractive to be a mum. That was four years ago. Since then she looked as though she'd aged more than a decade. Her hair was thinning along her temples, she'd put on a considerable amount of weight for her small frame, and she looked like she'd fallen out of a laundry basket. Her clothes were wrinkled and mismatched. But it was her eyes that struck Kjeld the most. Baggy and bloodshot.

She welcomed Kjeld into her home, a small but upscale house in Hovås, a posh suburban neighbourhood on the southern side of Gothenburg Kommun. A long-haired German shepherd raced out of the kitchen and began barking at Kjeld.

'Hush, Balder!'

The dog looked up at Monika and whimpered. Then he sniffed around Kjeld's legs.

'Sorry about him. He's Jonny's dog.' She paused. Her breath was accompanied by the thick stench of sour wine. 'Was Jonny's dog. I got him for Jonny after … you know. I thought it would help him with the grief. All I got out of it was a neurotic dog that can't walk on a leash.'

'You don't have to apologise,' Kjeld said, trying not to make too much of a face as he carefully walked around the canine and followed Monika into the kitchen. He felt a twinge of shame for being there. He was risking the integrity of the investigation by speaking to her and, in truth, there probably wasn't much more he could learn that Esme and Sixten hadn't already uncovered in their talk with her. And when the dog looked up at him with its sad eyes he felt even worse. But Kjeld couldn't let it go.

Monika slumped down at the kitchen table without offering Kjeld anything to drink. Kjeld sat across from her. Balder lay on the floor beneath the table, resting his head on Kjeld's shoes.

'I know I should be surprised,' Monika said. 'But I'm not. Not really. If you'd asked me five years ago if my son was capable of committing suicide I would have argued until my throat was raw. But the truth is Jonny wasn't the same person after all those kids died. People used to tell me it was because he lost his girlfriend. She was at the party too, you know. Young love and all that. But it wasn't that. Sure, that was part of it, but it was so much more. It was just …'

'Traumatic?'

Monika nodded. Her face twisted like she might cry, but her eyes were dry and red. 'I can't be angry with him. Not really. I might have done the same thing if I were him.'

'You said he was different after the incident at the cabin. How? Was he depressed?'

'Oh, God, no. If it had just been depression I could have handled it. No, he was uncontrollable. Eccentric highs. Heavy lows. And then there were the drugs.'

'Tell me about the drugs.'

'I hate to say it, but that was the only time I could actually stand to be around him afterwards. When he was high, that is. At least then he acted as though he was happy. They made him feel like things could be better. And that gave me hope, too. But it was short-lived. Once the high wore off he was unmanageable. Angry all the time. Once he went outside in the middle of the night and chopped down the cherry blossom tree next door. I convinced the neighbour not to call the police, but I had to replace it. Not that money was an issue, but none of the neighbours have spoken to me since.'

She hung her head.

Balder let out a whine and licked at Kjeld's shoes.

'Do you know where he was getting these drugs?'

Monika shrugged. 'Probably at that damn job of his. I was excited at first when he told me he'd found a job. It hurt me when he dropped out of university, but I didn't tell him that. I couldn't imagine what he was going through and knew he had to find his own way. But then he said it was at a club and I knew it would lead to trouble. He used to be such a good boy. He never drank. He never smoked. That's why he didn't die with the rest of them, you know. Jonny never drank. Not until after.'

'Which club was this?' Kjeld asked, searching his pockets for something to write on. But when Monika responded he realised he didn't need to.

'Portside.'

Kjeld raised a brow. 'Portside? The one in the warehouse district?'

'I know it's a hotbed of drugs and prostitution. I read about it in the newspaper.'

Kjeld had never been to Portside, but he'd heard some of his colleagues in the narcotics squad talk about it as a potential hub of gang activity. Nothing ever seemed to stick, however. The owners, assuming they were involved in any illegal activities, knew how to cover their bases. To Kjeld's knowledge there'd never been a successful raid on the popular nightclub.

'What about in the weeks leading up to Jonny's death? What was his mood? Was he hanging around any new people?'

Monika choked a laugh. A tear fell down her cheek and she wiped it off with the back of her hand. 'I'm sorry. I didn't mean to laugh. But that's the cruellest thing of it all. I barely saw Jonny for the last six months because of his new friends. If you can call them that.'

'Where was he?' Kjeld asked, his instinct already prepared for the answer.

'He joined that cult. I can't remember if I told the other officers that when they spoke to me. I was such a mess.' Monika sniffled. 'And I know they say it's not a cult. But what kind of place takes someone's boy away for six months and tells him he's not allowed to contact his friends and family?'

'They took him?'

'Well, no. He was an adult so I suppose that means he joined them willingly. Or, at least, that's what I'm sure everyone would say. But they must have said something to convince him. To manipulate him somehow. Why else would he go there?'

'Maybe they thought they could help him with his drug problem?'

Monika scoffed. 'What could a bunch of weird cultists – sorry, hippies – do for my son that I couldn't? They pushed him towards this. I know they did.'

Kjeld took out his phone and pulled up a photo of Louisa for Monika to see. 'Did you ever see Jonny in the company of this woman?'

Monika leaned forward, looking at the photo for a solid ten seconds before shaking her head.

'What about this photo? Do you recognise her?' Kjeld scrolled to a photograph of Andrea.

'Yes, that woman came by the house once.'

'Do you remember why?'

Monika shook her head. 'Nothing good, I'm sure. I just assumed she was the one getting him the drugs. She looked like the type. But I don't know for certain. As soon as they saw me she left.'

Kjeld slipped the phone back into his pocket. 'I appreciate you taking the time to talk to me today, Fru Lindh. Especially in light of everything. But if it gives you any solace I don't agree with my colleagues. I think Jonny was murdered.'

Monika sighed. 'Does it matter?'

'It does to me.'

Kjeld pushed out his chair and stood up. Balder crawled out from under the kitchen table and began clawing at his pant leg. Kjeld reached down and scratched the dog behind his ear. Then he turned his attention back to Monika. 'Is there anything I can do for you before I go?'

Monika frowned. 'No, thank you.' She paused. 'Not unless you want a dog.'

Chapter 49

Bengt hunched over the kitchen table, rearranging the dates in his agenda to account for Tove's appointment with the therapist. It hadn't been easy getting her in on short notice, but Liam had made some calls to a few colleagues and managed to fast-track her for an evaluation session with one of the city's leading child trauma therapists. Of course, the appointment was smack dab in the middle of the day, which meant that Bengt had to not only pull her out of school for the afternoon but also reschedule his own meetings.

He made a note to call that gallery owner he was working with in Stockholm about postponing the opening of the exhibit by a few weeks. That would give him the opportunity to spend more time with Tove and ensure that the incident hadn't caused any lasting emotional damage. Perhaps he could even have the paintings from his studio shipped ahead of time to save on extra travel. Then he could still attend all of his studio lectures at the university and make it to the meeting for the parents of the pupils of Stella's School of Dance.

Liam set a glass of white wine in front of Bengt and pulled out a chair to sit beside him. 'You've been poring over that calendar for hours. Why don't you take a break?'

'I think I've just about fit everything in.' Bengt crossed off a dentist appointment that he'd moved to the following week.

'I can take some of that responsibility off your hands, you know.'

'It's important to me that I work it out myself,' Bengt said quickly. A second later he realised that he might have sounded cold or ungrateful and turned his attention to Liam. A crooked smile crossed his lips. 'Not that I don't appreciate it. You do too much as it is. I already don't know how to repay you.'

'You don't have to.' Liam took a sip from his own glass before setting it down on the table.

Bengt closed his diary and pushed it to the side of the table. Then he picked up the glass and took a sip. Dry, just as he liked it. He took another sip, allowing the intense aromatic flavour of honey and citrus blossom to roll over his tongue, before setting it back down. The taste was delicious and he felt a twinge of guilt for enjoying it. Liam had been nothing but attentive to him since the day they met and Bengt couldn't help but feel slightly undeserving. He enjoyed being doted on. Loved the romantic gestures. That was something that he'd never received from Kjeld. Not overtly at least. But despite how much he craved the attention, he couldn't help but be awkward about it. Not to mention quietly ashamed for wanting it. And for wanting more.

'Have you thought about my proposal?'

Bengt ran his fingers back through his hair, sweeping that chunk of white, which had grown over the front of his dark hair away from his face. His hair was thinner than it used to be, but he was grateful to have it. Of all the traumas that came with radiation, the hair loss had been the one to truly break him. He could handle the aches, the pains, the gaps of lucidity from the abundance of medications, and the general lethargy that made even the simplest of tasks unbearably difficult. But seeing himself in the mirror, gaunt and hairless, had been the worst.

When his scans finally came back clear after months of waiting, he'd purposefully put on an extra fifteen pounds above his normal weight just to avoid seeing his cheekbones press out against his skin. And when his hair came back he refused to trim it above his ears as he used to wear it. Anything not to look like that shadow of a man he'd once been. It was vain, he knew, but he didn't care. He still had nightmares of accidentally pulling out clumps of hair in his sleep.

'Hm?' Bengt looked up at Liam, his thoughts distracted.

'London.'

'Oh.' Bengt took another sip of wine to avoid answering too quickly. The truth was he hadn't thought much about Liam's suggestion that the three of them move to London. Not because he didn't want to. London was an artist's dream. And the change would have been good for his relationship with Liam. A fresh start, so to speak. But the entire thing took him by surprise. And Bengt didn't know how to broach that subject with Kjeld. Nor did he think it was entirely fair for him to do so. 'I don't know if it's the right time. It feels so sudden. And with everything going on with Tove …'

'A new experience would be exciting for her. We could put her in a private school that would help her hone her interests and talents. She's still young so she'd learn the language quickly. And we could get a nice house with a garden. Maybe even a dog?'

Bengt cringed. 'No, not a dog.'

'I've been offered an amazing position at Guys' Hospital as clinical director of their cancer centre. Aside from being incredibly prestigious the salary is extraordinary. Tove would want for nothing.'

'She doesn't want for anything now.' Bengt ran his thumb over his lower lip, wiping off a stray drop of wine. 'Besides I really don't think it's fair.'

'Fair?'

'To Kjeld.'

Liam scoffed and leaned back in his chair. 'And when has Kjeld ever been fair to us?'

'Liam …'

'I'm serious. He has been a thorn in the side of our relationship since the very beginning.' Bengt opened his mouth to speak, but Liam cut him off. 'And before you say that it was your fault for not breaking it off with him before getting together with me, let me remind you *why* you cheated on him in the first place. Because he didn't put your needs and Tove's needs above his own. That man is selfish and irresponsible when it comes to other people's emotions. You've said it yourself that he'll never change. Why should you, and Tove for that matter, spend your entire lives waiting for him to get his act together? If he truly cares about what is going on in your life and in his daughter's life then why isn't he here?'

'You know his work hours are unpredictable.'

'Are they? Because it seems to me that he purposefully makes them that way.'

Bengt knitted his brows together. Liam wasn't wrong, but Bengt still had difficulty hearing other people say harsh truths about Kjeld. It was one thing for Bengt to be critical of him, but for reasons he couldn't quite explain he always felt a tad protective of the man in the presence of others. Part of it was because of their history and part of it was something Bengt didn't like to admit. A certain regret that maybe he'd made the wrong decision. This by no means diminished his love for Liam, which was entirely different from the love he'd had for Kjeld. But it did make him wonder if things could have been repaired if he hadn't been so starved for a certain kind of attention. Attention that Kjeld simply wasn't capable of giving him. Maybe anyone.

Liam reached out and placed his hand over Bengt's. There was a burgeoning bruise atop the skin of Liam's knuckles he hadn't noticed before. The colour was a deep purple and bulged against his darker skin tone.

'What happened to your hand?' Bengt knew that Liam had been working volunteer shifts at the prison hospital recently and suddenly the image of an inmate attacking him flashed across his mind.

Liam pulled his hand back and shifted his gaze to the wine. 'It's nothing. I caught it in the car door.'

He took another sip and quickly changed the conversation back to Kjeld. And while Bengt didn't feel like he was being lied to, he did have the odd sensation that Liam wasn't being entirely honest with him. But he shook off the feeling as a by-product of stress. Liam had no reason to be deceitful.

Liam cleared his throat. 'One of these days Kjeld's going to do something that really hurts Tove. And then what? I know you, Bengt. You'll carry that guilt for him. That's what you always do. You never let Kjeld take responsibility for his own actions. You always spare him the consequences by taking them on yourself.'

'Kjeld has a lot going on in his life. I don't think it's our place to judge.'

'You're too generous. You're always waiting for him to have an epiphany. Don't you think he would have by now? Honestly, I think us moving to London would be good for him, too.'

There was a roundabout logic to Liam's reasoning that Bengt couldn't deny. Maybe moving far away would be the kick Kjeld needed to put his daughter first. But that would mean leaving everything Bengt knew behind. Including the man he couldn't quite get out of his thoughts.

'Maybe you're right.' Bengt glanced down at his fingers. Bits of dried paint were stuck underneath his nails and stained the pads of his fingertips. He tried scratching it off, but it was too deep into the grooves of his skin. 'But if Kjeld doesn't agree then I'd have to take him to court for full custody.'

And that was something Bengt hoped he'd never have to do.

Liam reached over and placed his unbruised hand on Bengt's forearm. He smiled. It was a charismatic smile. Charming. The kind that reached his eyes and exuded true affection. But instead of soothing his worries, it made Bengt feel like he was at fault for something. 'One step at a time. First you have to tell him.'

Bengt exhaled a heavy sigh and drank the rest of his wine in a single gulp.

If only it were that easy.

Chapter 50

The motion detector on the outdoor camera activated, sending a message to Daniel's phone. It buzzed on the desk and he slipped off his noise-cancelling headphones to check the alert. The camera was connected to an app that let him know if anyone was in the vicinity of his house. Normally he used it to notify him when the postman delivered packages. He enjoyed listening to loud music while he worked and if he was wearing his headphones he very rarely heard the doorbell. But lately he'd been using the cameras to make sure no one was snooping around his lawn. He didn't have any proof that anyone was nosing around where they shouldn't be, but there had been a rash of break-ins around the neighbourhood and he didn't want to take any chances.

Daniel wasn't the sort of person who was willing to take chances. He'd always been a meticulous man. Meticulous about his business, about his contacts, about his finances. And after the events six years ago, he was meticulous about his safety.

He turned his phone horizontally to enlarge the image file. It was a short ten-second clip from the camera above the back door to the house. He played it to the end, but couldn't make out anything. There was too much rain.

Maybe that's what set it off.

He set his phone back down on the desk and refocused his attention on the computer screen. There had been a time when he would have paid someone else to do this kind of low-level financial work. But ever since the trial he'd been essentially barred from working with any reputable, high-paying companies. All he had was the occasional private client. Most of them didn't know who he was, which made doing business with them easier. Others did and refused to pay him his worth. That's what happened when you fucked up. And Daniel had fucked up big time.

But he was alive. Which was more than he could say for his old colleagues.

His phone buzzed again. This time the alert was from the camera on the side window. Again he opened the digital file and played the ten-second clip. The front of the lens was awash in rain. It was coming down heavy, hitting the roof hard. Might have even been hail.

'Stupid sensor,' Daniel grumbled.

His stomach grumbled with hunger and he glanced at the time on his computer. Shit, it was already late. Not that time had the same meaning anymore. He lived alone now. His wife had taken the kids and refused to call him except for his rare weekends with them. And even those were few and far between. His kids were embarrassed by him. They shared their mother's shame. He'd destroyed the family with his greed. And everyone knew about it.

He pushed his ergonomic chair away from the desk and stood up. He stretched his arms above his head, cracking the joints in his upper back. He needed to remember not to sit for such long periods at a time.

Daniel made his way down the stairs to the kitchen. He opened his fridge. All he had was some leftover takeaway, a block of smooth cheese, and half a bottle of pinot grigio. He groaned and took out the takeaway. When he opened the box, however, he was met with a sour stench. Spoiled. He closed it up and tossed it in the trash. Then he grabbed the block of cheese and set it on the counter beside a loaf of bread.

'Looks like you're back to the good ol' college meals, buddy,' he said aloud to himself.

He took a cheese knife from the drawer and removed the block from the package.

Upstairs his phone vibrated.

Daniel drew the cheese knife over the block, cutting off three thick slices. Maybe he would have that pinot, though. Shame to let it go to waste.

He turned back towards the refrigerator. From the corner of his eye he caught the image of a dark shadow crossing in front of the window. His heart leapt into his throat.

He scrambled into the living room just in time to see the shadow pass the next window, heading for the front door.

It's one of them. They're after me again.

He dropped the cheese knife and dashed upstairs to his office. His heart was racing and he thought he heard the sounds of someone tugging on the front door handle. His phone vibrated on his desk. He snatched it up and dialled 112.

A young woman answered after the first ring. 'This is the police. How can I assist you?'

'This is Daniel Santelmann. You have to send someone over to my house right away! Someone's trying to kill me.'

Chapter 51

Fredag | Friday

Portside wasn't exactly an exclusive club, but it catered to a particular clientele that was willing to splurge more on drinks than at the average city club. It was located in an unused shipping warehouse at the eastern end of the port of Gothenburg. On the outside the building was a brick and steel eyesore with a metal roof that had rusted green over years of disuse and lack of upkeep. The inside, however, boasted a large open dance floor and stage, where the current DJ was yelling out to a shoulder-to-shoulder crowd of throbbing bodies against a pulsating backbeat that made it impossible for Kjeld to hear his own thoughts.

The average age of Portside's clubgoers appeared to range from early twenties to late forties, but the frenetic flashing of strobe lights and hip-gyrating motions of the crowd made it difficult to tell one person apart from the other. Kjeld skirted his way around the edge of the club to the chic bar, which stretched nearly the entire length of the side wall. The endless bottles on the back wall were lit up by neon lights of blue and green. The music thumped up his body through the floor, reverberating an uncomfortable trill in his chest. He craned his neck over the cluster of skimpily dressed women and men reeking of sweat and an overabundance of cologne, in search of anything that might indicate whether this was the place the killer had kidnapped Jonny.

The bartender, a young man with a fake tan and teeth so white that they glowed translucent against the blacklight spot lamps from behind the bar, leaned over the counter. 'What can I get you?'

Kjeld took out his phone and held up a photograph of Jonny. 'You ever see this guy around here?'

The bartender's expression faltered but was quickly replaced with a cocky smirk. 'Who's asking?'

'I am.'

'You a cop?'

'Does it matter?'

The bartender wiped a wet rag over the counter, doing very little to clean up the sticky residue from spilled drinks. Then he shrugged. 'He's not here tonight.'

'So, you have seen him?'

'Of course I've seen him. The little shit used to work here. I say used to, but that didn't stop him from sneaking in after he quit and pouring himself some free drinks. I don't care about the cover charge, mind you, but alcohol is expensive.'

'What kind of work did he do?' Kjeld raised his voice. He could barely hear himself over the music, let alone the bartender.

The bartender nodded. 'He worked the cages.'

'Cages?'

The bartender motioned to the dance cages, which hung in the air above the crowd. They looked like they were floating, but Kjeld could see the extensive high-tension wire connecting them to the ceiling. In each of the cages, lit up by the black light strobes from the stage and ceiling, was a shirtless man or a bikini-clad woman dancing to the beat of the music.

'When did he stop working here?' Kjeld asked.

'About six months ago.' The bartender filled two beers and set them on the counter for his colleague who was bustling to keep up with the crowd.

That same pinch of guilt he'd experienced when he spoke to Monika Lindh behind his colleagues' backs prickled him. Kjeld took out his phone and sent Esme a quick text informing her that Jonny used to be employed at the club. It didn't go through. Dammit. He didn't have a signal. Then he glanced up into the rafters, searching for any signs of security cameras. 'Is there CCTV in this place?'

The bartender snorted a laugh. 'Hell no, man. I mean, this place is on the level. It's legit, but not everything that goes on in the dark is if you catch my meaning. Besides, the owner takes his privacy very seriously. And so do many of the people he entertains.'

The bartender motioned to a woman at the other end of the bar surrounded by a crowd of men. Kjeld recognised the woman as an actress made famous on one of those reality shows where people had to survive stark naked on a desert island. One of the men beside her looked like a city council representative, but Kjeld couldn't be certain.

'When did you last see him?'

'The owner?'

'The guy in the photograph.'

'Oh, shit, man. I don't know. A few nights ago?'

'Was he with anyone?'

'Look, are you going to buy a drink or what?'

Kjeld reached into his pocket and took out a five-hundred kronor note, slapping it on the counter. The bartender reached for it, but Kjeld held on to it. 'Was he with anyone?'

The bartender hesitated again, his eyes darting to the left.

Kjeld followed his gaze and caught a glimpse of a man in a purple tracksuit passing something in his hand to one of the clubgoers. The man smiled a toothy grin and gave the other person a half hug which almost, but not entirely, hid the action of the clubgoer slipping cash into his pocket.

'Hey!' Kjeld called out to the man.

The man looked up, eyes wide with surprise when his gaze locked with Kjeld's. They both froze in place. It only took a second for Kjeld to recognise him. And to see the handle of a pistol tucked in his slacks.

Vidar Rask.

'Son of a bitch,' Kjeld mumbled.

Then Vidar bolted.

Chapter 52

Kjeld broke into a run after Vidar, but his sprint was short-lived. The density of the people in front of the stage had increased and moving through them was like pushing against a wall. The only benefit to Kjeld's own difficulty manoeuvring through the congestion of bodies was that it was equally difficult for Vidar, who looked to be using brute force to shove people out of his way.

Kjeld felt like a salmon trying to swim upriver. He turned his body sidelong, trying to slip between the mob. Someone shoved him from behind. Another yelled at him. But Kjeld kept his attention glued to Vidar's bald head as he squirrelled through the horde of dancing bodies on his way to the opposite end of the club, ignoring the thick stench of sweat and alcohol as he tried to catch up to him.

When Vidar reached the edge of the dance floor he made a dash down a dark corridor along the side of the stage. Kjeld was a few seconds behind him. Not far, but enough for him to lose sight of him around the corner.

Kjeld rushed after him, following the irritated complaints of young women in the toilet queue whom Vidar had bumped into in the dark, middle fingers accompanied by an endless holler of colourful profanity. At the end of the corridor a door flapped closed. Kjeld threw it open and hurried out into a large open space that composed the back of the old shipping warehouse, separated from the rest of the club by a makeshift wall covered in soundproof tiles to ensure the deafening roar of music stayed in the front of the building. The odour of liquor and bodies was gone. Instantly replaced by the smell of dust, moulding pallets, and rusted metal.

Kjeld stepped out into the open. Above him the rain clattered against the metal roof, but the rest of the room was quiet. He waited, using the moment to catch his breath.

The sound of running footsteps resounded from his left. He caught a glimpse of a shadow out of the corner of his eye and made a mad dash in that direction.

'Vidar! Stop!' Kjeld called out. His voice echoed through the high rafters.

But Vidar didn't stop. He cut across the floor in front of him, ducking behind piles of pallets as he headed towards the main loading bay at the back of the warehouse.

'Vidar!'

His shout frightened a group of pigeons huddled together on an overhead beam and they frantically flew in front of him to another crossbar, blocking his view of Vidar, who'd already leapt down to a loading ramp. Kjeld waved the pigeons away and bolted after him. His heart pounded in his chest and his breath heaved against the damp cool air of the warehouse. He jumped down the ramp, stumbled as he nearly rolled his ankle, and then picked up his pace, following him out into the night and the rain.

But Vidar was gone.

He glanced from side to side, searching for any trace of the man. Outside was a large expanse of open tarmac with no cars in sight. In front of him were the tall smoking towers of the city energy plant. To the right was the port, the mouth of the Göta river, black beneath the night sky.

Where was he?

261

A reverberating clang rang out. Kjeld spun on his heel. Three drunken clubgoers laughed as one of their friends stumbled into a rubbish bin, dropping his beer. They didn't notice Kjeld in the dark and hurried through the rain towards the nearest bus stop.

When he turned back to the warehouse he was met with the barrel of a gun in his face.

Chapter 53

Kjeld slowly raised his hands in front of him, palms out. 'Don't do anything stupid.'

'What? Like chase a guy with a gun through a warehouse? Don't do anything stupid like that?' Vidar took a step closer, weapon still raised. He had a nervous sweat on his brow and his chest was heaving exhausted breaths from the chase. His eyes, already wide and protruding, had a glossy tinge to them. He was high.

'I'm an unarmed police officer, Vidar. If you shoot me you'll be in a hell of a lot of trouble.'

'Only if I get caught. And I know a thing or two about not getting caught.' Vidar turned his head to the side and spat out a glob of phlegm. Then he wiped his lips on the side of his shoulder. He waved the gun. 'What the fuck, Kjeld? You trying to get me killed or something.'

'That was never my intention.'

Vidar groaned and dropped his arm, slipping the gun into the pocket of his tracksuit jacket. 'You are a fucking blight on my life, man. Every time you show up shit goes to hell in a fucking handbasket. You know that?'

Kjeld lowered his arms before nodding to Vidar's pocket. 'Did you put the safety back on before you stuck that thing so close to your privates?'

Vidar furrowed his bushy caterpillar brows before checking the gun to make sure the safety was in place. It was.

'What the hell do you think you're doing chasing me through a club full of clients? Do you know who owns this place? Do you know the shit storm I'd be in if they saw me talking to you?'

'We're just having a chat, Vidar. Nothing more.'

Vidar laughed and then spat up another wad of yellow phlegm on the tarmac. 'Just having a chat! It's never just having a chat with you. It's always "tell me what I want to know before I slam your face into the pavement."'

'I don't think we need to resort to that, do you?'

Vidar waved a dismissive hand at Kjeld and started back towards the warehouse so as to get out of the rain. 'Just ask me whatever it is you've come to ask and get the fuck out of here before someone sees you. I swear to God, giving you some low-key gang gossip on a couple of occasions does not give you the right to roll up on me at my place of business.'

Kjeld followed after him, keeping a close eye on their surroundings to ensure they weren't being watched. For all of Vidar's yammering and complaints, he had a point. Being seen with him wasn't exactly good for the drug business. And even though Kjeld didn't know all of the ins and outs of Portside's management, it wasn't much of a stretch to assume the owners were involved in something illegal. Vidar's presence there was proof enough of that.

'I'm here about Jonny Lindh.'

'Jonny who?'

Kjeld took out his mobile phone and pulled up the photo of Jonny.

Vidar pursed his lips and rolled his head to the side, uninterested. 'Okay, yeah. I've seen that guy around. What about him?'

'When was the last time you saw him?'

'Why? He do something naughty? Did he sell some weed to

264

a few kids? Look, if you're trying to follow a drug trail back to me, you can forget about it. Once it's out of my hands, it's out of my hands. I'm not responsible for who shares what with who or anything that goes down. It's a free market, you see.'

'This isn't drugs, Vidar. It's homicide.'

Vidar double blinked. 'Jonny's dead?'

'He downed a punch bowl full of antifreeze.'

Vidar gagged. 'Jesus Christ. I didn't give him antifreeze, if that's what you're asking.'

'I know you didn't. But I need to know what you did give him and when you saw him last.'

Vidar shook his head. 'Fuck, man. I don't know. I gave him some pills, a bit of coke. Maybe some acid. Not much, just whatever I had on me. The guy was having a rough day. He was looking for something to chase away the demons. You know. So I gave him a cocktail of the good stuff. For a bargain, too, I might add.'

'When was this?' Kjeld asked.

'A week ago, maybe? It's not like I have a personal assistant keeping track for me.'

'Was he one of your regulars?'

Vidar frowned. Above them the rain clattered against the metal roof, scaring a group of huddled pigeons into a corner of the rafters.

'Was he?' Kjeld pressed.

'He used to be. You know the kid's story. He was a fucking mess. I don't think he worked a single day sober. Then one day he just left.'

'Where'd he go?'

Vidar smirked. A lightbulb seemed to go off in his mind. 'Ah, *that's* what you're interested in. Well, let me tell you, that is a very interesting twist to the story.'

'Don't jerk me around, Vidar. I've got other people I'd rather be wasting my time with.'

'Like that cute little partner of yours? This is twice in a row now without her. You two get into a fight or something?'

'You said Jonny left. Where did he go?'

'He shacked it up with those second-coming psychos.'

Kjeld frowned. 'If you're talking about Second Life, I already know Jonny was involved with them.'

'But did you know he got himself clean after he joined them? I know because I ran into him outside an Espresso House in the city centre one day. He looked good. He was off the shit. Lucid. And then last week he just shows back up here on my doorstep begging for anything to make the pain go away. Poor baby.' Vidar's lips curled in a fake pout. 'I have a mantra. Once an addict, always an addict. But this was different. Jonny was scared.'

'Scared of what?'

Vidar shrugged. 'Hell if I know.'

Kjeld took out his phone and pulled up a photograph of Louisa. 'Did you ever see him with this woman?'

Vidar shook his head. 'No, I've never seen her. But there was another woman.'

'Who?'

'Chestnut-coloured hair. Long, wavy. She was tall. Sexy face. But she was dressed weird.'

'Weird how?'

'She wore a high-cut turtleneck with sleeves that stretched over her knuckles. Like she was purposefully hiding her body. Pity, too. She looked like she was in good shape.'

Chapter 54

Daniel Santelmann's two-storey house in Lundby was less impressive than Esme expected after reading up on him. And if she hadn't already refreshed her memory of his case, she might have thought the myriad of security cameras he'd set up around his home's exterior were overkill for the neighbourhood. His case wasn't as memorable as Louisa's or Jonny's, although it had received national attention, but that was mostly because of the circumstances that resulted in the murders than the actual murders themselves.

Seven years ago, Daniel Santelmann had been a prominent businessman in Gothenburg's financial district. He was one of those movers and shakers. The kind who made million-dollar deals before lunch and considered that a slow day. When it was discovered he'd been embezzling money off the various companies he did business with and helping more prominent CEOs do the same, it erupted in a nationwide scandal.

The most prominent company, and the one that propelled the case into the media, was an overseas real estate investment firm that sold non-existent rental properties to small-time home-owners with the promise of a return on investment. Thousands of people lost their life savings, many falling into bankruptcy.

Daniel Santelmann hadn't been the only one involved in this scheme, he wasn't even the most influential or the most to blame, but he was the one it was easiest to pin it on. And he was the one who lost everything as a result of it. His career, his wife, his kids, his expensive high-rise apartment in the city centre. Even his dog. Most tragic of all, however, was the fact that he almost lost his life.

Arvid Wibe had been a well-meaning, carefree man preparing to enter retirement when he lost his entire life savings in the real estate scam. When his wife died after he could no longer afford her medical care, he snapped. He went out to the garden shed where he kept his great-grandfather's hunting rifle. Then he drove to the city, took the elevator up to the top floor of the firm where Santelmann worked, and walked mindlessly into the boardroom where he killed everyone he blamed for the deal that lost him everything. Everyone but Daniel Santelmann, who cowered beneath a dead man's body, praying not to be noticed.

But none of that seemed to change the fact that he was an insufferable arsehole. And after a few minutes of being in his house, Esme could understand why someone might want to kill him.

'You certainly have a fancy camera system set-up here,' Sixten said as he walked back into the living room from Daniel's office.

'Because unlike the police I anticipated the possibility that someone might come after me.'

'What makes you think that?' Esme asked.

Daniel shot her a dull, irritated glare. 'Oh, I don't know. Maybe because someone tried it once before?'

'Do you have reason to believe that someone might want to harm you?'

'Do I need a reason? If I understand you two correctly it sounds like this serial killer you're chasing doesn't need much of a reason to go after his victims. But why should I have a reason to think I could be one of them?'

268

Esme placed photos of Louisa, Jonny, and Andrea on the coffee table. She still didn't know if Andrea was truly involved in the same case, but she couldn't deny the fact that there had been multiple murders across the city and Andrea was one of them. And Kjeld had a hunch there was something more to Andrea's case than met the eye. It couldn't hurt to put her in the line-up. Maybe they'd accidentally stumble onto something important. 'Have you ever seen any of these people before?'

Daniel gave the photos little more than a cursory glance. 'Yeah, sure. Those two were in the news the other day.'

Esme motioned to Andrea's photo. 'And her?'

'Never seen her before.'

'Officers responded to an emergency call from your residence yesterday. Can you tell us about that?'

Daniel rolled his eyes. 'There was someone sneaking around my house.'

'Did you get a good look at them?' Esme asked.

'No. It was dark and it was raining.'

'What about your fancy cameras? Any of them pick this person up?' Sixten stood beside Esme's chair, using the backrest to casually lean his weight against. It struck her as interesting that he seemed so much more relaxed in Daniel's presence than he had in front of Andrea's widow.

'No, unfortunately they did not. Nothing more than shadows. I explained all of this to the officers who came by.'

'Not so fancy then, I guess.'

'I want to know what the police plan to do about all of this.' Daniel huffed as he poured himself a glass of whisky from a decanter on the shelf. He acted tough, but Esme had seen his hand shaking all night. He was scared. 'I'm sick of answering these inane questions. If someone is trying to kill me then I want protection.'

'We're here to assess the possible danger to you, Herr Santelmann,' Esme said. 'That's why we're asking all of these questions. They might not seem important, but they are. And if it looks like we have a reason to be concerned we will do everything in our power to make sure you're safe and protected.'

Daniel scoffed. 'Why do I not feel relieved? I have a state-of-the-art security system. Nothing is supposed to be able to get past these cameras. Nothing. Not even a fox.'

'You get a lot of foxes trying to break into houses here in Lundby?'

Daniel ignored Sixten's smug comment. 'It's the best equipment money can buy. And yet yesterday someone managed to get close enough to my door without being caught on the images. That means they know my system. They know the weak spots. Someone has been watching me.'

'We tried to get hold of you the other day, but you didn't answer.'

'I was visiting my sister.'

'And where does she live?'

'Jönköping.' Daniel drank the entire dram in a single gulp and poured himself another. 'I was there for four days. I got back late last night and spent the evening working.'

Esme glanced at Sixten. 'Let's do a search around the house and the perimeter. Check for any signs that someone has broken in or disturbed the surveillance cameras.'

Sixten nodded.

Esme returned her focus to Daniel. 'I'll make a call into the station about getting an officer to watch your house.'

Daniel gave a disbelieving snort. 'One officer?'

'You're welcome to hire someone else, if you prefer,' Esme said, knowing full well that Daniel couldn't afford personal security. She'd looked him up online. He was barred from working in any reputable financial position and was relegated to doing freelance assessment work for private clients. But from the look of his home, that work wasn't very successful.

Daniel sneered and slumped down on his sofa.

Esme stood up and motioned for Sixten to follow her. Once they were at the opposite end of the living room near the downstairs corridor, out of range of Daniel's hearing, she spoke. 'You check the ground floor, cellar, and exterior. I'll go through the upstairs. I remember seeing a basement window on the way in. Make sure it's locked.'

'Do you really think he could be one of the killer's targets?'

'I don't know, but it worries me that there was someone snooping around his house the other day.'

'Could have just been neighbourhood kids.'

'It could have, but I think we need to err on the side of caution.'

'Do you want me to make a call to the station?'

'That'd be great. See if Lindén is available.'

'You want to put a detective on guard duty?'

'I want someone I trust.'

'Yes, ma'am.' Sixten gave her a playful salute.

Esme shook her head to prevent herself from laughing. 'God, you really are insufferable sometimes.'

Sixten's expression faltered. 'Is that why Kjeld doesn't want me on the team?'

'What do you mean he doesn't want you on the team?'

'I know he doesn't like me.'

'He likes you. We all do.'

'You don't have to say that just to be nice. I know he just tolerates me because he has to. And given a choice I think it's clear he'd rather have someone else.'

'Kjeld doesn't just tolerate you, Sixten. That's just how he is. It takes time for him to adjust to change. You actually share something in common.'

'We do?'

'Yeah, he's equally insufferable at times.'

Sixten smiled in relief.

Daniel, a few more drinks in his system, knocked over the television remote from the coffee table, sending it clattering to the floor. 'I hope whoever you send to guard me is bigger than a twelve-year-old girl!'

Esme took a deep, calming breath. 'I'm going to check upstairs and use the bathroom. Meet you back down here in ten minutes?'

'Sure thing, boss.'

Esme flushed the toilet and washed her hands in the sink. Daniel had an array of various soaps sitting on the vanity, none of which appeared to be antibacterial, so she used all of them just to be safe. Then she looked at herself in the high-gloss mirror and tried not to let Daniel's drunken comment discourage her. She didn't think she looked like a twelve-year-old. People had made fun of her size before. It wasn't that she was below average height, but she was thin-framed and her fringe did give her a younger appearance. She'd had more than one boyfriend in the past suggest that she grow it out because it would make her look older and more attractive. More feminine. That only seemed to have the opposite effect on her. She kept it to spite those kinds of misogynistic comments. But now that she looked at herself in the mirror, she wondered if it was too harshly cut. Too childish.

Was that the reason why she was alone?

She swept her palm over her forehead, pulling her fringe back, and admired her forehead. The lack of fringe made her face look longer. Slenderer. Perhaps a little bit older. But it didn't change her bushy eyebrows or her small nose. Nor did it change the fact that her lips had the tendency to pull downwards at the corners in a natural pout when she made a neutral expression. She let go of her fringe and matted it back down with her fingers. It was thick and fell into place with little trouble. Then she tied the rest of her hair into a low ponytail.

Not that she cared what people like Daniel said or thought about her. Their opinions didn't matter. Esme liked how she looked. But more than that, she was comfortable with her appearance. It reminded her that she was an individual while also making her feel safe.

She stepped out of the bathroom and did another sweep of the upstairs bedrooms. There was an uncomfortable loneliness to the master bedroom that reminded her of her own apartment. She checked the windows and the closets. Locked and empty. Then she moved on to the second bedroom, which doubled as Daniel's office. Also empty. When she reached the third bedroom she paused in the doorway. It was a little boy's room. Probably one of Daniel's children. The wall above the bed was decorated in galaxy wallpaper with planets and shooting stars. The duvet matched, depicting a pattern of rocket ships against a dark blue background. Even the lamp was made to look like a configuration of the solar system. When she flicked on the switch, each planet lit up in various colours. Red. Green. Blue. Purple. The rings of Saturn were made of some kind of phosphorescent material that glittered under the light.

Esme felt a sentimental tug in her chest. Followed by an unexpected sorrow she couldn't quite explain.

Then the lights went out. The entire house shrouded in blackness.

She turned into the corridor, quickly removing her weapon from its holster.

'Sixten?' she called out. 'Daniel?'

She heard a rustle from downstairs, followed by a clatter.

'Sixten?'

She made her way to the stairs.

No response. Only silence.

'Sixten? Are you okay?'

The crack of a gunshot cutting through the silence was her only answer.

Chapter 55

Esme bolted down the stairs, gun drawn. She paused just before she reached the ground floor and peeked around the corner. She raised her weapon, checking her blind spots. The lights were out and she pressed her back up against a wall, waiting for her eyes to adjust. The low thump of her heartbeat echoed in her ears.

She stepped off the stairs and made her way into the living room where she found Daniel crouched in a corner behind the sofa. He nearly shrieked when he saw her, his face pale with fear. Esme held up a finger to her lips before mouthing, "Which way?" Daniel raised a shaky arm and pointed towards the kitchen.

Esme stepped through to the dining room. Empty. She tried the nearest light switch, but it didn't work. Someone had cut the power. She inched forward and checked behind the doorway before pressing on into the kitchen.

The room was a mess. On the floor a carton of tropical fruit juice had fallen, spilling out across the linoleum. Her gaze darted to the left where a knife was missing from the stainless-steel magnetic knife rack above the counter. She steadied her grip, stepping over the spilled juice. She searched the space for Sixten, but he was nowhere to be seen. That was when she noticed that the door at the back of the kitchen to the right of the pantry was ajar. The basement.

She quickly checked the corridor, which circled back to the living room, ensuring no one was hiding in the downstairs toilet. Then she headed back towards the stairwell.

She slipped a small torch from her back pocket and braced it against the wrist of her right hand. The light cast a sharp beam down the steps, illuminating Sixten's collapsed figure at the bottom. A bloody knife lying beside him.

Esme held back her instinct to rush down the stairs, taking each step in a cautious stride, until she was at the bottom. She searched the entire basement for signs of anyone else before making her way back to Sixten. Then she holstered her weapon, called in an "officer down" on her mobile phone, and checked the younger detective for a pulse.

Sixten was lying on his side, one hand dangling limply over his belly, which was bleeding out onto the mouldy concrete. He had a pulse, but it was faint.

'I took a shot, but I missed,' Sixten wheezed. 'I'm sorry, boss ...'

'Don't worry. Help is on its way. I'm going to move you so I can get a better look at that wound.' Esme rolled the younger detective over onto his back and tore open his shirt. Aside from a weak groan, Sixten barely reacted to being repositioned. There was so much blood Esme could barely see skin. She pressed her bare hands on the wound. A breathy hiss escaped Sixten's lips as he slipped into unconsciousness. 'Don't die on me, Sixten. Not after forcing me to listen to your stupid jokes for the last few months. Don't you fucking dare.'

The blood seeped through her fingers. Esme pressed harder. She yelled upstairs for help. Yelled until her voice was hoarse and the muscles in her forearms went numb from holding pressure to Sixten's belly.

'Holy shit. Holy shit. Is he dead?'

For a split second Esme imagined it was Kjeld's voice, but

when she looked up she saw Daniel, face taut in shock at the sight of Sixten.

'I need help! Get me something to push into this wound! I can't let him die.' Esme pushed down harder on Sixten's stomach, but the blood continued to seep through her fingers. She adjusted her position and bore her full weight down on his abdomen. 'Wake up, you stupid rookie! Wake up!'

Sixten's face went white. Still Esme continued to press on the gash in his belly. She couldn't feel her fingers anymore. They'd disappeared into the blood, which pooled fast, spilling out over Sixten's side and staining the ground around her knees.

In the background Esme heard Daniel shouting for help, but she kept her focus on Sixten. The younger detective's eyelids drooped. Skin sallow. The muscles in Esme's arms shuddered as she pushed her last bit of strength onto Sixten's wound.

By the time the paramedics arrived she'd lost all feeling in her arms and Sixten had stopped breathing.

Chapter 56

Kjeld stood in the corridor outside Sixten's hospital room, peering in the small window at the figure on the bed. Esme had called him on impulse soon after arriving at Sahlgrenska. She'd been in a panic, overwrought by what had happened and barely intelligible on the phone. Without thinking, Kjeld drove to the hospital to make sure she was all right. By the time he arrived, Esme was less frantic and in a subdued state of shock. Sixten, on the other hand, was in bad shape. Kjeld could barely recognise him for all of the tubes, lines, and equipment in the small space around him.

The doctors didn't have a prognosis yet. The wound to his stomach, which they'd later attributed to one of Daniel Santelmann's kitchen knives, hadn't been easy for the surgeon to repair, but for the time being it was stable. The bigger problem had been the injury sustained to Sixten's head. The doctor theorised that either by force or accident, Sixten had fallen down the stairs, possibly in pursuit of his attacker, and hit his head. The trauma resulted in a build-up of pressure on his brain that could only be relieved by putting Sixten in a medically induced coma. That was the state he was in now. Unconscious and unaware. And whenever Kjeld asked a passing nurse or physician about Sixten's condition he received the same practised reply: "Too soon to tell."

Esme walked up beside him, two cups of coffee in hand. She held one out to Kjeld. He accepted it with a grateful nod and took a sip. It was sweet. Disgustingly sweet. Creamy. And he winced from the taste.

'Oh, shit. That one's mine. Caramel cappuccino.' Esme took the cup from Kjeld and gave him the other.

'I don't know how you can drink that. Tastes like chalk.' Kjeld brought the new cup to his lips in a more cautious sip.

'Better than that nasty dishwater coffee you make.'

'Mm.' Kjeld's attention returned to the window, watching for any signs of wakefulness from Sixten's unconscious form. He knew it was ridiculous to expect to see anything. Until the doctors believed it was safe to pull him out of the coma, there'd be very little to see in the way of movement or activity. They said that even if Sixten did recover from the head trauma, there was a risk that a prolonged unconscious state, however temporary, could result in adverse effects. Many of which might be lifelong. It was possible that even if he did regain consciousness and the full range of his faculties that he might not be able to return to work.

It wasn't until he looked at Esme, however, really looked at her and saw how she was feverishly trying to hide her own emotions behind a facade of stoicism, the harshness of which looked peculiar on her normally soft features, that he realised she was trying to process the guilt of Sixten's situation. Esme had been in charge, after all. He'd been injured under her watch. She'd been responsible for his safety and well-being. And her refusal to show any emotion confirmed to Kjeld that she was breaking on the inside.

'He's going to be fine,' Esme said, holding the paper cup between both hands to preserve the warmth of the beverage in her palms. Her tone didn't waver in confidence, but Kjeld had the impression she was reassuring herself.

'You don't know that.'

'No, but I choose to believe it.'

Kjeld didn't know what to believe.

He sipped the coffee. It tasted better than the sludge they made at the office, but not by much. 'We're missing something crucial on this case.'

'Kjeld, you're supposed to be on leave …'

'I think we're wrong. I don't think these are two separate cases. I think they're the same case. Andrea and Jonny were both involved in drug-related crimes. Jonny was actively trying to recruit Louisa for Second Life. Louisa, Jonny, and Daniel were all survivors of former crimes. Andrea used to traffic drugs from Romania when she first moved to Sweden. And Second Life is under investigation as a front for international drug trafficking from Eastern Europe. We should be focusing on Second Life.'

'What about Daniel?'

'I don't know, but I'm certain he's connected to this somehow. He used to do finances for private organisations that weren't exactly on the up-and-up. It's possible he could be working for Second Life.' Kjeld paused. 'Also, I spoke to Vidar again and he claims he saw Jonny talking to a suspicious woman.'

'Did he say who it was?'

'He didn't know, but he gave me a description. You should bring him in and have him sit with a sketch artist.'

'How do we know this woman isn't just a girlfriend or a stranger at a bar?'

'We don't, but I have a feeling about it.'

Esme shook her head. 'You're too close to this.'

That comment took Kjeld by surprise. 'What?'

'Well, maybe close isn't the right word.' Esme sighed into her cup. 'What I mean to say is that I think you came back to work too quickly.'

Kjeld scoffed. 'That's absurd. Work is all I have to focus on.'

'But that's not true.' Esme looked up to him. 'You've just been through a traumatising discovery with your family, you're struggling to maintain your relationship and responsibilities to your daughter, you still haven't opened up to me or Bengt about what happened with Nils, you've thrown yourself in on another high-profile case, you're the subject of perpetual media backlash, someone blew up your car, and you're getting into fights with people.'

Kjeld raised a hand to the area around his eye. It was swollen and tender to the touch. He hadn't looked in a mirror recently, but he could tell from how sore the skin was that it was bad.

'I know how long it takes for a bruise to form, Kjeld. That wasn't from the explosion.'

'It wasn't a fight,' he mumbled.

'And now you're lying to me. That hurts, Kjeld. I thought we were closer than that.' Esme shook her head and looked away from him, turning her attention back to the window. 'You know the worst of it? It's the fact that you're not even working as well as you think you are because you refuse to deal with everything else.'

Esme's words felt like a stab to the gut and for a long moment he refused to look at her. He merely stared off at the wall opposite the window, reining in his urge to argue with her. His instinct was to tell her she was wrong. While, yes, those things had been difficult to deal with, he refused to believe they were affecting his ability to focus on the investigation. He'd put his father, sister, and Nils behind him. Liam had made it clear that Bengt was also out of his reach. Yes, he'd screwed things up with Tove again, but he could fix that. He could figure out a way to make that work. Just like he could figure out this case.

But logic told him that Esme was telling him the truth. His refusal to accept that he was incapable of sweeping these events under the rug and moving on was blinding him to his own insecurities.

'I can't change those things,' Kjeld said after a pause. 'I can't go back and change my relationship with my father or my sister. I can't change what Nils did or the fact that I didn't see it soon enough. Or didn't want to see it.'

'Nobody is asking you to change anything, Kjeld. *I'm* not asking you to change anything. But I worry about you and where all of this is headed if you don't confront what's happened to you. If you won't talk with me about it, fine. But you need to talk to someone.'

That was the problem, wasn't it? There'd been a time in his life when he could have talked to Bengt about these things. A time when Bengt would have listened without judgement. Or Esme. She'd offered more than once to listen to him. But he never gave her the chance. Why? Because he was stubborn? Because he hated feeling vulnerable? Or perhaps it was simpler than that. Perhaps he was afraid that others would see him the way he saw himself. Defenceless, exposed, weak.

'I am talking to someone. I've been seeing the station therapist regularly.'

Esme raised a disbelieving brow. 'Well, from what I see, it's not helping. Maybe you need to talk to someone else.'

Esme reached out and placed a hand on his elbow. 'It's gone too far. You need to do something before it gets worse. Before you start making decisions you can't turn back from.'

There was an ache in Kjeld's chest. It was pinched and heavy, weighing him down. When he took a deep breath it caught in his throat like a piece of food that refused to be swallowed.

Esme was right. He wasn't performing at his best. Not mentally, at least.

Esme gave his elbow a gentle squeeze, bringing him out of his thoughts and into the moment.

'I know,' Kjeld said. 'And if you think it's necessary I'll find someone else to talk to. I promise. And I know I'm not technically on the case anymore—'

'You're not technically at work anymore.'

'—but I need to see this through. I have to find the person who's doing this.'

Esme let go of his arm, placing both hands on the small paper cup before she took a sip. He had the impression she was doing so in order to hide her face from him. Her eyes glistened as she looked past the window to Sixten. Liam's words echoed in his thoughts. *You're a user, Kjeld. A parasite. You latch on to good people and suck everything out of them until there's nothing left.* Had he done that to Esme? Had he ignored her pain because of his own?

'It looks like there might be some viable prints on the knife used against Sixten,' Esme said without looking at him. 'There could be DNA, too. We're on the right track with the list. We know what to look for with the victims and who to focus on. That'll make it more difficult for the killer now. He's going to mess up.'

'I hope you're right.'

'I am.'

'There is one thing that bothers me about all of this.'

'Only one?' Esme tried to joke, but it fell flat.

'How could someone orchestrate all of this without leaving a single shred of usable evidence? Why hasn't this killer made a mistake yet?'

Esme looked at him with knowing sympathy, but didn't say anything. Instead that constant concern which always seemed to wash over her face when they were talking to each other pinched her brows near the centre of her forehead.

It took Kjeld a moment to make the connection with what he'd said. Nils had also orchestrated an unbelievable amount of chaos on his own. And when he was finally caught, Kjeld suspected it wasn't because he'd made a mistake but because he wanted to be caught. Why couldn't someone else be equally capable of staying one step ahead of them?

'You should go home and get some sleep.'

'What about you?'

'I'm going to wait until the doctor comes back.' She twirled the silver ring on her thumb with one hand as she stared through the window at Sixten, the beeping of monitors filling the soundless void between them. 'I think his mother lives in the area. I should probably call her.'

Kjeld finished off the rest of the gritty coffee and crumpled up the cup before tossing it in a nearby bin. He was about to head off when he saw the corner of Esme's lip tremble. When she caught him looking, however, she inhaled a deep breath and brought the cup to her mouth.

'Sixten and I didn't get off to a good start.'

Esme almost laughed. 'Neither did we.'

'Do you remember when he introduced himself?'

'I remember he brought up Nils and you almost punched him in the nose.'

Kjeld scratched the back of his neck. 'I shouldn't have been so hard on him. He just wanted to know what it was like when we first met. He wasn't interested in Nils as a murderer. He was interested in our working relationship. He wanted to know if I was nervous to be partnered alongside a detective with such a productive track record. Someone with a good reputation.'

Esme paused before responding. 'What was it like meeting him on your first day as a detective?'

'That's the thing,' Kjeld said. 'I'd already met him. Our paths crossed earlier in my career. Back when I was still passing out parking tickets, if you can believe it.'

'I didn't know that.'

'It feels like ancient history now. Anyway, I should have been nicer to Sixten. He's a good investigator and a good person.'

Esme fell quiet, her attention drifting to the window. Kjeld followed her gaze, watching as the monitor beside Sixten's bed continued displaying the same jagged lines. He supposed that was at least a sign of hope. But when he averted his gaze back to Esme she didn't look optimistic.

'Are you okay, Esme?'

Her eyelashes fluttered in surprise at the question. He thought he saw a dampness in her eyes, but she blinked it away before giving him a smile that only half reached her eyes. 'I'm fine, Kjeld. Go get some sleep. Don't worry about me.'

Chapter 57

Kjeld hadn't been home from the hospital for more than twenty minutes before there was a knock at the door. Tired and groggy from another long day of chasing dead ends, he trudged back to the entrance and opened the door without checking the peephole.

'What the hell happened to your eye?' Bengt asked as he squeezed past Kjeld and into the apartment.

Kjeld, having once again forgotten the dark bruise that had formed along the outer edge of his eye, floundered for an appropriate response. He quickly remembered Liam's threat about seeing Bengt and thought about turning the man away, but before he could say anything Bengt was removing his coat and slipping off his shoes.

'Yeah, sure, come in,' Kjeld mumbled.

Bengt shook off the damp snowflakes from his hair and hung up his coat on the rack on the wall. Then he bent down and neatly lined up his shoes side by side on the thin doormat Kjeld rarely used before making his way further into the apartment. He'd always been a stickler about shoes in the house. It was a tradition Kjeld had all but given up when he went back to living alone.

An awkward silence filled the space between them and when

Kjeld opened his mouth the apology fell forth before he realised it. 'I'm sorry.'

Bengt blinked, confused. 'Sorry for what?'

Bengt ran his fingers back through his hair, smoothing out the droplets of water from the melted snowflakes. A rosy blush coloured his cheeks. And the reminder that Bengt was healthy – in remission from the cancer that had stretched their relationship to the literal limits – caused a knot to form in Kjeld's throat.

'Everything.'

Bengt laughed. 'Well, that certainly covers it all then, doesn't it?'

Bengt brought a finger to the side of Kjeld's eye. Kjeld flinched, not so much from pain as from surprise, and Bengt pulled his hand away as though suddenly realising that their relationship wasn't supposed to include those kinds of affectionate concerns.

'Who are you picking fights with now?'

'No one,' Kjeld lied. 'I walked into a door.'

'Are you sure a door didn't walk into you?'

Bengt brushed past him and into the living room. Compared to the place they'd once shared together, Kjeld's apartment was stark. Bare. More akin to a college student's residence than the home of a man pushing forty. And Kjeld suddenly felt a twinge of embarrassment.

The rustling of Oskar digging up the clay granules in his litter box interrupted the silence, tugging Kjeld out of his thoughts. 'Drink?'

Bengt eyed him warily. 'I really shouldn't.'

'Shouldn't have a drink or shouldn't stop by your ex's flat at—' Kjeld glanced at the clock on the wall. 'Almost one o'clock in the morning?'

'Either.' Bengt paused. 'Both.'

'Isn't Liam up waiting for you?' Kjeld hid his sneer by taking out a beer from the refrigerator.

Bengt flinched. 'No, he's working a double shift today.'

'And Tove?'

'Spending the night at her friend's house.'

'So, she's doing all right then?'

'We talked about it the next day. She hasn't brought it up since. I'm still going to take her to the therapist, just to be certain. But whatever she saw doesn't seem to bother her. I think she was just upset about how uncomfortable the rest of us were.' Bengt slowly made his way into the kitchen. He seemed suddenly cautious about keeping a formal amount of physical distance between them, putting himself just out of reach of friendliness. It was awkward. Forced. And Kjeld wasn't exactly sure how he was supposed to respond to it.

Kjeld popped the cap off the beer bottle by hooking it against the edge of the counter. 'Kids are stronger than adults. Or at least stronger than we give them credit for.'

Bengt frowned. 'I guess.'

Kjeld took a swig from the bottle. 'What are you doing here, Bengt?'

Bengt crossed his arms over his chest. 'Do you have wine?'

'Red, I think.'

'That's fine.'

Kjeld dug through the back of a cupboard for a bottle of merlot that someone had given to him after Nils's arrest. It was a cheap brand with a screw cap instead of a cork and Kjeld poured it into a coffee mug.

Bengt gave him a look when he handed it to him.

'Haven't unpacked the good stemware yet.'

'You wouldn't know good stemware if it bit you on the arse.'

'True.' Kjeld brushed past him and slumped onto the couch.

Bengt followed after and sat down beside him. Close, but not too close. Certainly not as close as Kjeld might have wanted, but closer than he expected.

'Liam and I had a fight.'

Kjeld raised a brow. 'About what?'

'You *know* what.'

Bengt's gaze drifted to the bruise on Kjeld's eye and Kjeld turned his face sideways to hide it.

'He didn't agree with your decision to paint the living room that horrific shade of chartreuse? Is that it?'

'Cut the shit, Kjeld.'

'Okay, okay. I'm sorry the two of you got into a fight over me.'

'Are you?'

'No.'

Bengt groaned.

Kjeld turned to face him. 'But I do want to apologise for the way I've been behaving recently.'

Bengt took a sip of the wine, tried and failed to hold back a wince at the taste, and then set the mug on the coffee table. 'Look, if this is about the incident with Tove—'

'It's not.' Kjeld turned to face Bengt. 'I've been thinking about some of the things you said. Some of the things a lot of people have said, actually. And you're right. I'm not doing well.'

Bengt eyed him carefully but didn't say anything. Kjeld wondered what he was thinking. What was going on behind those sharp blue eyes? Kjeld searched his face for something. Disapproval, disbelief. But all he saw was the look of someone who was waiting. Waiting for the truth.

Kjeld tapped his finger on the neck of the bottle. He took a deep breath, steeling himself for what he wanted to say, but had to drop his gaze to do so. 'I miss you.'

'Kjeld …'

'Please, hear me out.'

Kjeld set the bottle on the coffee table beside the mug of cheap wine. Then he looked at Bengt directly, forcing himself to hold the other man's gaze. 'I really fucked up with us and with Tove. I know that. I've known it for a very long time. But I was so angry with myself—'

'And with me,' Bengt interrupted.

Kjeld sighed. 'Yes, but I knew it wasn't your fault. I pushed you away. I didn't know how to deal with your illness and a child. And I don't mean to say that as an excuse. There is no excuse. But I know I made the wrong choices and I regret them. More than I can express.'

Bengt pinched his brows together.

'I've never told you how important you were to me. How much being with you meant to me. I should have told you those things a long time ago. Maybe if I had been more open and honest then we might have been able to make it work.'

Thinking about those early years with Bengt filled Kjeld with stinging self-loathing. He hated that it had taken him so long to recognise that he'd had a good thing with Bengt. Something that he might not ever have with anyone else.

Bengt leaned forward, resting his elbows on his knees. 'You can't think like that, Kjeld. You don't know what would have happened. And it doesn't matter. I know you blame yourself, but I made mistakes, too. I pressured you into becoming a father when you weren't ready. That was wrong. And I should have ended it with you before getting involved with someone else.'

Bengt hung his head, hiding his face from view. 'But what's done is done. And, to be honest, we weren't really a good match for each other anyway.'

That final comment stung Kjeld in a way he wasn't prepared for and he turned away from Bengt, snatching up the beer bottle for another long swig before leaning back into the lumpy couch cushions.

Bengt, perhaps realising after the fact how harsh his comment might have sounded, picked up the mug and drank the entire contents in one go. Then he moved sideways onto the couch, facing Kjeld. 'But we did have some good times.'

'We did.'

'And I still care about you.'

'It's not the same.'

'What do you want me to say, Kjeld?'

Kjeld shot a hard look at Bengt. 'You *know* what I want you to say.'

Bengt hesitated, his voice lowered to just above a whisper. 'You know I can't.'

'Then what are you doing here?'

Kjeld set the bottle hard on the coffee table and stood up.

A flash of uncertain panic washed over Bengt's expression. Then he stood as well, catching Kjeld's hand before he had the chance to walk out of the room.

Kjeld almost pulled away on reflex. In truth he had no expectations of Bengt. And the fact that Bengt was there shouldn't have given him any, although it did give him a fragile hope. He just wanted to be honest with someone. Someone he'd once known well. But now when he looked at Bengt he didn't have any clue what the man was thinking. There was a time when he might have been able to guess. A time when he could read into the subtleties of Bengt's sober expression, the falter in his voice, the tenseness in his grip. But that had been long ago. And Esme was right. Kjeld couldn't be certain of his ability to see anything clearly anymore.

Bengt tightened his hold on Kjeld's hand. 'I can't say it. That doesn't mean I don't feel it.'

Kjeld placed his free hand on the side of Bengt's face, thumb tracing along the edge of his jaw. 'What's that supposed to mean?'

'I think you know.'

There was a weariness in Bengt's gaze that Kjeld recognised. It was the same tired look he used to get after they'd both apologised to each other after a vicious argument. This time, however, Kjeld thought he saw something else in that fatigue. A quiet pleading, perhaps. Or a wordless request for Kjeld to decide for them both. And as much as Kjeld wanted to think that this was Bengt's way of inviting him back into his life, he couldn't help but wonder if it wasn't also Bengt sparing himself from being the responsible party.

But while Kjeld had no trouble being irresponsible, his ability to close himself off from his feelings had become less reliable. And as much as he wanted things to be as they had been, he knew he couldn't handle another heartbreak.

Kjeld dropped his hand from Bengt's face. 'Are we really going to do this again?'

But Bengt surprised him by gently touching the burgeoning bruise along the ridge of his brow. 'What happened to your eye?'

Kjeld's expression was rigid, but weakly resolute. 'I think you know.'

Bengt nodded, the weariness in his gaze quickly replaced by a kind of unspoken awareness. As though Kjeld had just confirmed something he'd already suspected. He tightened his hold on Kjeld's hand. 'What else do you have to drink?'

Chapter 58

Esme collapsed on her bed and stared up at the ceiling. An anxious buzz trilled through her body. She could feel it start in her chest and travel down the length of her arms, ending with her middle finger tapping nervously on the duvet. She inhaled deeply, held her breath to a count of ten, and exhaled. When that didn't ease her unrest, she repeated the breath work until the trill subsided into a heavy limpness in her arms.

She'd fucked up.

She'd fucked up bad.

She tugged off her socks and tossed them in the corner of her bedroom where a pile of unwashed clothing was beginning to crawl up the wall. She was too tired to change into her sleep shirt, so she just lay there, looking up at the bland eggshell-coloured ceiling. Her thoughts were filled with self-doubt. It was as though every step she'd taken since the chief put her in charge of the investigation had been wrong. Worse than wrong. Disastrous. And no matter how hard she tried she couldn't get the image of Sixten on the ground, eyes pleading, stomach spurting blood with every rapid breath, out of her mind. Then there was the smell. That sharp odour of blood – a metallic pungency so acrid she could practically taste it.

What if he died because of her inaction? What if he lived but was permanently comatose, confined to a machine for the rest of his life? Or what if he lived, but could no longer return to duty? Her heart pounded in her chest with each passing thought. She could feel her pulse thumping through the artery on the side of her neck.

She needed a distraction.

Esme reached into the pocket of her slacks and removed her phone. She opened her Tinder app and scrolled through the potential hook-ups, but all of the nearby options were looking for dinner and a date first. Esme sighed. That wouldn't do her any good at two in the morning. A text message popped up from Miriam and she swiped it away without reading it. She couldn't deal with any more of her concern or advice. Miriam meant well, of course, but they'd clearly diverged on the friend path years ago. And Esme was too tired to explain her feelings again. She couldn't deal with having them be misinterpreted again. Nor did she want to hear any more digs about how she needed to grow up.

It was nobody's business what she chose to prioritise or how she lived her life. Least of all someone with a perfect family, a perfect husband, and a perfect house. But Miriam's earlier comments, well intended or otherwise, persisted in rolling around in Esme's mind, tearing down her self-confidence and filling her with unnecessary doubt. Later there would be a misplaced sense of shame, as well. One that had followed Esme since childhood.

She dropped her phone on the mattress and placed a hand on her stomach. She thought of Kjeld, wondering what he was doing. Had she been too hard on him at the hospital? Sure, she'd been distracted by Sixten, in shock from the botched operation. But she'd never before allowed her own stress and anxiety to get between her and the work. Or between her and Kjeld. He may have looked the tougher of the two, but deep down she knew he was hurting. She wanted to help him, but he was so insufferable. He refused to let her in, even when she sensed he wanted to. That hurt Esme. She knew not to take it personally, but she did. And she didn't know why. Kjeld just had that effect on her. He was so blind to the people around him. The people who truly cared for him. It made her want to scream.

She wondered if she should call him. Or maybe she should drive over to his flat and see if he wanted to talk. He was probably still awake.

No, that would be too intrusive. Besides, it wouldn't do any good. Pushing Kjeld to open up was like trying to get blood from a stone. And maybe that wasn't what she really wanted anyway. Maybe what she really wanted was someone to listen to *her* talk.

Her phone buzzed again and she groaned. She picked it up expecting it to be another unsolicited life tip but was surprised to see it was a message from Axel. Was he still at work? At this hour? She opened the message. Attached was the new report from ballistics on the gun used in the Hedebrant murder. She felt her pulse quicken in excitement. Maybe this would finally be the break they needed to figure out one of these cases. She opened the report and scanned through it impatiently. The gun in the evidence locker didn't match either the bullet used to kill Tobias Hedebrant or Andrea Nicolescu. Nor was it the gun that was registered to Emil Hermansson. Someone had replaced it with a similar make and model.

Shit. What did that mean? Was it possible that Kjeld was right? Did they have someone else in the police who was conspiring against them? Someone who was helping the murderer?

They had to find another way of tracking this killer.

But how?

Her phone pinged. Axel sent another text. *Forensics found DNA on the knife and two good fingerprints. Going to run them through the database. Will keep you posted.*

A rush of anticipation surged through her. Finally. A potential break in the case. Suddenly she felt wide awake. Like someone had just injected her with a dose of adrenaline. She opened up her Tinder app again, widening her search parameters. A bright-eyed, gym-obsessed face who was "looking for a good time with no complications" smiled back at her. Less than two miles away. Esme swiped right.

Chapter 59

Lördag | Saturday

The digital clock on his nightstand flashed into a new hour and the crooning voice of Michael Stipe losing his religion tore through the room. Kjeld smacked the snooze button with the palm of his hand and rolled over to find the space beside him empty. His thoughts were dishevelled, slowly crawling out of a dreamless slumber. The room was dark aside from a sliver of light peeking through the blackout curtains. He pressed his face against the other pillow, indented from the night before, and inhaled Bengt's scent. For a fleeting second, he expected to hear Bengt in the kitchen, putting together one of his overly complex breakfasts while Tove told him all about her fantastical dreams or plans for the day. But there was nothing. The apartment was quiet. He was alone.

There was a note on the duvet, folded in half with the letter "K" scrawled in artistic lettering on the front. Kjeld reached for the lamp switch on his nightstand and dragged himself up to a sitting position, allowing his eyes to adjust to the light before opening the note.

Sorry I had to dash. I have to pick up Tove from her friend's house and collect a few pieces from the studio for an exhibition later this afternoon. Tried to wake you, but you were out. We should talk later.

B

A half-smile tugged at the corner of Kjeld's lips as he set the note on the nightstand. He knew it was foolish to get his hopes up. The problems between him and Bengt couldn't be settled with one unexpected night together. And for all Kjeld knew the talk Bengt wanted to have was a confession that this unplanned relapse of feelings on their part was a mistake. But that didn't stop a tiny glimmer of hope from brightening the dark corners of his mind.

The radio kicked on again and this time he hit the stop button. It was a few minutes after seven in the morning. He couldn't remember the last time he'd slept so soundly and an unexpected thought crossed his mind.

Maybe it *was* time to change.

Kjeld had always used his career as a way of identifying himself. When he thought of the kind of person he was, it was difficult for him to separate Kjeld the individual from Kjeld the detective. But maybe it was time to make that distinction. Maybe that was how he would repair the problems between him and Bengt. Maybe the life he'd built for himself as a police detective had finally reached its pinnacle. Maybe it was time to put the murder squad behind him.

Kjeld crawled out of bed, slipped into a pair of sweatpants, and made his way into the living room. His phone was still sitting on the coffee table, untouched since Bengt's arrival. He picked it up to find multiple missed calls and messages from Esme. He skimmed through the texts. Despite the incident with Sixten, Rhodin had kept her on as lead of the investigation. That was good. If anyone was capable of putting together the missing pieces of the puzzle then it was Esme.

Her last message was a link to a new article on *The Chatterbox* accompanied by an exasperated emoji. Kjeld clicked on the link and quickly read through Henny's new outrageous piece of fiction. Only this time there wasn't much about it that was untrue. Even the headline was spot on.

Police Duped by Second Serial Killer in Span of a Year

The rest of the article followed Henny's usual pattern of pointing out the failures of the Gothenburg City Police to successfully trap the mysterious killer. She even went so far as to refer to one of the lead detectives as being personally responsible for botching up the operation and resulting in the near-death of a colleague, although she incorrectly referred to Sixten as an officer-in-training rather than a detective constable. To Henny's credit, however, she didn't mention Esme's name and Kjeld wondered if she hadn't done so deliberately in order to maintain some semblance of professional dignity.

The rest of the article was a lot of hearsay and unsubstantiated theories about who the killer might be and why he was tracking down these particular individuals. But that didn't bother Kjeld as much as the images she'd plastered between the article. Actual footage of Daniel Santelmann's kitchen, including close-ups of the bloodstained knife, as well as a reused photograph of Kjeld standing in the rain at the scene of the first murder.

Worst of all, however, was the photo of Sixten in his hospital bed, which Kjeld knew she couldn't have taken herself. Because of the likelihood that Sixten had seen the killer, he had a twenty-four-hour guard on his room. No one could get in or out without the officer on duty noticing. Henny must have had someone leaking information to her on the inside. The thought of which set Kjeld's blood to boiling.

He was about to set his phone back down and head for the shower when a live video popped up at the top of Henny's page.

He turned up his volume and listened as she spoke about the injustices of the police invading the sanctuaries of private citizens. But it wasn't the words she was speaking that caught Kjeld's attention. It was the location she was speaking from.

Small red buildings. Thatched roofs. A vegetable garden where two women in linen garments tended to the plants.

It didn't take long for Kjeld to recognise the scene although he stared at it for almost a full minute in astonishment. It was so unexpected that his brain took longer to process what he was seeing. Once it did, however, the realisation of what he was looking at hit him.

In the turmoil of Sixten's injury, Kjeld hadn't had time to think about the woman Vidar had told him about. The one Jonny had been seen talking to, possibly in connection to Second Life. Tall. Chestnut hair. Conservatively dressed.

Henny was that woman. And she was at the commune.

Chapter 60

Despite Liam's insistence that Bengt maintain a studio in the spare bedroom of their apartment or in a location closer to home, Bengt preferred the snug concrete-walled room he rented out of a converted church in the urban district of Älvsborg. While he didn't have an inspiring view of the Rivö Fjord, there was a crisp coastal scent in the air that energised his desire to create and the light that streamed in through the stained-glass windows when the sun began to set gave the space a dusky, almost ethereal hue to it. He'd often experimented with those changing afternoon colours on his canvases, overlaying most of his paintings with varying shades of orange, yellow, and that frail shade of blue reflected from a cold winter morning.

Today, however, he didn't have time to take advantage of that gloomy purple-grey that illuminated his messy workspace. In every other aspect of his life – Kjeld and art being the notable exceptions – Bengt was meticulous about order to an almost compulsive degree. He maintained a pristine household. Dustless surfaces, furniture arranged to the precise millimetre, nothing in the refrigerator within two days of the expiration date. But when it came to his art he let go of those orderly obsessions. The cold cement floors were stained in oils and acrylics. Rows of finished and unfinished canvases were stacked against an old wooden shelf that was scattered with brushes, paint tubes, crafting knives, and sketchpads.

At the centre of the room was a single easel holding up his current work in progress, a brown cloth draped over the canvas, denoting its incomplete state and protecting it from the multitudes of dust that fell from the rafters overnight. Pigeons always seemed to find their way in, despite his attempts to ward them off. On the wall opposite the stained-glass window was a hanging tarp that he used as a practice palette, testing out different colours and brush stroke techniques. In the bottom left corner were three handprints of various size and colour. Blue, green, and red. Him, Kjeld, and Tove.

'Can I draw something, Papa?' Tove asked, immediately making her way over to a small corner where she knew Bengt kept the charcoal pencils.

'We don't have time today, sweetheart. Papa has to take some pieces over to the gallery for an exhibition this weekend.'

'Just one drawing?'

'All right. Just one. But only on a blank piece of paper!'

Tove let out a whoop of excitement and began digging through a box of used sketchpads for one that had an empty page between its covers.

Bengt smiled. He wouldn't necessarily wish an artist's life on anyone, but it filled his heart with joy to see Tove express such an interest in anything creative. It almost made him feel whole. Of course, there was much more of Kjeld in her than there would ever be of him, but that didn't make him feel any less about his ability to provide her with everything she needed to grow up to be a strong, independent woman. If anything, that only reassured him that she would.

For all of Kjeld's faults he never failed to stand firmly on his own two feet, confident of who he was and the decisions he made. That confidence was one of the things that attracted Bengt to him in the first place. Bengt had never before met anyone so full of stubborn determination. As someone who'd always felt slightly moulded from the wallpaper, rarely commanding attention, it was an attractive quality. And might have remained so if that persistence of self hadn't become so inflexible. Or if Kjeld had focused it on them instead of his work.

Had he made a mistake in staying over at Kjeld's?

Bengt had no doubts about his feelings for Liam. Liam was everything he wanted in a partner. He was dependable, trustworthy, affectionate, and attentive. He had a respectable career and he cared deeply for people. He exuded a natural empathy that had brought Bengt to tears when they first met. Liam never missed a dinner or a date. He was supportive of Tove and treated her as if she were his own. On top of that he could hold an intelligent conversation about practically anything. He enjoyed entertaining friends, as Bengt did. And he had a charismatic charm that literally had the ability to make Bengt weak at the knees.

But, for better or worse, Liam wasn't Kjeld.

Bengt didn't know what it was about Kjeld that made him so crazy. Kjeld was almost the antithesis of Liam. Unreliable, irresponsible, an atrocious sense of style. But when Bengt was in the same room as Kjeld his stomach did somersaults. When he caught that intense blue-grey gaze on him, it was as though all of his insides turned into butterflies trapped in a jar, fluttering to get out. Kjeld was unexpected and irrational as a lover. When it came to passion there was no calculation. No thinking. And Bengt's attraction to him was similar. It had no sturdy basis in the logical world. It was like an elastic rope that tied them together. And the further Bengt tried to pull himself away, the more he just increased the tension and his desire to go back.

He had to stop thinking about him. If he continued in this way he'd end up at Kjeld's flat again. And if he did that then there'd be no turning back.

Bengt pulled out an abstract canvas from one of the stacks against the wall and set it off to the side. Then he set aside another. He didn't need too many pieces. Five or six should have been sufficient. But there was one in particular he was looking for. An oil landscape of three women walking along the rocky coast near the Älvsborg Fortress. Bengt didn't do a lot of realistic landscapes or portraits because they required a lot of emotional energy from him. Those paintings always felt more personal and penetrating. And he was more harshly critical of them than his expressive abstract work. Consequently, they were also the pieces he was most proud of. And they always fetched the highest prices when they were featured in a gallery.

If only he could remember where he put it. He really needed to invest in a better system. On the outside he was the epitome of equanimity. On the inside he was chaos. Just like this studio.

'Papa?'

'Just a moment, darling. I'm looking for something important.'

'P-papa?'

The stammer in Tove's tone sent an involuntary shiver down Bengt's spine. It was as though something primal had reached out to warn him, the hairs on the back of his neck instinctively standing on end. But the warning came too late.

The sharp sting of a needle piercing his neck caused him to recoil in the opposite direction, but from the corner of his eye he could see that the stranger's gloved hand had already pushed down the syringe. He stumbled into the stack of paintings leaned up against the wall. He tripped, his right foot breaking through one of the canvases. He reached out for the wall to steady himself, but the room was spinning. The sensation in his hands numbed to a buzzy tingle.

He fell to the ground. His left knee jabbed hard into the concrete floor, but he hardly noticed the pain. Only the reverberation through the bone up to his hip. He blinked, his vision clouding.

'Please,' he begged, his voice strange in his own ears. 'Please … Don't hurt my daughter …'

He crawled towards Tove. She was a blurry mass in front of him, distinguishable only by the bright red of her hair, like a surrealist sunset.

'Please …'

Bengt slumped onto his back.

The figure stood above him, blocking the polychromatic light from the stained-glass window. Bengt narrowed his eyes, but he couldn't tell who it was. In the background he heard Tove screaming. She sounded far away. So far away.

And then she was gone.

Chapter 61

Kjeld sat in traffic on the E45 southbound under the Partihallsförbindelsen motorway en route back to the city from the spot of land that housed Second Life Wellness Respite. Following Henny had proven to be another dead end. Once he'd driven into the area, he tried to locate her vehicle, but it didn't appear to be anywhere. Her broadcast, which had been little more than a twenty-minute diatribe against the Gothenburg police on behalf of the residents of Second Life who, in her opinion, were "undoing systematic persecution by local authorities without evidence to support their harassment", had ended not long before he arrived in the area.

Unfortunately, he couldn't approach the commune via the main entrance now that he knew Olsen had the area under surveillance. Instead he tried to get a glimpse of the commune from some of the tiny back roads, but there were too many to follow them all. For his trouble he ended up driving circles around half of the Änggårdsbergen Nature Reserve to no avail. If he wanted to talk to Henny about her potential connection to Jonny he would have to do it another way and at another time.

Kjeld turned up the volume on the radio when the DJ broke through the nonstop classic rock lunch hour to provide a traffic update. A turned-over semitruck was slowing traffic to a standstill from the next highway interchange all the way back to five miles behind Kjeld. The radio host said the accident could delay traffic into the city by more than forty-five minutes. But Kjeld didn't need to hear that to know it was true. The mob of automobiles packed around him hadn't moved in almost twenty minutes.

Kjeld turned off the ignition and placed the vehicle in park in order to give his foot a break and stared out the window. The sky was packed full of dark rain clouds, threatening a downpour at any moment. A gentle sprinkle of rain fell against the windscreen. It looked cold, but inside the car was warm. Kjeld watched as automobiles, unaware of the immobile queue beneath them, crossed the interchange above, slowly backing up from the on ramp.

He canted his gaze upward and felt his fingers clench around the steering wheel. His heart lurched into his throat as he thought back to that day sixteen years ago. The day Emma Hassan jumped out of his car and fell to her death on the opposite leg of the highway, not more than twenty-five metres from where Kjeld's car currently sat stuck in traffic.

Nils was driving, as he often did early on in their partnership. It would be three years of them working together, side by side, before Nils loosened up and allowed Kjeld the opportunity to take the wheel. When they were first assigned together, Kjeld assumed Nils's pretentiousness about driving was a control thing. A power play meant to show Kjeld, the rookie detective, who was in charge. Later Kjeld would learn that Nils simply enjoyed the act of driving. He once described it as an opportunity for reflection. Some people had their most illuminating thoughts in the shower. Nils had his in the car.

Years later Kjeld would cringe at what some of those thoughts might have been.

'Let me out of this fucking car! This is a violation of my rights!' Emma yelled from the back seat. She pounded her fist against the plastic barrier separating the front two seats from the back.

Kjeld turned in his seat to look at her. 'You were caught at school with a gun in your backpack. By my count that's at least two illegal acts. And since we have reason to believe that gun may have been used in a murder, that gives us more than enough right to take you down to the station.'

'I'm a minor.'

'And your parents have been notified that they can pick you up at the station. Just as soon as you answer a few questions about Emil Hermansson.'

'I don't know anything about him.'

Nils peered at her through the rear-view mirror. 'We know you were with him when he killed his business partner.'

'It's not that we think you were intentionally involved,' Kjeld said. 'Nor do we want to charge you with possession of a weapon. We know you were in the wrong place at the wrong time. We just need your statement to make sure Emil goes away to prison for murder.'

Emma kicked the back of Kjeld's seat. 'I'm not a fucking rat! I'm not talking to the pigs.'

'You really should be careful who you talk to like that,' Nils said, his tone placid but stern. 'It could get you in trouble one day.'

'Fuck you, pig.'

The highway separated and Nils followed the path of the interchange towards the city centre, back towards the main police station. Directly over the E45, however, traffic backed up to a stop.

Kjeld sighed. 'Why is this stretch of highway always blocked when you're in a hurry? Should I put a call into the station and let them know we'll be a little late?'

'I wouldn't worry about it,' Nils said. 'Emil isn't going anywhere. Let him sweat a little.'

'What about the girl's parents?'

'They'll be there when we arrive. Don't worry so much, Kjeld. It's not good for you.'

Kjeld slouched back, turning his gaze out the side window. Emma kicked the back of his seat again, hitting him right in the kidney.

306

A small jab of pain dulled his lower back and he glanced back at her. 'Cut it out.'

She stopped and Kjeld stretched upward to try to see beyond the vehicles in front of them. 'I wonder how long it's going to be.'

'Do you have somewhere you need to be?'

'No, I just don't like sitting still for too long.'

'You should cut back on the coffee. It makes you anxious.'

Kjeld laughed. 'Sure, if you want me sleeping during our shifts.'

Click.

Kjeld knew immediately that it was the door handle being tugged and the door pushed open, but in that brief moment his rational mind refused to acknowledge it. The door couldn't be opened. It had been locked. Kjeld himself had made sure of that. And yet, he heard the sound, he knew the passenger door on the driver's side was being opened, and he knew Emma was getting out of the car.

The events that happened next were so quick Kjeld didn't have time to think.

Nils yelled something just as Kjeld scrambled out of the car. Emma was already zigzagging through the stopped vehicles, heading towards the median at the centre of the highway. Kjeld followed after, shouting at her to stop. Cars honked at him as he weaved through traffic.

By the time he reached the concrete barrier separating the two different directions of traffic, Emma had already climbed over it. The vehicles speeding off in the opposite direction weren't in the same standstill as the branch of traffic heading towards the city. Cars and semis sped past without regard for a sixteen-year-old girl who'd suddenly bolted into traffic.

Panic propelled Kjeld forward. He leapt atop the concrete median but was held back from crossing because of an influx of automobiles. They whirred past him. He checked for an opening, stepped forward and then pulled back quickly as a motorcycle whizzed by.

Dammit.

He glanced up and saw Emma darting between the vehicles.

Motorists laid on the horns, filling the air with a persistent blare.

Kjeld saw an opening, heard a shout behind him, and jumped onto the road. He was halfway across the first lane when it happened.

Emma was mere feet away from the edge of the highway, practically within reach of that thin strip of road opposite the rumble strip, when a truck roared around the curve of the on ramp. Kjeld caught a glimpse of the driver's expression the second before he hit Emma head on. It was a look he'd never forget. Sheer terror packed in an infinitesimal nanosecond. Enough time for the driver's mind to recognise this would be a moment that would forever change his life. Not enough time to react.

Emma's body flung up in the air like a ragdoll, her arms and legs limp, her hair jerking loose of her ponytail. The truck swerved into the median, crashing the front end into the barrier. Another crunch. The air bags deployed at the exact second that Emma's body hit the low guardrail, which acted as an extra buoy against vehicles hurling over the overhang in bad weather. A thunk. And then her body fell over the railing and down into the oncoming traffic on the freeway.

Kjeld raced to the guardrail and glanced over the edge. Emma's body lay mangled and distorted almost fifty feet below.

A horn blared from the vehicle behind him and Kjeld jolted out of his own thoughts. Traffic had started moving again. Heart pounding, he turned the key in the ignition and rolled forward. Once traffic picked up he put the car in drive and accelerated. A moment later he drove over the exact spot where Emma's body had landed. The pathologist on duty at the time couldn't offer Kjeld or the family any reassurance that she'd died on impact with the truck. It was possible, but it was also likely that she'd survived being hit and was conscious as her body went into freefall over the edge of the highway.

Kjeld never forgot the look on Emma's mother's face. Pure uncontrollable agony. Kjeld had still been in a strange state of delayed shock when he was pulled into an interview room to give a statement. His memory of chasing Emma across the highway seemed slow and fragmentary in his mind. It was as though he'd witnessed it from someone else's perspective. But his memory of the moments before were clear. He'd locked the back doors. He knew he had.

He must have.

But if he had, how had she gotten out?

His gaze caught a glimpse of the centre lane and for a split second he imagined her body there and almost swerved to miss it. Then he dug his nails deeper into the wheel and pushed his foot down hard on the accelerator, speeding up to pass the spot before he saw her again.

Chapter 62

Kjeld had just pulled his car into an empty space in front of his apartment when he saw the dozens of missed calls on his phone. Esme, Axel, Rhodin. His heart nearly stopped in his chest. He was halfway through the first voicemail before he was pulling out of the space and speeding back to the main road. It should have been a twenty-minute drive with traffic from the station to Bengt's studio in Älvsborg, but Kjeld made it there in twelve. When he arrived, he barrelled his way through the officers in front of the renovated church, but it was Esme who stopped him from entering Bengt's studio by physically blocking the doorway.

'Esme, you have to let me in.'

'No, Kjeld. I don't. And I *can't*. Aside from the fact that you're not actively on this case anymore, this just became personal.'

'It was already personal.'

'But this is your family.'

'Where is he?' Kjeld leaned over her to get a better look at the scene. But between the mess of paintings scattered about the room, and crime-scene technicians scouring the area for evidence, he could barely see a thing. 'Where *is* he, Esme? Where's Bengt?'

'He's—'

'Kjeld!'

Kjeld turned to see Bengt rushing towards him. Bengt wrapped his arms around him in a frazzled embrace that felt more like a need to steady himself than anything else. His fingers dug into Kjeld's arms and he was shaking. When he pulled away after a few seconds, Kjeld got the first good look at Bengt's face and his heart leapt into his throat. It was an expression every parent recognised even if they'd never seen it before.

The muscles in Kjeld's chest tightened. 'Where's Tove?'

And that's when Bengt broke down. He tried to speak but he couldn't complete a full sentence for his choking sobs.

Kjeld grabbed Bengt by the shoulders and forced him to look at him. 'Where's Tove, Bengt?'

'She's—' Bengt cut himself off, gasping for air. 'She took her! Oh, God. What are we going to do? You don't think it's the same person who's been committing these murders, do you? It's my fault. I had my back turned. I didn't see her come in the room.'

'You didn't see who came into the room?'

'I don't know. I didn't get a good look at her. I felt a sharp prick in my neck and when I woke up, Tove was gone! She must have taken her.'

She? Kjeld's thoughts jostled in his mind as he tried to process what Bengt was saying. He kept his hands firmly gripped on Bengt's arms but turned his gaze to Esme. She didn't look surprised.

'The paramedics checked him out. We think he was drugged. When we got here he wasn't very lucid. One of the neighbours saw him stumbling around and called in a wellness check. We want to send him to the hospital for a blood test and to check him for evidence, but he refused to leave until he saw you.'

Bengt grabbed onto the front of Kjeld's shirt, wrenching his fingers around the fabric. 'She took Tove!'

Kjeld placed his focus back on Bengt. 'Okay, Bengt. I need you to tell me everything you remember.'

Bengt sniffled and coughed. 'I was going through my paintings,

311

looking for something for the exhibit. Tove was drawing in the corner. She tried to get my attention but I wasn't listening. Then I felt something on my neck. When I turned I saw a woman. It's hazy. It all happened so fast.'

'Can you remember anything about this woman? Was she tall? Thin? What colour was her hair?'

Bengt's face twisted as though in pain. His ragged brows bunched together at the centre of his forehead and his lips turned downward. He looked like he was going to be sick.

'I don't remember. I think she was tall.'

'How tall? Taller than you?'

'I'm not sure.'

'What about her size?'

'She was … thin. I think. God, it's so fuzzy.'

'What about her hair?'

'It was …'

Kjeld shook him. 'Focus, Bengt.'

Tears immediately fell from Bengt's eyes. 'I don't remember. I just remember hearing her scream.'

Bengt's knees gave out beneath him and he fell to the floor, sobbing into Kjeld's pant leg. 'Tove was screaming and I couldn't do anything.'

Commotion broke out at the end of the corridor and both Kjeld and Esme looked up to see Liam trying to barge his way through the police line. He was being held back by two uniformed officers, but when he saw Bengt on the floor he nearly barrelled right through them.

Kjeld helped Bengt to his feet and led him towards the end of the hall. Liam immediately pulled Bengt close to him, but Bengt was too much of an emotional wreck to speak. Esme carefully explained the situation. Each word brought a new look of terror and fury to Liam's face.

'What we need is for Bengt to be checked out properly and processed by a forensic specialist in case he has any evidence of the kidnapper on him,' Esme said to Liam. Her tone was sympathetic but stern. 'That's the most helpful thing you can do for us right now. The faster we can process the scene, the faster we can work towards bringing Tove home.'

Liam shot Kjeld an angry but frantic stare.

'She's right, Liam. Time is not on our side. We need to work quickly.'

'You call me the minute you learn something. Anything,' Liam said through gritted teeth.

'We will,' Esme said.

Liam nodded and then led Bengt back outside.

Esme glanced behind her, ensuring that no one was listening in over her shoulder. Then she turned her attention to Kjeld. 'Let's go someplace a little more private.'

There was a seriousness to Esme's tone that Kjeld knew not to question. He made his way back towards the entrance of the church, Esme following close behind him. It wasn't until they were both in his car, protected from the flurry of rain and snow outside, that Esme breathed out an exasperated sigh.

Kjeld turned on the ignition but not the engine. The heater immediately began blasting out cold air. He adjusted the fans to a lower setting until it had time to heat up.

'Tell me what's going on.'

'I shouldn't. This has already gone too far. The chief—'

'Dammit, Esme! She has Tove.'

And that was enough to get Esme to give in.

'Forensics came back on the knife that stabbed Sixten.'

'And?'

'We got a single fingerprint match.'

'Whose?'

'Maja Hassan.'

Kjeld stared at her blankly. 'What?'

Esme chewed at her lower lip. It was badly chapped. Enough that the skin looked like it was about to peel off. Kjeld hadn't noticed that the last time he'd seen her and wondered what else could have happened in a few days to increase her stress levels so dramatically.

'I can't explain it. We almost missed it. It was a partial.'

'How did we have Maja's prints on file?'

'They were taken to exclude her from unidentified prints found during the Emil Hermansson case.'

'But Maja Hassan is dead.'

'Apparently her body was never found. I pulled up the report that was filed after her vehicle was discovered in the river. A search of the river was done, but the water levels were high that week because of rain. There was evidence that she'd been in the car and at least two witnesses saw her drive off the bridge. The officers in charge of the investigation labelled it a suicide because that was the most likely explanation.' Esme grimaced. 'And that's not all. The gun in the evidence box for the Hedebrant case didn't match either of the bullets used to murder Hedebrant or Andrea.'

'What? That's not possible.'

'Either you had the wrong gun the entire time and someone falsified the ballistics testing in the Hedebrant case or someone replaced it after Hermansson's trial.'

Kjeld stared at the dash of the car, thoughts scrambling to put the pieces together, but he couldn't get the image of Maja Hassan out of his head. 'Maja Hassan wouldn't have been physically capable of some of these crimes. She never would have been able to drag Louisa's body into a cellar or carry Jonny into that cabin.'

'It's been sixteen years. A lot could change in that time.'

'But why would she be killing these people? What did they do to her?'

'I don't think they did anything to her.'

'What do you mean?'

'We've been looking for someone who's targeting survivors of violent crimes. But I don't think that's all of it.' Esme turned in the passenger seat so she was facing Kjeld. 'I think the killer we've been chasing is targeting *your* survivors of violent crimes.'

'What?'

'Louisa was the survivor of one of your first major cases after you were promoted to detective. You were lead investigator on the case involving the graduation homicides, with Jonny being one of the sole survivors. Daniel was also one of your cases. And Andrea—'

'I never worked a case involving Andrea.'

'When Sixten and I spoke to Ingrid Nicolescu she mentioned that Andrea's life was saved by a young police officer shortly after she moved to Sweden. I couldn't find any documentation of that incident in her file because, according to Ingrid, Andrea ran from the scene. But yesterday at the hospital you mentioned meeting Nils while you were assigned to parking ticket duty. So, I pulled up Nils's case files from that time. He was the one who first arrived on the scene to find the young officer handcuffing two assailants who'd fired off a weapon at a woman. It was you. That was the first time you met, wasn't it?'

Kjeld knitted his brows together in confusion. He was trying to catch up with Esme's breakdown of the events, but he couldn't believe it. 'That was Andrea? The woman who was almost shot?'

'I believe so. The description of the scene matches what we heard from Ingrid. Only we couldn't verify it as being relevant because there was nothing about it in the records. If she hadn't fled the scene then we might have realised earlier that her murder was related to Louisa's.'

'But how could the killer know that? We didn't even know who she was at the time. I certainly didn't know. How could Maja figure that out?'

Esme shook her head incredulously. 'I don't know. But they're all connected. And you're at the centre of that connection. This entire thing has been about you.'

'And about Emma …'

'Possibly,' Esme offered. 'The only thing that doesn't make sense is the drug connection and Second Life. Are they coincidences? Or something meant to lead us astray?'

Kjeld raked his fingers back through his hair. 'I don't know what to think anymore.'

'Did Emma Hassan have a drug connection?'

'We suspected there might have been something related to drugs at the time. She was mixed up in a bad crowd. And her father had a record. But we never had any solid proof. We were hoping she would tell us when we picked her up, but ...'

Kjeld didn't finish his sentence, but he knew that Esme understood. They'd never made it back to the station. Not with Emma alive.

Kjeld slammed his fist into the steering wheel, inadvertently hitting the horn and scaring a crime-scene technician who was carrying equipment into the building. 'Goddammit. We're spinning our wheels.'

And now Tove was gone. Missing. Kidnapped. Potentially by the same person who'd already committed at least two murders, maybe more.

'If it is Maja and she wanted revenge against me for what happened to Emma then why all the others? Why wait until now to go after me and my daughter?'

'She might have panicked because we interrupted her last kidnapping attempt. This might be her way of speeding things up. If anything, it's proof that this has been more than just murdering survivors from old cases. It's personal. And if it is Maja Hassan then we can assume it has something to do with her daughter's death. But we're not out of leads yet. We still have Henny.'

'You're right. Her last article proves she's getting information from somebody. If not the killer than somebody in the department. Either way she must know more than she's letting on.'

Esme pursed her lips in thought. 'Do you think Maja could be the one who was tipping her off to the crime scenes?'

'I don't know, but I think she might be the one Jonny was

seen talking to. She was reporting live from the commune this morning. I tried to drive out there to find her, but I couldn't locate her. I must have just missed her.' The heat finally kicked on, but Kjeld was no longer thinking straight enough to adjust it.

'If we need to we'll talk to her again. An active kidnapping changes everything. Henny might be a nuisance and she might only be looking out for herself, but I can't imagine she would hold back information if she knew a child's life was in danger.'

Esme was right, of course. Kjeld's bitterness towards Henny made it difficult for him to judge her rationally. It was one thing to post slanderous falsehoods on the internet to gain followers and subscribers. It was another thing entirely to help a murderer continue their killing spree simply to boost one's career. And as much as Kjeld despised Henny, he didn't think anyone who had gone through the traumas she had would knowingly put others in that same position. Let alone a child.

He turned back to Esme. 'What about Daniel Santelmann? Did you get anything from him?'

'Nothing useful. He didn't get a good look at Sixten's attacker.'

'And we're sure it was Maja's fingerprints on the knife?'

'I had them run the results twice.'

'How does this help us find Tove? We've had no leads to indicate where the killer's been hiding.'

'I've sent a team out to the house where the Hassans used to live. And Axel is poring over the records hoping to find something in the files.'

Kjeld turned his gaze out the window. It wasn't raining, but the sky was full of heavy clouds threatening to burst at any moment. How had they missed all of this? How had it gotten this far? And why? Esme's theory about Maja seeking revenge against survivors wasn't completely out of the question, but it still left him with so many questions. Why not come for him directly if she considered him responsible for Emma's death? Why go after innocent victims? And why recreate the scenes with the other victims?

317

But most of all, how did she find these people? Louisa and Jonny had been front-page news when they were found, but Kjeld's involvement in Daniel's investigation had never been publicly announced. Nils had been the lead back then. And what about Tove? Was that something else? Was that payback for Emma?

Esme placed a hand on Kjeld's arm. 'We'll find her, Kjeld. I promise.'

Chapter 63

But Kjeld couldn't wait to get answers. Nor could he simply leave everything in the hands of his colleagues. His daughter was in trouble. He needed to find her. And there was only one person in his mind who appeared to know just as much as the police about what was going on. One person who was matching their steps in the investigation. One person who seemed to know more than they were letting on.

Henny Engström.

When Esme left to continue coordinating the search for Tove and receive an update from the crime-scene manager, Kjeld checked Henny's blog for any recent posts. Nothing. He clicked on her YouTube page. No live recordings. Then he logged into his work account and pulled up the report he'd written after their interview with Henny. On the final page was her home address and contact information. It was finally time to pay her a visit. He pulled his rental car out of the parking space, swerved around the forensic vehicles collecting evidence from Bengt's studio, and sped through the city to Henny's apartment in Linné.

When Henny opened the door and saw the look on Kjeld's face, she immediately tried to slam it shut on him. Kjeld shoved his leg into the gap to prevent her from closing the door and when she stepped backwards he pushed his way inside.

She snatched an umbrella from the corner beneath the coat rack and brandished it at him like a weapon. Kjeld barely withheld the urge to roll his eyes.

'I'm not going to hurt you,' he said.

She laughed nervously and jabbed the sharp end of the umbrella at his waist. 'Oh? Says the armed man who just barged his way into my home? You think you can get away with this just because you're a police officer? That you can do whatever you want to me and sweep it under the rug like the rest of your crimes?'

'I don't want to *do* anything to you.'

'Then what the hell are you doing in my home?'

'My daughter is missing.'

'What does that have to do with me?'

'The murderer. The one you've been posting about. She might have her.'

Henny slowly lowered the umbrella. 'She?'

'Please, Henny.' Kjeld held his hands forward, palms up, in a display of goodwill. 'I need to know whatever you can tell me about this killer or about this person who has been tipping you off to the crime scenes.'

Henny eyed him a moment longer than necessary, no doubt searching his expression for any sign of deception, before she hooked the umbrella back on the rack beneath her coats. Then she turned her back on him and made her way into the apartment.

Kjeld followed her down the hallway and into the large open living space. Henny's home looked as though it had been plucked out of a magazine. And were Kjeld not desperate to find his daughter, he might have been impressed by the centuries' old architecture, high ceilings, ornate moulding, and high-end design.

Henny made her way to a large bookshelf where an ordered display of whisky bottles lined the lower shelf. She poured herself a glass, tossed it back in a single gulp, and turned to stare at him.

'I don't know anything about a woman. And I've already told you what I know about the man who called me.'

'There must be something more. He called you repeatedly. He must have given some hint as to who he was.'

'I didn't lie to you when you asked me if I knew who was giving me those tips. I didn't know. I *still* don't know. But when he continued calling ...' Henny trailed off. 'I suppose I always suspected that the caller could be the killer. How else could he know where the next body was? How could he know the details about the murders?'

'What details?'

Henny drummed her fingers on the bookshelf, her gaze lingering on the empty glass. 'That's how I knew the methods of their deaths. He told me.'

'And you posted that on your blog without confirmation?'

'Of course not! I'm not an idiot. I had it confirmed.'

'By whom?'

Kjeld caught her glance for a split second. Enough to know she was trying to figure out how to answer without incriminating herself or someone else. But eventually the stubbornness dropped from her expression.

'I have a source in the pathologist's office,' she said. 'He sent me photos of the victims from the lab.'

Kjeld clenched his jaw. 'Could your source also be the person who's been calling you?'

'No,' Henny said, confident in her certainty. 'Absolutely not.'

'How can you be sure?'

'Because there's something in his voice. The man on the phone. Something ... different. Unfeeling. My source at the pathologist's office is just looking for attention from a pretty face. His fifteen minutes of fame, you could say. And he's easily bribed with a bottle of cheap scotch. But the man who calls me ...'

Henny's face whitened as she thought about him. 'I can't explain it. There's something about his voice that's threatening even when he's being helpful. Something about him that's untrustworthy. And yet, he hasn't lied. Everything he's told me so far has been the truth.'

'And you're certain it wasn't a woman?'

'I'm positive.'

Kjeld tried to reconcile Henny's insistence that the man on the phone was the killer with the knowledge that Maja Hassan's fingerprints had been found on the knife at Daniel Santelmann's house. Was it possible there were two killers? Or was someone trying to lead them astray? But if that were the case, how could they possibly get Maja's fingerprints on the knife? Better yet, why?

'Is it someone from Second Life?'

The shock that sprung up on Henny's face couldn't be performed. She looked at him as though he'd just accused her of being the murderer. As though it were something impossible to believe.

'Second Life?' She laughed. 'What? No. That's ridiculous.'

'I know you were seen speaking to Jonny Lindh. I also know that until his death Jonny was a resident at Second Life Wellness Respite. A few days after he decides to leave the commune, he turns up dead. I find a witness who claims to have seen you speaking to Jonny. Then I overhear you in the coffee shop making a deal with somebody and shortly after you drive all the way out to Second Life and report from within their walls. Am I supposed to believe that's a coincidence?'

Henny shook her head. There was a frazzled glimmer in her expression, which she buried in another glass of whisky.

'No, no, no,' she muttered.

'You have been present at every crime scene. And you were with Jonny before his death. So, either you know more than you're telling me. Something this supposed caller told you about Jonny. Something that connects all of these killings to Second Life. Or you're involved.'

Henny slammed the glass on the shelf. It clinked against one

322

of the bottles. She winced, seemingly frightened of the sound. 'I am not a murderer.'

'Then who were you talking to? What did you say to Jonny? And what were you doing at the commune?' Kjeld took a step forward, closing the distance between them so he could get a better look at her face.

'It had nothing to do with the case. It was a coincidence. I knew Jonny was a Second Life resident, but when I spoke to him I had no idea he was one of the killer's targets.'

'What did you talk about?'

Henny bit her lip.

'If you don't tell me you could be charged with impeding this investigation. That carries a prison sentence.'

'It's not what it looks like.'

'You think your life is miserable because you lock yourself up in these beautifully furnished rooms? Wait until you're in a cell no bigger than a garden shed.'

'I was talking to him because I want to go back!'

Kjeld lowered his brows. Henny was shaking, her hands clenched together in front of her chest, fingers anxiously rubbing against each other. For a moment the sleeve of her turtleneck rolled up and he got a glimpse of a deep scar on her wrist. Her eyes welled up, threatening tears, but she refused to let them fall. Instead she pressed her hands to her eyes, waiting until her heaving breaths subsided before dropping them to her sides.

'What do you mean you want to go back?'

'I used to be a member of Second Life,' she whispered. 'After my attack. I didn't know what to do anymore. I didn't want to live. I was afraid to go anywhere. Second Life took me in. They helped me find a path back to myself. They gave me focus and a reason to go on. People think that survivors should be grateful. They should feel lucky for being spared death. Something horrible happens to you and people see you differently. Friends and family can't understand why you can't be happy. Why you can't just turn around and be the person you were before the event that changed you. They take their safety for granted. They don't realise that it's so much harder to live. Death would have been so much easier than the pain that follows.'

Henny took a deep breath. 'That's what I was talking to Jonny about. About going back to the commune. But I was afraid. It's been years. What if they didn't want me again? What if I'd lost my chance?'

Kjeld felt a twinge of guilt as Henny told her story. It didn't excuse the things she'd done and it didn't change his hatred of her, but it did strike a poignant chord with him. Perhaps he didn't understand her tragedy exactly, but he understood the pain of carrying the past with him. And the fear that he'd never be rid of it.

'It's possible that Jonny was trying to recruit Louisa Karlsson to Second Life. We think she may have attended a few meetings.'

Henny blinked out of her daze. 'What?'

'And there is some speculation that Andrea Nicolescu might have been involved in the drug trafficking that Second Life is being investigated for.'

Kjeld watched Henny closely for a reaction to that revelation, but her expression didn't change.

'And you're certain the voice of the man who called you couldn't have been from someone at the commune?'

Henny frowned, deep lines forming between her brows as she thought. 'I don't know.'

'What about Brother Björk?'

'Brother Björk? No, he would never. He's not that kind of man. He's peaceful. He's—'

'Charming? Convincing? Manipulative?'

Henny peered at him.

'Could he be the voice?'

'Maybe. I don't know. It's been so long since I've spoken to him.'

'But you were at the commune for at least an hour this morning.'

'It doesn't work like that. You can't just get an audience with him because you want to. You have to go through the steps. You have to be one of them. I left years ago. And they don't forget that. It's not a betrayal so much as a sign of weakness. I was weak. So was Jonny.' Henny hung her head. 'I tried to convince Sister Löv to let me speak with him, but she said I wasn't ready. That's who I was talking to on the phone at the coffee shop. And that's why I did the broadcast. I thought it might make Brother Björk change his mind. That's how it is with their philosophy. You have to be ready before you can move on to the next step. You have to give up your old life. I clearly have not.'

Kjeld crossed his arms over his chest and paced the width of the handcrafted floor rug. He still felt as though he were missing a piece of the puzzle, but he knew there were answers at Second Life. But if Henny couldn't get a conversation with the commune's leader, how could he?

'How did you get past the police watching the commune? Surely they would have recognised you.'

A small smirk tugged at the corner of Henny's lips. 'There's another path through the forest. You can't find it by following the main road. You have to know where it is.'

'I want to get into that commune.'

'Even if you got in, nobody would talk to you.'

'I assume Brother Björk has an office. A place where he conducts his business. A place where he meets people when they are ready.'

'He does, but it isn't easy to get to. It'll be guarded. He's a little paranoid.'

'What else would I expect of a cult leader?'

'It's not a cult.'

'That's what people keep telling me.'

325

Henny pursed her lips. 'All right. I'll show you how to get into the commune, but I want something in return.'

'What's that?'

'An interview. An exclusive with you on the Kattegat Killer. No holds barred. Nothing is off limits. I want to know everything.'

Kjeld stopped his pacing. This was not a deal he wanted to make. But Tove's life was on the line. He didn't have a choice.

'Fine. But if I do that then you retract everything disparaging you've posted about my department. And you take down the photos of my daughter.'

'Agreed.' Henny held out her hand.

Kjeld hesitated before clasping her hand in his own. He knew it was a bad arrangement. Somehow Henny would figure out a way to turn it on him, as she did everything else. But if giving her one little interview saved Tove's life, then it would be worth it. And he'd deal with the consequences later.

Chapter 64

Kjeld followed Henny's vehicle from her apartment to the Änggårdsbergen Nature Reserve. When she didn't take the same exit he had the previous time through Gunnilse, he thought she might have been jerking his chain. But a few minutes later she turned off the main street and onto a narrow strip of dirt road that stretched through the trees. Before she drove too far into the forest, however, she pulled the car off to the side and parked. Kjeld pulled up behind her. Henny climbed out of the car and made her way over to his driver's side window. He rolled it down.

'This is as far as I'm going,' she said. 'If anyone sees me here so soon after the last time, they might not talk to me again.'

'How much further is it?'

'You can drive another kilometre before the road ends. There's a fallen tree. You have to walk the rest of the way.'

'In which direction?'

'It's an almost straight shot from the road. There's a row of birch trees about halfway. Keep them to your left. There isn't a path, but you might be able to make out footprints because of the rain. You'll come upon some warning signs for guard dogs just before the commune. That's just for show. They're trying to discourage people from sneaking in and taking photographs.'

'What about the commune itself? I won't be able to walk through the front door. They'll remember me.'

'The exterior wall is shorter on the northern stretch. I'm sure you'll find a way to climb over it.'

'Which building is Björk's office in?'

'The second floor of the communal cabin. The same building where they have group meditations.'

The beanbag building. Kjeld had already been there once. That would make it easier.

Henny started for her car and Kjeld canted his head out the window to call back at her. 'Thanks, Henny.'

She stopped and glanced back at him. Kjeld expected to see a sneer on her lips, but there was an uncommon sympathy on her face instead. Esme was right. A child in danger changed everything. 'Don't thank me. Just don't forget about what you owe me.'

Henny climbed back in her car and drove off.

Just as Henny said, the road ended after another kilometre. Kjeld turned the vehicle around in the small patch of dirt so it was facing back down the road before he got out and headed out into the woods.

His pace was quick, spurred on by the worry for his daughter. Kjeld tried not to think about what the killer had planned for her. Ever since he'd learned about Tove's kidnapping he'd tried to mentally focus his priorities into simple well-defined compartments in order to prevent himself from losing track of what he needed to do. First, he had to get into the commune. Then he had to speak to Brother Björk. If his instincts were correct then that conversation might illuminate some of the discrepancies in the case. And, if he was lucky, it might even lead him to the killer. Kjeld wasn't entirely convinced that Tove might be held at the commune – even if much of the evidence seemed to point to them – but he hoped.

He increased his hike to a jog, zigzagging in between trees and over large stones, mindful to keep the birch trees to his left. The mossy ground was damp from the week's rainfall, but he didn't see any footprints. Henny better not have led him astray. Kjeld didn't have any time to waste. Every minute that passed was another minute closer to the killer's plans for Tove.

Assuming the killer hadn't already carried them out.

He shook the thought away.

Ten minutes after passing the guard dog signs nailed to the trees he came upon the commune.

And true to Henny's word, the northern portion of the fence was at least two feet lower, as though they'd run out of longer planks during construction and weren't concerned about trespassers wandering in from the forest. Kjeld jumped, high enough to see over the fence, and checked for any onlookers. Then he grabbed hold of the top of the planks and pulled himself up. A minute later he was over the fence on the other side.

Kjeld crept towards the back of the communal building that he and Esme had been in earlier that week. A large rain cloud passed overhead, darkening the ground beneath his feet and obscuring the afternoon hour. The murmur of voices caught his attention and he ducked down, waiting as two women left via the front door and crossed the lawn to one of the more barrack-styled buildings.

Just get in and find Björk, he reminded himself. Once the man was in front of him he'd have to talk.

Kjeld stood up and made his way around the opposite side of the house. When he turned the corner, however, a large shadow swung at him. His head buzzed with pain for a split second. And then everything went dark.

Chapter 65

Kjeld's feet dragged along behind him as the two men lugged him into the room. They dropped him into a chair and his eyes slowly blinked open. His head throbbed and it took a few moments before the disorientated blur of his vision came into focus. Once it did he found himself face-to-face with Brother Björk, whose dark and scornful expression looked considerably less peaceful than it had the last time they'd spoken.

'I'm afraid Brothers Alm and Ceder were a little too enthusiastic when they knocked you over the head. They don't often get the opportunity to catch trespassers.'

Kjeld glanced at the two men who stood side by side near the doorway. They, like Brother Björk, were dressed in khaki-coloured tunics and green slacks. The garments gave them the appearance of beachside masseuses at a tropical resort. Or maybe yoga instructors from a private spa. But judging from their rugged hard-bitten faces, arm-length tattoos, and Alm's rigid right hook, Kjeld didn't think they were much into the world of spiritual or physical healing.

'Alm and Ceder? Don't you think you're going a little overboard with the tree names? Besides, with arms like that they look more like redwoods.'

Björk laughed. 'They do, don't they?' He waved dismissively to the two men. They left the room, closing the door behind them.

Kjeld pressed the heel of his palm to his temple to ease the throb in his head. Then he turned his attention back to Björk.

'I hope you don't mind, I had your pockets checked before you were brought in.'

Kjeld caught a glimpse of his service weapon sitting on the desk and clenched his teeth.

Björk picked up his police identification. 'You're not the first detective to try to seek an audience with me on their own terms, but I have to give you props for being the most creative. No one's ever climbed the fence before. That goes against protocol, doesn't it?'

'Does it?' Kjeld knew it wasn't wise to be flippant, but Björk irked him and he didn't have time for pleasantries.

Björk chortled again, but the laugh quickly turned into a throaty cough. He picked up a tissue from his desk and hacked into it. Then he wadded the tissue up into a ball and tossed it in a bin. 'Did you think that by sneaking in through the back we wouldn't notice? I've known about your friends out on the main road for weeks. It's hard to keep a secret when the media is crawling all over you. Nobody is interested in drug trafficking. Not when the police department could be staffed with cold-blooded killers. Besides, surely if there was something to find they would have found it by now.'

Kjeld shook his head. 'I'm not interested in any of that.'

Björk raised a brow. 'No? The state of your vehicle says otherwise.'

Kjeld blinked. 'That was you?'

'Not me. I haven't left the commune in months. But my associates don't have patience for people getting between them and their profits. The bomb was supposed to be a warning. But now that you're here ...'

'I'm just looking for my daughter.' Kjeld clenched his jaw. He couldn't let his anger at discovering Björk's men were behind the car bomb on his vehicle distract him. He had to find Tove.

'Your daughter? You look a little young to have a daughter old enough to be one of our members.'

'She was kidnapped by the same person who murdered Louisa Karlsson and Jonny Lindh. And I suspect that person may also be responsible for the death of Andrea Nicolescu, who I'm almost certain was involved in your side business – the one my colleagues out on the main road are interested in.'

Björk gave Kjeld a scrutinising stare before sitting down on the edge of his desk, but he didn't say anything.

'Tell me what these murders have to do with Second Life. I know they're connected. I know someone from here is responsible.' Kjeld glared at Björk, his patience waning. 'Tell me where my daughter is.'

Björk pursed his lips. It was clear from the ridges in his forehead that he was trying to decide how to answer. But the rest of his expression was difficult to read. Kjeld knew he was hedging. He was hiding something, but Kjeld couldn't tell what.

'I don't know anything about your daughter. And those murders don't have anything to do with us. Yes, Jonny was recently a member of ours. And, yes, he was trying to recruit Louisa. She attended a few meetings. Sweet girl. But their deaths had nothing to do with Second Life. It's tragic, really. Perhaps if they'd both been here they never would have been murdered. That's what we offer here, after all. A sanctuary from the outside world.'

'You said you never saw Louisa.'

'I couldn't tell you the truth without potentially exposing what else we were doing here. And I knew we weren't involved. I didn't think it would hurt to tell a little white lie.'

'And Andrea?'

'Ah, Andrea. What can I say? We had an off-again, on-again business relationship. She wasn't exactly the most reliable employee, if you know what I mean. Never hire an addict to do a sober man's job.' Björk shrugged. 'But her death was as much a surprise to me as the others.'

'And I'm supposed to believe that bullshit? You can spin that story to your followers, but not to me.'

'It doesn't matter to me what you believe, Detective. But neither Jonny's death nor Louisa's had anything to do with what's going on at Second Life. And whoever killed Andrea didn't come to us for demands. If it was supposed to be a message about my side business, as you call it, then they failed to properly address it. You're looking in the wrong direction.'

Kjeld's hopes dwindled by the second. He didn't know what he'd expected to find in the commune. Perhaps he thought he'd barrel through the front door and find Tove there waiting for him. No, he'd just hoped there'd be something. Some sign that the murderer was connected to this place. Some sign of who they were and where they'd taken Tove. But despite Björk's vexing sneer and unbelievable story that the commune wasn't involved in any of the deaths, Kjeld had nothing to go on. And, if he was being honest with himself, he didn't get the impression that Björk was lying.

Kjeld stood up from the chair, caught his balance, and made his way to the desk. Björk eyed him cautiously as he picked up his identification card. He was about to reach for his gun when he saw the framed photo on Björk's desk and hesitated.

A rush of confusion filled his thoughts, scrambling to make sense of it.

The photo was of a teenage girl standing in front of a white cabin. She was smiling in a white summer dress, a *Midsommar* crown of flowers atop her head. Kjeld stared at it in disbelief. She had blonde hair, the same shade as Björk's. And the same small eyes. But it wasn't those qualities that made her familiar to Kjeld. He'd seen her face before. He'd seen her in his memories and his nightmares.

Emma Hassan.

Chapter 66

Kjeld reached for his weapon on the desk, but Brother Björk grabbed it quicker. Then he slid off the desk and took a step towards the centre of the room. He didn't raise the gun at Kjeld, but he had the upper hand between them. Kjeld cursed himself for not picking it up earlier when he had the chance.

His eyes darted from the photograph of Emma Hassan to the man standing in front of him. The similarities were uncanny and now he understood why he felt an odd familiarity when he first spoke to the man. Björk was cleanshaven now and he was older, but it should have been obvious to Kjeld from the beginning who he was.

'Jan-Erik ...'

Emma's father.

Björk's hand gripped the handle of the gun. He shifted his weight, his mouth drawn in a tense frown. Kjeld suspected Björk was trying to determine what to do next. He couldn't very well shoot him without attracting the attention of Olsen's team. Sure, they were a few kilometres away, but a gunshot in the middle of the forest was difficult to muffle when your location was under surveillance.

'Think about what you're doing.'

'Why the hell did you have to come here? Why couldn't you just stay on the perimeter like your colleagues? Why did you have to show up and unbury old memories?' Björk clenched his teeth. A vein bulged on the side of his head.

'You recognised me? From before?'

'Of course I recognised you!' He shook the gun at Kjeld. 'How could I not recognise you?'

Kjeld took a slow step away from the desk. 'Okay, let's take a breath and talk about this. Whatever you've got going on – whatever it is that those officers outside your property are interested in – I don't care about it. All I care about is getting justice for Louisa, Andrea, Jonny, and the others this killer has gone after. All I want is to find my daughter.'

'I told you I had nothing to do with that.'

'What about someone else here at the commune? Could anyone else be involved?'

Björk's brows pinched near the centre of his forehead. Then he shook his head. 'No, that's not possible.'

'You're certain?'

'Yes, I'm certain. I would know. This is a tight-knit community. And bringing about pain is not what we're about. Quite the opposite, in fact.'

'I thought all that healing bullshit was just a front for the drugs?'

'It didn't start that way. And the healing part is still true. Most people are here for help. And we do help people. But I still owe debts. And you know what they say about bad habits.'

'Tell me,' Kjeld said. He took another step closer to Björk. The man was shaking, his face contorted in the agony of memory. For the loss of his daughter. When Kjeld was within arm's reach he held out his hand. 'Give me the gun and tell me what you're really trying to achieve here. Explain to me why I'm looking in the wrong place.'

Björk hesitated. Then the tension in his arm loosened and he placed the weapon in Kjeld's hand. He wiped a panicked tear from his eye and made his way back to the desk. 'I wasn't a good father. I was the worst. I didn't give a shit about my family. Not in the way I should have. But after Emma's death I was overwrought. I couldn't get over my grief. It was my fault, you see. If I had been a better father none of this would have happened. And then when my wife – when Maja drove off that bridge – I couldn't go on anymore as I had been. I didn't want to live as the man I was.'

'So you became Brother Björk.' Kjeld holstered his weapon.

Björk nodded. 'That's what it was supposed to be. A chance to start a new life. An opportunity to be the person you couldn't be with your past clinging to you. Björk was a free spirit, no longer bound by the tragedies of his past. And I wanted to bring that new beginning to others. People like Jonny who'd lost everything. Or like Louisa who didn't know how to move beyond the trauma of her captivity. And all of it was in honour of Emma. She showed me who I should have been all along. But eventually some people from my past caught up with me.'

'Sandu?'

'He was still out for blood for what went down between Hermansson and Hedebrant. He wanted to be repaid his losses. And a place like this isn't cheap. No matter how many vegetables we grow, the commune doesn't pay for itself. The money from the drugs goes right back to the people who come to us for help.'

'We found evidence that Maja had been at two of the crime scenes.'

The look on Björk's face was pure shock. 'That's not possible. Maja is dead.'

'They never found her body. Either she lived or someone is making it look like she did. Someone who, perhaps, would like to see you implicated in these deaths?'

The furrows in Björk's brow deepened. He looked like a man straining to lift a heavy weight. But in the end, he merely lifted his shoulders in an exhausted shrug. 'I don't know what to tell you. But whatever it is you're looking for, you're not going to find it here. I never saw Maja again. And while there are people who may still have animosities towards me because of my former life, there's nothing any of them could do to hurt me. The guilt I have for my family's death is more painful than anything anyone else could ever threaten me with.'

Kjeld believed him. There was an honesty in Björk's voice that couldn't be faked. More than that, there was a look in his eyes. The shame. The guilt. It was a look he sometimes saw in himself when he stood in front of a mirror. This man might have been culpable in many things, but not in the deaths Kjeld was investigating.

Dammit. He was back to square one.

What if he was already too late? What if Tove was already dead?

Kjeld would never be able to live with himself if he failed to bring her back to Bengt alive.

He ran his fingers back through his hair. He had to think. What was he missing? What didn't he see?

Kjeld glanced back to the photograph of Emma.

'You look like a man who could also use a second chance,' Björk said. 'I don't blame you for what happened to my daughter. I know it was an accident. And I can see in your face that you've also had to live with the pain of her death. Maybe other things, too.'

Kjeld picked up the framed photo. There was something else about the picture, apart from Emma, that caused the hair to stand up on the back of his neck. What was it?

'If you ever wanted to leave your old life behind you and start anew, you would be welcome here.'

And then it struck Kjeld. He'd seen this photo before. No, not the photo itself. But another one similar to it.

He glanced up at Björk, his heart racing. 'Is this your cabin?'

'It was my father's. I sold it shortly after Maja's death. There didn't seem to be a point in keeping it anymore. I used some of the money to open the respite.' Björk paused. 'Why?'

But Kjeld had already dropped the photo back on the desk and was rushing out the door. It was clear to him now that there was only one place Tove could be. One place for Maja to take her final revenge for her daughter's death.

The motorway.

Chapter 67

Esme downed an entire glass of water and set it on the desk. Then she turned her back to the incident room whiteboard and focused on her team. 'What have we got?'

Axel twirled a pen between his fingers as he spoke. 'Preliminary results from the analysts in fingerprinting say that the prints on the doorknob to the studio match the one lifted from the knife at Daniel Santelmann's house. They're still going through the lot, but they said it's a high probability that they match Maja Hassan.'

'Any witnesses?'

Axel coughed, clearing his throat. 'No one in the neighbourhood saw a woman or a little girl leave the building, but it's not a high traffic area. I've been in contact with the dispatched technicians who are searching for nearby CCTV on the roads, hoping they might catch sight of them entering a vehicle, but so far no word back. Photos of Tove have been issued to all local law enforcement and we've issued an AMBER Alert, but as you know the National Police Authority just joined the European missing children network this past week so we're not certain how effective it's going to be. The system still has kinks that need working out. We've sent her photo to local media stations as well, just in case.'

'What about a photo of Maja Hassan?' Esme asked.

'We're having trouble tracking one down. She's only mentioned by name in her daughter's case file.'

Esme mentally cursed herself for not being more adamant about looking into the possible connections Kjeld might have to this elusive killer. She'd ignored her gut because she was afraid of making a mistake. She'd been so worried about proving to the team and the chief that she could lead an investigation that she'd failed to follow her instincts. This killer clearly had a more intimate connection to Kjeld than they'd realised. And if she hadn't been worrying about her career or the distractions in her personal life she might have discovered that connection earlier. And now Tove was missing. Or worse.

Esme had joined the Gothenburg police as Kjeld's partner just as his relationship with Bengt was beginning to crumble. She'd helped Kjeld out by watching Tove on numerous occasions while he tried to repair what remained of his marriage. It was one of the reasons their relationship improved as quickly as it had. Because Kjeld hadn't liked her in the beginning. And, truth be told, the feeling had been mutual. They'd clashed on everything. It took a long time for them to find a method of communication that worked for them. Tove had inadvertently assisted in bringing them together as colleagues. Esme quickly grew close to the girl. Loved her, even. And the thought that something horrible could happen to her made Esme sick with guilt and rage.

'What about the explosives used on Kjeld's car?'

Axel shuffled through his paperwork. 'The technicians are still combing through the mess, but they said it looked like a match to a string of homemade car bombs used by some gang members fifteen years ago. Apparently, there'd been a rash of them in Biskopsgården for a while. Police put it down to turf disputes due to the influx of immigrants in the area.'

'Were those disputes drug-related?' Esme asked.

'I'm not sure. Most of the victims didn't report it to the police.' Axel spread the papers over his desk. 'Hold up. There was a vehicle that was destroyed. The owner filed an official report. Let me pull it up on the system.'

Axel logged into the records system on the computer and typed in the file number. When it loaded on screen, his face flushed. 'Shit.'

'What is it?' Esme leaned around the desk to get a look.

'Tobias Hedebrant. Two months before his murder his car exploded in the street outside his house. He claimed Emil Hermansson was behind it.'

'The man who shot him? With the bullet that matches the one that killed Andrea Nicolescu?'

Axel nodded. 'And we received secondary confirmation from ballistics. The gun in the Hedebrant file is the same make and model as the one used to kill him and Andrea, but it's definitely not the gun from either murder. As far as they can tell it hasn't been fired recently. But they also insist that the original evidence bag and documentation hasn't been tampered with.'

'What are you saying?' Esme asked.

'The chain of custody is intact. It's the same gun that Kjeld retrieved from Emma Hassan when they picked her up.'

'So, she never had the actual gun from Hedebrant's murder? Then who did?'

Axel shrugged. 'Her mother? Assuming, of course, that she's the one who murdered Andrea.'

'No, it doesn't make sense.' Esme twisted a thick lock of her hair between her fingers. 'The gun would have been tested by forensics and matched to the bullet that killed Tobias Hedebrant. That means it couldn't be the same gun. Hermansson went to prison on the evidence of that firearm. The case had to be airtight for that to happen. Someone must have switched it out afterwards. Someone who was capable of forging the documents to make it look like the file hadn't been looked at in years.'

Esme turned her attention back to the whiteboard. She looked at the list of names. Louisa. Andrea. Jonny. Daniel. Tove. And in between them Kjeld's name, circled with a question mark, and an arrow leading to Maja Hassan and her daughter, Emma. Drug trafficking, serial murders, and the accidental death of a young girl. There was only one thing this could be. Revenge. But how did that help them find Maja?

The door to the incident room opened and Rhodin stepped inside, his face pale and sweaty. 'I just got off the phone with the hospital. Sixteen woke up. You're not going to believe who he says stabbed him.'

Chapter 68

Kjeld climbed over the construction posts set up to prevent motorists from driving onto the closed-off section of the ramp. He'd already removed his service pistol and held it pointed low as he jogged around the curve of tarmac. The road was broken up in places where the construction crews had yet to finish paving the overhang exchange, but Kjeld kept to the edge near the rumble strip to avoid the uneven terrain. It was still raining, but the bitter chill in the air told him snow was on its way. A brisk wind pushed against him and he thought he felt a few snowflakes dampen his cheeks. He hoped he was wrong. He hoped he wouldn't find Tove up there near the guardrail. Or worse, discover that he was too late and his daughter had already met a fate similar to Emma.

When Kjeld came around the curve in the road, he caught a glimpse of two figures. One upright and tall. The other small and shivering, the pink cast on her arm drooping, the weight of which had been made heavier by the earlier rain. He raised his weapon and slowed his pace on approach. There was no way to hide from view. They both saw him coming. But that made no difference. As soon as Kjeld saw them he knew he was expected.

'Daddy!' Tove yelled. She tried to rush forward but a hand caught her shoulder from behind, pulling her backwards.

'I wasn't sure if you were going to make it.'

Kjeld aimed his weapon at the woman who held back his daughter. She, too, had a gun raised, pointed directly at Tove's rain-matted head.

Kjeld's heart skipped a beat. The muscles in his forearms tensed. And he found himself having to forcibly hold back his quick-tempered rage.

'Alice,' he said, his tone steadier than his hand.

Alice laughed. 'You don't sound surprised.'

'Would you prefer I call you Maja?'

Alice shuddered, her face stricken with hate at the sound of that name. 'Maja Hassan is dead.'

'Is she? Because from where I'm standing, she just appears to have changed her appearance some.'

Alice laughed. 'How did you know it was me?'

'Your husband.'

'Jan-Erik? That dim-witted fool? How did he put it together?'

'He didn't. But he had a photograph of Emma at the commune. In the photo she's standing in front of the Hassan family summer cabin.' Kjeld cast a quick sidelong glance to Tove before refocusing on Alice. Despite the cold, a bead of sweat trickled down the back of his neck. 'The same cabin you have a photo of in your office.'

Alice rolled her head to the side and let out an exasperated sigh. 'I knew that imbecile was a dangerous risk. Honestly, I was afraid someone might have caught onto me sooner because of him. Thought about getting rid of him, but he was never part of the plan. Not the killing part anyway.'

'But you nearly implicated him in the deaths.'

'He deserved it. Do you think he's innocent simply because he opened a holistic hippy camp? It was his drug involvement that set Emma on the wrong path. If it weren't for him she never would have gotten mixed up with that crowd. She never would have met that bastard Emil Hermansson. And he never would have convinced her to cover for him.' Alice clenched her teeth.

'If it weren't for my idiot husband she never would have ended up in your patrol car.'

Kjeld's anger was near breaking point. He wanted to lash out, to protect his daughter, but he knew that any rash movement could end disastrously. He had to keep calm. He couldn't give Alice any more control of the situation than she already had. 'Why Daniel Santelmann?'

'Two birds with one stone. He matched the pattern of Louisa and Jonny, but he also had connections to the commune's side business. He was helping Jan-Erik cover his finances. I knew that I'd never be able to get close enough to Jan-Erik to kill him. He's always been paranoid. That's why he has those two buffoons watching him. But a long prison sentence is the next best thing. That's the least he deserves.'

'What about Andrea?'

'She was one of them too. One of Emil and Tobias's little runner girls. The ones they used to bring the drugs into the country. Afterwards she started working with Jan-Erik. Wellness respite, my arse. He's been using the commune to continue the work Emil started. The same work that resulted in the death of my little girl.'

'How did you find out about the day I saved her?'

Alice smirked. 'Oh, that's a good story. But sadly that's not mine to tell.'

Kjeld steadied his weight. The rain sprinkled over his arms, dotting the barrel of his service weapon in tiny droplets. He glanced over at Tove. Her eyes were red from crying and she winced against the pinching hand on her shoulder. Seeing the fear in her face nearly caused him to lose his composure.

He had to keep Alice talking. Maybe if he distracted her long enough he could convince her to let Tove go. Or get a better angle for a shot.

'And my daughter?'

'I was growing tired of the game. It was taking too long to get your attention. Truth be told, it was never supposed to be her. It was supposed to be you. I thought that would have been fitting, don't you? A final standoff. But when I saw her photograph on the news – well, I realised this was more poetic. And I knew it would be enough to push you. To get you to finally figure it out. And now that you have we can finally end this and ensure there will be no more senseless deaths like my Emma's.'

'The other deaths weren't senseless?'

Alice threw her head back in another laugh, mindful not to turn the gun away from Tove. 'No, of course not! No. Is that what you think? Goodness, you really haven't been paying attention, have you? You really do fail to see the obvious sometimes. Spending too much time burying yourself in minutiae. Thinking too hard about the problem. Haven't you heard of Occam's razor? The simplest answer is often the right one. No, their deaths weren't senseless. They were precision targets. The only people in this city who met the requirements.'

'Being survivors?'

Alice's expression broke into one of proud wonder. 'Not just any old survivors. *Your* survivors.'

'Why mine?'

'Because *you* didn't save my Emma. She didn't survive when she should have. These others are a mockery of her memory. How dare they have the chance to live when she didn't. What did they have to offer this world? A timid girl afraid to do anything with her life? An angry drug addict? A boy who gave up a promising future to dance half naked for a bunch of insipid socialites? A money-laundering arsehole who when given a second chance turns around and does the exact same thing he did before? My Emma never would have shied away from the gift of life. She would have become something bigger than herself. Something greater. The rest of them were just wasteful. Undeserving. They had to be returned to their fate. The clock had to be reset, so to speak. Only then could Emma's soul truly be at peace.'

Kjeld took a steadying breath. 'Emma's death was an accident.'

'Was it? I've been through every statement and every testimony of that day. The only thing that makes sense is that you left the door unlocked. You chased her across the highway. You're the reason she was hit by that truck. I tried to get you to admit to that in therapy, but you've somehow convinced yourself that it wasn't your fault. Just like you've convinced yourself that the end of your relationship wasn't your fault. Or the death of your real father.' She paused. 'And the Kattegat Killings.'

Kjeld stared at her. His thoughts wanted to frantically search his memory for any truth to her claim. Was she right? Had he made a mistake? But he shook the doubts away. 'You know how fucking crazy that sounds, right?'

Alice grinned. 'I never expected you to understand. You couldn't because you haven't been where the rest of us have been.'

'And where's that?'

An odd, almost obsessive gleam crossed her eyes when he asked his question. Kjeld couldn't quite place what it meant or where he'd seen it before, but it unnerved him.

'To that dark place where survivors go. To that jagged corner of your subconscious where you ask yourself, "Why me? Why did I survive when others didn't? Why should I have to suffer my fears over and over again?"' Alice's voice lowered, hypnotic. 'You don't know what that's like. You walk away from your fears and your troubles just like you walked away from all of them. From Emma. From Louisa. Daniel, Jonny. Your father. Bengt, who you walked away from when you thought he was dying. Even your precious little Tove. You couldn't cut it being a father so you handed off the responsibility to someone else. Why bother saving them if you're just going to forget about them?'

Kjeld watched Alice carefully. There was a steadfastness in her face that unsettled him. She believed what she said. And even though it didn't make any sense, he could see the obsession in her eyes. This had been her truth for years. A truth she was willing to stake lives on. This was a woman he would not be able to negotiate with. The realisation of that caught in his chest and it tightened. How had he not seen this madness in her before? All of those private discussions in her office and he never once suspected that there was anything wrong. Had he been so wrapped up in his own problems that he didn't notice? Or was he truly so easy to fool?

Kjeld looked quickly at Tove, her eyes wide with fear. It was the same look he saw in his nightmares after arresting Nils. Thick red curls soaked in the rain, a pleading whimper on her lips. Only this time it was real.

'I'm sorry I couldn't save Emma, but none of this can change that,' Kjeld said. He managed to keep his tone level and clear, but he could feel his confidence wobbling. He was fully sweating under his coat. 'You don't have to do this. Emma wouldn't want you to.'

'How would you know what my Emma wanted? She would have wanted to live! She would have wanted the opportunity to finish high school. To go to college. To get married. Have children. She had a beautiful and gracious spirit. She was innocent, caught up in something she couldn't possibly understand. And it was your job to protect her.' Alice let go of Tove and pulled back on the hammer of the gun. From his angle Kjeld couldn't tell if the safety was on, but he assumed it wasn't. One wrong move and the gun could go off.

Tove took a small step away from Alice.

'Don't move!' Alice snapped at her. Tove stopped in place, fearful tears welling in her eyes.

'Alice, please. Let's put down the guns and talk about this. Explain it to me. Help me understand how killing four innocent people can make up for the loss of your daughter. Because you're right. I don't understand. I don't understand how this will change anything.'

'This is all your fault!' she yelled, unconscious tears sliding down the sides of her face as she waved the gun at him.

'Tell me how I can fix it.'

'You can't! It's too late! You were supposed to protect my Emma. That was your job! Instead you frightened her. And you failed to follow protocol. It was your recklessness and inexperience that prevented her from being here now!'

Kjeld had gone over the events leading up to Emma's death over and over in his mind for years. Of all his cases it was the one that still plagued him with uncertainties. But it wasn't just his word against Alice's. There was no proof that he'd made a mistake. He'd locked that door. He couldn't explain how she got out. Nor could he have stopped her from running. That was a decision Emma made. One he'd never understand and had to live with every day for the rest of his life. 'I did everything by the book.'

'Don't lie to me!' Her voice cracked. 'I know you forgot to lock the door!'

Kjeld shook his head. 'I wasn't even driving. That was Nils.'

'Stop it! Don't lie to me!'

'I'm not lying. Listen to me. Maja—'

'No!' Alice tightened her grip on the gun, edging it closer to Tove's head. 'You're only saying that to confuse me. But I know you, Kjeld. I know how you think. I know the way your mind works. I've seen it. You've told me as much yourself in our sessions. You're trying to turn everything around on its head like you always do. Trying to make yourself look like the hero in all of this. But it's not going to work. I've been waiting years for this. Ever since I drove my car off Lemmingsgatan bridge and into the river. You won't take this from me.'

'Don't do this. It's not worth it.'

'It's the only thing I have left. The only thing I can do to avenge my Emma.' She paused long enough to catch her breath. 'Now you can know what it feels like to lose them. All of them. Your precious survivors. And the daughter you pretend to care about.'

Tove looked from Alice to Kjeld, her expression stricken with horror and confusion. Kjeld tried to offer her a reassuring glance, but every tendon in his body was pulled taut. He needed to make a decision. And he needed to make it fast.

'And now we finish this,' Alice said, her tone suddenly calm and composed, her earlier rage swept from her features.

Kjeld trained his focus on Alice, hammer cocked, finger on the trigger. He could wing her in the shoulder, but not without risking Tove also being shot. There was another option, but he didn't like it. And it went against everything he'd learned as a police officer. He could lower his weapon. He could try to convince her to give up. But, as she said, she'd been waiting years for this moment. And that waiting had distorted her perception of everything around her. He'd never be able to reach her.

But he had to try.

He slowly lowered his weapon.

'You're an intelligent, educated woman, Alice. You understand hurt and grief more than anyone. Losing a child? I can't imagine that pain. I wouldn't be able to survive as long as you have if anything happened to my little girl. If anyone knows that, it's you. As you said, I've told you everything. But if you truly believe that I am to blame, then blame me.' Kjeld nodded to Tove. 'Not her. She's just a child. She deserves the chance to grow up and be better than me. Let her go. Let me pay the price for Emma's death.'

Alice hesitated. The muscles in her cheeks slackened, exposing the weariness beneath the taut skin. Kjeld still didn't recognise her as the mother of the teenage girl from fifteen years ago. She'd lost at least half of her previous body weight and put on enough muscle to allow her to carry the bodies of the unconscious victims. And while she was physically fitter than she had been in the past, her face showed signs of ageing. But it was the callous determination in her eyes, built on grief and festering hatred, that struck him the most.

'I can't do that,' she said, resolute. 'That's not enough. It'll never be enough. The only way to even the score is to make sure you live with this forever.'

Alice turned her gaze away from Kjeld and onto Tove.

Kjeld's arm jerked upward and he pulled the trigger.

Alice's stare wavered, surprise shining through impassioned eyes. She looked like she was possessed, driven to this decision by all the pain and guilt she'd suffered from the loss of her daughter. The gun fell from her hand, blood seeping through the fabric of her coat. Then she stumbled backwards. She stretched her arm outward, grasping for Tove. Kjeld pulled the trigger again. Another shot cut through the air and Alice tumbled into the railing and over the edge.

'Daddy?'

Kjeld holstered his weapon and rushed across the motorway. He swept Tove up into his arms and held her against his chest. She buried her face into his jacket. A sense of relief tried to wash over him, but his mind was slow to respond. His body was tense, his thoughts swirling in delayed panic. But Tove was safe. She was unharmed. She was going to be okay. Still, that didn't stop his arms from shaking.

Chapter 69

The sleek linoleum floor glistened back at him with a tawny glimmer from the fluorescent lighting overhead. At the end of the corridor the chatter of nurses droned on between the beeping of monitors from open rooms. Kjeld glanced down at the toe of his boot where a smudge of Alice's blood – no, Maja's blood – had spattered after he'd shot her. He replayed the look on her face in his mind over and over. She'd been so calm and collected. So rational in her madness. That was what bothered him more than the spray of blood on the road. The sheer composure of her mental state.

She was crazy, of course. Kjeld wasn't a psychiatrist so he wouldn't even begin to fathom how to diagnose her, but he had no doubt that something had snapped in her years ago when her daughter died. Something that lingered and poisoned her mind into believing the absurdity she'd spouted as an excuse for committing one senseless murder after the next. But it was that calm in her expression and her behaviour that rattled him and left a permanent shiver at the base of his spine whenever he recalled her face in those final moments. It was a calm he'd only ever seen once before. On the face of his best friend. In the seconds before Kjeld shot him, too.

'You can go in now.'

Kjeld looked up at Liam. He hadn't heard the man approach. His normally broad-shouldered posture was slumped and leaning. His face was ragged, eyes bloodshot from lack of sleep and incessant sobbing. Kjeld, on the other hand, hadn't shed a tear. He was still in shock, mind reeling from the image of Tove with a gun to her head. And his emotional core, which had always been a bit slow to respond, hadn't quite caught up to him yet.

Kjeld stood up from the harsh plastic chair. Liam placed a hand gently on his shoulder and Kjeld was surprised that he didn't flinch in response. He looked into Liam's dark brown eyes, sombre but grateful.

'Thank you,' Liam said. He dropped his hand from Kjeld's shoulder. 'Thank you for not giving up.'

Kjeld nodded and stepped around the larger man, making his way into the private room across the corridor. The curtains on the window were drawn open, but the sky outside was cloudy and dark, belying the early hour. Kjeld crossed the room to the bed and took a seat in the chair Liam had just occupied. It was still warm.

Bengt sat in the chair beside him. Tove lay in the hospital bed, asleep. The pillow beneath her head was crooked and Kjeld instinctively adjusted it for her. Then he sat back and exhaled an exhausted sigh. When the paramedics arrived on the scene, they'd insisted on taking Tove to the hospital to have her checked. Thankfully she wasn't injured. Her cast had to be replaced, however, after sustaining so much exposure to the rain. And instead of the hot pink colour it had once been it was now a soft blue. No one had written on it yet. According to the physician on duty she could be taken home, but the entire experience had been so physically draining that none of them seemed to have the energy to get up.

Bengt reached out and took Kjeld's hand in his own, weaving their fingers together the way he used to. Kjeld looked him in the eye and tried not to think of the self-blame on Bengt's face when he discovered that Tove was missing. And the terror when he realised she was in the hands of a serial murderer. Kjeld pinched his eyes shut and shook the thought away. It wasn't important anymore. What mattered was that Tove was safe. That they all were.

'I don't know what I would have done if—' Bengt hung his head.

'It's not your fault,' Kjeld said.

'I know.' Bengt brushed a loose strand of Tove's curls back behind her ear. She stirred, but didn't wake. Then he looked back at Kjeld. Dark shadows discoloured the skin beneath his eyes. He looked like a man who'd been to hell and back. Kjeld could only imagine how he looked in return. 'And I know it's not your fault either.'

Kjeld winced. Even though it wasn't meant as an offence, he couldn't help but feel responsible for the tragedies of the last few weeks. If he'd done better on Emma's case, if he'd been more aware, perhaps none of this would have happened.

'And I'm glad you're here,' Bengt said, giving Kjeld's hand a gentle squeeze.

'Where else would I be?'

Bengt quirked a sarcastic smile. 'Work.'

'Touché.' Kjeld brought Bengt's hand to his face and placed a gentle kiss on his knuckles.

Bengt's face saddened.

'What?' Kjeld asked. 'Don't tell me I've crossed a line.'

'No, it's not that.'

'Then what is it?'

Bengt averted his eyes and Kjeld felt a tightness in his chest. The kind that preceded bad news. And his fingers inherently clenched around Bengt's hand. He didn't notice he'd done so until Bengt winced from the strength of his grip. Kjeld loosened his hold and inhaled deeply through his nose, waiting for Bengt to begin speaking before allowing himself to exhale.

'I love you,' Bengt said. The last word hovered in the air

between them, hesitating on the unspoken second half of that confession. Kjeld knew what was coming before Bengt gathered the strength to say it.

But.

'But I can't do this.'

The muscles in Kjeld's arm tensed. He didn't let go of Bengt's hand, but he no longer felt it. What had once been so intimate suddenly felt mechanical and performed.

Bengt sighed. 'Liam has been offered a position in London. He's asked me and Tove to go with him. I didn't feel right about it before, but after all of this ...'

Kjeld let go of Bengt and dropped both his hands in his lap. He sat hunched in the chair, thoughts drifting. He felt so many emotions simultaneously bristling beneath the surface that he couldn't distinguish one as being more poignant than the other. Anger, sadness, grief, regret, failure. And behind all of them was an uncomfortable relief. Not that Bengt had chosen to give up on the possibility of them having a life together again, but that at least the wondering and second-guessing were over.

'Kjeld?'

'Hm?'

'If you can promise me that we'll be safe, I won't go.'

Kjeld shook his head. 'How am I supposed to do that?'

'Leave your job.'

Kjeld looked up. There was no more sarcasm in Bengt's eyes. No smile on his face. Only grave seriousness. He was finally doing what he'd been too afraid to do years before. He was giving Kjeld an ultimatum. Him or the job. Them together as a family or the career that had given him a purpose.

He glanced back to the bed, watching Tove's chest rise and fall with each sleeping breath. 'What about Liam?'

'Forget about Liam. I'm asking you if you're willing to walk away from the police in order to be with us. We could leave the city. Find a place out in the countryside where it's quiet. A place where we can both give Tove as much of our time as she needs. Where people aren't being kidnapped and tortured. Where we can both sleep peacefully without the nightmares.'

Kjeld frowned. But who was he without those nightmares? Without the constant reminder that there were other people out there like Maja? And what about their victims and their families? Was he supposed to trust that a generation of Sixtens would devote themselves to their cases the way Kjeld had? Of course, that wasn't the real reason he did what he did. The reason he didn't leave the job was because the job gave him meaning. It gave him resolution when he closed a case or caught the killer. It made him feel like he was doing something right in a world full of so much wrong. And he didn't know how to convert those feelings into his personal life. Into being a father, a lover, a friend.

Bengt was offering him everything he'd ever wanted since the day they'd separated. Everything he'd ever dreamed of. And Kjeld could see it clearly. A small cabin near a lake. Painted yellow, no doubt, because that was Bengt's favourite colour. Tove playing in the garden. Oskar sunning himself on the porch. They could afford it. With his share of the Lindqvist fortune, Kjeld didn't need to work anymore. And Bengt could spend the entire day painting in his studio, a semi-attached shed built off the side of the house with a view of the water, glistening brilliant shades of blue in the summertime. The sweet scent of wildflowers on the breeze.

He would be a fool to say no.

'Kjeld?'

Kjeld blinked out of his thoughts, the pleasant image of their potential home in the country a distant fantasy at the back of his mind. His imagination had been interrupted by another image. The image of a young girl rushing into traffic.

Bengt raised his brows, waiting for an answer.

Kjeld smiled softly, tentative and cautious.

'I love you, too.'

But.

Chapter 70

Söndag | Sunday

Kjeld stabbed his fork into the bowl of Chinese takeaway, twirling it unsuccessfully around the slippery lo mein noodles as though it were spaghetti while Esme deftly used a pair of wooden chopsticks to pick up the vegetables in her fried rice and tofu dish. An evening of greasy, salt-saturated food to celebrate the end of the case had been her idea and Kjeld was glad for the company. He took a swig of beer from the bottle and leaned back in his chair. At Esme's request he'd removed the boxes, making it the first time in months that he'd eaten at the kitchen table. Oskar sniffed around the floor near his feet for any fallen scraps of food.

'Seriously. When are you going to take that damn thing down?' Esme nodded, mouth half full, towards the artificial Christmas tree lit up in the corner of the living room.

Kjeld craned his neck backwards to look at the twinkling coloured lights, a good third of which were burned out, and the string of Swedish flags still dangling on the floor where Oskar had pulled them out of the branches. 'When I move.'

Esme raised a brow. 'Are you moving?'

Kjeld took another bite and shrugged. 'I'm thinking about it.'

'I still can't believe you confronted Maja without telling me.'

'I wasn't thinking at the time.'

'That was a stupid thing to do.'

There was an aggravated edge to Esme's tone that Kjeld knew he was meant to hear. She'd nearly lost it with him when she arrived at the scene. She'd been furious to discover that he hadn't called in for backup, but she'd also been relieved. 'You're right. It was.'

'Don't do that again. We're a team, Kjeld. We work together. Always.' She looked him directly in the eyes. There was something pleading in her expression. 'One of these days I hope you'll trust me enough to believe that.'

'I do trust you, Esme.'

But he could see in her gaze that she wasn't entirely convinced.

'The chief called while I was on my way over. Sixten is finally out of the woods. Apparently he was singing your praises this morning. When he heard how you found Maja he immediately insisted Rhodin give you a promotion. Said that if any of those, and I quote, "pencil-pushing bureaucratic pricks" in administration didn't think you were deserving then they could take it up with him. The nurses had to give him a sedative to calm him down.' Esme smiled. 'He was a little out of it.'

'I'm glad he's all right. You didn't need that hanging over you.'

'No, I didn't.' Esme looked down in her bowl, moving the food around with her chopsticks. 'The doctors still don't know if he'll be able to return to active police duty. They say he's had some nerve damage. He's going to require a lot of physical therapy.'

'He's young and he's stubborn,' Kjeld said, thinking for the first time that he and Sixten shared that in common. They were both hard-headed and difficult to dissuade. 'If he wants it badly enough, he'll find a way to recover.'

'If he heard you say that his esteem for you would probably increase twofold.'

'He shouldn't admire me.'

'I know.' Esme smirked. 'But we don't always get to choose how other people see us. To him, you're a hero.'

Kjeld huffed before taking another swig of beer. He wasn't a hero. A hero would have found a way to save Emma Hassan all those years ago. A hero would have checked up on the victims whose lives he'd saved after their cases were closed. A hero would have trusted his partner with the truth. A hero never would have put his own family in danger. And a hero wouldn't have put his own problems above those of someone else. If there had ever been a hero in this world, it wasn't Kjeld. He wasn't even close to deserving that title.

'I should have seen it sooner. I'd been talking to her for months and didn't notice a thing.'

'Because she didn't want you to notice.'

'There must have been a sign. Something I missed. To allow myself to be so blind? Twice in a row?' Three times if he counted the situation in Varsund last year, but that was still too fresh in his mind for Kjeld to think about. It was one thing to be fooled by someone who knew him well like a close friend or family member, but by a complete stranger? Then again, Maja hadn't been a complete stranger. She'd been Alice. And he'd told Alice everything. She was supposed to be a confidante. Someone he could trust.

He'd never make that mistake again.

'She fooled all of us, Kjeld. Not just you. Stop taking all the credit,' Esme said, only half sarcastic.

They sat across from each other in silence for a full minute before Esme broke the quiet. 'Do you think there might have been any truth to what Alice said?'

Kjeld raised a brow. 'Truth to what? She said a lot of things.'

'That sometimes people avoid their fate. That some of us might not have been meant to survive situations in our past. That maybe we're just living on borrowed time.'

Kjeld stared at his partner carefully. There was an uncommon solemnity in Esme's tone that told him she wasn't joking. He had the feeling she was trying to tell him something else, something he probably should have noticed, but he wasn't sure what. While Esme had the ability to visualise problems in her head, Kjeld did not. And it didn't seem appropriate to guess or intrude. Not until she was more explicit.

'I think it's bullshit,' Kjeld said, a tad more flippantly than intended. Then he cleared his throat and took another sip. 'I don't believe in fate. I believe we make our own destiny and our own choices. She chose to believe I was responsible for Emma's death. And because of that choice she made the decision to kill three innocent people. So, no, I don't give any credence to the things she said. She was crazy. Good at hiding it, yes. But crazy just the same.'

But there had been something in the words she said that still stuck in his mind. One sentence in particular kept winding itself in his thoughts. Something he'd heard before from someone else.

Esme gave him a far-off look as though not entirely convinced. After a few seconds, wherein Kjeld assumed she was dissecting his response for flaws, she nodded, her face relaxed back to its more casual self. 'You're probably right. You know what still bothers me though?'

'The gun?'

'How did Maja get it in the first place? She couldn't have gotten into the evidence locker. She wouldn't have had authority. Which suggests that the gun you retrieved from Emma Hassan all those years ago came from somewhere else. But that couldn't have happened either because the gun would have been tested by ballistics in the original case to match the bullet that killed Tobias Hedebrant. So, who switched the guns and when?'

'I don't know. I still haven't figured that one out.' And Kjeld worried that with Maja's death they never would find out the truth of it. He wasn't looking forward to having that conversation with SU when they realised the same thing.

Esme pushed her food around on her plate until she'd created a centre pile of vegetables and rice. 'What have you decided about Bengt?'

'What do you mean?'

'Are you going to try to make it work?'

Kjeld stared at his plate as though he might find the answer to her question in the noodles. The truth was he hadn't decided yet. Part of him wanted to. The same part of him that wanted to be a better man and a better father. But there was another part of him that knew he'd never be fulfilled in that kind of life.

'I don't know.'

'You'll figure it out. And you know I'll support whichever decision you make.'

'I know you will.' Kjeld tried to offer a grateful smile, but it fell flat.

If Esme noticed the reluctance in his voice she didn't mention it. Instead she motioned to the takeaway carton near Kjeld's elbow. 'Pass the dumplings?'

Chapter 71

Kjeld watched from his window as Esme's car sputtered to a start before driving off down the road. His phone buzzed in his pocket. Another unknown caller. He declined the call without answering and set his phone to silent. Then he made his way into the quiet of the living room, the smell of leftover takeaway lingering in the air from the kitchen, and slumped down on the sofa. He wished Tove were there to break up the silence with one of her silly stories or to show him what she'd learned in her dance class. Kjeld wished Bengt were there, too, although he knew he couldn't see him until he had an answer to his question. And while Kjeld knew what he wanted, he couldn't help but feel like he wouldn't be ready to give Bengt an answer until he'd put all the troubles of his past behind him. And he didn't know if that was something he was capable of.

You think too hard about the problem. The simplest answer is often the right one.

Kjeld recognised the logic when Maja said it, but he'd been too overwhelmed in the moment to really think about what those words meant in context. And even though the case was solved, those words rolled around in his head. They were jarring. They didn't fit. It was as though she'd been repeating something she'd heard, almost mechanically.

Occam's razor. The simplest answer.

When Kjeld thought about it now it seemed obvious. The simplest answer to the case was a mother seeking revenge for the death of her child. A mother who resented the people who had survived where her daughter had not. A mother who then blamed the most likely suspect. The man who had her daughter in his care.

Him.

That was the simple explanation to what had happened. But that didn't feel right to Kjeld. It felt unfinished somehow. The motivation was simple, but the mechanism was not. How had Maja managed to orchestrate the entire thing on her own? She must have been planning it for years. Watching him, following his cases, securing a career at the station where he would eventually come in direct contact with her. While he didn't want to minimise her intellect, she'd clearly spent many hours of her life preparing for this moment and she did succeed in fooling them up until the end, something about it didn't sit well with him. It felt like there was something more to it than the obvious.

He stood up and made his way to the bookshelves on the opposite wall, fingers drawing over the covers of his favourites, reread so often that the spines were broken and illegible. When he came to the small section of classics, most of which he'd inherited from his mother, he stopped.

It was the phone calls that didn't sit well with him. Henny's anonymous caller. One of the first tasks Axel set himself to after Maja's death was to go through her phone records. She'd never called Henny. At least, not from a phone that they'd discovered. And Henny had been certain that it was a man's voice on the other end of the line.

And then there was the gun. Maja never would have been able to replace the weapon in the evidence locker.

The simplest answer.

He took a book off the shelf. It was older, antique, but in

good condition. The cover was hard, leather-bound. Not a first edition by any means, but probably worth something on a dealer's market. It was the only classic not belonging to his mother. The only book he'd ever received as a gift.

A gift on his first day as a detective.

The Count of Monte Cristo by Alexandre Dumas. An English edition, which was why Kjeld hadn't yet read it.

He opened the book. On the inside cover there was a handwritten inscription:

> *Kjeld,*
> *Remember not to think too hard.*
> *The simplest answer is usually the correct one ... Usually.*
> *But not always.*

A foreboding chill spread through his body as he stared at the name signed at the bottom.

> *Nils.*

Chapter 72

Måndag | Monday

The visiting booth at the Gothenburg Detention Centre was warmer than Kjeld had anticipated, but he kept his coat on. He didn't intend to be there for very long. The officer on duty said he could have up to twenty minutes with the prisoner on account of him being law enforcement, but Kjeld didn't think he'd need more than five. This wasn't a social visit. Well, on record it was. But for Kjeld it was something much more than that. It was closure.

Or as close to closure as he was going to get while they both lived.

The door on the opposite side of the glass opened and two officers entered, escorting a man wearing a grey sweatshirt and jogging pants. The man's arms dangled in front of him, wrists restrained by handcuffs. He was taller than both his guards and the way they tugged at his elbows caused the sweatshirt to rise up and expose the white undershirt tucked into his pants. The sweatshirt was too small for him and Kjeld imagined the jogging pants were as well, but he couldn't see his ankles to confirm his assumption. The officers shoved the prisoner into the chair on the opposite side of the glass, a motion that seemed to aggravate the man's left shoulder, which he was favouring with a stooped lean.

After he was seated the guards stepped back towards the far wall in a false display of privacy. The man looked down at the tiny cubicle counter in front of him, empty save for some dust in the corner near the glass that the morning cleaning crew had missed, then he raised his gaze and smiled.

Kjeld's abdominal muscles clenched.

Nils Hedin didn't look like a monster. He had a long face with a high forehead and hair that was a darker shade of blond. It was thinning on the sides, but that may have been the result of a bad trim on the part of the prison barber. He had a thinly trimmed goatee that was going white. And he looked awkward in that sweatshirt. It sickened Kjeld to admit that Nils was a handsome man. Not that unattractive people had the monopoly on serial murders, but it offended Kjeld that a man he'd once admired both physically and professionally could be capable of such grievous atrocities.

Nils used his sleeve to wipe off the telephone attached to the inner wall of the booth before picking it up and holding it to his ear.

Kjeld almost didn't respond in kind. The sight of Nils looking well nauseated him. But if Kjeld didn't speak to him now then he might never. And Nils was something Kjeld had to put behind him. For good.

He picked up the telephone.

'Hello, Kjeld.' Nils's voice was calm and soothing. It was the kind of voice that one wanted to trust. A voice that welcomed confessions easier than a priest. Friendly and warm. Fatherly. 'It took you a while to come and see me.'

'I've been busy.'

'So I've heard.' Nils smacked his lips. 'Tell me, what can I do for you?'

'I want to know how you did it.'

'How I did what?'

'Don't play games with me, Nils. I don't know how or why, but I know you're the one who was behind Maja Hassan. Somehow you helped her fake her death and hide all of these years as Alice Pihl. And you also provided her with the means to find surviving victims of crimes to appease her insane means of avenging her daughter. I checked the visitor list. I know she came to see you. Why? To get more names and information?' Kjeld leaned forward, nose close to the glass. 'How did you do it? How did you manipulate her into believing that killing other people would avenge her daughter's death?'

'Is that what you think I did?' Nils raised a brow and canted his head to the side. He shrugged with his good shoulder, but didn't offer any other confirmation of Kjeld's theory.

'I do. I think if you'd told Maja to walk into traffic, she would have. I think she was completely under your spell. Possibly for years.'

'Sounds like the poor woman was simply overwrought with grief.'

Kjeld narrowed his eyes. 'An officer almost died. *Tove* almost died.'

'But she didn't. You protected her. Just as you protect everyone.'

'This has to stop. This isn't a game. These are people's lives. Lives you once swore to protect. What happened to change that?'

Nils's lips curled a few millimetres higher on the right. 'Why did anything have to happen? Why can't this simply be the way it is?'

'Because I refuse to accept that you were always this way. You were an incredible detective. You must have believed in the job at some point. What happened to change you?'

'By your accounts, I changed. Not by mine.' Nils paused, staring at Kjeld like a scientist might a single-celled organism under a microscope. Unimpressed. 'But I have to admit, your concern is touching. Even if I know you'd much prefer to strangle me than hear my answer.'

Nils tapped on the glass. 'Pity there's this wall between us.'

'It was you, wasn't it?' Kjeld clenched his teeth. 'You were the one who left the car door unlocked. You're the reason Emma ran out into traffic.'

Nils lolled his head to the side, bored. 'All these accusations, Kjeld. One might get the impression you think I'm some kind of criminal mastermind.'

'No, that's not what I think. I think you're bored. I think you like playing games with people's lives and since you're about to be locked up for the rest of your life this is the only way you can do that. By manipulating vulnerable people into doing your bidding. No, I don't think you're a criminal mastermind, Nils. I don't even think you're a genius. I think you're a cockroach. You're a sick, bottom-feeding insect begging for attention.'

Nils laughed. His thin lips curled into a knowing smirk. 'I know self-reflection has never been your strong suit, Kjeld, but even you have to admit that sounds a lot like projection. Are you sure it's not you who's feeling ignored? Or are you just angry because you realise you're not meant for the same kind of happiness as others? That society's idea of the perfect little family is a concept totally unattainable to someone like yourself? Because the truth is you don't love them as much as you love *this*. This game we're playing.'

Kjeld hardened his face into a glower. Beneath the small counter, which Nils casually rested his elbows upon like they were two old friends catching up at a pub over a couple of beers, Kjeld was clenching his fist. Hard enough for him to lose sensation in his pinkie finger. But it was better than letting Nils see the frustration on his face. And it prevented him from losing his temper and showing his old colleague – his old friend – just how unhinged he'd become since the last time they'd seen each other.

'I also know that you're the one who switched the guns in the evidence locker. It's the only thing that makes sense. How long ago was that? After Hermansson's trial? Fifteen years ago? Ten? How long have you been planning this?'

'Let me ask you something.' Nils leaned in towards the partition, close enough for his hot breath to fog up the glass. 'When you're at home, alone because everyone you ever cared about has left you, and rightfully so, what is it that keeps you up at night? Is it the anger towards the people who never understood you well enough to stick by you? Is it the guilt that you put your calling before them? Or is it the realisation that you simply don't give a damn? That given a second chance you wouldn't have done anything differently. Is that what keeps you awake? Knowing that nothing else is as important to you as solving the case and catching the bad guy? Of trying to outdo someone like me?'

Kjeld's fingers tightened on the phone.

'You want to make comparisons? You're a dog, Kjeld. A dog with a bone. As long as you have something to gnaw on you manage to keep it together. But the moment someone takes that bone away from you, you break. You always have and you always will. People think they can change, but people don't change. People are what they are. And those who survive are the ones who accept that fact. The ones who take advantage of that self-knowledge and use it to become something greater.' Nils breathed out against the glass. Then he drew a smiley face in the smudge, waiting for it to fade away before he continued. 'Say what you will about cockroaches, but when mankind has long made itself extinct for its inability to accept what it is, it'll be the cockroaches who reign supreme. We'll be the only ones left.'

Kjeld shook his head. Then he shoved his chair out from the booth and stood up. It felt good to look down on Nils for once. But even standing and separated by glass, Kjeld had the unnerving sensation that he wasn't the one in control. 'You're fucking crazy, Nils. But at least you're crazy in here. And now that Maja is gone you won't be able to touch anyone else.'

There was a glimmer in Nils's eyes, reflected off the sharp

lighting above the booth, but for an instant it looked like something else. Like a warning light flashing for Kjeld's attention.

'Crazy?' Nils grinned. 'Says the man who could have ended all of this if he'd just picked up his damn phone.'

Kjeld flinched. He thought back to all of those missed calls from an unknown number. Had that been Nils reaching out to him? His brow furrowed in consternation. Once he'd found Nils's note in the book, Kjeld knew that he had been the one supplying Henny with the tips that led her to Andrea's crime scene. Nils was the one who picked out the victims from previous cases for Maja's revenge list. Nils was the one who orchestrated the connection to the Second Life commune. Nils had controlled everything from the very beginning. And Maja had been his eyes into the police's progress. Because Kjeld had told her – had told Alice – everything in confidence during his therapy sessions. And she told Nils. But the realisation that those unknown phone calls had been Nils, the idea that if Kjeld had only answered the calls he might have been able to end the murders, shook him to his core.

The rage that surged through Kjeld's body was so intense he could feel the muscles in his face twitch. And if there hadn't been a wall of glass between them he might have done exactly what Nils predicted he would do – thrown himself over the counter in an attempt to strangle him. And it wasn't even so much the fact that Nils had played a part in the recent killings and attempted murder of Tove that set Kjeld's temper to boil. It was the fact that Nils was so blasé about everything. About the murders. About the job. About the friendship Kjeld thought they'd had. None of it mattered to him so long as his ego was fed.

'Did you unlock the door?'

'Is that what bothers you the most? The fact that I might have unlocked the door and allowed that annoying little brat to jump in front of traffic?'

'Did you?'

'I didn't chase her, Kjeld. You did.'

Kjeld fumed.

'Speaking of children, how is little Tove?' Nils smirked. 'Poor thing. I heard she had a few nasty scares this week. I hope she's not too upset by everything that happened.'

'I hope you rot in here.'

Nils's smirk spread wider. 'I won't. In fact, I don't think I'll be in here for very long. And when I get out we'll have plenty to talk about.'

'I should have killed you when I had the chance.'

'Guess it's lucky for me you're a good shot and that you play by the book.'

'That's where you're wrong, Nils.' Kjeld's face remained firm, but a hint of a smile crossed his eyes. 'I missed.'

'Did you?' Nils lips parted into a toothy grin. 'Since you think I'm so calculating, let me ask you one question. Why did you shoot me? Because it was your only choice? Or because I wanted you to?'

Kjeld blinked, a rush of fear tightening in his chest.

'And here's another question for you to chew on …' Nils ran his tongue over his lower lip. 'What makes you think Maja was the only one?'

Epilogue

Outside the detention centre a dusky haze hung in the air. The temperature had dropped at least five degrees since that morning, reminding Kjeld that winter wasn't quite finished. It had merely been lurking behind the rain, waiting to rear its head again. The tip of his nose felt the chill first. Then his ears. He reached into his pockets for the gloves he thought he'd brought with him only to find them empty aside from his phone and an unopened pack of chewing gum. He looked at the thin paper wrapping and sighed when he realised he'd accidentally grabbed sweet mint instead of peppermint. He hated the sweet mint taste. It was too artificial. But the packaging was almost identical to the peppermint chewing gum and since he'd quit smoking he'd probably purchased the wrong flavour at least three times.

He shoved the pack of gum back into his pocket and stood on the edge of the pavement, trying to collect his thoughts and shake off the nauseating sensation Nils had left him with. It was like a stale taste in his mouth. Or an eerie shudder that sometimes prickled beneath the skin when he was alone, but felt like someone was watching him. A feeling of self-induced paranoia that Kjeld now realised wasn't entirely unwarranted. Because Nils *had* been watching him. Through Maja's eyes.

Which left him wondering about Nils's final threat. If he'd been manipulating Maja for almost fifteen years, then who else did he hold under his spell? And how much would it take for Nils to push them out of obscurity and onto a path of devastation?

The thought chilled him deeper than the icy breeze that stung his face.

A young woman, probably in her late teens or early twenties by the state of her fashion, walked up beside him. Her hair was red like Tove's, but straight, sharply angled to be longer in the front than in the back. She dug through her pockets, feverishly removing a single cigarette from a crumpled carton, before letting out an exasperated huff.

'You got a light?' she asked, fingers anxiously twirling the cigarette between her index and middle finger.

'I don't smoke,' Kjeld replied.

She rolled her eyes. 'Figures.'

After a pause, the sickening feeling of being in Nils's presence nearly worn off, Kjeld undid the top button on his coat and reached into the inner pocket where he took out the lighter he hadn't used in months.

The red-haired woman who, when he looked at her now barely seemed much more than a girl, gave him an approving grin and leaned towards him while Kjeld held back the breeze from the flame with his palm. She took a deep drag and exhaled, the smoke hovering in the cold air.

'If you're waiting for the bus you're in the wrong place. It doesn't stop at the entrance,' she said.

'I drove.' Kjeld inhaled the acrid scent of cigarette smoke. He could almost taste it in the back of his mouth and while it did nothing to wash off the grimy taste of his conversation in the detention centre, it did help to distract him.

The girl heaved another melodramatic sigh. 'Lucky. I hate how the bus times never match up with visiting hours. And, of course, you can't wait inside. Not that I'd want to. Place gives me the creeps. I always feel like I have to shower afterwards.'

'Yeah, I know how you feel.'

'But it's the outside that's scarier. You know?' She took another nervous drag on her cigarette. 'At least the crazies in there are locked up. And you know who they are. Out here they could be anyone.'

Kjeld glanced over at her, one brow raised slightly higher than the other, his justified paranoia silently questioning if he was supposed to make more of her spontaneous chit-chat. But the girl wasn't looking at him. She was too busy staring off into the ever-darkening clouds in the distance. Maybe she was talking more to herself than to him. She flicked the ash to the ground and leaned her weight on one leg, canting her hip in typical teenage posture, as though posing for an invisible group of friends. There was a stubborn sadness in her face that Kjeld sometimes recognised in himself. And he wondered if she'd been visiting her father.

'You want a smoke?' she asked.

'I said I don't smoke.'

She looked at the lighter in his hand. 'Yeah, I heard that.'

Kjeld glanced at the outstretched cigarette and thought about his daughter. Bengt was right. Tove deserved to live some place safe. Some place where Kjeld's world of murder and violent crime had less of a chance of touching her. Somewhere she wouldn't grow up to be like this girl, jaded and angry, more afraid of the evil outside prison walls than within them. Or worse, grow up to be like him. And for that to happen Kjeld had to make a choice. Them or everyone else.

'Well?' the girl said, impatient. 'You want it?'

Kjeld reached out and took the cigarette. 'Yeah, I do.'

THE END

Acknowledgements

Writing a book at any time is hard. Writing a book during a pandemic is an entirely different animal. Anyone else trying to be creative during a period of uncertainty knows that the real struggle of an artist has very little to do with the art and everything to do with one's self. The biggest challenge of that process is trusting someone else to be honest and to see the good in your work even when you can't. So, while there are many names listed here, the one most deserving of my gratitude, is my editor, Sarah Goodey. Her patience, dedication, and belief in the characters made this book possible. Thank you, Sarah. And thank you to the countless others at HQ Digital for bringing this book to readers the world over.

Dark times often have a silver lining. Over the course of the last year I made many friends in unexpected places, without whom I may never have finished this novel. Thanks to Diana Marie Hall for her optimism, inspiration, and for sharing with me her own story of perseverance. To Darin Nagamootoo for his boundless positivity and encouragement. (All my love to Leia and Rey!) To Terry Holman for taking time out of his busy schedule to support all of my ridiculous Instagram posts and for his kind messages. Thanks also to Katri Soikkeli for her infectious humour, cat videos, and for making me laugh every morning with her memes.

Thanks to Niklas Broberg both for answering my questions about life in Gothenburg and for his tireless support of so many writers. (And for helping me choose the location of Kjeld's apartment!)

Writers write alone, but very rarely on their own. I owe a huge debt of gratitude to my writing group, with particular thanks to Pine Irwin, Lex Snyder, Kasia Grabiec, Rebekah Barkhauer (Jace), and Lemon Beckham, who spent hours workshopping some challenging plot points in this book.

A very special *tack så mycket* to Hanna Hattson who not only reminded me of the accomplishments I should be proud of, but for going out of her way to help me clarify some aspects of the Swedish judicial system and for brainstorming Esme's story. Thanks also to Anne Alcott for her enthusiasm, friendship, and overall zest for life. Also, for reminding me of the importance of the love of writing. I am truly honoured to know both of these incredible women.

And to my dearest Becky Youtz – thank you for being with me since the very beginning of my writing journey and for challenging me to improve my craft. Words can't begin to explain how important our friendship is to me. You're one of the best people and writers I know.

Readers are the reason authors exist. A huge thank you to the bloggers and early reviewers who have supported this series. I sincerely appreciate your love of these characters and your enthusiasm for their stories.

To my family for believing in me when I didn't believe in myself. And to all of the friends, colleagues, neighbours, and people from my past who came out to spread the word about my books. It means the world to me.

Every writer needs someone to remind them to take a break now and again. Thank you, Feiko, for that reminder. And for your love and patience.

And, of course, thanks to Watson, the cat who always gets the final word.

Turn the page for a thrilling extract from
Where Ravens Roost, a gripping crime thriller featuring
Kjeld and Esme.

Out now!

Prologue

The call of the ravens was what woke him.

Stenar pulled back the curtains and peered out into the night. The clock on the nightstand read a quarter past eleven, but the engulfing darkness of the sky made it feel much later than that. Stenar rubbed his eyes and focused on the long walk between the house and the old barn thinly illuminated by the waning glow of a crescent moon. The barn and its attached rookery had been his grandfather's doing, but Stenar had learned to love those birds. Unlike members of his own species, they had been a consistent presence in his life. They understood him. They never left him.

They were his true family.

The low guttural *kraas* became more frequent and mutated into high-pitched shrieks like the phantom wails of the mythological *draug* after it tugged mariners into the sea.

Stenar went downstairs, pulled on his heavy wool-lined coat, and stepped into his mud-stained work boots. There had been an uncommon amount of rain in the last week and the distance between the house and the old barn had become a marshy length of matted grass and slick earth. His boots stuck in the mud with each step and he wrapped his arms about him to hold back the cold. Autumn had come early this year and the shorter days made for cooler nights. He would be glad for winter. Then the ground would freeze and he could make this walk with less strain on his arthritic joints. There had been a time when he would have been able to bound across the yard in a matter of seconds. Now it took minutes. But the mud made it feel like hours.

The barn wasn't as sturdy as it once was. It was listing to one side and there was a hole in the roof that Stenar's son had promised to fix more than ten years ago. It hadn't been much of a hole then, but the heavy weight of snow over the years had turned it from a crack that let in an annoying amount of rain to a window-sized skylight offering a view of the stretching birch trees that surrounded the edge of the property. Stenar could see the hole as he approached the barn and the thought of it filled him with a weight of spiteful regret.

The closer he came to the barn the more flustered the caws of the ravens grew. He reached into his pocket and removed an old metal torch. His eyesight had diminished over the years and the copper red colour of the barn blended into the pitch-black of the night, concealing the edges of the door. He used to be able to find it by memory. Could reach for the handle with his eyes closed. But his memory, like his knees and his eyes, had become less reliable over the years. He pressed his thumb against the torch knob but stopped when a voice cut through the calls of the ravens.

Stenar froze, his boots sinking deeper into the mud.

Didn't he know that voice?

He slipped the torch back into his pocket and listened. The voice was muted against the high-pitched cries of the birds, but Stenar could hear anger in the speaker's tone. Anger followed by a mocking laugh that almost mimicked the provoking *toc-toc-tocs* that Stenar had heard in his youth. He slowly crept around the side of the barn, his boots mucking through the thick sludge with each step, bypassing the closed door until he came to a small broken window on the side of the rookery. He peeked in through the frosted glass but was met with the flapping of sable wings, blocking his view of whoever was in the barn. He placed one hand on the side of the building and used it to guide his steps around the back where a portion of the wooden planks had rotted away, resulting in a jagged peephole. All he could see were shadows.

Another voice, sharper and more frazzled than the first, cut through the ravens' crying and Stenar felt his heart skip a beat. He was certain he knew that voice. There was no doubt in his mind.

Stenar turned and headed back around the edge of the barn towards the door. At the corner of the building he slipped in the mud and reached out for the wall to brace himself. He impaled his hand on a loose nail. The sharp pain that tore through his palm sent him down hard on his left knee. His leg burned like it was on fire. He heard a pop and knew he'd dislocated something. He tried to stand and realised that pop was probably the hip he was supposed to have replaced last summer. A gripping cramp seized his leg but he ignored it, dragging himself through the mud towards the barn door. The birds clamoured in their pen, rattling against the mesh chicken wire and snapping at whatever intrusion had disturbed the sanctity of their barn.

He had to get up. He had to help.

The cawing of the ravens drowned out the voices. Stenar hoisted himself up on an old milk crate. The pain in his knee radiated down his calf. He took one hard step forward and his hip popped back into the socket. He winced, wiping his mud and blood-stained hand on his jacket. Then he limped back towards the door. A harsh metallic clang rang out in the night and both the sound of the voices and the birds ceased, leaving behind them an unearthly silence in the dead air. Stenar stopped. A minute passed before he heard the sound of someone shuffling inside the barn. He leaned against the wall to support himself, the wet wood splintering against his coat, and peered in through that same broken window beside the rookery. He wiped at the frost-covered window with his uninjured palm. The ravens sat still on their perches, clearing a view to the main open space of the barn.

What he saw both shocked and confused him. As he tried to process the image before him, one of the birds nearest the window craned its neck and stared at him with two dark voids for eyes. Its unnaturally hooked bill gave the impression that it was sneering. Taunting. The bird had seen what Stenar had seen, but unlike him it understood.

It understood and it would never forget.

Chapter 1

Onsdag | Wednesday

Kjeld's phone rang nonstop from the bustling rain-slick streets of Gothenburg to the winding frost-covered roads of Jämtland county. Even when he stopped at the Shell off the E16 near Mora to take a piss and refill his coffee amid the crowd of tourists scrambling to try an authentic Swedish cinnamon roll and purchase discounted painted horses, his phone wouldn't stop buzzing in his jacket pocket. A busload of tourists en route to the Dala horse museum caused the queue for the single toilet to curve through the gift shop and outside the front entrance. Kjeld grumbled and relieved himself on the backside of the building beside an industrial waste container.

His phone continued to vibrate against his chest, but Kjeld didn't answer. He knew who it was: Detective Sergeant Esme Jansson who had been, until recently, his partner in the Violent Crimes Division at Gothenburg City Police. That was before his suspension. It was temporary, they said. Just until the investigation into the Aubuchon murder was cleared up, but regardless of how that turned out Kjeld didn't have high expectations of the chief going easy on him. Apparently the line between good police work and breaking the law was finer than Kjeld realised and as far as the police commission was concerned, he'd not only stepped over that line, but completely ignored its existence. He didn't disagree with them that he'd made mistakes. He had. But there had been circumstances that he thought warranted those mistakes. Esme understood. She was there when the aptly named Kattegat Killer made his final demands. But she wasn't the ranking officer on the scene. He was.

His phone buzzed that he had a voicemail. He grabbed his coffee from the ledge of the trash container and retrieved his messages. *You have three new voice messages*, the soft computerised tone informed him.

There was a pause and then Esme's voice, firm and direct, was loud in his ear. But it was the increasing heaviness of her southern Scanian dialect, accented by unnecessary diphthongs and an aggressively rolled "r" that told him she was livid.

'What the hell is this about a temporary leave of absence? Don't you know we're facing an inquest in a couple of weeks? And you just up and disappear to leave me with this mess? You're a fuckin' arsehole, Nygaard. I've got the commission breathing down my neck about my statement, the Special Investigations Division is asking me to provide a witness testimony for your actions covering the entire Aubuchon case, and your neighbour called me about feeding your cat. When did I ever say you could give my number to your neighbour? I'm not your fuckin' cat-sitter. You can't just head out of town and expect other people to cover your shit for you.'

End of first message. New message.

Esme's voice was louder this time.

'Pick up your goddamned phone, Nygaard! I've got a shit ton of your paperwork sitting on my desk and I am not cleaning it up for you. I don't care if you're on a fuckin' beach in Tahiti, you need to get your arse back here and fix this problem. The chief says you haven't turned in your deposition yet. I swear to God if I get demoted because you're an arsehole, I will never forgive you.'

End of message. Last message.

'Your apartment is a shit mess. You know that? Where do you keep the cat food? Call me back.'

You have no new messages. To replay these messages, press—

Kjeld punched the end-call button on his phone and slipped it in his pocket, walking around the petrol station and back towards his car. He felt guilty for avoiding Esme's calls, but he knew that she would try to get him to open up about everything that had happened during their last case. She would pester him until he shared his feelings and Kjeld didn't want to share them. He wanted to bury them just like he wanted to bury so many things in his past. But Esme was right. He should have told her he was going out of town. She deserved that at least. Hell, she deserved a lot more than that for covering his arse for the last four years, but Kjeld hadn't been thinking about her when he got into his car and started driving. If he was honest with himself, he hadn't been thinking about anything related to the last few months. Not her, not the chief, not the case that got him suspended, not the testimony he was supposed to give, not the possibility that he would lose his job or worse, serve time for impeding the course of a criminal investigation, not the fact that Bengt was threatening to contest his visitation rights to his daughter. Nothing.

All he was thinking about was the strange call he'd received from his father, a man he hadn't spoken to in almost twelve years. It was uncanny. Seeing his father's number pop up on the notification of missed calls was the last thing he'd expected to see that week. And his first thought was that it hadn't been his father calling at all, but someone else using the phone to give him news of the old man's death. Then he heard the familiar voice on the recording and was surprised by the severity of his gut reaction – hard disappointment.

He listened to the message three times, but it didn't make any sense. The context was unclear and the voice on the other end of the line was disorientated and vague, but it prickled at something in Kjeld that urged him to drive home.

Whether that prickle was hatred or sympathy, however, Kjeld didn't know. What he did know was that nothing short of an act of God would cause Stenar Nygaard to break his vow to never speak to his son again. And that act was worth driving almost ten hours across the country to confront.

'Take our picture?' a middle-aged woman asked. She was bundled up in a thick down coat with a blue and yellow Swedish football scarf wrapped around her neck. When Kjeld didn't respond right away she waved a large Nikon camera in his face. Behind her were three other women with similar short, cropped haircuts and puffy jackets, smiling with their cinnamon rolls and Daim chocolate bars.

Kjeld sighed and took the camera. He must have looked like an anomaly standing among them. While his appearance rarely stood out in a crowd of Swedes, at just over six feet, with ruddy unkempt hair, a thin scar above his top lip, and the scruff of what would be a full beard if he didn't shave soon, he was the physical antithesis of the tourists hovering around the bus. One of the women stared at the side of his head and Kjeld felt a moment of self-consciousness. She said something in a language he didn't understand. He assumed she was talking about the piece of flesh and cartilage missing from his left ear. He snapped four quick photos with the Shell petrol station in the background. The women thanked him in broken English, nodding their heads enthusiastically before hurrying off to the group conglomerating around a man waving a green flag attached to a long staff.

Kjeld quickened his pace to his car so as not to be bothered by any more tourists and pulled out of the service station just as another bus turned into the car park to continue the cycle of the never-ending toilet queue. It wasn't until he took the exit onto the E45 heading north that he realised he forgot to remove the lens cap.

* * *

November was usually a rainy month in Jämtland, but an early cold front had moved in, glossing the roads with a thin layer of ice. The gravel road that led up to Kjeld's old family home was unmaintained, interrupted with patches of long grass, fallen tree limbs, and potholes that could snap the suspension of a small car. In truth it could hardly be considered a road at all. It was more a narrow winding path cut out of the surrounding forest with so many sharp turns that Kjeld imagined his great-grandfather must have been three sheets to the wind when he decided to pave the old horse trail connecting his property to the township limits. The story was that his great-grandfather was so enamoured by the beauty of the birch and spruce trees that he refused to chop down a single one to build the drive from the town to his home. But Kjeld's impression of the story after hearing it ad nauseam during his childhood was that his great-grandfather was either too damn stubborn to cut down any trees or he just wanted to limit the possibility that anyone would visit him.

And if Kjeld looked to the other men in his family, himself included, for insight into which explanation was more likely, he would put his money on the latter.

The drive dipped downward just before reaching the house. Kjeld parked his car further up the road on the hill, not wanting to risk the possibility of getting snowed in should the weather take a turn, and walked the rest of the distance to the house. There was a bitter chill in the air that nipped at his neck and he hunched his shoulders against the cold.

It was a typical Norrland farmhouse with the red exterior and white trim, although much of the paint on the northern side had chipped and peeled over the years. Most of the clay roof tiles were covered in moss and the rain gutter on the right side had fallen and was lying in a pile of uncut brush beside the house. The picket fence that he'd painted as a child was missing some planks and someone had permanently tied the gate to an open position against the remaining pickets where it was over-grown with ragweed and arctic violets whose petals had broken off and withered due to the unnatural wetness of the season. In the distance Kjeld could see a spiral of smoke coming from the chimney of the nearest house, which was at least eight kilometres away.

He walked around a fallen garden gnome that he vaguely recognised as once belonging to his mother, and up the steps to the porch. When the doorbell didn't work, he rapped his fist against the metal screen that someone had recently fit over the yellow door. It was loosely hinged to the side of the house and made a hard clanking sound as it hit against the wooden frame.

Kjeld looked out over the yard. The disarray of weeds, aban-doned garden tools buried beneath a pile of broken shutters and rotten firewood, and an overturned wheelbarrow once filled with shattered kitchen tiles caused his face to burn with anger and guilt.

What the hell was he doing here?

It was late afternoon and the sun was just beginning to dip towards the horizon, sending an orangish-yellow gleam through the trees. He was kicking himself for leaving Gothenburg in the middle of the night. It had been an impulsive decision. Now he was tired and regretting making the drive at all. If he got back in his car right now, he could probably make it to Östersund before the local businesses closed and get himself a room for the night. If he could find himself a decent cup of coffee then he could probably make it all the way back to Mora. Neither coffee nor desperation would get him back to Gothenburg before tomorrow, but at least he wouldn't be here, questioning his good sense.

He was already down two porch steps when the front door opened. Kjeld turned around and looked back at his sister as she stared at him through the mesh of the metal screen. Her expression was rigid, the age lines in her face pulled taut around thin pursed lips. After an uncomfortable pause that seemed to Kjeld to last minutes she pushed open the screen door with her hip and snorted a laugh.

'Well, I'll be damned,' she scoffed. 'It must be snowing in hell.'

Dear Reader,

Thank you for taking the time to read my book. I hope you enjoyed solving the crime alongside Kjeld and Esme and that, like them, you were shocked by a few surprises.

After the release of *Where Ravens Roost* I received numerous questions from readers wanting to know if Kjeld was going to keep the promises he made to himself and his family. This novel was the first step in answering some of those questions. But as I discovered along the way while writing, some questions don't have easy answers. And not all promises can be kept. The dynamics of family was a significant theme in Kjeld's first story and it was important to me to continue that thread because family, in all its forms, is something that connects each of us. I hope to explore that more thoroughly in the future, particularly as Tove grows up, begins to develop her own identity, and faces the ramifications of both her fathers' choices on her own life.

But let's not forget Esme. I know she's a reader favourite. She's one of mine, too! And I hope you enjoyed getting a deeper glimpse into her life outside of Kjeld and the police. Of all my characters in this series she is the most fun to write, but she's also the most difficult. I see in her a lot of myself and women that I know. It will probably come as no surprise that she has a difficult journey ahead of her. One that will challenge her relationship with Kjeld and determine the future of their partnership. But if anyone is up to the task, it's Esme!

And then there's Nils. Finally, we can put a face to that figure in the background. He's the kind of character who makes an impact despite remaining offstage. Many people have asked me if we'll get to see his betrayal first-hand. And I'll answer that by saying I don't think this is the last we've seen of Nils or of his crimes.

I love hearing readers' thoughts on characters and learning what they connect to most in the books they read. I also love hearing their questions. Sometimes they inspire ideas! If you want to get in touch, you can find me on Instagram – where I spend too much time posting silly videos instead of writing – @karinnordinauthor. I'm also on Twitter @KNordinAuthor. And if you enjoyed this book I'd be incredibly grateful if you would consider leaving a review so other readers can meet Kjeld and Esme as well.

Hope to see you again soon!

Happy reading!
Karin

Dear Reader,

We hope you enjoyed reading this book. If you did, we'd be so appreciative if you left a review. It really helps us and the author to bring more books like this to you.

Here at HQ Digital we are dedicated to publishing fiction that will keep you turning the pages into the early hours. Don't want to miss a thing? To find out more about our books, promotions, discover exclusive content and enter competitions you can keep in touch in the following ways:

JOIN OUR COMMUNITY:

Sign up to our new email newsletter:
http://smarturl.it/SignUpHQ

Read our new blog www.hqstories.co.uk

🐦 https://twitter.com/HQStories

📘 www.facebook.com/HQStories

BUDDING WRITER?

We're also looking for authors to join the HQ Digital family!
Find out more here:

https://www.hqstories.co.uk/want-to-write-for-us/

Thanks for reading, from the HQ Digital team

If you enjoyed *Last One Alive*, then why not try another gripping crime thriller from HQ Digital?

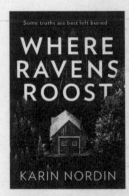

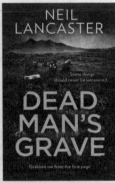